The Sons of Animus Letum

By Andrew F. Whittle

© 2015 Andrew Whittle
All Rights Reserved.

No part of this book may be reproduced in any written, electronic, recording, or photocopying form without written permission of the author, Andrew Whittle

For my family:

When I was broken, I didn't rebuild me...

We rebuilt me.

Special Thanks To:
Marc Plamondon, Ph.D.
It is impossible to measure the amount of work you contributed to this project. I could not have done this without your help. Thank you so much for your insights and honesty

Evin Bekeschus (Cover Artist)
Thank you for your creativity. Your artwork pinpointed the style I was looking for

Sarah "Sarock" Cotnam
Thank you for getting the ball rolling

Meg Parker
Your insight helped shape the novel into what it is

The "So Crazy It Feels Like Home" Peddle Family
Grimey ... Dougie Pacino ... The list goes on... Thank you for being in my corner

Denis Stokes
From start to finish, thank you for your contributions to this project

Dr. Jean Guy Gagnon
Who would have thought that the kid you met twelve years ago would write a novel? Thank you for all of your help.

And Last But Not Least, Pat "The Restless Hobo" Kirk
Thank you for your editing and Photoshop expertise. See you on Wednesday

Cast of characters

Serich Lyran (SER-itch LEER-an) – King of Animus Letum
Rhea Lyran (RAY-ah LEER-an) – Serich's queen
Charon (SHAR-on) – historian of Animus Letum
Perian Lyran (PAIR-i-an LEER-an) – ancestor of Serich
Jerub Lyran (JARE-ub LEER-an) – father of Serich
Odin (OH-din) – son of Serich and Rhea, brother of Galian
Galian (GAL-i-an) – son of Serich and Rhea, brother of Odin
Forneus (FORE-ni-us) – Serich's general / Serpent Messiah
Haren (HARE-en) – young Deathrider
Morello (mor-ELL-o) – Haren's brother
Tholyk (THO-lik) – cleric of Haren's village
Aeroh (AIR-oh) – monk of the Throne's Eye
Igallik (i-GAL-ik) – head monk of the Throne's Eye monastery
Wylak (WHY-lik) – Throne's Eye herbalist
Raine – Throne's Eye warrior
Losik (LOH-sik) – Haren's father
Yilas (YIE-las) – Haren's mother
Usis (YOU-sis) – Raine's apprentice
Nile – Logic totem of the High Order
Bysin – Instinct totem of the High Order
Raeman (RAY-ah-men) – Justice totem of the High Order
Palis (PAL-is) – Mercy totem of the High Order
Eiydia (EYE-di-ah) – scout in the rebel faction
Tyrik (TEER-ik) – monk of the Throne's Eye
Jasil (ja-ZEEL) – monk of the Throne's Eye
Cole – monk of the Throne's Eye
Lizin (LY-zin) – monk of the Throne's Eye
Shylam – leader of the rebel faction
Malum Ludus (MAL-um LOO-dis) – embodiment of evil
Symin – monk of the Throne's Eye
Craine – monk of the Throne's Eye
the MacEnrow – family of miners
Evelyn – head mistress of the Sisterhood
Chloe – nun of the sisterhood
Sykos (SYE-kose) – leader of the Scale
Adara (a-DAR-ah) – member of the afterlife's resistance
Azean (AZ-i-en) – member of the afterlife's resistance
Rysan (RYE-sen) – member of the afterlife's resistance

Lilas (LYE-les) – member of the afterlife's resistance

α

There is a world that awaits you – each of you. By your breath you are promised it. By your death you are given it. I speak of the afterlife. My pen pledges this truth, for, dearest reader, I am dead. I write to you from the hereafter. With only the scythe between us, I write to you from a short distance – much closer, I assure you, than you realize. Time, the inescapable venom of death, promises our meeting. But you know not what you are destined to enter. Many of your earth realm's mystics have claimed knowledge of the afterlife. I tell you now that your prophets are false. The faiths of your earth realm demand surrender and penance. They choose to breed sheep instead of shepherds. My world cannot afford such a price. When the swords of good and evil clash in war, a sheep is of little value. God lives in my world just as He lives in yours. He is the invisible presence of which we are born. But make no mistake: He has grown tired of your realm's endless strife. It is true that your religions are the rivers that lead to His Ocean, but you have sieged your rivers with blood. You have warred upon fallacy and died upon delusion. Your religions have blinded you to what is next. Allow me to lift the veil: there is no heaven, there is no hell. There is only Animus Letum.

Animus Letum is not estranged from the politics that reign in your earth realm. Government is necessary; but where your governments employ mediators, Animus Letum employs warriors. We need our kings to wield more than words. War was the trade of our gladiator kings, and by their brawn, our ironclad rulers were the great compass of the afterlife. The land heeded to them. Just as a righteous soul on the throne brought us heaven, a wicked soul would bring us hell. It was that simple: so simple, in fact, that wars were repeatedly waged to claim the throne. However, there exists only one royal lineage incumbent to the throne: the House of Lyran. Never once defeated, the House of Lyran have proved themselves to be invincible guardian of the afterlife. The truths of the Lyran kings' power are disgraced by the limits of my pen, for they, the great tenders of the throne, are more god than man. Heavy but worthy lie their crowns. In praise of the Lyran it must be said that they are much more than a throne. Their veins, their blood, in fact their very souls define the rhythm of the afterlife. Each king, like a heartbeat, is the very core of Animus Letum's being, and I attest my land is the better for it.

Andrew F. Whittle

In Animus Letum, the most important detail of any king's reign, in fact the defining element of his dominion, is the Soul Cauldron. The Cauldron, a massive ninety-foot high cylinder in the king's Throne Room, contains the greatest energy in the afterlife. It is so powerful that its condition affects the entire hereafter. The Cauldron is an exact representation of the king's thoughts and actions. Every act the king commits – good or evil – is reflected by the Cauldron's nature. Depending on the king's actions, the Cauldron could grow to be a source of great virtue or malice – it could spread heaven or hell across the entire afterlife. Through the House of Lyran, the Cauldron had brought ages of heaven.

The Cauldron is also a refuge. In my realm, time does not reap its due consequences – we are in an age of forever. Yet, we still fear Death. Death and his scythe could strike their second blow. The only form of asylum for the souls having twice died is the Soul Cauldron. For these souls, the Cauldron is the last state of existence – a final resting place. Like the land, the souls in the Cauldron are completely affected by the Cauldron's nature, and they, depending on the king's morality, would become either angels or demons in his service. By the House of Lyran, only angels were formed in the Cauldron. As each reign of the Lyran House stretched over thousands of years, the Cauldron became the great icon of the Lyrans' righteous reign.

Millennia had passed before the House of Lyran's lineage led to Serich, son of Jerub. No king was more powerful than the Great Serich. His reign, succumbing to no vice, to no fault, embodied the spirit of the throne. He was our king, our saint, and our idol. Serich's might was without equal, and in the portraits of our kings, he was the rendering of the divine stroke. Serich was the perfect incarnation of his bloodline – and this was proven the moment that he inherited the crown. The great power of the crown was that it held all the powers, thoughts, and memories each king of Animus Letum had ever possessed. With each new reign, these powers were passed down from king to king. However, the crown could heed to only one man – it knew intimately its wearer and obeyed only him. If the crown were worn by any man or woman who had not been anointed, then no power would be inherited. In Animus Letum there are only two ways to be anointed: the first is to be awarded the throne by the will of the king, and the second is to kill the king. Being of the most royal Lyran house, Serich was willed the crown by his father. His inheritance was great. By way of Jerub, his father, the crown bestowed patience and wisdom. From Perian, the great warrior king,

Serich inherited incredible skill in combat. But to his greatest credit, Serich possessed a unique power of his own – he held mastery over his own soul. This power was limitless. Serich could see into the hearts and minds of all within his sight. He could move objects without touching them. He could even lift the very soul within himself: he could fly.

Under Serich's rule, Animus Letum shone with the might of its king: it was heaven.

Not long into Serich's reign, the great king took his queen, the beautiful and graceful Rhea. In any world, Rhea's beauty humbled even the most stunning horizon of earth, sea and sky. It was not only a beauty of form, but of mind and soul as well. Like Serich's Cauldron, Rhea seemed to shine more brightly upon each new day. Her spirit was so radiant that upon touch, her emotions were transferred to other souls. Any life that brushed against hers became better. More than any power or possession, Rhea was whom Serich held dearest.

Centuries passed under Serich and Rhea's rule. And as the afterlife thrived, the king began to desire the one thing he was without: an heir. Thankful for the blessings of his blood and monarchy, Serich wished to sire a child in his world. He hoped to continue the cycle of his lineage. And soon, by God's grace, our land rejoiced as Serich announced that Rhea was with child. It was I, however, while tending to Rhea, who discovered the great blessing of her pregnancy. The queen was carrying twins – both male. I brought the news to Serich. Any lesser king would have delved long and hard into the problems posed by two heirs, but our king was joyous, refusing to challenge the hands of fate.

The people of Animus Letum eagerly awaited the arrival of the new royal blood.

But I speak not of all in our kingdom.

With great regret I must introduce you to the dark shadow of Animus Letum: the Dark Pool. The Dark Pool is an evil cavern that is determined to bring anarchy to the afterlife. It remains the great bane to the throne of Animus Letum.

The Dark Pool's soldiers are known as the Vayne. The Vayne are not people, they are not human. They are serpents in the guise of man. They are the drones of the Dark Pool, and they serve their master's malice with callous execution.

The Dark Pool and Vayne, having warred with the House of Lyran for ages, despised the possibility of another royal heir. So as news of Serich's heirs reached the Dark Pool, acts of gruesome violence began to grow closer and closer to the throne. The Vayne, so absolutely pathetic and futile in their attacks against Serich, took immense pleasure in manipulating the only thorn they had managed to dig into Serich's side: corrupting the people of his kingdom. A small number of attempts – all by men who were spellbound by serpent whispers – were made on the Queen's life. The king was easily able to neutralize the threats, but the Vayne's methods had become a growing concern.

The king, no longer believing the Queen to be safe in his absence, turned to his most faithful ally: Forneus. Forneus had been the king's lifelong friend, and aside from Serich, he remained Animus Letum's strongest warrior. Forneus spoke few words, but his was a silence deep in thought. Having read the hearts of all in his quarters, Serich knew that Forneus was endowed with the strongest of all. And so it was that Serich requested a service from his great friend. The king asked Forneus to suffer the descent into the Dark Pool so that he could destroy the threat posed by the serpent menace.

Forneus obliged.

Animus Letum would never be the same.

In service to the king he admired, Forneus took up his duty with vigilance. As he trekked into Animus Letum's shadows, he believed himself to be the hunter – the opposite was true. The Dark Pool had targeted his heart with weapons of corruption. While stationed at the Dark Pool, Forneus delivered countless Vayne to their deaths and, on the surface, he appeared to be depressing the morale of his serpent foe. However, with weapons of shadows and whispers, the Dark Pool and its Vayne were making tactical advances on Forneus's mind. What a pleasure it would be for them to twist Serich's most trusted ally. With great regret, I must inform you of their success. In the wicked hiss of the Dark Pool, Forneus was driven mad. He was robbed of his loyalty, and soon his corrupted heart began to beat with a rhythm of anarchy. Forneus came to despise his king. Insanity led to initiative, and in his weakness Forneus offered himself to the Dark Pool. The denizens of the Dark Pool received Forneus as their messiah, and then, with thousands of the slithering Vayne, Forneus marched on the throne.

War was upon Animus Letum.

The first and only night of war swayed between the extremes of virtue and vileness. The pendulum of Animus Letum's soul, swinging to Serich and then swiftly to Forneus, seemed to possess no allegiance. The tides of war seemed uninterested in right or wrong – there was only madness. Blood was shed. It still pains me to report that ours was spilled more than theirs. The trail of destruction that Forneus left on his way to the crown was merciless, and as the Serpent Messiah grew closer to the Royal Throne, the task of the kingdom's defence fell solely on Serich's shoulders – Forneus and his hundreds of Vayne against the king. Serich was outnumbered at least three hundred to one, and still I favoured our king. That is a testament, without boast or ignorance, to Serich's might: pit against the very devil of his land, with his opponents numbered in the hundreds, the king would overcome.

Forneus led his three hundred Vayne up the grand staircase to the Throne Room. His dark skin blushed a hellish orange against the smouldering hail that fell from the stormy skies of Animus Letum. His orange eyes – no pupil or iris – raged with the blazing hue of the falling debris.

Those eyes had set their mark on the prize.

The throne was the massive golden centerpiece within Serich's roofless court, and it stood directly in front of the luminous blue Soul Cauldron. The azure glow of the Cauldron dominated the Throne Room's pallet, reflecting an electric blue onto the Throne Room's dark marble base and forty surrounding pillars.

With his orange eyes burning through the blue, the Serpent Messiah was followed by his hundreds of malevolent Vayne.

The serpent soldiers marched under the comfort of darkness. Thunderous flashes of orange light snaked down from the storm clouds above and coloured the serpent army with a haunting amber. Under the harsh light, the Vayne's muscular pale gray bodies lit up, highlighting the ancient symbols that were carved into their skin. The Vayne's faces, all masked from the eyes down, were also carved with the sacred symbols held by their serpent brotherhood, and as the orange light cascaded from above, the symbols burned like hot coals. Above their masks, the Vayne's eyes were solid and soulless yellow, and above their brow their hair emerged like thick, black, serpentine dreadlocks. The Vayne, armed with swords and spears, followed Forneus into view of the great king.

Rising from his throne, Serich's mighty voice boomed through the very core of his kingdom.

"Forneus," he bellowed. "What have you done?"

As the king's eyes burned an electric blue, he stared fearsomely across his court, his long gray hair blowing madly in the ripping winds.

"Answer me!" he demanded.

Hunched in his vile madness, Forneus offered his reply.

"Destiny awaits a new king, sire."

After spitting upon the court he once served, the Serpent Messiah ordered his Vayne to converge upon Serich. Like a wave, the Vayne spread methodically throughout the Throne Room.

Serich paid them no attention.

Instead, with the flare of betrayal burning in his eyes, he managed one mournful look at his great friend. But as the king read Forneus's soul, he knew: Forneus was truly dead.

The king's ensuing rage, brought by the pain of losing his great friend, would be ruthless.

As I stood in hiding with the queen, even we were startled by the great pain that streaked across Serich's face. As Rhea's hand braced my shoulder, her heartbreak swept through us both.

"God have mercy," she prayed.

"The king will be fine," I assured her.

"Not on Serich," the queen said, "on the Dark Pool. They have killed my king's best friend and for that Serich will seek retribution," she said. "They have no idea what they have unlocked."

As I looked back over the courtyard, and watched Serich bow his head and shoulders to the earth, I understood the queen exactly. It was not mercy that the king had decided upon for the Vayne – it was extinction.

With furious eyes, Serich knelt and crashed his massive fists into the marble beneath him. As the floor cracked and fractured, sparks began to flare from the king's hands. The sparks quickly grew, and as a torrent of blue light spewed from the king's fists, an electric fire began to scorch around his entire body. The flames circled the king like a windstorm. The Cauldron began to churn, and suddenly, with the Throne Room painted entirely blue, Serich erupted upwards, and an explosion of blue fire blasted across the Throne Room. As the massive wave of flames barrelled over the royal court, every Vayne member within forty yards of the king was incinerated.

Forneus and those of the Vayne not destroyed by Serich's great power were tossed to the Throne Room floor. As Forneus and the Vayne rose back to their feet, Serich summoned his mighty staff and moved deep into the center of their numbers. Foolishly, the Vayne again attempted to converge on the king, but Serich tore through their ranks with vicious, precise, and powerful strikes of his mighty staff. After dealing dozens and dozens of the Vayne into death, Serich focused himself even deeper into the well of his wrath. The great Lyran smashed his staff to the ground, igniting it with blue fire, and with a powerful leap, he launched himself high above the

Throne Room. With his foes scrambling beneath him, Serich descended out of the skies and slammed his staff mightily into the floor of the Throne Room. Like thunder, another blue shockwave erupted from the marble base of the king's court, and again the Vayne and Forneus were thrown to the floor.

As the godly Serich surveyed his helpless foes, his mind burned with the hate and disdain he had for the Vayne. They had broken his greatest friend, and for that, they would die.

His only weakness, his only form of vulnerability was his queen.

As his heart led his eyes back to Rhea standing beneath the blue Soul Cauldron, the king committed a crucial error. Forneus was quick to follow Serich's gaze, and as he learned of the queen's position, he rose to his feet and howled out into the night air.

"We are honoured here tonight my brothers!" he wailed. "The queen has yet to withdraw from our presence!"

Wildly, the Serpent stabbed his sword at the queen.

"You were unwise not to lead your queen away from here," he spat at the king. "You will suffer for your arrogance."

As the determined king prepared to vindicate his only battle mistake, the Serpent grinned with delight.

"My Vayne!" he cried. "Bring me the heirs of Animus Letum!"

The Vayne, still paying no heed to the king's great power, rose to their feet and set their yellow eyes on the Queen. As Rhea shuddered and held tightly to my shoulder, the mighty Serich roared in fury.

"YOU WILL NOT," he bellowed as he raised his hands to the sky, "HARM MY QUEEN!"

Serich's body began to burn once more, and as the fire raged around him like a tornado, the very foundation of the Throne Room began to tremble. With cracks and splinters, dozens of the giant stone pillars surrounding the Throne Room broke loose, and as Serich suspended the boulders high above his court, his eyes threatened any Vayne who would think to move.

The Vayne would not listen.

As the serpent soldiers continued to rush the queen, Serich plunged his hands downwards, and immediately, the suspended pillars barrelled down and began to crash heavily into the Throne Room. As the Vayne fell in droves, the impact of each massive stone sent swells of thunder throughout Serich's court.

After the last of the thunder echoed away, the king retrieved his staff and stood ominously over the destruction in his Throne Room. Many more Vayne were destroyed, leaving only a dozen of Forneus's initial three hundred.

Forneus took note of his casualties but remained poised. With an arrogant wave, he ordered his remaining serpents to continue their pursuit of the queen. As they tore across the court, the Serpent turned his hellish eyes upon the king.

"You will see, Sire, that even your great power bows to persistence."

Serich made no reply. Instead, while effortlessly defeating every member of the Vayne within reach, he grew closer to Forneus.

As Serich reached him, the traitor grinned in amusement. "You will not find this an easy task," he grinned.

With a snarl, Serich drove his massive fist into Forneus's cheek. The Serpent Messiah, in spite of the deep and dripping laceration under his eye, did not seem fazed. His eyes glowed an even more devilish orange, and with a wicked smile he scolded the king.

"Surprised, Serich? How about another?"

The queen and I were in shock. Even the king halted in confusion. Never had an opponent withstood his fist, let alone remain standing, begging for more.

"Come, Serich!" Forneus screamed. "You owe me more than that! Destroy me, oh brother! Strike me down!"

"As you wish," Serich consented.

With devastating force, the king delivered five furious strikes to Forneus's body, targeting pressure points that would result in permanent paralysis. As each shot rocked the Serpent's core, Forneus let out a series of whimpers, and then crumpled lifelessly to the ground.

The Serpent Messiah was silent. Curled in a fetal position, his voice seeped out weakly, whimpering as he squirmed like a wounded snake.

Serich stood over him, his eyes heavy with regret.

"You left me no choice," he whispered.

A tear fell from the king's eye as he surveyed the broken shell of his old friend.

"Damn you," he cursed. "You were of my throne."

Forneus seemed to be gasping for air through his sobs, but the serpent's voice slowly turned from a painful whimper into a deep, menacing laugh. With a cackle, Forneus began to rise to his feet.

"Impossible!" the king protested.

The Sons of Animus Letum

Slowly, Forneus rose completely, and as he cranked his neck back and forth, each loud snap of his vertebrae broke the Throne Room's silence. With menace in his eyes, he turned back to the king, grinning as he tasted the blood the king had drawn from his cheek. Already stunned by his opponent's recovery from the attack, Serich looked at Forneus with even more confusion. Forneus's tongue was thin, black and double pronged like a serpent's.

The Serpent offered another grin, letting his black tongue dart and lash across the streaks of blood on his face.

"You were arrogant," he spat. "You assumed that all power in this land belonged to your throne. Has it never occurred to you that despite all your efforts, the Dark Pool only grows?"

The king would not hear such blasphemy. "You're mad. You know the Pool only speaks in deceit."

"You're mistaken," Forneus replied. "The Dark Pool abides by rules older than your house. And as you waited for your heir, so too did the serpents."

Forneus's devilish eyes met the king's. "I, Serich, am that heir."

"Then you shall die with their cause," Serich promised.

"I am beyond the hands of death," Forneus crowed. "Each strike, any infliction of pain against my flesh only grants me more power. I now feed on pain," he cried. "The Dark Pool has allowed me to feed upon despair. Hit me again," the Serpent provoked. "Prove my words true."

Serich held his regal pose.

"You must only build on what can never be taken away," he said.

"I disagree," Forneus countered. "I will build on *what I take* from you."

With another motion of his hand, fifty more Vayne ascended the royal staircase into the Throne Room. As the Vayne began to surround the king, Forneus lunged several times at Serich, driving his sword at the king's heart. The king parried each attack and after a quick step, he used Forneus's momentum to send the Serpent tumbling across the Throne Room floor.

With a furious scream, Forneus bounded back to his feet.

"Enough games," he roared. "Bear witness to my true power!"

With his eyes raging like coals, the Serpent Messiah cast his hands violently over the Throne Room, and almost instantly the marble floor erupted into a blazing orange wildfire. Amid the flames, the Vayne stood still, immune to the fire's burn. As the falling debris began to descend thicker and faster, suddenly, from all directions, a cold wind ripped through the Throne Room. The fire swayed in feral bursts, but soon the wind seemed to bond with the fire and two amber silhouettes began to take form.

"Here is the proof of my bond with the Dark Pool!" Forneus screamed.

As the blazing figures quickly assumed their complete form, the Serpent narrowed his gaze onto the king.

"Dragons, my lord. Your forefather Perian would remember these beasts well."

The dragons stood fifteen feet high and had ebon black talons and fangs. Their massive flaming wings stretched across their backs, and their torsos were like giant pieces of coal held together by veins of fire. As the dragons seemed to unfold their limbs and wings, each movement of their joints released an exploding ball of flame.

The dragons scraped their claws against the marble. The Vayne surrounding the king charged inwards, trying to stun Serich. The strategy was insulting to Serich's greatness. With a powerful leap, the king exploded into the air and began to use his power of flight as his battle advantage.

As he floated mightily above the court, Serich stretched his hand out over the Throne Room, and with a sudden flare, blue fire began to spring from the marble floor. With hisses and snaps, the blue and orange fires clashed and curled at each other – the Lyran and Dark Pool – in a war of flame.

As the flames burned throughout the court, Forneus's dragons rose onto their hind legs, and after extending their long thin necks, they launched up into the skies to face the king.

Serich was ready. Masterfully, he caught the first dragon by its long thin throat and began to squeeze the life out of it. In retaliation, the second dragon spewed its fire at Serich, but the king used the dragon in his grasp as a shield.

Down on the floor of the Throne Room, Serich's blue fire had begun to overpower its orange counterpart. Forneus's voice – maddening at the futile state of his attacks – barked orders to his Vayne.

"The queen!" he yelled again. "Destroy the queen!" The Vayne undertook the mission immediately. While still quarrelling with the dragons, Serich managed to call down to me.

"Charon!" he bellowed. "Hold them back! Use this!"

With a lob, Serich tossed his mighty staff to my feet. The staff, unlike the royal crown, could be used by anyone. I quickly retrieved it and struck it into the Throne Room floor. The blue fire instantly burned more intensely, and as it burst and popped over the marble, it consumed all of the Vayne approaching the queen.

I was holding them at bay, buying the king the time he needed. As I used the staff to cast even more power into the blue flames, suddenly a dagger shot through the air and pierced into my right ankle. With a wince, I fell back, and as the staff fell from my hands, the entirety of blue flames extinguished.

No longer held back by the blue fire, Forneus approached to claim his dagger. Shamed by my failure, I watched as the Vayne began to close in on the queen. My heart pleaded and begged for Serich to somehow undo my failure, but the dragons' relentless attack on the king had left Rhea open to the Vayne's pursuit. I attempted again to protect Rhea, but the Vayne quickly pinned me to the floor. Acknowledging my defeat, The king somehow coursed his voice, like a gentle thunder, through my head.

"Charon, my friend," he spoke, "this is not the end."

Even amid the carnage, the king's voice put me at ease. That calm was turned to disdain as another voice sounded out in the Throne Room.

"Leave Charon alive," Forneus ordered as he slowly approached. "He may prove useful."

With another tongue lash, the villain turned his attention to the queen, pinning her against the Soul Cauldron.

"As for the beautiful Rhea..." he seethed, grinning at the prospect of hurting Serich through the queen. "You, my dear, will embrace a different fate."

Ashamed of her old friend, Rhea spat in the Serpent's face.

"You have disgraced yourself," she scolded.

The Serpent Messiah only beamed with amusement.

"Oh, my queen," he revelled, "your words mean nothing. Can you not see this is your end? Your world has ceased. Mine has begun."

"Are you mad?" Rhea cried. "Look at what you've done! You were of our house! You were our brother!"

Forneus offered a sinister grin. "Better a king than a servant."

Rhea looked the Serpent dead in his eyes. "You know damn well that you were more than that."

"Yes, and today I prove it."

"You have not earned this world," the queen said. "Only the worthy will reign."

"Perhaps," Forneus weighed, "but fortunately, there is about to be a vacancy on the throne. My Vayne!" he cried, "bind the queen's arms! Let's see how bravely this heart beats."

Forneus looked pleased with himself as he waited for his serpent brothers to seize the queen.

Rhea smiled at him coldly.

"Your arrogance has blinded you," she said.

"My Vayne!" Forneus bellowed.

None came.

With a hiss, Forneus turned furiously toward the center of the Throne Room. His Vayne all lay bloody and lifeless, their heads and appendages strewn across the marble floor. Two giant mounds of smouldering ash, topped with broken and battered wings, lay burning in the center of the Throne Room.

Serich stood ominously over the chaos, blood and ash streaked against every inch of his towering frame. The king's eyes burned an even wilder electric blue, and as he set his gaze upon Forneus, the Serpent Messiah stumbled back.

In desperation, Forneus clutched the queen by the neck, but even with Rhea in the Serpent's grip, the king continued to approach.

As the king's eyes burned at his old friend, a tempest of winds began to rip through the Throne Room,

"Your Vayne are dead," Serich growled. "Your dragons are dead. And your cause," he promised, "is destroyed. You have lost."

"Back!" Forneus hissed as he drew his blade to Rhea's throat.

Serich slowed his march.

"I still stand," Forneus cried. "Your victory will only be achieved with my defeat. And as for my cause?" he said as he pounded the butt end of his sword over his heart. "It still beats."

Forneus clutched his arm tightly around the queen's frame. "But you, Serich," he said while tapping his sword against Rhea's pregnant stomach, "will watch your cause die!"

With another hiss, Forneus wrenched the queen's hair back, and after exposing her bare neck, he sliced wildly at her throat.

"No!" the king screamed.

With urgency, Serich leapt to the queen's aid, but Forneus had already completed the stroke of his blade. As the king lunged at the traitor, he quickly summoned his mighty staff, and as it reached his hands, he pierced the weapon through Forneus's chest. The king's strike narrowly missed Forneus's heart, but Serich used it as leverage to volley the Serpent back across the Throne Room. As Forneus sailed overhead, Serich dropped his staff and quickly caught Rhea's fall.

Forneus's blade had cut deep. Rhea's life was dwindling.

With whimpers and coughs, Forneus lay still on the marble. But as the blood spilled from the deep puncture in his chest, the pain, by way of the bond he had made with the Dark Pool, began to make him stronger.

"Brothers!" he raged as he rose to his feet. "Come! Both lord and legacy fall by my hand!"

Dozens more serpents ascended the royal staircase. As the Vayne immediately set across the Throne Room in hunt for the king, Forneus crept slowly behind them, swinging his blade in small maniacal arcs.

Serich ignored them and knelt, holding his Queen in his arms. His electric blue eyes dimmed considerably as he wiped a tear from her cheek.

"Rhea," The king's voice trembled, "forgive me."

The queen, severely bleeding from the deep wound on her throat, could barely speak. As she shook in tremors and her breath seeped out of her, Serich clutched to her hands. Bravely, Rhea forced her gaze up, but as she saw the emotion locked in Serich's eyes, she began to shake her head.

She could see what her king was planning.

"No..." her strangled voice protested.

The king offered a gentle smile as he removed his crown and placed it on her pregnant stomach.

"We live on," he whispered.

As gently as he could, the king caressed Rhea's cheek and then handed her the mighty staff.

"Hold on to these," he begged, "as tightly as you can."

The queen nodded as tears streamed down her face.

As he sensed the Vayne growing closer, the king acknowledged their proximity with an unforgiving grimace. With a grunt, his eyes flared with blue fire, and after gathering what strength he had left, the king bowed his head. Suddenly, a thick wave of blue energy exploded from his body, and as the energy scorched back across the Throne Room, it decimated the Vayne close to him and restrained the movement of the Vayne further away.

With another smile at his wife, Serich placed his hand over Rhea's wounded neck, healing her wound as best he could. It would not save her, but it would buy her the time she needed. The king's hand then moved over the queen's heart, and with another sudden burst, Lyran fire emerged from his hand and began to encompass the queen's body.

As the fire lifted Rhea into the air, Serich whispered his last words to her.

"I love you."

The words seemed to echo in the air, and as Rhea looked over Serich's shoulders to the approaching Vayne, she said the same.

As the Vayne hacked through the energy, they began to inch towards the king. Inches were not enough for their leader. With a primal yell, Forneus's madness erupted into a wild sword-slashing offensive, and as his blade hewed through the blue matter, he began to advance directly towards the king's back.

The queen, still hanging in the blue flame, still holding to Serich's crown and staff, watched helplessly as Forneus sliced his way closer to her king.

"No..." she cried.

The whole of Serich's power had been exhausted in summoning his great energy, and with his life force drained, he managed a final smile to his queen.

Then, as the Serpent grew within reach of the mighty Serich, and a wild hiss sprayed from his mouth, the villain struck.

Forneus stabbed his blade into Serich's back, piercing his sword directly into the king's heart. As the king collapsed, the blue energy he had conjured evaporated. The fire surrounding the queen, however, grew instantly more intense, and with a thunderous boom the fire imploded in on itself and Rhea vanished into the air.

Forneus wasn't aware of what had happened. He would forge countless unrewarding searches for the answer, but his mind would never claim the knowledge that mine held: Rhea, pregnant and fading, was sent to your earth realm.

Indisputably, Forneus had killed the king, and taken the throne. However, Serich's deed would never be undone.

This is the story of the sons of Animus Letum.

The Sons of Animus Letum

1

Haren was a girl of seventeen years with a soul aged five decades more. Within her village, Haren's wild dark hair and bronzed skin attracted more attention than she desired. However, close up, it was her violet eyes that captured the stares of her peers. Within her lilac eyes there was a faith most mistook for stubbornness. It was not a faith in God or religion, but a faith that she mattered like no one before her. Somehow, Haren knew there had to be something more to her world. As she learned about the world that man had made, she felt like an outsider. She found that religion obscured her view. Haren had sought out every religious text she could. She had hoped to find a creed to subscribe to, but she was never satisfied. Worship seemed wasteful, guilt and penance even more so. It was as if a compass lay within her and no matter what factors pulled or dragged or deceived her, her heart always pointed to what was right. Her compass was also influenced by a very particular and very frequent phenomenon. Haren often heard a voice – a booming voice that spoke to her soul – that made her believe that there was a world behind the one she could see. The voice, the best friend that she had never met, always announced his arrival with the smell of bergamot. When the rain would fall, Haren would smell the powerful aroma, and although she didn't know why, in those moments she knew a purpose awaited her. The voice only ever said two words: "Hold strong." They were simple words, but they were potent – potent enough to promise a young girl that greatness would come.

Within her small village, Haren was the victim of her mother and father's dishonor. Her father, Losik, was a soldier who had retired because of bad health, and her mother, Yila, was a housewife who had been deemed mad and unfit for society. Haren's mother had once been highly esteemed within the village, but after giving birth to Haren's only brother, she experienced a very public depression that never healed. It was in this crisis that Haren's father was measured poorest. Against the slander of his wife, Losik remained silent. Betrayed by his failing body and dishonored by his early retirement, Losik chose to remain agreeable in the public sphere and continuously chose beliefs that the village mob perpetuated. This included ostracizing his wife. He became a broken man, trying to rebuild himself with another's bricks.

While the supposed pillars of her family cracked, Haren had to begin construction on herself. Instead of mortar, she had her mind. Instead of brick, she had her body. Haren sacrificed her ambitions and health to support her family, and in doing so, she became the rare miracle that builds itself. The miracle was simple: Haren followed her inner compass. For her, there was no need to debate or second-guess her actions and responsibilities – her compass pointed to what was right, and her heart followed. Haren suffered hunger and nearly every other deprivation she could to benefit her family. She endured food-famished shifts in the village infirmary and performed many meagre deeds to care for her crumbling kin. Such a weight, at such an age, should have surely drowned her. But in the form of her brother, Haren had reason to swim. Morello was eight years younger than Haren, but his appearance was that of a shorter doppelganger. He shared Haren's wild hair and eyes, and as he aged even his meditative posture and sauntering walk matched his sister's. Haren and Morello had been paired by dire circumstance, but they had been bonded by something far greater. When the voice told Haren to "hold strong," Haren knew it was just as much for her brother. Because of her mother's illness, Haren began as Morello's mother, but soon, she became his sister and great friend. They were two staffs perfectly balanced against one another, strong on each other's shoulder, but if one were to shift or fall, the other would do the same.

On a spring evening, weeks after Haren's seventeenth birthday, she lost her balance.

Each year, years that are now centuries in the past, Haren's village gathered for a feast during spring. It was the rare occasion where invalids like Haren's mother were able to congregate outside the house. However, in the revel of that spring evening, Haren had lost track of Morello. Her young brother had been absent at least an hour, and this sort of disappearance was more than rare: it was unprecedented. As the feast carried into twilight, a worried Haren began to search. Half an hour later, a scared Haren had still not found her brother. With night falling, Haren made a frantic plea to the villagers for help. But a girl of her caste – the village decided – should receive none. No one knew and no one cared.

"He'll be back around," Haren's father assured her once the crowd had lost interest. Losik was a tall man, but his body had been beaten into a beleaguered hunch.

Haren's purple eyes stung him as he tried to shuffle past her. "You're just going to wait?"

As some of the villagers watched the exchange, Losik hushed his voice to drop their attention. "Yes," he replied, "as should you."

"I won't," Haren asserted. "This is not right. It doesn't feel right."

Losik shed an irritated shrug. "Maybe he went to the stables."

Haren grinded her teeth to subdue her scream. "I'm sorry I have troubled you with the disappearance of your son," she said. "I'll check the stables *again*."

As a furious Haren left and shouted Morello's name over the cobblestone roadways of her village, she saw the village's cleric make a slow exit from a nearby barn.

"Tholyk!" she called to him.

Tholyk's fat and balding head twisted nervously until his eyes found the approaching Haren.

"Have you seen Morello?" Haren asked as she grew close.

"Is he missing?" Tholyk asked with an unsteady voice.

"For too long," Haren replied. As she approached him, Tholyk's drunken breath hit her, and Haren flinched, craning her neck away from the cleric.

Tholyk seemed ashamed, and after he hid his hands under his black robe, he nodded his head down the road.

"You know, I think I saw him walking that way. I figured he was headed home."

"Thanks, Tholyk," Haren said. "That's the most help I've had all night."

"It takes a village," Tholyk said with an awkward smile. The fat cleric then began a quick walk back to the feast.

"If you can't find him in an hour," he shouted from up the road, "I'll get some of the villagers to take a look."

"I'd appreciate it," Haren called back as she squinted down the dark lane. "Hopefully it won't be necessary."

As Haren began a furtive survey of the road to her home, something about Tholyk seemed suddenly and sickly wrong. For as long as she could remember, Haren possessed a sixth sense that allowed her to read situations beyond the ears, eyes, and nose. As she looked back to the barn Tholyk had exited, her sense was ringing. Something horrid was pulling her back towards the barn.

As she grew close to the barn door, a intense sensation began to overwhelm her mind and she braced her hands on her knees. She began to inhale the horror of an unfolding heartbreak. Tholyk's drunk preaching was always at the center of village feasts – so much so that you noticed when it wasn't there. Haren's jaw slacked numbly as her thoughts crashed like a sequence of earthquakes: Tholyk had been absent from the feast just as long as Morello had. Rumours had followed Tholyk from the last village he lived in. It *was* true that he had always shown an interest in the village's young boys.

As Haren's trembling hand pushed through the barn door, horror escaped from her mouth.

"Morello!" she cried.

Morello lay naked, bloodied, and barely alive on the barn floor. As Haren's screams filled the barn, she quickly knelt next to her broken brother and cradled his head.

No one should meet such terror.

As Haren's violet eyes bled tears over her best friend, her heart fought vainly to damn the accuracy of her senses. It was no use: by the sight of Morello's concaved chest and the sound of his tortured breath, Haren knew that his lungs were collapsing. As an apprentice in the infirmary, Haren had seen enough to know when death was certain. As her brother's anguished wheezes wrung the whole of her mercy, Haren, at age seventeen, drew a dagger from her belt and chose to break herself beyond repair. With Morello's innocent eyes pleading for help, Haren gave the only aid she could.

"No monster will ever ruin us," she whispered to her brother.

With a swift stab, Haren plunged the dagger precisely into Morello's heart, and as he fell dead into her arms, she cradled him and rocked slowly in the silent hell of a mercy kill.

Tragedy has a way of its own. It can numb both the heart and the senses. It can be so greedy that it stops time for the sake of playing out its own torture. Tragedy is the drunkard who wastes not a drop. Haren felt its greed.

It was twenty minutes before the raucous din of the feast reminded Haren that there was a world outside of the hell she found in the barn. With her brother's blood soaking her burgundy gown, she heard her village with fearsome ears. After closing Morello's eyes, she stood up upon hatred and then ran out of the barn upon vengeance. With her dagger white-knuckled in her grip, Haren sprinted in murderous pursuit of the village's holy man. Her fervent strides and furious breath became the rhythm of a monster, and as her back curved forward like a hunting predator, her amethyst eyes scavenged the crowd for the villain.

However, it was he who found her first.

"There!" Tholyk shouted as he pointed five soldiers to her.

The soldiers reacted immediately, and with spears drawn they cut their path on top of Haren's and then circled around her.

"I told you!" Tholyk yelled as the soldiers and Haren stood at a combative stalemate. "She killed her brother! She's mad!"

"Don't you dare!" Haren screamed as she pointed her dagger. Her voice was shrill. "You killed him! You took him from me!"

As the crowd circled around the scene, Tholyk knew he could use them as the mob they were.

"Look at her gown!" he accused arrogantly. "Soaked in her own brother's blood! A murderer!" he shouted.

Haren had no choice but to try and claim the mob.

"It was him!" she yelled as she stabbed the dagger wildly in his direction. "It was Tholyk, I swear! I told you all that Morello was missing! Tholyk stole him and killed him! I found him in the barn!"

As if expecting a rebuttal, the mob turned back to the cleric.

"We've heard this lunacy before," Tholyk said as if he were burdened by his memory. "Haren's mother fell into this very state years ago. I hate to voice logic amidst this tragedy, but people, we must see the heredity of this sickness."

After receiving the only fact they could verify, the mob seemed to pledge an allegiance. At first the murmurs and whispers sounded individually, but soon the mob made the slight shift into a jury and – without trial – announced a unanimous verdict.

"Lashes and mark!" they shouted. "Lashes and mark!"

Lashes referred to the whipping punishment that was dealt onto the village's criminals, and mark referred to the hot coal brand that was pressed onto the faces of criminals who would henceforth be outcasts.

For the crime of murder, Haren would have to suffer ten lashes.

"Damn you all!" Haren cried. As she held her dagger, she scanned the crowd for support. There was none. "I will not be punished for this!" she cried. Haren was trying to remain fearsome, but her voice was cracking and breaking against the mob's accusing stares.

"Apprehend her," Tholyk ordered. "We have had enough spectacle for now. We will whip and brand her tomorrow."

As the soldiers advanced, Haren knew she couldn't miss what might be her last chance. She drew back her dagger, and after savouring the fear that rose in Tholyk's eyes, she launched her blade at his chest. It was to no avail. The ferocity of Haren's pitch defeated its accuracy, and the wayward blade cut only a minor shoulder wound into the cleric. Haren's vengeance had been rendered bitterly inert.

Indeed, that was Haren's last chance. In the minutes after, she was arrested, beaten, and then thrown into the village's lone jail cell.

The cleric, however, sought one more blow. He needed to avenge the intimidation that Haren had struck into him. With the natters of the village crowded in front of Haren's cell, Tholyk approached and flaunted his political brawn.

"There is news, Haren," he said, his voice projected purposely to the gossip mongers. "I have laboured to lighten your sentence. The punishment you've incurred does not reflect the crime. The brand was non-negotiable, but I've worked your lashes down to five. No less, no more."

As Haren sat on the cell's stool, her purple eyes burned through the cleric. Arrogantly, Tholyk circled in front of her, tapping the cell bars to further illustrate his victory. Then, as if to twist the blade he had struck into Haren's heart, Tholyk explained the logic that had emended her sentence.

"You see, although you've hurt your family, we believe you've done the village no injustice. Your brother was a beggar. It was unlikely that he would rise to any promise. Be thankful that —"

In an instant, Haren's hands and words shot through the cell bars.

"If you think for one second you've won," she seared, "you are coldly wrong. If you think five, or ten, or fifty lashes will stop me from ripping your heart out, you have not met my stare. You should kill me, cleric, for there has never been a hatred like the one you've unlocked in me."

Tholyk coiled back from Haren's words like a threatened snake. With his body cringing backwards, his eyes and head dropped under Haren's certain and steady stare. It took him several moments to remember that there were bars between them.

"I see now that my labour was extraneous," Tholyk said as he tried to feign his calm. "Five lashes are not enough to curb your insolence. I will see to it that you are served twenty."

Haren made no reply. She instead looked on Tholyk with such cold and callous eyes that the cleric stumbled back.

After catching his steps, Tholyk had to make another conscious grab for his wits. "You *will* be broken," he promised as he slowly stepped away from the cell. But as Haren's eyes continued to cut into him, Tholyk's returning gaze suggested that even he didn't believe it was possible.

"A lunatic," Tholyk mocked as he turned back to the village. "She is her mother's daughter. A lost cause."

"I assure you," Haren called after him, "I have found a new cause and it is far from lost."

After Tholyk made an intimidated shuffle out of sight, the natters collectively noted his honorable conduct and then began to leave. However, as Haren's mother and father began to approach the jail cell, the mongers cancelled their exit and stealthily attuned their prying eyes and ears.

With a deep exhale, Haren looked intently onto her approaching parents. She expected their support and understanding, but as she read Losik and Yila's sunken posture, she realized neither would come.

With her gaze focused down, Yila's words whispered weakly towards the cell.

"How could you? How could you do this to our family?"

"Do this to our family!" Haren blurted. "How mad are you? I would never! I would never hurt Morello!"

Yila lowered her gaze even further and then hid herself in Losik's shoulder.

"You didn't hurt him?" Losik challenged grimly. "Haren, his blood is still on your hands."

Haren's heart broke for the second time that night.

"I have given you everything I could," she said with a fierce stare. "I would never take – I never took. I sacrificed everything for your survival, and when I need you, you give me this? I didn't kill him. You know I could never."

Losik looked sternly at his daughter. "You have ruined who we are in this village. The brand you receive tomorrow might as well be on our family."

Haren's eyes bulged with anger. "The village!" she screamed as her hands wrenched the cell bars. "Your son was murdered and you care about your public standing!"

"Accept your punishment," Losik said with repulsion. "Accept it and then leave our village. Both of my children died today."

As Haren's eyes conveyed her heartbreak, Losik turned pitilessly from her, wrapped his arm over Yila's shoulders, and then ushered her away from the cell.

After Haren's parents had left, the crowd did the same. They had claimed what they had intended. Soon the village would know of poor Haren and her even poorer plight. A cleric had beaten her, and an ignorant village would applaud him.

After she was alone, Haren could not bear her pain any longer. She had hardened her heart for her pride's sake, but now, after being dammed for too long, her pain surged out in a stream of sobs and tears. As her body crumpled over on the stool, there was a fracture growing so deep within her that her mind and heart began to seek Death. Amidst her hell, it was only the grimmest of reapers who could offer a next move.

When the heart breaks this way, the scythe seems to promise less hurt than breathing does.

In the midnight hour, Haren removed her gown and tied it into a noose.

As her shaking hands fastened the garment to the bars above her, she felt numb inside and out. However, just as she stepped onto the stool and placed the loop around her neck, the smell of bergamot filled her cell. Seconds later, a gentle rain began to fall onto her village. For most, rainfall would not have impeded a suicide. But Haren was not most. Haren had an inexplicable relationship – almost friendship – with the rain, and the moment she heard its patter she removed the noose from her neck. Every time the rain fell on her village, Haren would inhale the scent of bergamot – a scent that she could not trace to any visible source. When the aroma came, Haren would need to find somewhere to remain still, because every time the scent came, Haren was soothed to the point of trance. Although many noticed her trance, Haren never disclosed the mechanics of it. The truth was that the voice – the booming voice Haren had heard her entire life – always spoke in the rain's drops. Like a letter, Haren could read the rainfall's patter as if it were written specifically for her. It was as if the voice penned the rain, and let it fall solely for her.

As Haren studied the rain from her jail cell, one phrase spoke through the rain: "Back up."

Even amid her anguish, she knew she had to consent – a friend was asking.

As Haren pressed herself against the cell's back wall, a blue flash flared in front of her cell and then immediately disappeared. The peculiarity of the blue light was enough to draw Haren off the wall. As she approached the cell bars, she nervously scanned the roadway to see if anyone else had seen the flare. There was no one. Then, as Haren's nose twitched from a burning smell filling her cell, a snap of electricity struck against the steel bars, and a blue flame sparked onto the cell door. In seconds the blue fire engulfed the jail's metal bars, and as the flames grew wild around the jail door, Haren instinctively recoiled back and guarded her face with her gown. Shielding herself, Haren was hit with the strange realization that there was no heat coming off the blue fire. With the azure glow of the fire beaming onto her, Haren tentatively lowered her gown and stood aghast before the inexplicable flames. Her mind protested its possibility. Then, with a sudden snap the cell jolted with intense warmth and the fire extinguished.

The aftermath of the blue fire confounded Haren. In prudence, her reason tried to comprehend what she was seeing, but it was to no avail. As gray ash floated and settled in every corner of her cell, Haren's disbelieving eyes were fixed on a miracle. The jail door had been completely disintegrated by the blue fire. Haren examined the open cell with an element of fear in her breath. She was too stunned to exit. The shock of the fire had pushed her against the cell's back wall, and as she eyed her exit, she was cripplingly confused by how it had happened. Vainly, Haren fought to disprove the event, but as the proof continued to stare back at her, she surrendered her disbelief. With gritted teeth, she found enough sense to make a tentative step off the cell's back wall. As her foot landed in front of her, her ears perked, and she immediately recoiled back from the threatening sound of large flapping wings. As the flapping grew louder, another distinct pitch rang in Haren's ears. She began to wince from the sound, and as she leaned against the cell bars for stability, the voice, somehow even more thunderous, rang in her head.

"Follow the heron," the voice boomed.

As the voice seemed to echo back and forth in Haren's mind, all confusion evaporated from her being. All of her tension and pain seemed to fade. Haren's posture grew erect in the serene calm, and as the sound of flapping returned, she embraced the tranquil sound and watched a blue heron land gracefully in front of her cell. As the giant bird extended its long neck and eyed her, Haren felt something inside of herself that she couldn't define. There was a spark growing within her that burned with more promise than anything she had ever felt. It felt like the actualization of the strange feelings she had experienced her whole life. Indeed, her abilities and destiny had collided. As the voice and heron beckoned her to follow, the reality of Haren's cell compelled her to stay.

"I have something to finish," Haren said apologetically. "I cannot follow."

"It is already finished," the thundering voice said.

Haren heard the voice's words, but felt something much more. In the voice's reply Haren had been assured of her vengeance. Haren could feel that Morello would be avenged, and that there was a hell waiting for Tholyk that even her own hatred couldn't match.

Haren's eyes welled thankfully for Morello's justice.

"Follow the heron," the voice repeated.

As Haren wiped her eyes, she looked onto the mighty bird and then onto the village that had tried to break her. She spat at the latter, and as she paced out of the cell, she looked sternly at the heron.

"I don't have much left," she said, "but I am giving it to you."

The great heron seemed to understand the pact, and after opening its wingspan it launched effortlessly into the air and flapped headlong into the east.

Although Haren would follow, it was not her faith that forced her steps. It was desperation. Any exit from her village would have sufficed.

Your realm had tried to break her, but mine was trying to build her. It is a sad truth that your realm destroys more legends than it builds. In this instance, we were wise to intervene.

2

Destiny disguises herself in many different cloaks. It is not often that she reaches out her naked hand. Winged and blue, Destiny had landed in Haren's village. A cold air – far too cold for the season – had followed the bird. The chill had touched the town with a layer of frost, and under the bright moon, every line and angle in Haren's village sparkled with the white shine of astral light. A strong wind crashed through the village's surrounding trees, and as the branches moved like waves, a madness of whispers spread across the freezing leaves. In such a costume, most would mistake Destiny for something far more sinister.

Haren saw what she wanted – an exit.

Destiny had said "Follow the heron" and had exclaimed the message with an opus of sight and sound. Destiny had proclaimed entry – to a purpose, to a higher path. But after the great bird had ascended out of the frosted village and had soared into the night with a grace somehow unaffected by the powerful winds, Haren had followed only to escape. The further the better.

Without Morello, the village offered nothing.

Wearing her brother's blood, Haren escaped for eight days.

The mighty bird maintained an eastern course, and strangely, even after eight days, Haren had had no desire for food, water or even sleep. There was a bond – a trance induced by the great bird – that had enabled Haren to escape even the most basic human needs. Like the bird, Haren seemed to be fuelled by the phenomenal. It was as if every step brought more energy. Haren had left her village with a famished body, but like a fading candle held to a burning flame, the exile had begun to feed upon a greater source of fire.

As the trance pushed Haren's body forward, Haren knew that something incredible was happening. But even though the walk felt amazing and purposeful, as if the blue fire had freed her from more than just the village cell, a heart like Haren's can never let go of the past. For her there could be no fresh starts – even if a mystical heron was promising otherwise. There were facts – truths like shackles – that Haren was dragging away from her village. The worst and heaviest was that Morello was gone. Haren had often felt like a gardener while she was raising Morello. There was a thrill to waking him every morning, giving him what he needed, and then watching how the day would shape him. The ritual was consistent, and the yields were fulfilling. Like any gardener, Haren was forging greatness at the root. The growers – of man or of nature – seem to practice this more than most. In so many ways, they build themselves as they build their crop. However, in very much the same way, gardeners are lost when their crop is destroyed. Although she was being led by a guide, Haren knew that she was completely lost. The aftershock of her brother's murder was that she had lost her purpose.

The fear that Haren had lost her purpose was worsened by the idea that another one was waiting. Although Haren was trying her best to outrun it, there was a thought stalking her from her village. The thought was that she had reaped a benefit from her brother's death. There was an argument within her that condoned and then condemned what had happened. The heron, the blue fire – they promised something *more*. The thought was like an elixir that served a dose of medicine and then a sting of poison. Haren knew that she was worth *more*. She had always known. But like a monster looming over her past, *more* asked a sequence of morbid questions: wasn't Morello enough? Did Morello have to die for Haren to be found? It is a sick feeling to think you've been freed by your little brother's murder. Even sicker is to be glad it happened.

As Haren kept to the mighty bird's brisk pace, she wanted so desperately to know what was happening. She threw her questions to the heron, but the bird was uninterested. Its gentle squawk said simply to walk on. Haren felt she had no other choice. She had promised Morello that no monster would ruin them. It was up to her to hold the promise. Although she hated it, Haren knew that if she was going to honour Morello, she needed to embark on the awful duty of leaving him behind.

After Haren had walked under the suns and moons of nine days, she arrived at the mouth of a massive forest. The forest was composed of staggeringly tall pines that were lined like the wall of a fortress. Both sides of the wall stretched further than the horizon. The greenery of the massive woodland was vivid. The hues before Haren seemed somehow unreal, somehow too healthy. It was as if the rain, sun, and earth had impregnated the woodland with too much life. Haren felt the same aura from the forest as she did from the blue heron. It seemed that both the bird and forest belonged to a time before man, a time when nature ruled the earth and the forests were a kingdom.

As Haren watched the sun rise and drench the green woodland with light, the heron perched upon a massive pine directly in front of her. The great blue bird then cocked back its long neck and made three gentle squawks. After a small moment, Haren heard the rustling of leaves. Expecting an animal, she clenched her dagger;

however, as she eyed the forest, there was a flash of blue fire, and with a sound like sawing wood the undergrowth in front of her began to twist and spread. At first it seemed that a narrow passage was burrowing into the treeline. Upon her second look, Haren realized it was not merely a burrow; it was a perfect tunnel. Vines, trees, and undergrowth had grown, stretched, and knotted themselves into a hallway of nature's design. Twisting roots framed the gateway, and ivy, flora, and dark earth coloured the hall into a bouquet of green, ivory, and lilac. It was as if the woodland was a vast being, and the earthy tunnel was the vein leading to its heart.

As an astonished Haren approached the gate, she leaned over to search for its end. It was not in sight. As she looked, the tunnel created a sense of vertigo, and Haren was forced to balance her hands on her knees. However, even after she had averted her gaze, it was as if a piece of her had forged ahead into the burrow, and like some mystical rope, it was trying to pull her in tow. There was something about the pull that said there was no going back. After a tentative step into the treeline, Haren glanced to the great bird for confirmation. The heron replied with an affirmative squawk, and then launched back into the air.

"I can't go back," Haren whispered to herself as she breached into the tunnel, "because there is no back."

As Haren pushed into the tunnel, the rich hues of the tunnel as well as the sun breaking through the thick green overhead created what Haren could only call a dream walk. The sun danced upon her from all angles, and as its light reflected off the tunnel's moisture, an aura of gold light sparkled over the passageway. Small gusts of wind rustled the green hallway and there seemed to be a rhythm to the sound. Like music, the wind blew across the tunnel's sides and played a melody of rustling leaves. The experience was so extraordinary that as Haren pushed thirty minutes further into the tunnel she had to remind herself of Morello just to keep a piece of herself in reality.

After forty minutes of wonder, Haren began to see an end to the burrow. As she neared her exit, she saw that the hallway opened into a massive clearing surrounded by enormous trees. The clearing was as incredible as the tunnel. The base of the giant trees, widely spaced from one another, formed the glade, but as the trees grew eighty, ninety feet high, their branches began to stretch across the hollow like the ceiling of a massive cathedral. Like the tunnel, the morning sun surged through the branches overhead and cast the rich earth in deep hues of brown and green.

Andrew F. Whittle

Haren stood in awe. The clearing seemed unkempt; however, as she studied the landscape, its motions – the wind, the swaying grass, and the dancing light – began to untangle the undergrowth into a visible supernatural path for her. Haren – a foreign presence in the sacred meadow – began to chase the unfolding path. After reaching the end of the path, she found herself at the clearing's center next to a giant stone. Haren was unsure of her next move. As the wind threw her burgundy gown into the same motions of the waving meadow, Haren knelt slowly and began to search the clearing – for anything. There seemed to be nothing out of the ordinary. The clearing, aside from the wind, seemed to be typical. Regardless, Haren knew, deep in her heart, that something profound had drawn her to this place. Then, as she remained kneeling, a deep hush suddenly overtook the glade. It was a powerful silence: a deep, imposing, nearly maddening stridence of nothing. The quiet sustained for a long moment, until with a sudden howl, a chorus of shrieking winds crashed over the meadow. The winds began to scream through the perimeter of the clearing, bending and cracking the trunks of the glade's border trees. As the wind wailed like a fearsome siren, the clearing's branched roof collapsed powerfully and drowned the meadow in darkness. All sound and all light were lost.

As the madness that possessed the meadow frightened Haren into a scared huddle, a kindling of blue sparks began to appear on the glade's center stone. The sound and colour of the sparks were enough to lift Haren's head out of her crossed arms. Peeking out from between her arms, Haren watched the fire burn its blue hue across the entire meadow. Then, with a giant blast, the blue fire exploded into a wild blaze that consumed the entirety of the meadow. Somehow immune to the fire, Haren watched the blaze in awe. There was a feeling amid the flames that Haren found soothing. She stood upright, and with the fire circling her, she attuned her ears to what seemed like words slashing around in the flames. But as she strained to listen, a sudden scorching snap rocked her frame, and the blue fire drew rapidly back to the stone. The shockwave of the fire blasted the upper branches of the trees back into their cathedral-like roof, and as the valley flooded again with light, a slender blond woman in a white gown lay sprawled on the stone at Haren's feet. The woman's throat was badly wounded, and over her pregnant belly, she was clutching a giant staff and a golden crown. Haren hovered over the woman for a moment, overwhelmed by not only her, but also the great fire that had brought her to her feet. As Haren looked her over, the woman's body was clenched tightly in panic.

Her breath escaped in an erratic rhythm of wheezes, and her eyes were wide as if she had just seen a murder. Not knowing what else to do, Haren carefully knelt over the woman and placed her hand over her forehead to comfort her. The moment Haren's hand connected with the woman's skin, Haren's body jolted, and a sudden wave of fear rolled over her. As she began to wheeze exactly in time with the woman's rapid gasps, Haren withdrew her hand. The break in contact seemed to dull the fear, but even still, the panic was enough that Haren had to brace herself on her knees. Although she didn't understand the phenomenon, Haren felt a tangible connection to the woman, a bridge that seemed to balance the woman's fear equally between both of their bodies.

After Haren caught her breath, she leaned back to the woman. Haren was compelled to help, but after the first transfer of fear, Haren was afraid to re-open the bridge.

"Just keep breathing," she said finally. "You're safe now. Just breathe."

It was unclear if the woman heard. The look in her eyes said that her mind was elsewhere. It was as if a scene of horror was playing repeatedly in her mind, and no matter what she did, she could not escape it. After another minute, Haren began to slap the stone next to the woman's ears. There was an immediate response to the sound, and in increments, it seemed like the woman was breaking out of whatever daze had claimed her. When she awoke completely, the woman's eyes began to well with tears. She seemed tormented by her presence in the meadow. She began to sob with a jaw gritted so tightly that her skin flushed a crimson red. From her damaged throat, the woman let out a deep sorrowful moan, a heartbroken wail that, without words, still screamed the anguish of watching a loved one die.

Haren recognized the sound.

As the woman cried, Haren heard the exact pain that she had felt in the barn with Morello. It was the sound of a dying soul. It was not fair that Haren was forced to bear that pain alone. It was not fair for anyone to bear that pain alone. As the sound of tragedy bled from the woman's mouth, Haren knelt next to her and wrapped an arm around the woman's shoulders. As the woman collapsed into Haren's arm, the exile took a deep breath and allowed herself to share the heartbreak.

After five minutes, the woman's sobs had slowed and weakened. As she remained on Haren's shoulder, a strangled whisper seeped weakly from her mouth.

"Thank you…"

Haren could feel her gratitude.

She could also feel the thump of the woman's heartbeat fading.

"Your injuries are grave," Haren said as she examined the woman's throat. "We need to get you help. Can you walk?"

The woman's eyes were doubtful but she nodded yes. As Haren braced her arm around the woman's torso and helped raise her to her feet, it suddenly dawned on Haren that she didn't know where to go. She had no bearing of direction or destination.

Haren looked the woman in her vibrant green eyes and saw something that seemed beyond human.

"You know where to go, don't you?" Haren said.

The woman nodded, and then placed her right hand on Haren's forehead.

In an instant, gentle warmth took over Haren's body. However, it was not only warmth that overwhelmed her – it was information. As the heat subsided, Haren was left with the knowledge of exactly where to go. It was as if a map had been transferred directly into her mind.

Haren braced the woman more tightly. "Hold on," she said as they began their stagger out of the glade. "We'll get you to the Throne's Eye."

Haren assumed that the Throne's Eye was a place.

She was only half right.

3

Hidden deep in your earth realm's history there lies a secret that you are not meant to know. This truth has been active in each century of your recorded past. Your tyrants have denounced it and your historians have omitted it, but nevertheless it is there. The motives that have kept you unknowing are vast. However, there is one key root to this deception: the rulers of your realm are afraid. They are afraid to let you know the truth.

I've decided to incite their terror.

Your existence, and in fact the very shapes of your nations, have been formed by design. In each dark chronicle of your earth's history, in the midnights of your worst wars, there have been a group of moral architects. They have walked among you, they have surveyed you, and ultimately they have saved you. Through blood and bone they have revised the course of your future from countless calamities. They are your secret guardians and they call themselves the Throne's Eye.

As Haren led the dying woman to these guardians, she had no concept of the situation's gravity. She had no idea that she was going home.

Like Haren, the monks of the Throne's Eye possessed a sixth sense. Each of them, like Haren, heard voices and often felt people and places in a manner that was beyond sight, smell, and sound. The name for these gifted souls is Deathrider.

Deathriders populate every corner of your realm. By the fault of your earth realm's philosophies, most Deathriders are unaware or confused by their ability. They are deemed mentally ill by your medical arrogance, and then exiled to asylums to have their gifts drowned in medicine.

Amid the medicines and doubt, every Deathrider is usually aware that something great awaits them.

For most, this means the Throne's Eye. In a way, the Throne's Eye monks were collectors. Once a year, small bands of Throne's Eye monks were tasked to traverse the globe in search of gifted souls. If found, the uninitiated Deathriders were lessoned in their abilities, and most often adopted into the Throne's Eye brotherhood.

However, adoption was only offered to the males. In fact, no woman had ever stepped foot in their inner sanctum.

Organized as a monastery, the monks of the Throne's Eye lived simply on the outland of your societies. Their existence was rooted and actualized as a medium between your world and Animus Letum, and upon this greater consciousness they had become your realm's unacknowledged saints. The Throne's Eye were masters of the spiritual and martial arts, and the great skills bred by these disciplines have been used to end your wars and facilitate your peace. They have sacrificed their lives and limbs to uphold the balance of your realm's morality, and as recompense, the great shadow walkers of your realm have requested nothing but to be forgotten – and so they were and are.

While their footprints have been barely pressed upon your earth, one great deity had always been aware of the righteous deeds of the Throne's Eye. Serich had long witnessed the masterful strokes the Throne's Eye had brushed across your histories. He watched the flames of impending wars and rising tyrants be doused by the tactical hand of the Throne's Eye brotherhood.

It was, aptly so, no mistake that unto them he sent his pregnant and dying queen.

With the queen on her shoulder, Haren staggered slowly to the endpoint Rhea had given her. With each passing minute the queen's breath became more erratic, and as she lost more and more of her breath, her weight fell heavily onto Haren's frame. At first, Haren accepted the weight in her stride, but after twenty minutes of staggering, the queen's weight had become almost too much to support.

Although it was not announced by either party, both Haren and Rhea knew that time was not on their side. Haren had seen enough in her village infirmary to know the queen's chances, and Rhea simply knew the truth. The queen knew that her wounds would be fatal. Knowing her fate, Rhea tried her best to speed up the journey to the Throne's Eye. But unlike the soul, the body has limits. No power or bravery could mend her wounds. As Rhea did her best to oppose and suppress the pain, she acknowledged that time was her greatest foe. Time threatened the lives of the Lyran heirs. Time was threatening a legacy. As she pushed on, Rhea could feel Death growing close. Even from my vantage, it was unclear who was walking to whom. Was it Death striding coldly to finalize a tragedy? Or was it Rhea sacrificing her wounds even further into Death's dominion so that her sons could live?

After another ten minutes of limping through the forest, Haren's body was pleading for rest. Her stamina had found and then exhausted her second wind, and as she and the queen pushed on, Haren's fatigue began to influence her hope. Noting the pace of their stagger, as well as the landmark that the queen had transferred into her mind, Haren's confidence had become tempered by reality. The chances of the queen arriving alive were not good. Bravely, Haren tried to labour on, but as she braced the queen, a sudden splash of water wet her legs. Haren was confused for a moment, but after looking down, her eyes grew wide.

"Your water," she said to the queen, "your water broke…"

The trembling queen was aware. As tears rolled down Rhea's cheek, it was clear that she was overwhelmed. It was as if hope and surrender were warring for her heart, and surrender had started to win.

"Its okay, my lady," Haren tried to assure her. "We just have to move more quickly."

The queen managed a nod. At the very least, she would go down fighting.

With the stakes even higher, Haren seemed to find a third wind. As she cut through more of the unkempt greenery, Haren began to hear three distinctly male voices.

"Hello!" Haren called desperately. "Is there someone there? Please! I need help!"

The reply was immediate.

"There, Aeroh!" one voice yelled.

Before Haren could detect from which direction the voice came, the bush on her left side rustled, and a young man in a brown robe leapt in front of her.

The man quickly surveyed Haren and her passenger. "It's her!" he yelled back into the bush. "Igallik was right!"

In an instant another two brown robed monks bounded out from the brush. One was as young as the first, but the other had a long and light gray beard.

"Aeroh," the older one barked. "Get back to the monastery. Inform Igallik that he was right. Tell him Rhea…" the monk seemed to pause with the gravity of what he was about to say. "Tell him Queen Rhea has been found."

Haren was shocked. A queen?

After the older monk made the order, Aeroh – the first monk who had arrived – disappeared back into the bush. The remaining two monks were quick to take the queen's weight from Haren, and after they had replaced her, the older monk looked to Haren and then nodded back to the heart of the forest.

"It would be best if you headed back," he said to her. "We will take her from here."

"But I have nowhere to go," Haren protested. "I don't even know where I am."

"You have been a great help," the monk said, "but there is no role for you where we are going."

"Just let me follow until…"

"Please, miss," the monk implored, "just walk away."

Haren was too tired and confused to formulate an argument. As her uncertain steps slowed, she felt compelled to finish the journey, but instead of walking, she froze. She somehow believed that the moment was too big for her. The queen could not allow it. Before Haren was out of arm's length, Rhea threw her hand back and grabbed Haren's red gown. As Haren's frame added to the weight that the monks were pulling, the older monk turned pleadingly to Rhea.

"My queen," he said, "we cannot bring her. There are rules. We cannot allow her in our home."

The queen looked sternly at the monk and angrily forfeited one of her limited breaths. "She comes…"

The two monks looked to each other: neither had the audacity to argue.

The older one looked reluctantly back to Haren.

"You can come," he said finally. "Stay close and don't get lost."

Haren nodded once to him, and although she didn't know why, she folded into a bow before the queen.

After her passage was assured, Haren's eyes studied the queen.

"Where is she from?" she asked the monks as she trailed behind them. "A queen from where?"

The older monk seemed uninterested in answering.

"At this point, you are not owed a history lesson," he said firmly.

The monk's tone conveyed clearly that he would not entertain any questions from the violet-eyed girl.

Even still, Haren was compelled to ask one more.

"Can I help carry her?" she asked. "I can take some of the weight."

"Take her belongings," the older monk said. "Take them, and keep close."

Haren nodded, and reached for the queen's crown and staff. The queen would only relinquish the staff.

After Haren accepted the weapon, the monks resolved to take all of the queen's weight, and with Rhea completely off the ground, the convoy headed quickly for home.

With the monks as navigators, the queen's journey was drastically quicker. It was only minutes before the giant gated entrance of the Throne's Eye monastery appeared. The dark wooden gate was thirty feet high, and on each of its sides, log walls stretched sideways to form a giant fortress. There were two wooden perches above the gate with two monks occupying each. After the elevated monks spotted Haren's convoy, they called out orders to each other, and after a few strenuous grunts and the sound of grinding and cranking gears, the giant Throne's Eye gate opened.

The monk Aeroh had been sent ahead of the convoy, and indeed he had brought the news. In addition to notifying Igallik, he had subsequently alerted nearly every monk in the monastery. The gravity of the situation had snapped each monk out of his routine and brought them all to the entrance to the monastery. The monks quickly made a path as Rhea was escorted through the gates. Haren was not as fortunate. As Haren entered through the gates, her path seemed to close. The monks blocked her path as if she were an intruder, and it was not until Rhea waved emphatically for her to follow that the path re-opened.

From behind the crowd, Igallik, the head monk of the monastery, emerged.

Igallik's green eyes and slow walk appeared as if they had seen one thousand years. His face was weathered with deep lines that deepened even further upon his every expression. A long gray beard fell from his jaw to his belt, and he wore a gray robe for the specific purpose of identifying himself as the senior monk in the monastery. Igallik was the enigmatic entity of the Throne's Eye. In the archives of the monastery's history, Igallik was accounted for in chronicles that were centuries past. No one knew his age, and no one knew his origin. It was only his wisdom that was fully acknowledged. The levels of Igallik's awareness and foresight remained the Throne's Eye's greatest instrument of direction and survival.

As Igallik broke into view of the queen, there was unmistakable relief in Rhea's eyes. The exchange was that of old friends. Igallik allowed his hand to fall onto Rhea's forehead, and after he removed it, his gaze and posture fell as if he knew every detail of her condition. After a mournful shake of his head, Igallik quickly began directing Haren, Rhea, and the other monks through the giant courtyard of the Throne's Eye monastery.

The inside of the monastery was a massive acreage completely surrounded by the thirty foot high perimeter wall. The monastery's central courtyard was a perfectly symmetrical circle with a base of dark red interlocking stone. The stone was carved and organized to form the symbols of the Lyran House, and within the stone there were small plots of soil that allowed for an abundance of massive cherry blossom trees. Like the points on a compass, there were eight paths branching out from the circle of red stone. Seven of the paths led to chapels, living quarters, horse stables, and training areas. The eighth path, which represented north on the compass, stretched one hundred yards to the aesthetic marvel of the Throne's Eye monastery: the High Temple. The High Temple was a golden chapel built at the summit of the monastery's grand staircase, a staircase that, step by step, ascended nearly two hundred feet.

Understanding the incredible stakes at play, Igallik rushed the monks and queen down one of the stone paths to the Throne's Eye infirmary. Once they had entered, Igallik instructed the monks to lay Rhea down on the table in front of an open window. The infirmary's contents were what one would expect; however, the room's dark wooden floor, grandiose stained glass windows, and golden tapestries seemed far too imposing for a sick room.

As the morning sun surged onto the monastery, its beams breached through the infirmary's windows and began to animate the stained glass's colours and characters onto the polished floor around the queen. The dozen monks present began to light and then place candles around the room, and Igallik, after calling for the monastery's herbalist, knelt next to the dying Rhea. Although no words were spoken audibly between them, it appeared as if the queen and head monk were having a conversation with their eyes. It was then that Rhea relinquished the golden crown into Igallik's hands.

Haren had been directly in tow of the procession, but feeling somewhat alien to the monastery and its monks, she had halted at the infirmary's door frame. As she watched the mysterious men in robes, she made sure not to encroach onto what seemed like privileged space.

While Haren watched, Igallik made sparing glances back to her. At one point, Igallik's face seemed to protest whatever the queen was saying to him; however, before he could return an argument, Rhea's body clenched and a strangled and painful scream burst out from her damaged throat.

"Wylak!" Igallik shouted as he rose to full posture. "Wylak, we need you now!"

In seconds, Wylak, the monastery's herbalist, pulled a wooden herb chest past Haren and into the room. The young and slender herbalist wore a green robe, and his cool blue eyes seemed to contrast his wild blonde hair and natty beard.

The man in green went quickly to work. He pulled his chest next to the queen, and after cracking it open, he quickly administered plant roots to the queen's throat. The roots immediately soothed the queen's wounds. With the pain managed, the herbalist dug deeper into his medicines and pulled out two vials of glowing blue water. Wylak poured the first vial over the queen's scalp, and almost instantly the tension in Rhea's body released. As the queen's face conveyed her relief, Wylak pulled a small golden apparatus from his chest and then held it over Rhea's pregnant belly. The tool's top half was shaped like a compass, and the lower half was a dangling golden chain with a small blue crystal bound to its end. After Wylak administered the second blue water vial to Rhea's belly and chest, he studiously held his tool over the queen and seemed intently focused on his gadget's dangling crystal. After studying the tool's movement over the queen's belly and heart, the young herbalist turned to the head monk with heavy eyes.

"In a way I don't understand," Wylak said sorrowfully, "the children have been affected by crossing realms." The herbalist looked apologetically to the queen, but had to look back to Igallik to fend off his own tears. "Every breath she takes is damaging her children. If the queen lives ten minutes longer with her sons in utero, the children could be very damaged – mentally and physically. The window of their survival is almost closed."

Every heart in the infirmary sank – all but one.

After Rhea heard that she was harming her children, her hands clenched around the bed sheets beneath her, and with a painful scream she charged unrestrained into the motions of childbirth. It is true in your realm that the good hearts must be led by the great ones. As the screaming Rhea clenched and pushed and the wounds on her neck tore even further open, the monks of the Throne's Eye, solely by witnessing the queen's strength, came to know courage in a way they never had before.

Even so, there was no time for reverence. There was barely time for action.

With his eyes remaining fixed on the struggling queen, Igallik nominated the herbalist. "Wylak, we need you to deliver the children."

Wylak's eyes grew wide with surprise. "This is the first woman we've ever had in the monastery," he said apologetically. "I can help her pain, but I am in no way practiced in childbirth. None of us are."

"I am," said the second woman to ever enter the Throne's Eye.

Every monk turned immediately to the purple-eyed girl at the door frame.

"I apprenticed in the infirmary of my village,' Haren said. "If you let me, I can deliver the children."

There was no time for rules or tradition.

"What do you need?" Igallik asked.

"Towels," Haren replied as she looked over the tools spread on the medical counter. "Towels and those clamps."

In seconds, Haren was given her tools. Wylak nodded affirmatively to her, and as he began to administer more herbs to the queen, Haren knelt at Rhea's legs and prepared to receive her babies.

Even in Rhea's broken state, when it was obvious that the throes and motions of childbirth were stealing the last reserves of her life, the queen would not relent. The conditions of her arrival on earth demanded nothing less.

Finally, after five minutes, the first child was born. Haren inspected the child, and after nodding to the queen to affirm that the child was healthy, Haren handed the small boy to Igallik. Rhea seemed to bite back her relief. Her duty – to Serich, to herself, and to her sons – was not yet complete.

As the seven minute mark passed, Rhea's will was nearly destroyed. The second child was crowning, but the queen was almost lifeless. As Rhea's eyes began to roll backwards, Wylak looked worriedly to Haren. His face conveyed far too clearly that he had no other herb or option for the queen. Haren couldn't allow it to end like this. Although the queen had shown her more courage than she had ever seen, Haren stood up and demanded more.

"My lady!" Haren shouted. "It is your life for his! One last push! For a life, my lady! Just push!"

Tears streamed down the queen's face. She feared the incredible pain she needed to inflict upon herself. She feared the immense courage that she needed to find. Her scared stare acknowledged the impossibility of a final push with a pleading and praying look up to the heavens. With her eyes still saying no to Haren, the queen managed to nod her head yes.

After a deep and intense breath, the queen's jaw gritted completely shut. As her eyes steeled with intent and each muscle from her neck to her thighs flexed and beaded with sweat, Rhea wailed and forced out a final push.

The second child was born.

The second, however, did not share the first's healthy form. As feared, the queen's injuries had affected the child. His body mass was greatly reduced, and his bones were frail and slightly deformed. Haren kept her gaze down and away from the queen; she could not bear Rhea learning that she had a deformed child because of the look on her own face. As Haren kept her eyes down and surveyed the child, she was unsure if the boy would survive.

Igallik could read Haren's fear.

As the head monk looked regretfully over the drained and destroyed queen, he feared burdening her last moments with the knowledge of her son's condition. Sensing the queen's end, Igallik made a decision on instinct, and then offered each of the children to his dying mother. The queen held her boys for her first and last time. As Igallik had feared, Rhea became aware of the second boy's condition. However, her reaction confounded him. She nestled the small child against her cheek, and as a smiling tear fell from her eye, she kissed the child's forehead. The queen smiled on her boys, and she seemed at peace. There was tranquility in her eyes. As Rhea savoured the moment, suddenly, her body broke into a sudden fit of seizure. Igallik quickly lifted each child out of Rhea's arms and gave them back to Haren. As the head monk then looked back to the queen, her eyes seemed to invite his unspoken responsibility. The head monk understood. He placed his hand over Rhea's forehead and began to recite a Throne's Eye prayer. Upon hearing the incantation, the queen closed her eyes and took in a deep breath. While the queen held her breath, the air in the infirmary seemed light, and with each passing second it seemed as if the candles in the room were burning more brightly. Then, as Rhea exhaled, the candles extinguished, and Rhea's body began to slowly transform from flesh to a thick white smoke. For a moment the smoke held to Rhea's silhouette, but soon, almost like a spreading puddle, the smoke dispersed and streamed slowly across the infirmary floor. The smoked disappeared in seconds, and at the exact moment it vanished, the candles in the infirmary flared back into flames. The candlelight emphatically stressed that the queen was gone; the only traces of her left were swaddled in Haren's arms.

For the queen, it was the end. The laws that governed Animus Letum could not allow her to cross again into the afterlife; a soul cannot journey twice past death. Rhea had perished on earth and would be survived only by her two sons.

As Igallik's balance wavered, forcing him unwillingly onto a stool in the infirmary, he eyed the royal heirs and then the young woman who was holding them.

Wylak opened his herb chest and seemed intent on attending to the head monk, but Igallik waved off his efforts.

After a long moment, Igallik gave the herbalist a task. "Assemble the High Order," he said. "We will meet in the High Temple in one hour."

He then looked to Haren, and although he didn't share what he was thinking, his eyebrow rose with a contemplative arc.

"Everything has changed," he whispered to himself. "We may have to follow suit."

4

The High Order of the Throne's Eye brotherhood was the monastery's elected government. The Order was responsible for all major decisions within the monastery, and through a collective vote, they determined and orchestrated the best interests of the monastery. This included whom they allowed to live within in their walls.

With three new arrivals, the Order needed to deliberate.

The Order was comprised of five monks. The five were known as totems and each represented a specific school of judgement. Raeman, a tall, pale, and slender man who possessed the uncanny likeness of a vulture, represented Justice. Palis, an Indian man half Raeman's size, represented Mercy. Nile, an Asian man adorned with glasses, was the youngest monk ever elected to the Order, and he represented Logic. And Bysin, a superstitious, ginger-haired man, who insisted on the aid of Wylak's mind-altering herbs, represented Instinct. The Order was completed by Igallik, who served as the group's chancellor, multi-talented totem, and tie-breaker if the four other members found themselves in a deadlock.

Using their individual judgement, each totem of the Order decided upon a verdict, and then collectively they decided upon a ruling. For each Order ruling, the five totems were relied on to explore the depths of their speciality and offer a vote based on their efforts. No totem was more important than the other, and likewise, no individual verdict was weighed with greater value. Ultimately, the Order had built its method such that there was little chance of bias or mistake. The monks had used their insight and foresight to develop a system where they could judge and scrutinize any scenario – even the unlikely. These considerations included scenarios where a totem could defer his vote to another's speciality or even a circumstance where an exceptional force became a higher authority than the Order. The latter statute was called Providence, and it occurred very rarely. Essentially, when Providence was enacted, the Order conceded its ruling to an exceptional force. The will of a Lyran King, for example, was exceptional. If Providence were recognized, the Order forfeited all votes and the exceptional force became the decider.

All assemblies of the High Order were held in the monastery's High Temple. The Temple was located at the summit of the monastery's grand staircase, two hundred feet above the monks' central court and living areas.

Andrew F. Whittle

The Temple resembled your earth realm's mosques, and was built with golden stone. Two dark marble statues of Serich posed ominously at the staircase's final step, and behind the royal effigies there were two lines of cherry blossom trees that led to the Temple's massive bronze door. A portion of the Temple's roof had a retractable glass ceiling to allow for the monastery's occasional smoke rituals, and there were exactly five crystal windows on the Temple's wall, each grafted with the blue *L* crest of the Lyran House.

With the afternoon sun beaming brightly off the Temple, the High Order began its ascent of the grand staircase. Haren was in tow.

As the Order monks and their guest approached the Temple's bronze door, they were ushered through by Raine. Raine was the Throne's Eye's strongest warrior, and he served as the honour guard each time the Order assembled. Raine was a massive black man with an English accent. With hands like bricks and shoulders as wide as the Temple door, he was a picture of strength. Like all of the monastery's soldiers, he wore red and gold armour instead of robes. And although his physical brawn was intimidating, most in the Throne's Eye thought of him as a gentle giant. Raine liked to wisecrack – typically with a foul mouth – but his warm disposition was so immediate that he could enter a room with twenty strangers and leave with twenty friends. He was the prototypical older brother, greatly strong and greatly loyal. However, that is not how his enemies knew him. In battle, Raine was fearsome. The Greeks of your realm would have lauded him, for when he was armed with his sword, Raine became a war god, surging with the ichor of Aries.

As the Order passed by the great warrior, Haren paused, struck by the shocking size of the Temple's guard.

Raine dropped his head. "It's noticeable, isn't it?"

"Your size?" Haren stammered.

"I've got a grievance with the Maker," Raine said with his heavy accent. "The bastard gave me the body and brains of a shithouse. Wanted to be a dancer, you know. Instead, he gave me a talent for getting bashed in the face."

As the warrior's eyes put her at ease, Haren smiled and played along. "You could always dance while you get bashed in the face."

"That's not half bad," Raine said. "Hell, I'd swing twice as hard if the prick in front of me was dancing. Thanks, birdy. My face is indebted."

Haren curtsied, but before she could say another word, Igallik's voice called back to her from inside the Temple.

"Raine wastes enough of his own time, Haren. We try not to let him waste ours."

Haren smiled; his name was Raine. However, as she looked to Igallik inviting her into the Temple's interior, the smile slowly faded. The Order monks, and in fact the entire situation, seemed far too imposing. Like the tunnel that had burrowed into the treeline, the Temple doors seemed to signal that there was no going back.

Raine knew all too well what Haren was feeling. "The Order's like a grain sickle," he said. "It's pretty scary until you see how it works."

As Haren's uncertain eyes looked up at him, Raine winked.

"You're home, love. Choose strength."

It was far too soon for Haren to believe that she had found a home. But as she stood at the precipice of her next chapter, she could not escape the coincidence of the giant warrior's name. As a symbol, rain had always been her guide. Rain had always been at the start of something good. Haren had known for a long time that she was worth more than the life she had lived. And although she hadn't been the breaker of her broken faith, it was still her task to rebuild. She just needed a chance. As she eyed the Raine that fell on her in that moment, she thought she could hear the patter of something good.

"I'm Haren," she said to Raine with an extended hand.

The warrior received Haren's hand and laughed. "Dear God, the bird's a bird!"

Haren smiled. "Better a bird than a storm's piss."

"Listen hear, birdy —"

"Raine," the head monk interrupted. "We're ready for her now."

Raine rolled his eyes such that only Haren could see, and made a formal gesture for her to enter the Temple.

Haren's apprehension subsided. After another curtsy to the warrior, she walked through the Temple door.

Once Haren had passed him, Raine closed the door behind her and continued to stand guard outside the Temple.

The inside of the High Temple was wreathed with royal class. As Haren walked down the center aisle of golden pews and claret rug, the hue of her burgundy gown matched the colour scheme so closely that she seemed to become a moving piece of the decoration. The glass roof and five windows of the Temple allowed a substantial volume of light to enter, and when lit by the sun, the room's gold and burgundy palette appeared so vividly that it seemed like the Temple should serve as a celestial lighthouse, a room tasked to hail the heavens, because if contact were ever made between them, their grandeurs would not be unequal.

At the back of the Temple there was a giant altar surrounded by a library of leather-bound books. Igallik had placed the golden crown of Animus Letum on top of the altar, and just in front of it there were five thrones situated in a semi-circle. Each throne belonged to a specific Order member, and upon that ownership, each throne was specifically designed.

Raeman, who represented Justice, sat at the far left in an imposing and gothic throne built out of steel, the strongest metal forged by man. Palis, the Mercy totem, sat at the far right, and his black and round-edged throne was built from lava rock, a material that had become strong and unmalleable even after suffering the heat of hell. Nile's Logic throne was on the inner right, and its simple design was built from the same glass that he wore in front of his eyes. The throne was transparent, and, like Nile's glasses, its lens was used to see more clearly. Bysin, who represented Instinct, was on the inner left and he possessed the only living throne. His chair was carved into the trunk of an Adansonia tree that required water and still yielded leaves. The roots of Bysin's throne spread beneath the Temple floor, and the spirit of the tree, like the totem that sat upon it, possessed an instinctual awareness of the present and ensuing future. Igallik's versatile throne was centered within the four totems. It was made of oak, and each of its four legs sunk one foot into a pool of water, a substance that adapts specifically to the conditions of the environment. Additionally, there was a tobacco hookah built into the right arm of the head monk's oak throne.

As Haren approached the Order, Igallik drew from his hookah. After a gentle nod to the Order's guest, the head monk spoke and exhaled his smoke in the same breath.

"Let it be understood, the verdict for this hearing will be final unless an exceptional force decrees otherwise." His voice was stern, and within the Temple a faint echo followed his words. "Because the verdict is final, the totems of the Order shall be permitted any length of time to make their verdict. However, if a totem is uncertain about a verdict – even in the least – he will defer his vote to another totem's speciality."

Igallik looked to the Order monks on his left and right, and after receiving each of their affirmations of understanding, he took another puff from his hookah. "It is pledged."

The words *hearing* and *verdict* were expected by the Order. But for the girl standing before them, they were surprising, big, and threatening. Haren could not escape the feeling that the Order had put her on trial. A mob had done the same nine days prior, and only a miracle had spared her from its grim sentence.

"I don't understand," Haren said with a weak voice and posture. "Am I in trouble?"

"No," Igallik said reassuringly. "For now, you are simply under discussion. We are very interested in why you are here."

Haren looked disheartened. "I'm not sure that I know."

"Quite right," the head monk smiled. "But even though you have no answer, this doesn't mean that there is no answer." Igallik tilted his head, choosing to revise his earlier statement. "I suppose I should have said that we are very interested in what has brought you here."

"It is not the prettiest of tales," Haren admitted.

Igallik took another puff from his hookah. "All the same, we are very interested."

After a deep breath, Haren recounted her last nine days. With heaviness, she remembered Morello; with disdain she described Tholyk; with relief she told of the blue heron; and with awe she detailed the incredible path that had led her to the queen.

Such a story should have rendered any audience speechless, but Igallik was quick with his reply.

"It is a shame that we must be measured by tragedy," he said sadly. "It seems, though, that you have been measured highly – by more than just our realm."

As her eyes fell away from the head monk, it was clear that Haren did not know how to respond. It is difficult to accept praise when you believe that it is undeserved. Instead of pride, Haren carried a heft of guilt; it was punishing to think that Morello had to die for her to be measured highly. Haren did not feel as if she had won – by any means. In her mind, she had lost. She had lost her brother, and she knew that his absence, like a hole in her spirit, would damage her for the rest of time.

As Haren's fidgeting hands and elusive gaze became the conduits of her heavy heart, Palis offered a reprieve.

"My dear, your past was what we required. We thank you for your candor. I estimate that the conditions of your last nine days have warranted you some rest. Find Raine at the door, and he will see to it that you get some food and drink."

Haren managed to claim some focus. "I am to leave?"

"For now," the head monk said as he swept a slow hand through his long beard. As he studied Haren, Igallik wondered if he should explain to her that the Order was about to debate whether or not they would offer to adopt her. He chose not to. "We will call you back when you're needed."

Haren nodded, trying unsuccessfully to read past Igallik's stoic eyes.

"As you wish," she finally consented.

With a curtsy, Haren backed away from the Order and paced back to the Temple door. Raine greeted her, and after Haren disappeared, the Order was left with varying impressions of her.

"I don't want her here," Raeman announced firmly. "The rules that have governed us shall always govern us. I cannot support her living within our walls."

"Our rules were tailored to reflect our world," Igallik reminded. "As of this moment – with Serich fallen from the throne – I contend that our world has vastly changed."

The head monk looked to the Instinct totem for affirmation.

Bysin nodded grievously. "I sense that our paths have breached completely from what they were."

Raeman shook his head. "So we are to follow the chaos? Brothers, now is when we must hold to our convictions. We cannot forfeit our ways. They are a weapon, a source of order with which to combat the disorder. We are strong as we are. To alter our makeup would compromise our strength."

Nile adjusted his glasses, and then pushed them back against the bridge of his nose. "Raeman's reasoning is strong, but not absolute. And unless Bysin will endorse it, I think our considerations should be relevant to what we know."

Bysin did not seem intent on endorsement.

"In that case," Nile said, "What we *know* is that Haren had a brother. And that she raised him from infancy. We also know that we have been given two infant boys, whose immediate care is of a variety not studied by the Throne's Eye. I see a set of circumstances that can resolve themselves."

Palis agreed. "I see a girl who could use us as much as we could use her."

Igallik turned back to Bysin. "How do you measure her as a Deathrider?"

"I felt her soul the moment she walked through our gates," Bysin replied. "And let me tell you that it was no coincidence that Serich chose her to find the queen." The Instinct totem looked down the row enthusiastically. "She is gifted, brothers. I believe it is right to adopt her. May I remind you that Serich sent us the very same message that he sent to her. He said…"

"Gentleman," Raeman interrupted, "the message was coincidence. I would not endorse a strict interpretation."

"Would you care to repeat the message?" Igallik challenged.

Raeman scowled and reluctantly agreed. "Serich said, 'Follow the heron.'"

"Coincidence?" Igallik asked.

Bysin and Palis shook their heads.

"I too have to say no," Nile said. "Although it is not completely sound, there is a line that can be reasonably drawn between these events."

The head monk exhaled the smoke from his hookah. "Shall we vote?"

The Order monks nodded.

"In favour?" Igallik asked.

By a show of hands, the monks voted. With a show of four to one, the Order moved in favour of adopting Haren. The motion was really an invitation. The Order had voted to *offer* Haren sanctuary at the Throne's Eye. The decision to stay was hers and hers alone.

"With that settled," Igallik said, "we can move onto the issue of the twins. I believe we are all in agreement that their arrival was an act of Providence. Nile, do you see it otherwise?"

"I do not," Nile replied. "It is evident that Serich went to great measures to send his queen and sons here. They were meant most certainly to arrive at our gates."

"And to live within them as well," Bysin added.

"Very well, then," Igallik said. "Upon Providence, it seems that we have adopted the boys. Are they any contentions?"

There were none.

As Igallik prepared to adjourn the Order, he opened the floor to any last thoughts.

"Are there any other matters concerning these rulings?" he asked. "Speak now, brothers, for these decisions will soon become canon."

"I have one," Nile announced. "A consideration regarding the twins."

Igallik nodded. "Proceed."

"I move to separate the boys," Nile said. "I think it is reasonable to deduce that the murder of Rhea was equally aimed at the twins: an attempt to kill a line of successors. Forneus's actions were predatory, and I suspect that he will continue his hunt even across realms. In the interest of survival – and I mean odds of survival – I move that the boys be separated."

"I disagree with separation," Igallik said. "Providence gave us both. I contend that their division would conflict with Serich's will."

"Furthermore," Raeman added, "if they are to be hunted, we offer them the best protection."

"I cannot endorse separation either," said Palis. "These boys – their origin, their fates, and truly the blood that courses within them – are of a class that makes them very different, perhaps too different for us to fully understand. It would serve them best to have each other."

"Anything to add, Bysin?" the head monk asked.

"I sense that there is already a bond between these twins," the Instinct totem said. "They are strong on their own. But I sense that they will be greater together."

"Show of hands," Igallik said.

By a show of four to one, the Order moved against separating the sons of Animus Letum.

"Are there any other matters?" Igallik asked.

There were none.

The head monk puffed once more from his hookah. "Brothers, we are adjourned. Today's verdicts are indisputable unless an exceptional force or event decrees otherwise. You may return to your quarters."

And with that, the Throne's Eye chose to become three stronger.

Only time would prove by how much.

5

After Haren had left the High Temple, Raine escorted her to the monastery's library. The library was a two story building shaped like an hourglass. The first story was built with red brick, and the second floor was built out of the same crystal as the High Temple windows. Raine ushered Haren through the doors and then welcomed her into a communal space known as the Spine. The Spine was a massive oval chamber that had a giant brick fireplace, numerous sitting areas, and a series of fifteen foot tall bookshelves that lined its entire circumference. Every monk in the Throne's Eye was allowed access to the Spine and its resources. There were thousands of books dedicated to world histories, religions, martial arts, and nearly every other topic that had been recorded by pen or print. The library's only other room was called the Ichor, and only a few monks were allowed entry. The Ichor was much smaller than the Spine in size and incredibly smaller in resources. In fact, the Ichor was a small study with one desk and only one book. *The Book of the Eterna* was the highest level text in the practice of the Throne's Eye monastery. Within its pages there were rituals and incantations that could hail the afterlife, ensure a soul safe passage between realms, and even merge the souls of two separate individuals. There was great power within the pages of *The Book of the Eterna*, and the privilege of reading it had to be earned. The Order monks were the only ones allowed access to the hallowed text; however, there were rare accounts where exceptional circumstances had allowed other monks to read its pages.

As the sun pushed through the second floor crystal of the library, Haren spun slowly at the center of the Spine, marvelling its impressive bookcases.

"Even if I had one hundred years," she said with a smile, "I still don't think I could read all of these."

Raine watched her for a moment. "So you're a reader?"

Haren's gaze would not leave the bookshelf. "When I had the time I was."

"The world's got enough readers, birdy. What we need are writers."

"I didn't say I couldn't write," Haren said. "I just figured that I wasn't that gifted with a pen."

Raine stepped next to Haren and joined her gaze. "Our bookshelf is filled mostly with history books," he said. "The authors aren't really writers. They're recorders – they write the stories that have already happened."

Haren's eyes fell off the bookshelf. "Are you making a point?"

"That I am," the warrior laughed. "Point is, you don't even need a pen to be a writer. You can write a history with your actions."

Haren smiled. "And I thought the bookshelf was grandiose."

"You wrote history today," Raine said matter-of-factly. "Up until this morning, no woman had ever set foot in this monastery."

"Hell of a book," Haren said sarcastically.

"It could be," Raine replied.

Haren was silenced by the giant warrior's stare. "Look," she said finally, "a lot has happened to me over the last nine days. To be honest, I'm not really thinking about writing the future. I'm paralyzed enough by the present."

Raine nodded, certain that he knew what Haren meant. "It's 'cause you've got a question," he said. "Trust me, I've had the same one. It's not the present that paralyzes us, it's the question."

"I have more than just one," Haren replied.

"But there is a big one," Raine guessed. "One that all others follow."

Haren looked up at Raine, sensing that he knew exactly which question was at the front of her mind.

"What is happening to me?" she said.

Raine nodded. "That's the one. Fortunately, history holds your answer."

After giving the bookshelf a quick survey, the old warrior pointed and then followed his finger to a particular section.

"Although I think it's better to write history," he said as his hand traced a line across the bookshelf, "it's not so bad to read every once in a while."

After his finger brushed down the spine of the book he wanted, Raine retrieved it and blew the dust off its cover.

"You've never seen this book," he said. "But I'll bet you recognize one of its characters."

With a heavy thud, the old warrior dropped the thick leather-bound book on the table nearest to Haren.

"Give it a read," he encouraged. "It has given me more than a few answers."

Haren studied the warrior for a moment, and then approached the book. In large script, there were two dark blue words carved onto its cover: *Animus Letum*.

"Latin?" Haren asked.

"Soul Light," Raine interpreted.

"And my answer is in here?" Haren asked skeptically.

"Mostly," Raine said.

Haren eyed the giant text. As her hand traced over its cover, her fingers moved slowly, tapping the leather as if she were measuring more than just the book's aesthetics.

"The author is fond of poetry," Raine said, "but nevertheless, it is history."

As Haren sat down, she was reminded of something her father used to say: "If you seek the future," she quoted, "you must consult the past."

"Sounds about right," Raine agreed. He then nodded back to the book. "While you consult, I'll rustle up some food and drink."

Haren offered her thanks, and after Raine had left, she carefully opened the leather-bound text to its first page.

Inked onto the page were quatrains of verse written with black script.

A death is not a death
When it serves as a door;
Instead, it takes a breath
And breathes in evermore.

There is time after here
And a path for the soul:
This grim road most souls fear
For your death pays its toll.

Heaven waits, as does Hell,
Both are under one sun;
Good and evil do dwell
In a land that is one.

In this land there's a fight
The war waged for all souls,
A war of dark and light,
And the prize is a throne.

There are Kings and their Queens
In wars of great mention;
There are serpentine fiends
And men who are Legend.

These Legends hold the throne
As Kings of hereafter,
With blue light in their souls,
Of might they are masters.

The Lyrans are these Kings
Who rule as the righteous;
With shining hearts they bring
Great light to the lightless.

As Haren's eyebrow rose skeptically, her reason told her to dismiss the book. With an airy exhalation, she pushed her chair back from the table and looked up to the library's crystal windows. In her village, Haren had explored every religious text she could get her hands on. She had hoped and prayed that one religion – or any religion – could help her understand herself. For so long, Haren had felt that a world awaited her. She knew somehow that she mattered to the world, a pivotal piece in its destiny. She just needed some help to understand how. The voice – the one she had heard her entire life – seemed to convince her that help was on the way. It seemed to promise something more than a poem.

"Just like all the others," she muttered.

"Then surely," a calm voice said from behind her, "there is no harm in reading a few more pages."

As Haren's body stiffened, she sprang up from the chair and turned to see the head monk behind her.

"Sorry to startle you," Igallik said. "I have an unintentional habit of sneaking up on people."

Haren offered a weak smile, trying to avoid eye contact. She felt a small wave of guilt washing over her. The head monk had surely heard her dismiss the book. And as Haren's gut churned, she hoped it had not been a grave insult.

Igallik brushed a hand through his beard, and after a moment, he pointed to the book.

"The poetry is a little much," he said, "but you should know that truth is not limited to a single medium." There was omniscience in his voice – as if his words had been formed over one thousand years of thought.

Even still, Haren felt a pang in her gut – the moment when you begin to pity someone. She respected Igallik, but felt sorry for his philosophy.

"Igallik," she said, trying to ease the blow, "it is a poem – a legend. There are many writers – even a few in my village – who pen this type of fiction. It is simply a poem."

"Was the heron just a bird?" the head monk replied.

Haren had many thoughts, but no answer. She had no way to explain her last nine days.

"Read the next three pages," Igallik said. "I would think – given the details of your arrival here – that these three will be a little more convincing."

Feeling that she owed Igallik and the monastery some level of thanks, Haren conceded. She nodded to the head monk – a nod more like a surrender – and then reseated herself. As she flipped the giant text to its next page, her eyes settled on a portrait centered at its top. The portrait was of a giant gray-haired man staring up from the page with electric blue eyes. The man wore a suit of golden armor, and there was a crown resting on his head. As Haren examined the crown's details, a sudden thought caused her to back away from the book. With her fingers pressed against her temples, Haren examined the crown once more, but soon her wide gaze rose onto the bookshelf in front of her. However, her purple eyes were not looking ahead. They were looking behind. Haren knew that she had seen the crown before – that very day in the meadow.

Igallik could sense her confusion.

"Three pages," he repeated. "I will answer any questions you have after then."

Haren rubbed her temples once more, and then tapped her finger on the table next to the book.

"Three pages," she agreed.

Beneath the portrait there were six more quatrains.

Perian was King first,
The war God of great might:
To conquer evil's worst
He drew from his blue light.

Andrew F. Whittle

> *Vile Dragons did hunt him*
> *With great fires and grand scales;*
> *But his light never dimmed*
> *And his heart never paled.*
>
> *He suffered hellish pains*
> *And endured hellish Pools;*
> *Through his foes he took reign*
> *And established his rule.*
>
> *A blue Cauldron became*
> *The spirit of the land;*
> *Burning its righteous flames,*
> *It shined noble and grand.*
>
> *In the light of his reign*
> *Heaven's bloom had begun;*
> *Cherry blossoms proclaimed*
> *That the Lyran had won.*
>
> *Through sheer might and blue light,*
> *The afterlife was won;*
> *And after siring knights,*
> *The great King sired a son.*

After a look to Igallik – a gaze that was moved by the crown, but unpersuaded by the verse – Haren turned to the next page. Again, a giant portrait of a man was centered at the top. This man had the same electric blue eyes and crown that the first one wore, but he had no suit of armour, and his body was set into a contemplative pose with his right fist set meditatively under his chin. There were another six quatrains.

> *The crown passed to Jerub,*
> *The King of patient mind:*
> *He was the wearer of*
> *The grand traits of mankind.*

His eyes saw through evil,
His heart saw through pain;
He sought the retrieval
Of the souls evil claimed.

His father won great wars,
Through his brawn, he was Lord,
But Jerub won far more
With his mind than his sword,

With wits, thought, and mercy
The first heir chose to build
His own theocracy
Where blood need not be spilled.

Choosing a new flower
That would hallmark his age,
He honoured his power
And elected the sage.

He built upon greatness
And thought upon grace,
Though all saw his greatest
When his son took his place.

Haren looked flatly at Igallik.

"One more page," she said. There was a cynical tone to her words, as if she were challenging the head monk – as if they had made a bet and Haren was certain that she was about to win.

"I suspect one will be enough," Igallik replied calmly.

Haren eyed the head monk for a moment, unsure if his confidence was foolish or wise.

The next page would decide.

After her fingers slipped between the leaves, Haren turned carefully to the next page.

Again, there was a portrait centered at its top. This portrait was of two people: a man and a woman – a king and a queen.

Haren's eyes quickly noted the king's electric blue eyes, wild gray hair, and golden armour, but as her stare shifted to the woman at his shoulder, one word – one whisper of shock – escaped from her mouth.

"Impossible…"

"I prefer unprecedented," the head monk said. "Recognize her?"

Haren did. She had watched the woman die that very morning. The woman was Rhea – an exact likeness. She wore the exact same white gown, she had the same blonde hair, and even her facial features were uncannily alike. The only difference was that in the portrait, Rhea's emerald eyes had no pupil or iris; they were completely green.

As Haren looked even more closely over the portrait, she ran her hands through her hair, making small noises like someone putting a puzzle together. The exile seemed to sense what she was being told. However, the truth – the secret that she had sought her entire life – seemed far larger than she had supposed. The world that Haren had waited for seemed to nullify the one that she had waited in. If the book was true, Haren's world had changed. It had broken. Without looking at the head monk, she began to speak, but after a few broken words, she cut herself off.

"Was it a charade?" she said finally, a small tremble in her voice. "Was my world a farce? Is *everybody's* world a farce? What about religion? What about god?"

Anxiously, Haren tapped the page in front of her. "If this is true, everyone is living a lie…"

"I wouldn't consider it a lie," Igallik said. "Religions are simply the different costumes we put on the same god. They are variations of the creator."

"But I had a brother, Igallik. I had a life. I don't know if I'm ready for this. I don't want my past to mean nothing."

"But you can feel it," Igallik said, pushing the revelation.

Haren seemed burdened by the truth. "I think I always did…"

"Then read."

Haren inhaled deeply, and returned her eyes to the book. Even with Morello in her mind, she knew she had tasted the truth and needed more.

The third portrait was followed by another six quatrains.

The third King was Serich,
The greatest King of all time;
His soul was the marriage
Of warrior and wise.

The Sons of Animus Letum

The invincible Liege
With unstoppable strength
Bore impossible siege
Of indefinite length.

His mind out-thought his foes,
His brawn out-duelled his bane;
He defended his throne
And slayed malevolent Vayne.

His rivals fell in droves,
His great staff was his scythe;
From him and him alone
Was the Serpent's demise.

In the rains of his reign,
The King grew Bergamot,
And so his bloom became
The plant he shaped and wrought.

With peace struck in heaven
And peace further foreseen,
The King who was legend
Took Rhea for his Queen.

Haren backed away from the book and repeated the one word that was breaking her heart.

"Bergamot..."

As she dropped her forehead into her palm and pushed her hand slowly back through her hair, a heavy sigh fell from her lips. It was as if a weight – a pressure that had been building for her entire life – suddenly fell through.

"It was him," she whispered. Her wide and amazed eyes turned to Igallik. "All this time, he was the voice. He *is* the voice."

Igallik was uncertain what she meant. "The voice?" he asked.

"My great friend," Haren said with tears welling in her eyes. "The bergamot... the rain. Serich has spoken to me my entire life," she cried. "He is the reason I'm here."

"You're sure?" Igallik asked.

"Deeper than anything."

Igallik smiled. "Then you are ready."

"For what?" Haren asked.

Igallik pointed back to the book. "To know about the chapter you are writing."

6

After learning that Serich had been the voice, Haren felt compelled to return some act of thanks to the fallen king. Her first act, although miniscule in comparison, was to learn more about Serich's world. Igallik proved to be a knowledgeable teacher. The head monk revealed everything he could about Animus Letum. He explained to Haren that she was a Deathrider, and then explained how many of the monks at the Throne's Eye shared the same gift. Then, using the different kings of the Lyran House, Igallik chronicled every age of Animus Letum. He described the look and power of the Soul Cauldron, he explained the evils of the Dark Pool, and he introduced Haren to the afterlife's newest king.

"So Forneus will rule until someone kills him?" Haren asked.

"I doubt he would concede the crown," Igallik said. "So, yes, if we want to restore heaven, we must kill him."

"There must be people in Animus Letum who will try," Haren said.

"Try and fail," Igallik replied. "With Serich gone, and his entire army destroyed, Forneus and the Vayne will meet little opposition as they forge their new regime. With the throne under their complete control, the afterlife will become Hell."

"So what will you do?" Haren asked. "Surely, you will make a move."

Igallik eyed the young Deathrider for a long moment. "We do intend to make a move," he said finally. "However, our first move will not be made across realms."

Haren's eyes shifted, trying unsuccessfully to decipher the head monk's meaning.

"I don't quite understand," she admitted.

"We must make our move from a position of strength," Igallik began to clarify. "The divide between the earth realm and Animus Letum has become a weapon. We can cross at will, whereas those in Animus Letum cannot. A war is inevitable," the head monk predicted. "Our advantage is that we can decide when it begins."

"So you will wait to act," Haren realized.

"Until the only possible outcome is our victory," Igallik confirmed.

"Could be a lengthy wait," Haren said cynically. The notion of letting an entire world suffer did not agree with her – even if it was temporary.

"You may be right," Igallik said. "But we believe we have been given two very important reasons to wait."

"The twins?" Haren guessed.

"The heirs," Igallik corrected. "We have been given Lyrans, and we intend to make them throne-worthy."

Haren's eyebrow rose as she calculated the timeline. "So your move is to raise the boys until they are men," she said skeptically.

"We were hoping it would be your move as well," the head monk said calmly.

Haren's neck tilted back from Igallik. Her immediate reaction was alarm.

"Forgive my boldness," Igallik said, trying to ease Haren's panic. "I was uncertain how to time this conversation. Sometimes it is easier to climb over the mountain than to go around. Quite plainly, Haren, we are inviting you to live among us. We have voted to offer you a home."

Haren's anxiety was still controlling her pulse. "In return for what?" she asked.

"Your help raising the boys," Igallik said.

Haren was stung. "Because I raised a brother," she said, hurt by the apparent reasoning.

"That played a part," Igallik admitted. "But not all of it. You were chosen, Haren – selected by minds and hearts much greater than our own. We believe you were sent to us, a belief I think you share."

Haren became quiet.

The head monk *was* right. With the revelation that Serich had been the voice, Haren believed that she had always been destined to arrive at the Throne's Eye. It seemed very much that her arrival – and possible adoption – were intended by Serich's will. However, there was a terrible thought that followed this belief. It burdened Haren to think that Morello had somehow been a hindrance to her destiny. It was heartbreaking to sense – even in the slightest – that Morello's life had been insignificant. More and more, it felt as if Haren's future had the terrible agenda of erasing her past.

With her gaze fixed ahead and her mind only loosely engaged in the present, Haren gave the only reply she could. "I will need some time to consider."

"Take as much as you need," Igallik said. "No one should rush one's future."

As Haren nodded her thanks, Igallik made a slow sweeping gesture to the Spine's bookshelves.

"Our library is at your disposal," he said as he stood from the table. "You never know, you may find your answer in here."

Haren sat back and looked once more onto the impressive bookshelves.

"I promise to take a look," she said.

Igallik offered a gentle smile. "As you please."

The head monk made a slight bow, and with almost inaudible steps, he turned and exited the Spine.

After Igallik had left, Haren felt very lost within the library. She sauntered along the circular bookshelves, uncertain where to start or what to think. As she walked, she traced a finger along a dark wooden shelf, drawing a straight line through the dust that had accumulated. After the line had overlapped twice, Haren realized that she was no closer to a starting point. Inevitably, her focus and steps returned to the book entitled *Animus Letum*.

After reseating herself, Haren turned the pages and examined the portrait of Serich and Rhea.

As the great king looked up from the page, Haren's tear fell onto the paper.

"I don't know how to say thanks," Haren whispered to her friend. "I don't know if I can. I should feel awake. I should feel reborn. But all I feel is guilt."

Haren looked skywards for a moment, contemplating and revising a question that she needed to ask. "Did I really need Morello to die?" she asked weakly. "Did you?"

The question hurt. Especially with no answer. As Haren shook her head, she brought her hand to her forehead, and leaned into it for a moment. After exhaling deeply, she sat back, and used both hand to sweep away the tears in her eyes.

"I'm sorry, Serich... I owe you more."

After another deep exhalation, Haren sank into the chair, wishing somehow for rain and bergamot.

Staring at nothing, Haren's mind fell blank and her head began to nod off. As her body began to recline to sleep, she barely noticed the door to the Spine slide open.

Until a male voice screamed.

As the war cry registered, Haren leapt from the chair with her senses clenched and survival instincts engaged.

"Aw hell, birdy," Raine laughed. "We're gonna have to shape you up. You move like a mule!"

"Why would you do that?" Haren cried. "Why would you yell?"

"You looked like you were sleeping," Raine replied casually.

"I was, Raine! I was sleeping!"

"Figured you'd wanna eat," Raine said as he presented a plate and water. There was a glint in his eye that was thoroughly enjoying Haren's alarm.

Haren managed to catch her breath, and despite her resistance, a smile began to surface on her face. "In the name of... Raine, what is wrong with you?"

"No one's been able to figure that out," Raine said as he placed the plate of meat and vegetables on the table. "I think it might have something to do with my astrology."

Haren's curiosity rose. She had studied some astrology in her village.

"When were you born?" she asked.

"Don't know," Raine replied. "But I figure it'd explain something."

Haren shook her head. There was no adequate reply. After she gave up trying to offer a response, Haren examined the plate of food.

"I didn't notice any livestock around here," she said. "Where do you get the food?"

"We have some friends in a village not far from here," Raine said. "Town called Northton. They like to take care of us. The villagers are mostly miners, but a few of them farm."

Haren was surprised. "So they just give you food?"

"More or less. We've sorted out a few of their messes," Raine said. "I think they like to keep themselves in our favour."

"And what favour is that?" Haren asked.

Raine smiled. "I don't play games, birdy. I know the old man told you what we do. If you have a question, be honest about it."

Haren took the advice to heart. "Have you killed people?" she asked.

"Many," Raine answered.

"Does it bother you?"

"Not in the least."

"What if they were innocent?"

"They weren't."

"How can you be so sure?"

"Trust."

"Trust with whom?"

"The Deathriders."

Haren backed away from the warrior, and played with her food for a moment.

"So you're not a Deathrider?"

"I told you when we met," Raine said, "my talent is getting bashed in the face. It just so happens that I can dish it out too."

"And you will dish it out to anyone the Deathriders say deserves it?"

"Yes."

"But how could the Deathriders know?" Haren asked. "How could they know who should be killed?"

Raine nodded, understanding the confusion. "Igallik explained it to me this way: imagine you had a flower in a crystal vase. And in that vase you can see two colours: orange and blue. When you see blue you know the flower is healthy and is going to bloom. When you see orange you know the flower is going to wither and die. If you saw orange, would you intervene? Would you try to get rid of it?"

"I suppose I would," Haren said.

"I figured so," Raine said, "because I would too. But wanting to get rid of the orange is not as common as you might believe. In this world there are many people who like the orange. They like to breed it. We are at war with them and we have been for centuries. Igallik and the other Deathriders are able to sense the two colours. They've learned to detect where orange is growing. And when they do, me and the brawlin' boys head out and dish out some blue."

"And they're always right?"

"Always. And let me tell you, birdy, orange looks mighty sinister in person."

The expression on Raine's face suggested that there was no need for description.

"So how did the Throne's Eye find you?" Haren asked. "I mean how did you get here?"

Raine sat down in the seat across from Haren. "I suppose it's not so different from how you got here."

Haren leaned into the table, quiet, attentive, and expecting the tale.

As Raine detected Haren's curiosity, he seemed tentative about sharing. The old warrior seemed to shake off some emotion, but after he adjusted his collar, he wiped his eyes and reclined further in his chair.

"Not many know my story," he said with a small waver in his voice. "I'd prefer if it were kept between us."

Haren put her hand over her heart. "I promise."

Raine tilted his head for a moment and rapped his fingers onto the table. The hardest part of his story was starting it.

"I had a boy," he began.

Haren choked up instantly – there was so much hurt in Raine's voice.

"Named him Ruscai," the old warrior said. "His mother left when he was young. His mum was a dreamer, and I guess one day she had a dream that meant more than me. Either way, I raised Rus by myself. I was scared at first, you know, raising him on my own, but I learned pretty quickly that all I needed was the two of us."

Haren smiled – she knew the feeling.

"Ruscai was pretty quick," Raine continued. "A lot smarter than me. Figured he was meant for something special."

The old warrior looked skywards and then shook his head. "I guess I figured wrong. Or at least, I figured he'd have more time to show it. When he was nine, me and Rus were on our way back home from a day in the field. All of a sudden four men jumped out on the roadway. The four of them started coming at us. It was a real strange thing to see on the way home from work. I got in front of Rus, preparing for the fight …"

Raine shook his head, paused and took a long, heavy breath. "There must have been a fifth behind me," he said. "I never saw him, but he had to be there, 'cause when I woke up a few hours later there was blood gushing from the back of my head." Raine shrugged and wiped a welling tear from his eyes. "My money was gone, and Rus was lying dead on my lap."

Haren slumped, her posture broken by Raine's trembling voice. "I'm so sorry," she said as she placed her hand over his.

Raine let out a strange laugh. "Me too, birdy."

The old warrior wiped his eyes again. "Anyway, I sort of wandered for a few weeks. I didn't know where I was headed – only that I knew how to get there. It was like there was a compass in my head. I could hear a voice sometimes. I couldn't hear the words, but I felt something that was giving me hope."

"Serich…" Haren said.

Raine nodded. "The greatest king of the afterlife led me right to these Throne's Eye gates."

"It's a strange feeling, isn't it?" Haren said. "To know that he cared."

Raine nodded with a small smile. "Boggles my mind."

Haren and Raine looked away in unison, leaving a long silence between them. Finally, after considering her question and its timing, Haren broke the quiet.

"Do you think it was your destiny to end up here?"

Raine smiled. "What'd I say about games, birdy? Be upfront with it."

Haren dropped her head, avoiding Raine's eyes. "Do you think Rus needed to die for you to end up here?"

Raine nodded. "I've considered it," he said. "But I soon realized that I was looking at the question backwards."

Haren looked up, hoping that the old warrior knew something she didn't.

"The Throne's Eye isn't a penance," Raine said. "It is a prize. It is where we go to salvage our tragedies. We got wrecked, Haren. This world smashed our hearts like a hammer to ice. But was it destiny that brought us here? No. It was mercy. Rus didn't die so I could end up here. I ended up here so that I could honour Rus. The Throne's Eye is my second chance."

Something turned in Haren's mind.

"Are you happy here?" She asked.

"I have a purpose," Raine replied. "Happy is when I see my boy again."

Haren tilted back, suddenly realizing that Morello was in Animus Letum.

The rush of knowing that she would one day see him again hit her like sunshine through a window. As a series of thoughts aligned in her mind, Haren realized that she had an answer for the head monk.

With beaming eyes, she let the old warrior know first.

"You know, I think I might stay," she said. "I think I can manage having a purpose."

7

After Haren had joined the ranks of the Throne's Eye monastery, the monks turned their attention to the sons of Animus Letum.

The twins were given the names Odin and Galian. Their crib became a regular stopping point on every monk's schedule. The boys had lost their parents, but had inherited one aunt and two hundred uncles. The children were so revered that there became a title for not only their arrival, but also for the clearing where their mother had crossed realms. The term was Sanctus Donum – *sacred gift*.

Both twins were born with blonde hair and blue eyes, but both of them were not born healthy. As Haren tended to the twins, it became clear that Galian – the second-born child – had been seriously damaged by the conditions of his birth. His muscular composition was far weaker than his brother's, and he had an irregular skeletal structure. It was as if Galian's body had shifted – his spine was curved significantly to the left, and the rest of his body had been forced to adapt. His left side hung lower than his right, and his ribcage had a non-symmetrical formation that constricted the functioning of his lungs. Furthermore, Galian failed to respond vocally to any stimuli that Haren presented. After a collection of specially-aimed tests, Haren came to a painful realization. The child had been born mute – he would never speak.

With all of these complications, Galian's prognosis was not good.

However, no doctor's tool can measure will. When all expected surrender, Galian persevered.

After weeks of struggle – after weeks of Galian's body betraying him and depriving him of air – there was a sudden and inexplicable improvement. Suddenly, with no explanation but the miraculous, Galian was able to breathe normally. There were no indications of how it happened, only the proof that it had.

Diligently, Haren performed a few more tests, but the results were the same. Somehow, Galian had escaped from the condition that had threatened his life. It was as if Destiny had quarreled with Death and the maiden had worked a miracle.

As Galian began to breathe more easily, every monk in the Throne's Eye did so as well – every monk except Igallik. After he had been assured of Galian's health, the head monk began work on a grand stratagem. The Lyran House and the Dark Pool had warred with each other for ages. The two foes had been trading moves on a chessboard where one false move could mean complete destruction. And even though the Dark Pool had won the latest exchange, Igallik believed that he had two new pieces that promised a checkmate. To the Lyran name, Igallik swore that he would make Galian and Odin throne-worthy. Any lesser goal was an insult to Serich. The head monk's goal was daunting, but it was also unflinching. There would be no compromise or surrender – especially with Galian. Igallik would acknowledge Galian's disability, but he would not yield to it. Regardless of either boy's condition, they would be trained – they would be initiated into the sacred arts of the Throne's Eye brotherhood.

Igallik's plan was understood by every monk in the monastery. Fittingly, nearly every monk wanted to help the twins achieve their destiny. Odin and Galian would never be sheltered from their origin, and, similarly, they would never be sheltered from where they were destined to be. The undeniable truth was that Odin and Galian were the heirs to the throne of Animus Letum. As a collective, the High Order acknowledged that the only option for the Throne's Eye was to help Odin and Galian take back their birthright. They also acknowledged that such a task would require many hands. Accordingly, only one month after the birth of the sons of Animus Letum, the Order called every monk who was older than fifteen to a meeting in the Spine.

The sun was sinking when the one hundred and twenty three monks moved into the library. The glow of the setting sun was pouring through the Spine's windows, and as the monks settled themselves, Igallik stood stoically before the room's giant fireplace. The Order was seated next to him, and at the back of the room, Haren sat with the infant twins.

Before long, Igallik raised his right hand, and after the monks had quieted, he explained the reason for their attendance.

"Brothers," he began, "I have decided to be forthright with this assembly. I am telling you now that for each one of us, a critical decision is only minutes away. In moments, brothers, I will be asking for your life." The head monk paused a moment and allowed his words to resound. The words most definitely registered, and after watching the monks shift and murmur, Igallik proceeded. "I hope we are all in agreement that we have entered into an age of unprecedented circumstance," he said. "Hell has begun in the second realm. This is an undeniable truth. The serpent Forneus has established his rule over Animus Letum, and, now, beyond the curtain of death, a great wickedness awaits. Our deaths have become his domain. That being said, there is an even more important detail concerning Forneus's rule: in our realm, more specifically, at the back of this room, we harbour hell's greatest threat – we harbour the last of the Lyran legacy."

The monks nodded their consensus. Igallik had given them indisputable facts.

"Upon these truths," Igallik continued, "I wish to give you one more: the Lyran and Forneus are destined to clash once more. A war is waiting for our adopted sons, and it is a war in which we must play a part."

A young and eager monk named Gieler, who was somewhat swept away by the head monk's third truth, attempted to rally his brothers.

"We will play our part!" he shouted while beating his chest. "We will train them! Hell will crumble before the Lyran!"

As a chorus of shouts and cheers moved throughout the Spine's younger audience, Igallik and the Order remained patient. The rally eventually faded, and after Igallik regained the room's attention, he looked directly at Gieler.

"We will train them," the head monk assured, "there is no doubt. But in that spirit, I have another question for you and every other monk in attendance: are you prepared to die with them?"

Gieler's neck flexed back. "Die with them?" he repeated.

As the question registered, more whispers and murmurs spread throughout the Spine. Igallik quickly raised his hand and restored the quiet.

"I did say die with them," he restated. "Brothers, in the last month, myself and the Order have considered absolutely every factor regarding the twins. The most obvious truth – one that has been hinted at but not stated explicitly – is that one day Galian and Odin will have to return to the afterlife. They will have to reclaim the throne. I believe we are the key-holders of this destiny. I don't believe Serich sent his sons so that we could help them in only this realm – I believe we are intended to help them in the second realm as well."

Nile, the Logic totem, chose to clarify what the head monk was saying.

"We intend to build the twins an army," he said. "One that will cross with them into the afterlife. For further reference, this army will be known as the Forge."

Aeroh, the monk who had helped find Haren and the queen, seemed to sense the implication.

"You intend a mass suicide?" he said.

Igallik nodded. "We do. When the twins are ready, I am proposing that they, and the monks of the Forge, die and bring war to Forneus's throne. The curtain of death has become our ally," the head monk said. "Our great advantage is that we can start this war the moment we are best prepared."

"But when will we know the twins are ready?" Aeroh asked. "How much time do we have?"

"At this point," Igallik replied, "we have decided that we have twenty-five years to complete the proper training. When the boys are twenty-five, we intend for them to die."

The plan was met with silence.

As the monks shifted in their seats, Palis, the small Mercy totem, broke the quiet.

"I know this sounds drastic," he said, "but we are also being very honest about the situation. Hell grows every day, brothers. We have delved very far into this fact, and we have deduced that twenty-five years is our window – a milestone that ensures that the twins are ready and that Hell has not grown too strong."

As a few more murmurs came from the mass of monks, Wylak, the herbalist, was still struggling with the idea of the Forge.

"So everything is already set?" he asked. "We are all in the Forge?"

"No," Palis replied. "With regard to the Forge, we are offering you a choice. The army will be voluntary, and only monks older than fifteen will be able to volunteer. Furthermore, there will be an annual meeting where monks can reconsider their position in the Forge – they can sign up or resign."

"Starting when?" Wylak asked.

"This is our first meeting," Palis replied.

Aeroh felt the need to point out the obvious. "But the twins are infants," he said. "They are not ready to be kings."

"What if death finds them before they are ready?" Igallik challenged. "Should we let them fall into the afterlife and hope for the best?"

The point was well taken.

After brushing his hand through his long beard, Igallik pointed towards the Ichor.

"You are all familiar with our burial rite," he said. "In death, we pay the boatman two coins for his service. There are one hundred and twenty three monks in this room, and in the Ichor, there are two hundred and forty six silver coins. I am asking each one of you to be a coin-bearer. I am asking you to claim two coins and carry them always as a gesture of your rank in the Forge."

"And what if we don't?" Aeroh asked. "Will there be any backlash?"

"No backlash," Igallik confirmed. "But before you choose, let me make one thing clear: never has a greater purpose been so close. This is an opportunity, brothers. We call this army the Forge because it is our chance to forge heaven."

With a small thunder in his voice, the head monk pointed back to Gieler. "Gieler was right," he said, "we *will* train them and make them throne-worthy. But is that enough? Shouldn't we, ourselves, force the hands of fate? Brothers, the coin-bearers can alter eternity. Think of this – imagine building heaven – as you consider your choice."

The words were a call. Even so, the monks in the Spine were very still. The idea of signing away their lives had turned one hundred and twenty three monks into statues. The gravity of the situation was felt by all, and it seemed no one wanted to make the first move. That was, until a violet-eyed girl at the back stood up.

With the twins still in her arms, Haren projected her voice throughout the Spine.

"This is not a moment to fear," she said to her brothers. "This a moment to be brave. Don't fear this moment because it is bigger than all of us: embrace it because we can hold on to it together. Many of you haven't met Hell," Haren said. "I have. I met it the day I killed my best friend…"

Although many of the monks were listening intently, Aeroh rolled his eyes.

"Are you making a point?" he asked, "or are you telling a story?"

"Both," Haren replied. "The short form of my story is that hell took everything from me, and my point is that we can't let it do the same to these twins. I believe, even in my short attendance here at the Throne's Eye, that each of you can help take back the throne of Animus Letum. That is not all these boys lost, but it is something. Hell struck these twins hard, there is no doubt. But for them, we can strike mightily back. On the grandest scale, we can swing our fists into Hell."

Haren looked to Raine, and then carried her gaze throughout the Spine. "Many of us have lost someone we love," she said. "On their behalf, we can honour what is right. On their behalf, we can give our best to these twins."

"No one has ever disputed that," Aeroh argued. "All of us plan to give the twins our best."

Haren nodded calmly back. "And now we prove it," she said.

With a poised stride, Haren moved through the monks and became the first person to collect her coins. As the studying eyes of the Spine watched her, there were a few whispers. But then, with a clap, Raine rose to his feet and began to follow. There was more silence and then four more rose. Then twenty. And soon, there was a lineup to the Ichor.

As Haren exited the Ichor with her coins, Igallik watched her every stride.

"Follow the Haren," he whispered to himself.

After all was said and done, there were ninety-six coin-bearers.

Suddenly, the sons of Animus Letum had an army.

Suddenly, the Forge had formed.

8

After the Forge was formed, the ninety-six coin-bearers showed an even stronger interest in the sons of Animus Letum. In shifts, the monks would watch over the boys, and when the shifts changed, the departing monks would share their observations about what they perceived to be the best care. Even without a throne, Galian and Odin were treated like royalty – they were the Sanctus Donum. However, for as much attention as they received, it was clear that Odin and Galian favoured the company of three: Haren, Raine, and Raine's nine year old apprentice Usis.

Usis was a slim and tall boy of Asian descent, with a set of strikingly dark eyes. His irises were a dark gray, and when any monk met his stare, it always appeared that Usis was looking through them. In fact, he always seemed to be looking past the present. He was not aloof, but considerate. However, his long-sight was not a weakness. There was an almost mechanical quality to his thinking, which resulted in a very adept ability to read situations and people. Usis also shared a similar backstory with the sons of Animus Letum. His past, like Galian's and Odin's, had made him an orphan. On his fourth birthday, a very dangerous cult had murdered his parents. The Throne's Eye monks, led by Raine, had arrived too late to save his parents, but after destroying the cult, Raine assumed the responsibility of Usis's care as a penance for their failure. It became a wise decision. Usis's methodical mind took so naturally to the martial arts that his skills marked him as a prodigy. As Raine kept Usis under his study, it was clear that Usis had the potential to be the Throne's Eye's greatest warrior.

For years, Usis thrived as the promise of the Throne's Eye soldiers.

That was, until Odin. If Usis's potential was sunbeams, Odin's was supernova. Even young, Odin exhibited an almost unnatural combination of physical abilities. He walked at a half year and ran soon after. Having watched over other boys at the same age, Raine and Haren knew how far ahead Odin was. As most children do, Odin mimicked the movements he observed; however, before his second year he had already exhibited an abundance of improvisational skills. The incredibly fast development of his balance and agility were unprecedented – even when measured against Usis. To predict Odin's future, the mind had to look further than greatness.

The Sons of Animus Letum

Unfortunately, Odin's physical promise was not his brother's. Because of Galian's physical limitations, he could not explore his world as well as his brother. For Haren, Raine, and Usis, the awareness of Galian's limits was painful – especially with the acknowledgement of Odin's strengths. There seemed to be no scenario where Galian wasn't in Odin's shadow. The boys' mentors honestly feared that Galian would hold Odin back. Pre-emptively, they devised a plan where the twins' individual strengths could be fostered and neither of them would be left in the shadow. Raine and Usis began a daily routine where they challenged Odin's physical abilities, and at the same time Haren spent time with Galian in an effort to create a sign language. Galian proved to be a quick study. The quiet Lyran showed exceptional mental resilience, and soon, by Haren's persistence and the great willingness of the other monks, the entire monastery was versed in Galian's quiet lexicon. As Galian's language continually evolved, no one was more versed in it than Odin. The two young brothers would share conversations in sign that even Haren could not read – although this, as every monk present in the boys' infancy could attest to, was not new. There was a bond – a born strength – between the twins. As infants, Galian, never able or even motivated to cry, could silence his brother's wails with a look. The roles of that bond, considering Galian's handicap, came as a surprise. It was Galian – even though his physical disability drastically limited his movement – who led the two. It was no secret that Odin was an exceptional child with a propensity for adventure. His toddling and unaccompanied steps had twice found the forest outside the monastery's walls. But as he grew and continued to cut his own paths, he always looked back to the quiet Galian. It was as if somehow, even in his young mind, Odin understood Galian's limitations, and as only a brother could, he ran for the hearts of two. Only joy was painted on Galian's face when he watched his brother – it was a love few are worthy to hold.

The early years of the sons of Animus Letum passed as such – with the young adventurer's steps made for, and adored by, his quiet anchor.

When Serich sent Rhea to your earth realm, he sacrificed more than just his life and throne. When he gave his sons to the Throne's Eye, he stripped the boys of what you may consider a normal childhood. The Throne's Eye was often more school than home, and within their walls the monks fostered a very different kind of play. Friendships were made in the training grounds known as the Damns, and instead of playing with toys, the youth sparred with weapons. The Damns held to strict conditions, but they were named for a time-honoured and proven purpose: they bred masters of war, gladiator souls conditioned to damn the rise of hell on earth. From youth, the monks were trained to inherit and uphold this colossal weight.

Galian and Odin would be no exception.

At the first sign of readiness, Galian and Odin entered the Damns. The schedule set for the youth of the Throne's Eye was arduous. From morning to dusk the young monks were instructed in the martial arts and drilled in their application. Strengths were identified and nurtured; weaknesses were discovered and rectified. To fail a task in the Damns was to volunteer another attempt. It was a test of heart, and it was the breeding ground of battle gods. In this arena, Odin thrived. Odin's exceptional physical ability, as well as his almost unnatural aptitude for learning, had made his skills in the martial arts beyond reasonable expectation. He was a phenom. In his many triumphs in the Damns, Odin's peers jokingly called him The Mighty Odin. The name would stick. However, the Damns of the Throne's Eye ultimately revealed strength, and of the twins, Odin was surprisingly the weaker of the two. Galian, born both mute and physically disabled, compensated for both limitations with his mind – twentyfold. Galian looked back on genius. His mind was in fact so powerful that he, like his father, learned to move objects without touching them. To spar with Galian was to invite great challenge. As you might expect, due to Galian's physical condition, almost every monk was able to push the silent monk over, but to get close enough to impose that advantage was essentially impossible. With his considerable mental power, he could trip, toss, or strike foes down from a distance as far back as four yards. Galian's power was still young and limited – his mind could not lift more than forty pounds, and he was unable to focus his power on two separate objects. But with the strategic employment of his abilities, Galian had made himself the juggernaut of the Damns.

When the twins reached their sixth year, and, more importantly the level of mental maturity that Igallik deemed fit, they were told the complete truth of their special heritage. The Throne's Eye had never guarded Odin and Galian from the realities of Animus Letum – their heritage had come up many times in the Damns – but at age six, the twins were lessoned extensively. The lessons were taken in stride. Galian and Odin had always been told that they were Lyrans, but at age six they were told exactly what that meant. They also learned who Forneus was. Igallik explained the nature of the

Dark Pool and then told the twins that Forneus had killed their parents and taken the throne. Additionally, he explained what the Forge was, and that because the twins were Lyrans, they were destined to return to the afterlife. At their age – or any age – this type of news could be daunting. Imagine knowing that you were the heir to the throne of heaven, or that an army of soldiers had promised to die with you to reclaim your birthright. Fear or resignation could easily follow. I am proud to report that Galian and Odin were neither afraid nor resigned. In fact, the sons of Animus Letum were bettered by the truth of their destiny – Galian especially. The Lyran legacy became his pride and direction. He became inspired by the Forge and also the blood within him. Serich, Jerub, and Perian became more than ancestors – they became beacons that called him to greatness. In honour of Perian, Galian would learn war-craft. For Jerub, the quiet monk sought to understand peace. And for Serich, his father, Galian would seek inwardly to discover the power of his soul. The moment his destiny was disclosed to him, Galian knew that he could attain it. He knew he could become worthy of the Lyran name. Somehow, just like a bird knows to fly south in the winter, Galian knew that he could lead the Forge and take back the throne.

Odin was also inspired by his Lyran destiny – but not to the extent of his brother. The adventurer saw promise in his blood. When Igallik regaled him with the tales of his ancestors' triumphs, Odin was thrilled to think that his Lyran name ensured him some great challenge or journey. But with regard to the idols of his birth story, Odin was disconnected. To Odin, Forneus was in some intangible realm. He could not imagine his serpent foe, and this failing forced a disconnection between Odin and his destiny. Furthermore, the Lyran kings seemed unreal. His father was more myth than man, and the further Odin looked back into his lineage, the more the fable grew. In fact, the only Lyran that Odin truly cared about was Galian. It was that simple. Children – as Odin still was – often see more clearly than adults. They tend to see people as they truly are. And although he felt far from his ancestors, it was when Odin looked at his brother that he could not deny that they were descended from kings. Galian's power and promise were undeniable. To Odin, Galian was a king. And so it became that when Galian found his purpose with the Forge and Lyran legacy, Odin found his purpose in Galian. Somehow, even in his young heart, Odin knew what his role was in the Forge: Galian was the king, and Odin was his protector.

Within the monastery, the training of the Throne's Eye youth was consistent throughout early development. However, at age twelve, each monk was assigned to a speciality. There existed two: Torch and Sight.

Torch monks were the designated soldiers of the Throne's Eye. To be designated a Torch meant that aside from an amplified study of combat, the young monks' routines would remain the same. They would continue to brawl and bleed in the Damns.

The far less frequent designation of Sight, however, drastically changed a monk's routine. Sight monks were the spiritual sages of the Throne's Eye, and their training grounds were within themselves. They were relieved of the rigours of the Damns and were set on an entirely different course. Sight monks became trained in meditation, spiritual rite, and most especially as Deathriders. With these abilities, the Sights became the strategists of the Throne's Eye army. Using the channels between earth and Animus Letum, Sights would access knowledge of both realms. They would learn of great deeds, but also of great injustices. Some were so great that intervention was necessary, and thus, the great battle skills of the Throne's Eye Torches were put into play. Based on the information of the Deathriders, units of Torches, accompanied by one or two Sights, would travel when and where they were needed. The commanders of these convoys were given the title Aeris. Aeris monks were the few and fierce gods of the Damns. They were champions of both physical combat and battle strategy, and they were the generals of the Throne's Eye soldiers. Each Torch trained with the ambition of becoming an Aeris – a goal most would not achieve.

Sight monks trained to become a Seraph. The title Seraph was awarded in even greater scarcity than that of Aeris. In fact, in the nearly two millennia history of the Throne's Eye, only twelve Sights had proven worthy of the Seraph title. A Seraph was defined more as a state of mind than as a rank. It was an achieved enlightenment. Seraphs were masters of the soul. They epitomized the harmony of mind, body, and spirit, and were wise in the affairs of both peace and war. Incredibly, each came to inherit his own specialized power. Some could read minds, others could heal mental and physical ailments, and one could even slow down time. The Seraphs were the rare glimpses of earth-born deity. However, the title and supernatural abilities of the Seraph were not achieved by will. Instead, they were earned by an excruciating trial called Descent. The aim of Descent is to split the bond between a Sight's body and soul, and then challenge the monk to reunite his halves. The great danger of this trial is that the body and soul are split over earth and Animus Letum – the body remains on earth, and the soul resides in the afterlife. Descent is made possible by a ritual whereby the Sight consciously separates his own body and soul, and then links his soul to a person experiencing death, essentially hitching a ride to the afterlife. Once they are separated, the body and soul incur great stress and pain – one can barely live without the other. In the throes of this suffering, the Sight must employ the extremity of his spiritual strength. Descent is a test of all that the Throne's Eye teaches, but the greatest test is of the monk's will. Because the consciousness of the Sight is bound to the soul – it is in Animus Letum – the struggle to reunite body and soul is a battle waged against the curtain of death. The Sight must pass backwards through death to reunite body and soul. To accomplish this feat necessitates near-godly willpower – it is the greatest spiritual challenge in existence. As such, success brings great prize. Each monk who successfully passes backwards through death emerges with the title and specialized powers of Seraph. However, the separation of Descent is torturous, and most often deadly. Only twelve Sights have ever been able to reconcile their body and soul through Descent. One hundred and nine Sights have tried – such is the price of chasing godhood.

On their twelfth birthday, Odin was designated Torch, and Galian was designated Sight. Haren, Raine, and Usis were not surprised. The boys' strengths had made the designations a foregone conclusion. However, despite the divergence in their paths, the truth remained that Odin and Galian would be greatest together. The bond that united them was an invincible force steady in one certainty: to hurt one was to incur the wrath of the other. The brothers had suffered at the hand of a ruthless villain. Their childhoods were stolen, and their parents were slain. But against that great misfortune, they had been given each other. Each lived and would die to spare the other pain. To test their bond was to crack diamonds with your fist.

When Haren agreed to live at the Throne's Eye, Igallik chose to spare her the Damns and designated her a Sight. As a result, there were times when her position as a Sight and Raine's post as an Aeris called them both away from the monastery. During their absences, it was Usis who was charged with the care of the sons of Animus Letum. The responsibility would prove to fall on able shoulders. Usis, still a teen, was young enough to be their friend, but experienced enough to be their mentor. Odin took full advantage of

Usis's instruction in the discipline of combat, while Galian began to study the eastern arts in which Usis was well practised.

As the three became like brothers, the shared trauma of orphanhood forged an even deeper kinship. In very much the same way as Odin and Galian, Usis's childhood had been stolen. Usis was told that the Metus Sane – a cult pledging allegiance to Malum Ludus – had committed the murders of his parents. Ludus was a phantom of the afterlife, and his penchant for torture had made him one of Animus Letum's most notorious villains. In service to Ludus, the Metus Sane had intended to kill Usis, and by using his blood, resurrect their fallen master. Their attempt had come dangerously close, but fortunately the Throne's Eye had managed to thwart them before completion. Even though Raine and the Order monk Raeman had arrived in time to save him, Usis could never fully accept his fate. He could not accept that his parents were killed because of him. While never mentioned in the presence of the elder monks, he knew that his purpose was vengeance. By his hand, he swore, Malum Ludus would die. In his care of the sons of Animus Letum, Usis nurtured a similar purpose in the young twins.

"We must honour our parents," he would preach over and over again to them. "By us the flames of evil will come to doubt their burn."

The three grew up with this vision – individually and as brothers. In fact, their bond grew so strong that when the monks mentioned the sons of Animus Letum, they always included a third.

In his long-vision, Igallik saw the trio as a perfect unit. With the right guidance he knew that they could be the trident at the forefront of the Forge. The three, with an army behind them, could end Forneus's reign. However, if they were successful in reclaiming the afterlife, one very important question followed their triumph: who would take the throne? A crown cannot rest on three heads – or even two.

This truth gnawed at the thoughts of the High Order – especially because of Usis's strength. The Order monks were in agreement that the sons of Animus Letum were the rightful heirs – the Forge had been assembled upon that truth. However, after a series of hearings, a few totems on the Order began to wonder if it was blood that made the most worthy king. Galian and Odin had their strengths, but so too did Usis and an assortment of other monks. Suddenly, the Order was divided. Was blood more important than vigour? Was the throne an heirloom, or a seat for the most worthy? They were questions that required answers.

The Sons of Animus Letum

After days of debate, the Order decided to nominate an heir.
And so, for the throne, a test became necessary.
For Animus Letum, there would be a fight.

9

Igallik's motive to test the boys was clear – but only to him and the Order. The head monk had kept his intention very secret, and only spoke of his plan within the High Temple. The Order was in complete agreement that an heir needed to be elected; however, they disagreed on who the heir should be. Ten debates passed with no semblance of solidarity. The Order had scrutinized the merits of the sons of Animus Letum, Usis, and even other monks within the monastery. They had measured mind against muscle, will against wisdom, and still were no closer to a decision.

After the totems of the Order had employed their logic, mercy, justice, and instinct, they had found that there were essentially four candidates: Odin, Galian, Usis, and a sixteen year old Torch monk named Tyrik. Tyrik was a hulking, ginger-haired boy who had been recruited from a village, not far from the Throne's Eye. Although Tyrik had much to learn about leadership, his brute strength had made him one of the Damns' strongest warriors. It was true that Tyrik did not have the intellect of the three others, but his sheer physical strength was undeniable – it was his inherent asset.

After ten debates, the Order had voted as such: Igallik and Palis had chosen Galian, Nile had voted for Usis, Raeman had chosen Tyrik, and Bysin had selected Odin.

Although Galian had received two votes, the three remaining Order members had consistently used their votes to stave off a majority.

With no promise of breaking the deadlock, the Order chose to invite three more voices to the debate: Raine, Haren, and the herbalist Wylak.

It was evening when Haren and Raine were called to the High Temple. In the twelve years that she had been at the Throne's Eye, Haren had matured into a striking young woman. The violet eyes, dark hair, and bronzed skin that had made her a pretty girl, now made her a beautiful woman. However, her greatest beauty was still actualized by her mind. She had become a surgeon, and even a stylist to the monks of the Throne's Eye, but to her greatest credit she had become a sister. Many monks sought her wisdom when their own failed, and with great care Haren gave what she could. Although Haren was still hurt by losing Morello, she had come to terms with the opportunity that his death provided – it had given her a home.

As Haren and Raine ascended to the top of the grand staircase, the sun was bowing after another day, leaving a red glow in the horizon. The cherry blossoms in front of the High Temple rustled above them, some falling and floating down, gleaming with a red that had absorbed the crimson sun.

"I'm telling you," Raine said as he bumped Haren with his shoulder. "This is it. They're kicking you out."

Haren shook her head. "Do humour me, Raine. What have I done now?"

"Aw hell, birdy," the old warrior said. "You didn't hear? Turns out you're useless."

"Anything else?"

"There's loads more," Raine said with a smile. "On top of being useless, you were voted least attractive woman in the monastery."

"Raine, I'm the only woman in the monastery."

"Your name did come up a lot."

Haren exhaled deeply. "Just open the door."

With a small bow, the old warrior turned and opened the Temple's massive bronze door.

"After you."

Haren offered a sarcastic curtsy, and one after the other, the two entered to meet with the High Order.

As the setting sun pushed through the western window, the Temple's red and gold palette was even more vivacious. The claret rug and drapery and the golden pews seemed to glow, and as Haren's red robe and Raine's golden armour melded into the colour scheme, the two walked down the Temple's aisle in a picture of pageantry. As they neared the Order thrones, each bowed to the crown of Animus Letum that was set on top of the Temple's altar.

Wylak, the blonde herbalist, had already arrived, and as his hand brushed through his natty beard, his cool blue eyes were set intently on Haren and Raine.

"I like your entrance," he said. "Entrancing."

Haren smiled as she stood next to him. "I must ask, Wylak, would you be so entranced if you were not using your herbs?"

"All herbalists must know their plants," Wylak replied with a wry grin.

Raine lightly jabbed Wylak's shoulder. "Just try and stay with us, medicine man."

"Fear not, warrior," Wylak said. "I've got herbs for that."

From above them, the head monk forced a cough. "Are we quite done?"

Haren, Raine, and Wylak quickly chose silence.

"Very well," the head monk said from the center of the five totem thrones. After looking to the totems on his left and right, Igallik took a puff from his tobacco hookah, exhaled, and addressed the monks before him.

"Let me begin by informing you that this will not be a typical hearing of the Order," he said. "For this hearing, and only this hearing, we are opening a debate beyond our own minds – beyond the five of us. We have asked you here for your thoughts, your voice, and especially your honesty."

Igallik looked sternly onto the three. "Can we expect your cooperation?"

After an affirming nod from each, Igallik continued.

"Allow me then to explain our dilemma. As a collective, we have begun to wonder about who is the rightful heir to Animus Letum. We have debated many candidates with no answer. In fact, this has become a very difficult quandary."

Haren's head tilted back, her brow creasing as she replayed Igallik's words in her mind. "I was not aware that there was a quandary," she said, her tone sounding almost defensive.

"Nor were any of us," Igallik replied, "that is, until we opened discussion."

Haren couldn't believe there had been debate. "I think the choice is fairly obvious," she said matter-of-factly.

"Let me challenge that," Igallik said. He then looked on all three guests. "When I raise my hand, please speak the name of who you believe should be heir."

The three nodded, and as the head monk raised his hand, they each spoke.

The result was a mishmash of three different names: Haren said Galian, Raine said Odin, and Wylak said Usis.

As Haren looked almost contemptuously upon Raine and Wylak, Igallik took another puff from his hookah.

"Do you see, Haren?" he said. "It is not so clear-cut. In fact, our debate has centered upon four monks."

"I see," Haren admitted, "but I do not understand. First of all, Galian has consistently proven to be much wiser than Odin. And second of all, Usis and whoever else is in the debate are not even Lyrans. May I remind you that the Forge was assembled to see that the Lyran took back the throne – no other bloodline was even considered."

Nile pushed his round glasses up the bridge of his nose. "Allow me to explain our thinking," he said, "at least with regard to Usis and Tyrik. We are choosing to look beyond bloodline, because blood, simply put, is a weak way to measure a man. Instead of blood determining the heir, we intend to elect the heir with wisdom."

"That does not change anything," Haren said. "Galian is still the right choice."

"And if the afterlife goes to war?" Raeman asked, his skeptical eyes piercing onto Haren from behind his long hooked nose.

Raine nodded reluctantly, trying not to antagonize Haren, but also knowing that the Justice totem was right.

"He could not lead an army," the old warrior said, "at least not as well as the other three candidates."

Haren's throat closed a little, and as she turned her eyes down and away from Raine, she knew that she couldn't be mad at him – he was simply being honest.

"This awareness is why you are here," Raeman said to Raine. "You have trained our Torches and sparred with them in the Damns. We have asked you here because we would like you to rate our warriors."

"In what context?" Raine asked.

Raeman sat back with a confused expression: he had not expected that any further context would be necessary.

"Skills should suffice," he said finally.

"In that case," Raine said, "Usis is our strongest. Odin is not far behind. And Tyrik is clearly third. There is a substantial gap between Tyrik and the monk that I would consider fourth."

The Justice totem was pleased by the analysis. Raeman had found and recruited Tyrik from a village not far from the Throne's Eye, and to know that Tyrik's skills were in a class with Usis and Odin allowed the elder monk a bit of pride.

Igallik was still considering what Raine had said. "If I may, Raine," he said. "In what other context would you measure a warrior?"

"There is skill," Raine replied, "and there is will. A warrior must have both, but the will must always be greater than the skill. If you want to measure a warrior, do not survey him when he is winning a fight, do it when he is losing. Measure them when their survival is on the line."

"And have you measured this?" Igallik asked.

"The occasion has not presented itself fully," Raine said. "But in glimpses I have seen that Usis and Odin have great will – almost equal."

"And Tyrik?" Raeman asked.

"He fades under this light," Raine said. "But he is still near the top of the pack."

Igallik swept his hand through his long gray beard, and after a moment of thought, he looked back to Raine.

"You say the occasion has not presented itself fully," he said. "What if we were to devise a way to present it completely? A test as it were."

Raine's reply was immediate.

"Without the imminent threat of death, it would be very difficult to measure our Torches. A proper test is almost impossible."

Igallik nodded, respecting Raine's assessment. After the head monk appeared to calculate the Order's options, he turned to Wylak.

"Is Raine right?" he asked. "Are we without a test?"

"I was beginning to wonder why I was here," the herbalist said.

"And?"

Wylak smiled. "Raine's insight has given me an idea."

"We need more than ideas," Raeman asserted.

The herbalist smiled confidently. "Fortunately I have ideas and herbs. If you give me three days, I will show you who the heir should be."

Igallik looked pleased with the herbalist. "Very well, Wylak. Shall we reconvene here in three days?"

"In three," Wylak agreed. "But not here. We will meet in the Damns."

10

Just as the herbalist had requested, Haren, Raine, and the Order reconvened at the Damns three days later. The Damns were a log pen built in the southeast corner of the monastery courtyard. Its perimeter was twenty feet high, and aside from the routine sounds of war coming from within, it was an unimpressive structure. As the hot sun hung over the early morning and Wylak's guests arrived at the Damns, they noted an unusual silence coming from behind the wall.

Just before they pushed the gate open, Wylak slid out to greet them.

As the herbalist looked over the group, he was noticeably fatigued, but there was also a mischievous glint in his eye. "Here for the show, are we?" he asked. "Today's spectacle will –"

Raeman cut him off. "We do not need a show, Wylak. Do you have a test or not?"

"That I do," Wylak replied, unaffected by Raeman's impatience. "In fact, today's show is the test."

As a collective, the confused faces of the Order solicited an explanation.

"Follow me to the Perch," Wylak said. "I'll explain on the way."

The Perch was an area built into the top of the Damns that gave an elevated view of the entire training ground.

As Wylak walked in front of the group, he began to explain, articulating his words with the paintbrush-like strokes of his right hand. "Three days ago," he recalled, "when Raine was explaining will, I was struck by something he said. I have altered his original quotation to my taste, but basically he said that a warrior is defined when he is losing a fight, not winning."

"We all heard him," Raeman said.

"But did we all think?" Wylak replied. "Did we all wonder if there is a way to simulate a losing fight – if there is a way, without hurting our Torches, to push them to the brink of themselves?"

As Wylak ascended the final few steps to The Perch, he made a grand sweeping gesture towards this inside of the Damns. "I thought over this question," he said, "and then I solved it."

The inside of the Damns had two sectors. The first sector was a simple rectangle with a floor of clay and an arsenal of weaponry – it was the area where the Torches fought. The second and bigger sector was called the Mount: it was a long narrowing pathway of rock that ascended towards a fifty foot pinnacle. The Torch monks would often compete in a game to see who could claim the Mount's summit and hold it for the longest.

For the purpose of Wylak's test, there were thirty monks – including Galian, Odin, Usis, and Tyrik – at the start of the Mount. At its end, there was a golden flag perched on the pinnacle of the rock mountain.

After gazing once more over the Damns, a proud Wylak turned back to the monks behind him. "My brothers," he said. "I give you the show."

"Is it a race?" Igallik asked.

"Yes," Wylak replied. "But not quite against each other. This race is against themselves."

The head monk broke a smile – there was a small thrill tied to his curiosity.

"How so, Wylak?" he asked.

"Over the last three days," the herbalist explained, "I have developed a very special tonic. I call it Quicksand. Its effect is quite extraordinary. When taken, it will counteract any physical or mental exertion with a depressing agent. That is to say, the more someone acts, the more it sedates them. It creates a losing fight. Or in this case, a losing race."

Nile's eyes closed for a moment of calculation. After reaching his conclusion, the Logic totem applauded Wylak with a pat on the shoulder. "Genius," he said. "Truly genius."

Raeman was confused. He peered over the Damns, and then looked back to Wylak, trying unsuccessfully to understand the herbalist's feat.

"I don't understand," he said. "How is it applied?"

Wylak smiled, and then nodded to the Logic totem. "Would you care to explain?"

"My pleasure," Nile said. "What Wylak has given us is a completely tangible way to measure willpower. There are thirty young monks at the start of the Mount, and assuming that our herbalist has administered Quicksand to each of them, when they participate in the race for the golden flag, each will be in a fight against his own will. The more they exert themselves, the more they will fall into sedation." Nile removed his glasses and polished them for a moment. As he placed them back on, there was a small smile growing on his face. "What we will be left with is a line of bodies," he explained. "Quite simply, the monk who is closest to the flag has exerted the most willpower. He will be our heir."

"And," Wylak added, "for future reference, there will be a clear line of who is second, third, and fourth."

Igallik offered a congratulatory nod to the herbalist. "Well done, Wylak. Better than could be expected."

The Mercy totem agreed. "Quite clever," Palis said. "Though, if I may ask, how have you motivated the racers?"

"Quite simply," Wylak replied. "They have been told that whoever claims the golden flag will earn one day in the Ichor."

The Ichor was the small room in the Throne's Eye library that housed *The Book of the Eterna*.

Upon hearing of the prize, Raeman's eyes burned onto Wylak. "You have overstepped your bounds," he said sternly. "No one but the Order is allowed in the Ichor."

Igallik was not as panicked. "There have been exceptions, Raeman. I believe this can be one."

"I had to motivate them," Wylak argued. "Simply put, a day in the Ichor is a chance every monk would fight for. And," the herbalist added, "for the record, I don't expect anyone to claim the flag. I have given each racer a substantial amount of Quicksand."

"So there may be no winner?" Raeman said.

"*We* will undoubtedly determine what we need." Wylak said. "But for the racers, yes, it is probable that no one wins."

Even against Wylak's prediction, a glint of promise sparked in Haren's eye. She turned from the group, considering the race as if she had inside information. When she finally turned back, there was hope in her eyes. "I must thank you, Wylak," she said. "I don't think you realize the degree to which you have motivated Galian. I believe he will make a very good show of this."

Raeman scoffed. "Please, Haren. Galian will be lucky if he comes in second last."

Haren shifted her head, and after weighing the odds, she met Raeman's eyes dead-on. "Care to make it interesting?" she asked.

"Ridiculous," Raeman dismissed. "You are in no position to make a wager."

The head monk – who had also endorsed Galian as the heir – saw it differently.

"I believe her position in the wager has been established," he said. "She is the challenger. It is your position that needs clarification."

"Igallik," Raeman argued, "this is beneath us. It is ludicrous. Galian has no chance."

"Then there is no harm in making the bet," Haren said.

Raeman scoffed again, and after a moment of deliberation, he offered Haren a very confident smile. "What are your terms, my dear?"

Haren was quick with her reply. "You may pick a racer as well, and whoever's pick ends up closest to the flag wins."

"And the prize?" Raeman asked.

"If Galian is closer, I too will be given a day in the Ichor."

"Very well," Raeman agreed. "I am picking Tyrik, and if he is closer, you my lady will be going on a walk. A long walk. You will pack your provisions and go at once to live among the women at the sisterhood."

"Raeman!" Igallik snapped. "Now you are overstepping your bounds."

The Justice totem waved off the head monk, and with a pompous grin, he offered Haren a final exit. "I will give you one last chance to back out," he said. "Consider it a charity."

"She will not make the bet," the head monk asserted.

"I appreciate your help, Igallik," Haren said. "But I will take the bet."

Before Igallik could intervene, Haren's hand extended to Raeman, and the two finalized their bet with a quick handshake.

As Igallik shot a deadly look at Raeman, Wylak clapped his hands excitedly. "This *will* be a show," he grinned. "Allow me to get the ball rolling."

After a quick turn, Wylak held up his right hand and grabbed the attention of the racers.

"Brothers!" he yelled, "You have all been briefed on etiquette. No harm is to be inflicted on any other racer. Let me you remind you that a day in the Ichor is on the line. For the Ichor, let us see your best!"

As the racers nodded and began to take their starting marks, the tall, slender Usis arrived at the center. The hulking orange-haired Tyrik was at his left, and the much smaller and younger Odin was at his right. Odin's body and features had begun to announce his coming adolesence, and as he stood among the racers, he was a picture of young strength. As his thick blonde hair blew across his lightning blue eyes, Odin dropped into his starting pose, stretching back and flexing his muscles with an air of godhood. The three were flanked by many other Torch monks, and at the back of the group, Galian stood by himself. The blonde Galian wore a brown robe and was easily the shortest of the group. As he hung at the back, he paced a little, his disproportionate body leaning to the left. His body, like

Odin's, had been affected by the onset of adolescence, but unlike his brother, Galian was growing lanky. His left side hung lower than his right, and his limbs were skinny and connected by bulbous joints.

With a small wrench of nerves pulsing through the racers, Tyrik dug his toes into the earth.

"Keep out of my way," the hulk said to Usis. "I don't care much for etiquette."

"Why would you?" Usis replied. "Rules are for men, not pigs."

As Tyrik's hands hardened to fists, Wylak called out from The Perch.

"Get ready!" the herbalist yelled.

Usis dug his toes into the earth.

"Go!"

As the mass of racers sprang forward, Tyrik swung his arm against Usis, and after his elbow careened into Usis's collarbone, Tyrik launched himself into the lead position. With a wince, Usis launched back at Tyrik, and with elbows and dekes, the two began to jockey towards the flag. As Odin kept just behind their pace, the monks on the Perch were shocked to see that Quicksand was already beginning to take effect. Like a wave, the mass of monks began to slow. Usis and Tyrik were first, and then, like wind blowing over a field, Quicksand spread throughout the racers. Some began to lull, keeling over and crawling forward, while others dropped to their stomachs, surrendering to the tonic that was sedating them.

Within twenty seconds, ninety percent of the field had dropped.

"I did not expect it to take effect so soon," Palis said.

Wylak offered a sheepish smile. "Neither did I."

Tyrik and Usis had continued to creep forward, and with their postures beginning to sink, they reached the halfway point to the flag. Odin was five steps behind, and as he lunged and leapt in pursuit, the toll of Quicksand began to overtake all three. Tyrik tried once more to push off Usis, but as he tried to throw his weight, he knocked himself off balance, and with a solid thud and a sprawl of rocks, Tyrik's large frame fell unconscious against the hill. Odin managed a clumsy jump overtop of Tyrik, and with only Usis ahead of him, he began a desperate scramble up the Mount.

As Raeman surveyed the race, he was pleased with Tyrik's performance. Every monk near Tyrik – except Usis and Odin – had fallen to Quicksand.

"Third isn't bad," Raeman announced.

With a pompous grin, the Justice totem turned to Haren. "Your horse has some ground to make up," he said.

"Galian works at his own pace," Haren calmly replied.

The confidence in Haren's words turned the monks' attention to Galian. The quiet monk was still upright, and with his strange steps, he was slowly advancing on Tyrik. Because Galian's spine curved left, his entire body was forced to adapt. There were many different ways in which Galian's deformity showed, but the most prominent was his walk. The quiet monk took a fairly typical step with his right foot, but his left foot always appeared to stumble as it caught up. It almost looked like he was bobbing down a river current.

As Usis and Odin became even more affected by Quicksand, Galian continued to bob along.

After a few furious strides, Odin had caught Usis, but as each of them stood only ten feet below the Mount's summit, Quicksand began to overwhelm them. Usis's balance began to waver drastically, and as he tried to scale further up, his limbs became limp like the flag ten feet above him. Desperately, he swung himself at the next plateau, but his trajectory was far off, and with a crack, his body jolted against the stone and he fell unconscious against the Mount.

After watching Usis's fall, Odin altered his own trajectory, and as he laboured against his hunched posture, he too launched himself at the next plateau. His revision of Usis's attempt proved vital. Odin's body just barely carried over the rock, and as his weight shifted onto the next level, he skidded against the stone and fell unconscious amid a small cloud of dust.

With only one monk still active, the attention of the Perch panned back to the quiet Galian.

With his bobbing steps, Galian passed the largest mass of unconscious monks, and moved officially into fourth place.

Because of Galian's natural posture, it was difficult to detect the effect of Quicksand. And as Galian's almost toddler-like climb began to close in on Tyrik, Raeman cried foul.

"There is no way he took Quicksand," he protested.

"I assure you," Wylak said, "each racer was administered the same dose."

The Justice totem turned emphatically to the herbalist. "What game is this, Wylak? Why hasn't he slowed?"

Wylak gave a wry smile. "I don't think you want the answer, Raeman."

Raeman seemed to suddenly recognize the weakness in his voice. With a small scowl, he sunk into silence.

However, as Galian approached within steps of Tyrik, Haren made sure to twist the blade.

"And..." she said, drawing out the ruling, "Galian passes Tyrik. A day in the Ichor will be very nice, gentleman. My thanks to you, Raeman."

As Raeman dismissed Haren with a flippant wave, the only question left was how much further could Galian climb?

As the monks on the Perch watched Galian's slow and steady ascent, Wylak moved quietly next to Igallik and hushed his voice so that only the head monk could hear.

"Just so we are clear," he whispered, "what Galian is doing is beyond human."

Igallik's gaze remained fixed on the quiet monk. "How far beyond?" he whispered back.

Wylak patted the head monk's shoulder. "Godly."

As a smile formed on Igallik's face, the head monk bowed his head, believing somehow that his words would reach a fallen king.

"We will guide him," he whispered.

As Galian climbed slowly up the Mount, it was like watching a toddler on stairs. Nevertheless, the quiet monk had caught Usis, and stood only five feet back from the plateau where Odin had crashed.

As the Perch watched, Raeman felt it necessary to point out Galian's shortcoming.

"You see," he said, "this is why Galian is not fit to be heir. He cannot make that jump – ever."

Haren rolled her eyes. "Really, Raeman? Must a king have *jumping* ability?"

"A king must have physical ability," Raeman replied. As if there could be no further argument, the Justice totem looked frankly to the rest of the Order. "Do any of you disagree?"

"I understand your point," Nile said. "I don't know if I agree with it."

As Palis began to weigh in, Igallik hushed him and pointed back to the Damns.

"It is possible," he said, "that physical ability has a formidable cousin."

On the Mount, Galian was still standing between Usis and Odin, but instead of climbing forward, his eyes were closed and his arms were outstretched towards the golden flag above him. With a few small ripples, Galian's power brought the previously limp flag to life, and as Galian's hands continued to draw it in, the flag began to flap loudly. As the flag flew and stretched open, Galian wrenched his hands back, and with a loud snap, the flag broke from the pole and sailed delicately into his hand.

The quiet monk inspected his prize for a moment. As Galian began to raise his hand in victory, his legs convulsed with an odd jig, and he dropped like a stone.

"Quicksand," Wylak said with a laugh. "Sooner or later, it wins."

With each racer down, Igallik took a few steps towards the edge of the Perch, and after brushing his hand through his beard, his head tilted with a satisfied nod. Each monk on the Perch had witnessed what he had.

After weighing his thoughts once more, Igallik turned to the Order with certitude in his eyes.

"With regards to the heir," he said. "I believe we have reached a consensus."

11

After Galian had claimed the flag and each racer had fallen to Quicksand, Wylak sauntered slowly through them, administering the first of two tonics that would counteract their sedation.

The first tonic was designed to wake the monks' bodies, and the second tonic was designed to wake their minds. The second tonic had to be ingested at least ten minutes after the first, and in between the two stages, the monks were in a much more primal state. They were in charge of their actions, but were far less inhibited.

After the first tonic was given, the monks awoke in nearly the same order that they had fallen, and like a line of sheep, they were herded into the library to await stage two.

Tyrik was fourth last to arrive, and soon after, Usis and Odin followed.

As Tyrik watched Usis's and Odin's entrance, seeing that neither of them had the flag relieved him, and with a satisfied grunt, he cocked his head back and offered an arrogant smile.

"Usis and the mighty Odin," he laughed. "Empty handed."

Usis offered a confident smile. "Better than empty-headed," he replied.

"Didn't matter much, did it?" Tyrik growled. "You didn't beat me out there. No one did."

On cue, Galian bobbed into the library, his right hand holding the golden flag.

Odin immediately raised a victorious fist. "Someone did," he beamed.

As Galian stood next to Odin, and a few of the racers applauded him, the quiet monk bent into a bow.

"The gimp?" Tyrik scoffed. With a sarcastic smile, Tyrik joined in the applause. "The Lyran mishap," he mocked. "I suppose you were due for something."

With no hesitation, Odin swung a hard kick into the back of Tyrik's legs, and the hulk collapsed to the floor.

"Speaking of due," Usis jested.

As Tyrik's only three friends, Cole, Lizin, and Jasil, assembled behind him, the hulk rose furiously to his feet and began to rush at Odin.

Usis was quick to intervene. The exact moment he read Tyrik's intent, Usis's tall and slender frame sliced in front of Odin, and with an impossibly quick stab, Usis struck his hand into Tyrik's throat and dug his fingers around Tyrik's windpipe.

As Usis met Tyrik's stare, he tightened his grip and leaked the rage out of Tyrik's eyes. With a fit of desperate coughs and gasps, the hulk fell to his knees, but even with Tyrik at his feet, Usis did not relent. With Tyrik's face flushing with red and panic, Usis controlled his prey, staring into him with eyes like Death. Usis seemed to grow stronger upon Tyrik's fear. However, as Usis's grip persisted, a large and heavy hand fell onto his shoulder.

"He's had enough," Raine said firmly.

After Usis's eyes shot a final dagger into Tyrik, Usis spat at the floor and relinquished his grip.

As Tyrik clenched his throat and strained for air, Haren, who had arrived with Raine, knelt down to examine the hulk's neck. With a push, Tyrik refused her help, and stumbled back to his feet. The return of air, brought the return of anger, and like a boulder gathering speed, Tyrik turned on Usis. With one step, Raine moved his massive frame between them. Raine was the only monk in the monastery that Tyrik had to look up at.

"Figures," Tyrik spat. "You protect your sheep, don't you, Raine?"

Raine took a slow step forward, closing the distance to less than a foot.

"And are you the wolf?" he asked. His tone was too deep, too strong. No one, not even the raving mad, would have dared a next move.

As Tyrik slunk away, the library was silent. The quiet seemed to amplify Tyrik's embarrassment. With no place to hide, the hulk paced loudly back and forth, looking to spot another monk's weakness. He settled on Galian.

"Well done," he laughed, with another mocking clap. "The flag and the Ichor is yours! Giving you power is like giving Haren a try in the Damns!"

Haren's violet eyes zeroed in on Tyrik. Targeting Galian had become like targeting Morello. "And giving you another second," she seared, "is like giving shit to an outhouse. Do you know why there was a race today?" she asked. "We wanted to see who had the strongest will among you. You lost. Badly. Pathetically. The gimp, as you so eloquently branded him, embarrassed you beyond reason. So take a walk," Haren said. "While you're gone, the Lyran mishap will claim his prize."

Amid the stares of every monk present, Tyrik's eyes burned onto Haren.

"You poke the wrong fire," he said angrily. "I promise you, it burns if you get too close."

Like a rolling thunder, Raine's voice became low once more. "You've got three seconds, Tyrik. Take your walk."

The hulk waved Raine off and narrowed his gaze on Haren.

"Sooner or later," he promised, "Raine won't be close."

Raine's head tilted slowly to the left. Any monk who had witnessed Raine's ferocious battle skills knew that the head tilt always preceded the fury. Tyrik knew it as much as anyone.

After glancing back to the old warrior and seeing the tilt, Tyrik backed off like a threatened dog. Without another word, the hulk and his three friends barged out of the library.

As the four stormed out, Wylak was entering with a handful of vials.

"You can't go, boys," the herbalist said as he held up the vials. "I've got one last tonic."

With a growl, Tyrik bowled through the door and jolted the herbalist into the door frame. The jolt was enough to make Wylak juggle the tonics, and as he balanced awkwardly against the door, Cole, Lizin, and Jasil barged passed him. After Wylak managed to reclaim the vials, he turned urgently back to Haren.

"Why are they leaving?" he asked. "I need to give them the second vial."

"I don't think they're coming back," Haren said frankly. "Do they need it right away?"

"Well, no," the herbalist said. "Actually, they don't need it at all. It just speeds up what the body does on its own. It'll take about a day for nature to sort them out."

"Then don't worry about them," Haren said. "They're nature's problem."

Wylak looked back out the door, his foot tapping out a frantic beat as he considered his options.

"As you wish," he said finally. He then held up second part of his tonic. "Racers, line up."

After Wylak had administered the second tonic, Haren and Galian chose to collect their winnings. As the library emptied, Haren and Galian retreated into the Ichor and set their eyes upon *The Book of the Eterna*. Just before they delved into the book, Haren explained to Galian why there had been a race. Her thinking was that if Galian knew he was the heir, he would use the time he had with *The Book of the Eterna* in a much more purposeful way.

She was right. Being the heir seemed to fuel Galian with a combination of excitement and responsibility. It seemed to bolster his desire to become a worthy Lyran.

Without break, the two soaked in the book's knowledge for twelve hours. They read about rituals and incantations that could hail the afterlife, and even a ritual where the souls of two people could be merged. The two were immersed, but even with their focus, twelve hours was not enough time to fully appreciate the book's power. One day had given them only a glimpse.

As the midnight hour fell over the monastery, Haren and Galian made their way out of the Ichor. After a day with *The Book of the Eterna*, the two walked slowly, drunk on the knowledge and potential that the human soul could achieve. The weight was heavy, but precious. It was as if they carried one thousand diamonds.

Against all rules, one of them also carried something else.

Haren had recorded an incantation from the book. The incantation was called Scour, and it could be used to find any person in the afterlife. If Haren's trespass were discovered, she would receive five reeds to the back. A small price, she thought. A small price if she could find Morello…

With a crescent moon peeking out from behind the clouds, Galian and Haren crossed through the courtyard to their quarters. As they walked, Haren offered Galian counsel. Although she would gladly accept the punishment for her crime, she couldn't allow Galian to bear any backlash.

"If they ask you, don't lie," she said to the quiet monk. "I took it. I will pay the price."

As Galian bobbed along, he replied with his sign language. "If they ask, I will lie," he said. "It is not even a debate. I can't imagine losing my brother. If I were you, I would do anything to get him back."

Haren smiled. "Let's hope we never walk that road." she said. "Besides—"

Haren cut herself off as Galian made his sign for silence.

Haren also knew the look in Galian's eye. Something was wrong. As a sense of panic grabbed Haren, Galian positioned himself in front of her, and he scoured the shadows for a predator.

In seconds, he found him – flanked by his only three friends.

"I warned you," Tyrik said from the shadow. "I told you not to poke the fire."

The Sons of Animus Letum

There was a wildness in Tyrik's voice – a primal, threatening tone that made his intentions very clear.

As Haren gripped Galian's shoulder, Tyrik and his friends emerged into the moonlight.

Galian stood fast.

"Back down," he signed. "There is no fight here."

"Back down?" Tyrik laughed. "Why would I do that?"

"Because of this," Galian replied. The quiet monk closed his eyes, and as a tremor shook the courtyard floor, he used his power to shake loose one of the floor stones and suspend it in the air in front of Tyrik.

Tyrik offered an arrogant smile. "Take your best shot, gimp."

Galian obliged. With a swing of his hand, Galian hurled the red stone forward. As the stone cut through the air, it missed Tyrik by a great margin and sailed over his head towards the barracks of the Throne's Eye monks.

"Tough break," Tyrik grinned. "My turn,"

With hatred in his eyes, the hulk dropped his lead shoulder and charged his prey. As Tyrik rumbled forward, he hit Galian first, and as the hulk's massive shoulder cracked into Galian's head, the quiet monk was tossed headlong across the stone, spiralling over the earth like a bird hit with an arrow.

After Galian had crashed in a heap, Tyrik looked Haren over.

"I told you Raine wouldn't always be close," he whispered.

As Haren tried to scream, Tyrik swung his massive palm against her temple and knocked her helplessly upon the courtyard stone.

The crash was there... He had heard it. As the sound resonated in his mind, Odin woke. The young Lyran's training engaged, and as his senses became alert, he surveyed his dark room. There was no sign of change. Still, he knew he had heard the crash. Furtively, Odin crept his way to the window. As his body leaned through the open window and he looked down, he could see pieces of cracked stone scattered beneath him. He knew that the red stone was from the courtyard. With studious eyes, Odin examined the sprawl of debris, and after calculating the point of impact, he followed a rough trajectory line back into the courtyard.

As Odin's eyes pierced through the dark, suddenly panic overtook his senses. Galian was in a heap, and Tyrik and his friends were lying overtop Haren.

Time stopped.

Fury took its place.

"Grab her legs," Tyrik ordered as Haren fought from the ground. "Hold her down."

As Tyrik's friends mauled her, Haren delivered fists and kicks in retaliation, but it was no use. Cole, Lizin, and Jasil quickly subdued her, and after they had captured her arms and legs, Tyrik grabbed Haren's burgundy robe and ripped it in half at the seam.

"Now who has the strongest will?" he seethed.

With a snarling smile, Tyrik made sure to catch Haren's eye, but to his surprise Haren's eyes were focused to his left – at the incoming knee. With a loud crack, Odin barrelled a flying knee at Tyrik's jaw, and as the hulk collapsed, Odin pounced on him, striking his neck as fast and as hard as he could. Tyrik was unconscious before he realized who was hitting him. As Odin sprang back to his feet, Tyrik's three friends converged on him, trying to use their numbers as the advantage. Like a net, they swarmed at him, but as they approached, Odin leapt forward and swung a ferocious kick at their jaws, hoping to connect with all three. The kick only smacked into Jasil and Lizin, leaving Cole standing and in a far better battle position than Odin. Before Odin could ready himself for the next attack, his ears were already ringing, buzzing from the impact of Cole's fist. With a stagger, Odin tried to return fire, but Cole, like all Throne's Eye monks, was expertly trained in combat. After a few evasive weaves, Cole threw a combination of jabs at Odin, striking hard into the Lyran's ribcage. The onslaught was enough that Odin abandoned striking and put up his arms to guard his head and torso. As Odin bundled, Jasil and Lizin re-entered the fight. The two came at Odin from his sides, and with their superior strength, they ripped and wrestled Odin's arms into submission. Desperately, Odin threw a series of kicks at Cole, but in moments, the fight tilted completely out of his control. With both of his arms locked in submission, Odin hung helplessly, his body snapping back and forth from the barrage of Cole's elbows and knees. As Odin began to falter, Cole wound back his arm, cocking his fist for the final blow. As he shifted his weight into the haymaker, suddenly a slab of red stone crashed against Cole's back. Cole staggered forward from the impact, cancelling his attack and saving Odin from the final shot. With a furious huff, Cole regained his balance and as he spun on a heel, he saw Galian upright and levitating three more of the floor stones.

"Make them count," Cole snarled.

With a wave of his hand, Galian launched the three slabs. The first two connected hard with Jasil and Lizin, exploding against their heads and freeing Odin from their grip. With a diving roll, Cole had evaded the third stone, and as he sprang back out of his tumble, he stood only a foot in front of Galian. Frantically, Galian cast out his hands and tried to raise another floor stone, but before he could shake one loose, Cole swung his hand into Galian's neck. The quiet monk toppled over, and with another furious huff, Cole grabbed a fragment of the red stone and began to pummel Galian against the ground. As the sound of brick hitting flesh filled his ears, Odin fought back to his feet. His balance was off: he was teetering from the damage of Cole's attacks. However, as he staggered, blinking and grimacing through the fog that had overcome his senses, suddenly, the silhouette of Cole burned through his stupor. Galian was in trouble; Odin's best friend was being mauled. Like fire to oil, Odin erupted. With a surge, Odin's heart willed him past his wounds, stoking his body with the blaze of a brother's love. As rage coursed through him, Odin launched himself at his foe's back, blasting his knee into Cole with spine-cracking force. The impact was immense. Like a cloth doll, Cole crumpled, expelling airy yelps as he writhed like a broken insect. Mercilessly, Odin leapt on top of him, bashing him like a hammer to a nail. Cole went limp, but the onslaught didn't stop. Odin was consumed. Amid Haren's screams for help, Odin continued. Amid hundreds of candles and monks flooding the courtyard, Odin wouldn't cease. Finally, with Cole's face bashed and bloody, Raine's massive hands latched onto Odin and ripped him off of his prey. As Raine restrained him, Odin spat foam from the corners of his mouth, staring wildly at the hundred monks that filled the courtyard.

Igallik was one of them.

As the head monk surveyed the madness, he was quiet, analyzing the pieces of the puzzle and doing his best to make them fit: Odin was irate, Haren was naked, Galian was bloody, Tyrik and Cole were unconscious, and Lizin and Jasil were sprawled on the stone holding their heads.

As voices, theories, and accusations filled the courtyard, Haren stood up awkwardly, contorting her naked body and trying to cover up. She backed out of the inner circle, and as she tried vainly to slink away, an Order monk, Palis, made a quiet and stealthy retrieval of Haren's ripped robe and draped it over her shoulders. With a shudder, Haren accepted the robe, but as Palis tried to tend to her, she pushed through him and walked quickly to the beaten and bloodied Galian.

Finally, with monks' fingers pointing blame in all directions, the head monk took rein of the bedlam.

"Silence!" he ordered.

With a hush, the courtyard obeyed.

The head monk turned first to Haren, who was holding Galian tightly against her shoulder.

"What am I to make of this?" he demanded.

With the bloodied Galian cradled against her, Haren snapped back her response.

"Which part?" she seared back. "The attempted rape? Or the beating?"

"Rape?" Igallik blurted. His eyes turned fearsome. "Who?" he demanded.

"Tyrik," Haren said coldly. "With a helping hand from Jasil, Lizin, and Cole."

With anger brimming in his eyes, Igallik turned to Wylak. The head monk's voice was disturbingly steady.

"Wake Tyrik and Cole," he said firmly.

With a nod, the herbalist retrieved the appropriate herbs. Igallik pressed his own palms together, his eyes smouldering forward as he made a concentrated effort to compose himself.

"And Odin fended them off?" he asked, his body rigid with anger.

"Yes," Haren answered flatly.

The Justice totem, Raeman, threw his hands up. He had heard enough. "This is slander," he protested. "It is but one voice."

The look that Igallik returned to the Justice totem could have silenced the wind.

As Raeman wisely chose quiet, Igallik looked back to Wylak.

"Are they up?" he asked.

Wylak looked back with heavy eyes. "Tyrik will be in a moment," he said. The herbalist paused for a long moment. "As for Cole...," he said finally, "...Cole's dead."

Somehow the courtyard became even quieter. The punishment for killing another monk was ten reeds to the back. There were no exceptions.

As if strings were pulling their heads, every monk in the courtyard turned slowly back to Odin. There was no doubt that he had been Cole's killer.

Raine, who was still hugging Odin in restraint, looked pleadingly over Odin's shoulder.

"Igallik," he protested, "ten will break him. He's too young. Too small."

The Sons of Animus Letum

Igallik knew that the old warrior was right. Ten could kill him. Even so, a murder could not be swept away.

"There will be a hearing," Igallik said.

It was the best he could do.

As murmurs spread throughout the courtyard, Tyrik began to wake. The hulk sat up slowly, cradling his head in his palm as he rocked in a small arc. With only a look, Igallik ordered Lizin and Jasil to help the hulk to his feet. Amid the stares of every monk present, Lizin and Jasil had no choice but to move fast. As they reached Tyrik, they tucked their shoulders under his arms and propped the hulk up between them.

Igallik walked slowly to their front.

"Welcome back," he said, as Tyrik looked groggily forward. "How are you feeling? Like a bashed nail, I'm sure."

The tone was too pleasant, like a smile before the guillotine.

"Are you with us?" Igallik asked.

Tyrik nodded, forcing a grunt as affirmation.

"Good," the head monk said. "You know, I never asked before, but now seems an opportune time. What's the furthest you've been from the monastery?"

Tyrik's head bobbed. "Northton," he grumbled.

Igallik nodded and then addressed Lizin and Jasil. "And you two?" he asked. "How far?"

"Northton," they said in unison.

"Very well," Igallik said.

With a quick hand, Igallik grabbed Jasil's wrist, and after a squeeze, Lizin, Tyrik, and Jasil fell unconscious like a line of dominoes.

The head monk turned calmly back to Raine.

"After Odin returns to some level of calm, pack these three in a carriage and drop them past Northton. Far enough that they never find their way home."

Raeman immediately muscled his way into the head monk's space, shouting wildly in protest.

"There are rules!" he yelled. "There are hearings! You have no right!"

Igallik met Raeman with stern eyes. "If you see a snake, Raeman, you kill it. You don't debate the pattern of its scales."

Furiously, Raeman took aim at the only weakness in Igallik's makeup – his position as the Order's Chancellor.

"I'll have your throne for this!" he threatened. "This is whim, not order!"

"Why wait?" Igallik fired back. "We'll vote right now." The head monk turned emphatically to the other three Order monks. "Brothers, is Raeman right? Has my ruling cost me my throne?"

Typically, such a vote would have been cast in the High Temple. However, as Igallik's fiery eyes called them to action, Palis, Bysin, and Nile each signified a vote of no. By majority, Igallik retained his chancellorship.

Igallik seared his eyes onto Raeman. "Is there anything else?"

The Justice totem returned a cold stare. "Apparently not."

"Very well," Igallik said.

After returning his mind to the bloody mess of the courtyard, Igallik raised his voice to all monks present.

"This night has fallen," he said, "and with it, a mockery of our ways. Retire," the head monk ordered. "Retire from the day."

With heaviness in his eyes the head monk turned to Odin.

"Tomorrow," he said, "we will deal our justice."

Upon Igallik's orders, the monks of the courtyard filed out. As a few of the monks lifted Cole's dead body and began to carry him to the infirmary, Haren helped Galian back to his feet.

"Are you alright?" she asked.

Galian nodded. "Beaten, not broken."

Haren kissed his forehead. "I know the feeling."

As she braced her arm under Galian's shoulder and her torn robe compressed between them, suddenly Haren's eyes grew wide with panic. With abandon, Haren threw off her robe and knelt naked above it, urgently searching its different folds. With no success, her eyes rose to the courtyard, hunting for what she had lost.

"Someone took it," she whispered fearfully. "Someone's taken the page."

Galian retrieved Haren's robe and threw it back over her shoulder.

"There was no page," he signed sternly. His eyes were pleading for Haren's cooperation.

Haren's looked frantically left and right, her mind searching desperately for her best option.

"There was no page," she said finally.

As Haren met Galian's stare, their eyes made a pact. It was a lie they would hold to even if it cost them their lives.

But there was a page… and it was in the wrong hands.

12

The morning after Cole's murder, Odin was called to the High Temple. The Order awaited, and a sentence was impending.

A rainstorm had laid claim to the morning, and as Odin ascended the final steps to the golden Temple, he marched slowly under the downpour, his clothes and blonde hair drenched against him. Raine was at the door, soaked and standing guard as he always did.

As Odin grew close, Raine tilted his head up, forcing a stream of water down his nose. "How are you feeling?" the old warrior asked.

Odin threw his blonde hair out of his eyes. "No worse for wear," he replied. As he ambled under the wet and wind-swept cherry blossoms, Odin's calm walk seemed to vouch for his words

"You know what's coming, don't you?" Raine said.

"I'm expecting ten," Odin replied.

Raine shook his head, scattering rain drops from his brow. "Expected or not, ten reeds could kill you."

Odin remained unfazed.

With worry, the old warrior forfeited his formal pose. "Odin, you need to formulate a defence. You need to realize…"

"Raine," Odin interrupted. "I know what I did last night, and I know what I will do within those doors. I will not lie, and I will not ask for forgiveness."

Odin's unabashed honesty troubled the old warrior. As Raine began to campaign once more, Odin nodded sternly through him.

"Can you open the doors?" he asked. "I am expected."

The tone did not offend Raine – it brought more worry. It was too composed. Too cool.

Knowing no other recourse, Raine finally obliged, and drew open the doors.

"You should know," he said as the rain splashed between them, "it is not weak to ask for mercy."

As he walked past Raine, Odin's words cut over the storm. "If I wanted it, I'd ask."

Without another word, Odin proceeded coolly into the Temple.

As was customary for a hearing, the five totems were present: Justice, Mercy, Logic, and Instinct each sat in his throne, and at their center, Igallik sat stoically.

The five watched Odin intently, somewhat struck by his unruffled demeanour.

As Odin approached, he bowed to the crown of Animus Letum on the altar, and then sat down in the foremost pew. The young Lyran threw the rain from his hair, and after a deep breath, he looked fearlessly up at the Order. With all parties present, Igallik took a puff from his tobacco hookah, exhaled, and commenced the hearing.

"Let it be understood, the verdict for this hearing will be final unless an exceptional force decrees otherwise. Because the verdict is final, the totems of the Order shall be permitted any length of time to make their verdict. However, if a totem is uncertain about a verdict – even in the least – he will defer his vote to another totem's speciality."

Igallik looked to the Order monks on his left and right, and after receiving each of their affirmations of understanding, he took another puff from his hookah.

"It is pledged."

The head monk turned to Odin. "You understand why we are here?" he presumed.

"I do," Odin replied.

"Have you anything to say?"

"That depends," Odin said.

"On what?" Igallik asked.

"Whether you want to excuse my actions or understand them."

Nile adjusted his glasses, raising an eyebrow as he looked over their frame. "I see no reason why we can't do both," he said. "One should lead to the other."

"Then you don't understand my actions," Odin replied.

Nile looked down the line of thrones, and then back to Odin. "Please, enlighten us."

Odin stood from the pew, his eyes and posture as calm as ever. "Cole's death was not an accident," he said. "It was not a crime of hot blood."

The words confounded the Order: Igallik more than anyone.

"You mean to destroy your one hope at mercy?" he asked.

"If it based upon a lie," Odin said, "then, yes."

"And what is the truth?" Igallik asked.

"Cole's murder is a warning," Odin declared.

The head monk was shocked, jostling on in his throne before he leaned intently to its edge. "To whom?" he demanded.

"Anyone," Odin replied. "Anyone who would ever think to hurt my brother."

With even more shock, the Order stared in silence.

As Odin stared daringly back, Palis, the Mercy totem, leapt to Odin's defence.

"Brothers, let us take these words with a grain of salt," he said. "I don't think that Odin is completely present today. He is still fuming with the fire of last night."

"You are mistaken," Odin said calmly. "I am merely giving you the truth."

As the Order monks turned and began to consult with each other, Odin raised his voice to break their huddle.

"I *am* my brother's keeper," he said commandingly. "Know this now and forever. Fate divided our strengths at birth, but make no mistake, his is the greater. Galian met with me before I came here this morning," Odin said. "He told me why we raced yesterday. Obviously, if you have elected him as the heir and leader of the Forge, you know his worth. He is greater than the five of you. Greater than me. And know this: I am not burdened by him being the successor – I am fuelled by it. I was given a body so that I could defend his heart. You may have made a decision to make him heir, but it is my mission to make it so. Serve me your ten reeds." Odin said. "Serve twenty, if you must. My bones will break far sooner than my word."

Igallik pressed his fingers hard into his temples. "You do not leave us with much choice," he said. "And worse, you seem proud of your actions."

"I am not proud," Odin said. "But I did kill Cole, and I meant to do it."

With his hands clasped together, Palis studied Odin with a grave seriousness.

"You court more than reeds," he said finally. "I will be honest with you, Odin. Your lack of remorse raises very unsettling questions."

"Feel free to ask them," Odin replied.

Raeman, who had purposely chosen to remain quiet the entire hearing, began to rap his knuckles against his steel throne.

"It was a murder," he said. "Plain and simple. He will be served ten reeds. No more, no less."

Nile agreed. "Ten it is. The punishment shall not be amended."

For a majority ruling, only one more totem had to agree.

"Ten," Igallik approved. "At this eve's close."

The head monk's ruling seemed to hang within the Temple, lingering like the words of a hurting father. Even so, Odin remained unfazed.

As Igallik met Odin's unflinching stare, the head monk took a final puff from his hookah.

"Brothers," he said, "We are adjourned. You may return to your quarters."

Odin turned, and before any of the Order monks had even stood from their thrones, he had left the Temple.

As the Order began to filter out, Igallik called Bysin aside. The head monk allowed the Temple to empty, and after arranging his own thoughts, he looked intently into the Instinct totem's eyes.

"What do you make of him?" Igallik asked.

"He was honest," Bysin said matter-of-factly.

"But was he – as Palis suggested – burning with the fires of last night?"

"He was," Bysin said.

"So he should come back to his senses?"

Bysin scratched his head and then shrugged his shoulders. "I didn't say that. Nor did I say that the fire was a bad thing."

Igallik tilted his neck back. As if to remind Bysin of Odin's behaviour, he pointed back to the Temple's foremost pew.

"He was livid," Igallik said. "Scary, even. No man, especially a Lyran, should live with such an edge."

"I do not sense that this edge is a weakness," Bysin said. "For a moment, just feel. Feel *how* his fire burns. And then feel *why* it burns. This a blaze of love, Igallik. Imagine this fire at the forefront of the Forge – it could reclaim Animus Letum – almost by itself. At the very least, we will need it soon."

Igallik's eyes grew with alarm. "Soon?" he repeated. "Why? What do you sense?"

"Something happened last night," Bysin said, "something with Haren that is still guised in secret. Worse, I sense that this secret will bring Death to our monastery."

"You have facts?"

"Only feeling," Bysin replied. "Strong feeling."

Igallik brushed his hand through his beard. "So what do we do?" he asked. "How do you feel we should proceed?"

"For starters," Bysin said, "we make sure that no other monk hurts Galian."

Igallik nodded gravely. "That aside."

"That aside," Bysin said, "We are limited. If I am right about this impending doom, I believe that our only move is to surround Odin's fire with tar. If we can do that, when he truly erupts, his fire will become unstoppable."

"The Forge is in place," Igallik reminded. "It is now nearly two-hundred monks strong. I don't know if there is much else to surround Odin with."

"We must surround him with more than an army of me," Bysin said. "The Forge is sound, there is no doubt. But we must surround Odin with an army of skills. If Odin can become great without the fire, then he can become godly with it."

Although he still felt some concern with regard to Odin, Igallik saw promise in Bysin's instinct. With a small sense of relief, the head monk patted Bysin's shoulder.

"So I gather ten reeds won't extinguish the fire," he said.

"He'll survive," Bysin replied.

Igallik nodded. "After the breaking, we will start the building."

That night, as the sun fell, Odin was served ten reeds. The first was taken with a grunt and gritted teeth. The second was followed with a whimper. The third, fourth, and fifth forced a shrill scream. The sixth and seventh broke his ribs. And the remaining three bashed him into a broken heap.

After the tenth reed, Death had circled. He had done so in vain. Underneath Odin's broken body was an unbreakable spirit. Even the hunter of life had to bow.

But Death would return – soon and in far greater form.

Bysin was right about the impending doom.

The day of the Blood Cael was looming.

13

Death is the great thief of your realm – the uncatchable and unforeseeable bandit of breath. However, Death should not draw your ire. Instead, your ire should find his accomplices. It should be those who force his hand. If Death is called on, he arrives – consistent and unbiased. The Great Reaper does not choose his victims: he is dealt onto them. Death has the regrettable duty of attending all tragedy. I beg you: pity the servant whose arrival brings heartbreak.

On the day of the Blood Cael, Death was dealt one hundred and forty-six times. The only victory by any monk witness to that day's horror was that he survived. The day of the Blood Cael was one of the most violent attacks on the Throne's Eye in the monastery's history. It was devised by hands foreign to the first realm, and carried out just the same. The number of monks that held guard that day was in the hundreds. Half of them died. My breath turns short and cold remembering that day's death-dealer, for there was only one. One hundred and forty-six monks were killed by the beast owning title to that day: the Blood Cael.

The day of the Blood Cael began in storm. The dark billowing skies churned above the monastery, commanding the moment, and stealing the monks from their routines. With sheets of rain and lightning falling from the skies, the monks took cover, attuning their eyes to nature's great ire.

As the thunder growled above the monastery, Usis emerged from one of the monastery's chapels, and with the wind and rain abusing his balance, he sprinted across the courtyard. As he grew close to Odin and Galian's quarters, the door opened slightly, and with a nimble slide, Usis sleeked through. Once inside, Usis shook the rain from his hair and clothes, and as he looked to Galian who was crouched fifteen feet away at the window, he nodded in appreciation. Galian smiled and then with a nod of his head the door closed shut.

"Hell of a storm," Usis said as his eyes shot around the room. His voice was quickly hushed by the crouching Galian.

"What?" Usis joked. "Your girly ears are too sensitive in the morning?"

"Not mine," Galian explained in his sign language. With a roll of his eyes, he pointed to Odin asleep on his bed. "Our lazy brother is taking the morning off."

"Oh," Usis whispered as he assumed a stealthy crouch. "So he probably won't like this."

With silent steps, Usis crept over to Odin's bed, and after gripping Odin's covers tightly, he ripped them off and tossed them to the floor.

Odin reacted with a deep exhalation. "You're not going to ruin this," he groaned. "I don't care how, but I'm sleeping in."

"That's going to be tough," Usis said as he reached his hand towards Odin's pillow, "without this!"

With a quick grab, Usis ripped the pillow from under Odin's head and tossed it across the room.

Odin calmly rose to his feet, retrieved his cover and pillow, and walked out the door.

"It's cold out there!" Usis called after him.

Odin made no reply as he walked to the Temple next door.

Usis turned back to Galian. "I'll give him credit," he laughed. "That took dedication."

Galian nodded, but then returned his attention to the storm crashing outside his window. As Galian surveyed the storm, Usis walked to the window sill, and after taking another look at the gale, he patted Galian on the back.

"I needed Odin out of the room," he said.

"Why?" Galian signed. "What's going on?"

Usis sat back against the window sill. "I received some news last night," he said. "Haren and Raine are to return this afternoon."

Galian turned his attention to Usis.

"Both are well?"

"Apparently quite well," Usis replied. "Their mission was a success."

"Good," Galian judged.

Usis's eyes darted around the room, and after his hands fidgeted, he stared back out into the storm.

"They have a prisoner," he said. "Someone linked to my past."

"How early in your past?" Galian asked.

"The earliest," Usis answered.

"How do you know?"

Usis retrieved a piece of paper from his belt.

"Because of this," he replied.

Galian's eyes grew wide. He immediately recognized the paper. It was the page that Haren had lost when Tyrik had attacked her. Written on it was the Scour incantation.

"Did you use it?" Galian asked. There was readable anxiety in his eyes.

"You and Haren are safe," Usis assured. "I am not going to tell Igallik."

"That is the least of my worries," Galian said. "Did you use it or not?"

"Of course I did," Usis said, not quite understanding Galian's anxiety. "I figured you would understand. You were going to use it anyway."

"Not me," Galian signed. "Haren was going to use it."

Usis looked back into the storm. "For her brother," he realized.

Galian nodded. "And you," he presumed, "you've used it for your parents?"

Usis nodded and then looked back to the quiet monk. "The ritual worked," he said. There was a flare of excitement in his eyes. "I found them, Galian. I've been speaking with them for two months."

Galian was washed of his worry.

"What have they said?" he asked, his face was excited by Scour's success.

Usis grinned. "They've said a lot. Mostly, they ask about my arrangements here. But they've also told me things about the afterlife."

"Like what?"

"Like who Malum Ludus is, and who his allies are."

"Hasn't Igallik told you the same thing?" Galian signed.

"Not quite," Usis replied. "For starters, Ludus's cult – the Metus Sane – have been using a ritual to resurrect fallen allies from the afterlife. They call them Caels."

"Is that possible?"

"My parents say yes. In fact we should meet a Cael today."

"Today?"

Usis nodded. "Haren and Raine's prisoner," he said.

Galian suddenly understood Usis's intent.

"You're going to kill the prisoner?"

"I am," Usis replied.

"You must wait for permission," Galian signed. "You must only kill him if Igallik says so."

"And if he says no?"

Before Galian could reply, Usis reminded the quiet monk of their pact.

"Make the flames of evil doubt their burn," he said. "We've talked about this before, Galian. And I was very clear that if fate were to offer me a chance like this, I would exact my revenge." Usis began to pace from the window. "This is my chance," he campaigned, "I can strike retribution for my parents' murder this very day."

Galian shook his head.

"What if we need the prisoner?" he said. "What if there is a reason Raine and Haren brought him back here?"

Usis continued to pace, weighing Galian's thoughts against his own. Then, almost as if an emotion had swept quickly upon him, Usis turned back to Galian.

"You're afraid," he challenged.

Galian looked to Usis in surprise.

"How do you always know?"

"I'm not sure," Usis answered. "I can just feel it sometimes." Usis shook his head as he studied Galian's eyes. "I felt it first when I pulled out Scour, but now I feel it tenfold. What are you holding back?"

Galian motioned his hand to the storm.

"Something is off today," he signed. "I've never felt energy in a storm like this. There's chaos in clouds and it's almost maddening."

"I'm sure it'll pass," Usis said.

Galian found it hard to agree.

"Promise me, no matter what happens today, you will choose control. You have your parents now, perhaps there is no need for vengeance."

Usis's eyebrow rose, his foot tapping out a slow rhythm.

"I wouldn't have come here if I didn't trust you," he said finally. "And although I hate to admit it, your mind has consistently proven wiser than mine. If you are telling me to wait, I suppose I should."

Galian nodded. "Wait does not mean abandon."

After a conceding smile, Usis examined the Scour incantation. "Do you need this?" he asked. "I've got it memorized."

With a wave of his hand, Galian used his power to snatch the paper and float it towards one of the room's candles. After giving the act a second thought, the page stopped and levitated just above the flame.

"Do you think I should give it to Haren?" he asked.

Usis shrugged. "It closed a wound for me," he said. "I don't know if it is the Order's business to delegate who should heal."

Galian smiled at the logic, and then with a snap, the paper flew into his hand.

Usis watched Galian tuck the paper away, and after a nod of approval, he turned towards the door.

"Where are you going?" Galian asked.

"Next door," Usis grinned. "I have some business in the chapel."

Galian shook his head with a smile.

"Let him sleep."

"Can't do it," Usis called back as he walked out the door. "Young men need structure."

There were no breaks in the storm until midday, when a fleeting burst of sun fell over the monastery. It was in that break that two monks caught their first glimpse of Haren and Raine's convoy. The returning convoy was nineteen monks strong – somewhat fewer than the thirty who had departed. Aside from Haren, who was a Sight, the convoy was populated wholly by Torch and Aeris monks. However, it was the convoy's prisoner – the Blood Cael – who demanded the greatest attention. Raine was a huge man. He was at least six foot six and two-hundred and fifty pounds, but standing next to the Cael he was dwarfed. As news of Raine and Haren's return – and the immense size of their prisoner – sounded back to the heart of the monastery, it took only minutes before a large congregation of monks had gathered at the front gate. Usis, Galian, and Odin were purposefully excluded. Igallik had decided that they would stay indoors until their safety was assured. As the convoy grew closer, the monks were awestruck by the fantastic size of the prisoner. However, as more distance was closed between them, the real shock proved to be the beast's gruesome condition. The Blood Cael was nine feet tall and was draped in a giant black cloak that covered most of its skin. The skin that was visible was polar white with blood red symbols carved and gouged into it. The monster's eyes – crimson red and lacking both pupil and iris – appeared like deep pools of blood, staring through reality like a soulless ghoul. The worst of the beast's gore was its hands: each hand had been pierced clean through with massive chains that were being used to haul the giant forward.

As a visibly distraught Raine ushered the convoy through the Throne's Eye gates, the monks did not have to be told to keep back – the giant's gruesome state was enough to keep the monks at a safe distance.

From the window of Galian and Odin's quarters, Usis and the sons of Animus Letum were intently watching the procession. The three became shocked by the sight of the prisoner.

"Holy God!" Odin cried. "That thing's monstrous!"

"Indeed, it is," Usis solemnly agreed.

Galian managed to catch Usis's eye, and after seeing the disbelief on Usis's face, Galian shot him a wry smile.

"If you're still set on revenge," he joked, "you can start by getting a ladder."

Usis broke a smile against his frustration, and after shaking his head again in disbelief, he returned to the window.

Outside, Igallik had just descended from the High Temple and was walking calmly to the front of the convoy.

"First," Igallik said as he reached Haren and Raine, "I wish to commend you on a successful mission."

Raine and Haren both bowed.

"I have been informed that there were losses," the head monk continued. "I trust their deaths belong to courage, not cowardice. Take heart that at this eve's close we will pay tribute to those lost."

Raine and Haren offered another bow to their head monk.

"But as for the issue at hand," Igallik said as he pointed to the prisoner. "What do we know of this monster?"

Haren was first to speak.

"It is of the Metus Sane cult," she explained. "From what we witnessed in the cult's lair, it seems to be worshipped as some sort of deity. Almost like Malum Ludus."

"Is it hostile?" Igallik asked.

"As much as you can believe," Raine snapped.

The old warrior was instantly regretful of his tone, and offered an apologetic bow to Igallik.

"This bastard," Raine explained as he calmed his voice, "is the reason we lost our men." As flashes of dying monks filled his eyes, Raine slapped his own cheeks to break his daze. "You better tell him, Haren," he said. "I don't want to relive this one."

Haren patted the old warrior's back, and then looked to Igallik in regret.

"The cult wasn't a problem. We picked them off quickly and precisely. But when we descended into the basement of their stronghold, we met this thing. It was in the center of some sort of spiritual rite, and the remaining cult members were chanting verse."

Haren inhaled deeply and shook her head. "Within thirty seconds of our guys engaging this monster, eleven of them were dead. And Igallik," Haren said, "I don't mean just dead – they were ripped to god-damned pieces."

As Raine was again reminded of his lost men, a great pain took to his eyes. The old warrior began to curse madly, and as words and spit flew from his mouth, he walked deliberately to the beast. After snatching a spear from one of the monks in the convoy, Raine hacked the back of the monster's legs, bringing the giant to his knees.

"I hope you feel pain!" Raine screamed, "'cause you're in for a world of it!"

Haren and a few of the convoy monks quickly latched onto Raine's shoulders and ripped him back. As they restrained him, Raine spit again at the monster, his eyes bulging as he kicked his legs at the monster's head. Finally, Raine fell to a defeated knee, whispering the names of his fallen brothers. As the old warrior mourned, Igallik approached him and placed his hand on Raine's shoulder.

"There will be retribution for this beast," the head monk promised. "But we will not lose time to anger. Raine, I trust you can pull yourself together."

Raine wiped his eyes again and slowly rose to his feet, forcing a strange grunt as an affirmation.

The head monk turned back to Haren.

"How were you able to subdue this monster?" he asked.

"After we lost our first wave of men, Raine arrived in the basement. He gave us the edge we needed. Raine and the remaining nineteen of our brothers managed to subdue the beast, and it was Raine who drove those chains through his palms."

"The prick didn't even flinch," Raine muttered.

Igallik swept his hand through his beard as he surveyed the Blood Cael.

"As you might have guessed," he said, "this monster is not from our realm. I have read about such beasts, and what we have is a very dangerous prisoner."

As Haren studied the head monk, she knew what Igallik's next question would be.

"Imprisoning the monster was our decision," she explained to Igallik. "We had to bring it here. Believe me, if this monster could die, Raine would have killed it. We decided that our monastery was the best place to learn how to kill the giant, or at the very least detain it."

"This is wise," Igallik praised. "You two have done well."

"There is something else," Haren said.

"What is it?" Igallik asked.

"The monster had this."

Haren handed Igallik a small painted portrait.

"We believe the beast is connected to one of our brothers."

Igallik looked over the painting, and a deep chill ran up his spine. The portrait was of Usis's parents. Igallik's eyes glanced to the window where Usis, Galian, and Odin were watching. He quickly returned his attention to Haren and handed the portrait back to her.

"Burn it," he instructed.

"Do we tell Usis?"

"No," Igallik sternly answered. "Just burn it."

"As you wish," Haren said.

As she began to tuck the small painting back into her satchel, the giant's eyes locked onto her. At first, the crimson stare startled her, but after studying the beast, Haren regained her poise and held the portrait up to the monster.

"Whatever ambition was bound to this painting," she promised, "will die with you."

With authority, the violet-eyed Deathrider drew a match from her belt and lit the small painting, scolding the giant as the portrait burned. As the canvas smouldered, a slow wind picked up in the monastery, blowing the flames back onto Haren's hand. With a flinch, Haren dropped the painting. As she knelt to retrieve it, she could hear the sound of light rain falling onto the courtyard floor. Haren dismissed the change in weather, but as she reclaimed the wet portrait, her eyes zeroed in on the colour of the precipitation.

"What in the hell?" she whispered as the rain beaded on the black and white picture. Haren drew the portrait to her nose to smell the red precipitation, and after inhaling its scent, she was taken with shock.

"The rain…" she realized. "It's blood…"

Haren turned back to Igallik who had also recognized the nature of the rainfall. As Igallik met Haren's eyes, his expression of confusion suddenly gave way to alarm.

"Haren!" he cried. "Get back!"

With her body rigid with panic, Haren spun back to see that the hulking Blood Cael was rising from its knees. As the beast rose to the height of his nine-foot frame, its dark cloak fell from its shoulders and the falling blood soaked its ghostly skin with a layer of crimson red. In what seemed like slow motion, Haren fell back and began a desperate crawl to safety. As she scraped herself out of range, Raine marched to the monster's front. The monks holding the monster's chains fought desperately to rein the prisoner, but as the monster thrashed its powerful arms, it ripped the chains free from their grips. Raine stood five feet in front of the monster, his fierce eyes staring up at the beast that had slaughtered eleven of his men.

"Let's have at it then," Raine growled.

As the blood cascaded down Raine's face, the old warrior ripped his sword from its sheath.

"It's you or me!" he snapped.

With a snarl, the monster flexed its massive hands back, and as the sound of slicing metal hummed through the monastery, the beast began to swing its chains as weapons. As the massive chains slashed towards Raine, he dodged the first attacks, but ultimately the whirlwind of chains overcame him and he was whipped across the upper torso. Raine dropped hard to the ground, but used what strength he had left to roll out of range of the monster's attacks.

As more monks drew their weapons and rushed in, Igallik turned fearfully from the fray and began to sprint to the monastery's High Temple.

As the first wave of monks converged on the beast, the tornado of chains quickly destroyed them. Some of the fallen monks managed to roll back to safety, but most were left immobile, and amid the bloody rainfall, the merciless monster stomped them to death.

From Odin and Galian's window, Usis watched one monk after another die, and after his rage had forced his action, he turned from the window and addressed the young twins.

"Alright boys," he said as he rushed to Odin's closet. "The time has come." Usis retrieved two staffs and a sword from the closet. "Don't argue with it, don't fight it," he said as he handed each brother a weapon. "We fight today for the losses of yesterday." Usis grabbed the door handle and threw it open. "Let's go!" he cried.

Galian and Odin looked to each other in agreement, and together they stormed after Usis. However, they quickly halted as they ran into Haren outside the door. Haren was using all her might to hold Usis back, and as Haren cast his irate eyes onto Galian and Odin, the twins retreated immediately.

Usis refused.

"Not now, godammit!" Haren yelled as she restrained Usis. "You have a death wish?"

"They're dying, Haren!" Usis screamed.

"They are, you're not!" Haren yelled back. Haren finally pushed Usis back into the room, and after she quickly slammed the door shut behind her, a defeated Usis began to pace in frustration.

"Haren," he pled, "we can help. Let us help."

"Not today," Haren firmly ruled. "Now sit down and shut up."

Usis's eyes continued to beg Haren, but it was clear that Haren would not yield. Haren locked the door, and after issuing Usis a threatening look, she stood with Galian and Odin at the window. Usis could barely calm himself, but he knew he needed to witness the beast, and soon he joined Haren and the sons of Animus Letum at the window.

Outside in the courtyard, it seemed that with each monk the giant killed, it grew more powerful. As the moments passed, the death toll was amassing in pace with the monster's blood lust. The giant continued to slice its enormous chain shackles through a radius of fifteen yards, until, as the blood-fall became torrential, it ceased the violent arcs of its chains. The blood-drenched monks, noting the standstill, rushed the monster, but as they drew close to the giant, the beast brutally lashed the chains into its own back. Confusion reigned over the monks as the monster's eyes began to burn with a wild, glowing red.

Igallik, who had begun his ascent of the High Temple staircase, halted in panic and began to scream back at his brothers.

"Get back! Get back and cover your ears!" he cried.

The monks who heard obeyed, but the ones who didn't continued to advance on the Blood Cael. As they arrived within yards of the monster, suddenly the giant's eyes exploded in flame and it bellowed a wicked roar into the monastery air. The eye sockets of fifty monks within range of the beast's bloody roar instantly burst into flames. With their screaming voices slicing over the bloody massacre, the Throne's Eye courtyard looked and sounded like hell. As the fire scorched fatally through the monks' eyes into their brains, the victims of the monster's scream suffered their torture for over a minute.

As a merciful Death finally collected them, the giant paraded in the destruction it had dealt, its eyes burning with flames as it readied its chains for the next wave.

Igallik watched in horror. He felt each monk's death as if was the death of his own son. But knowing his responsibility, he quickly turned from the courtyard and again rushed up the stairs to the High Temple. The head monk knew that there was only one weapon that would kill the giant.

By command, Raine held the remaining monks back, and as the monster lashed his chains, Raine called out his orders.

"Archers! Grab your bows!"

Immediately, twenty monks rushed to the Throne's Eye armoury.

"Whoever's left," Raine screamed, "grab those chains!"

The monks all leapt into action. Raine led the first wave. Nimbly, the old warrior dove successfully between the whips of the two chains, but as the swings of the monster's attacks slashed behind him, the chains crashed into the rest of the first wave. Excluding Raine, each of the ninety monks within fifteen yards of the beast were dead. As the monster scoured the heap of lifeless bodies below, Raine had no option but to feign his own death. The beast ruthlessly stomped onto the corpses, and it missed Raine's head by only inches. Raine lay deadly still, holding his breath as the beast passed him by. As the archers emerged from the armoury with their bows, the beast looked up from the heap of bodies, snarling and pounding its chest in boast. The archers drew their arrows back in unison, but the beast was not phased. It again lashed the chains into its own back, and as the metal tore into its white flesh, it prepared for another of its thunderous roars. Like sinister rubies, the monster's eyes began to burn with a wild red. Another roar was imminent. Urgently, Raine leapt to his feet, and after retrieving the dagger on his belt, he lunged at the beast's throat. The giant's eyes again exploded in flame, but just before it could scream, Raine plunged the dagger deep into the monster's windpipe. The giant's roar was muted, and as the beast staggered back, Raine began to twist the blade into the monster's flesh. The archers held their arrows as their leader wrestled with the giant, but after a few staggers the beast recaptured its wits and locked its grip around Raine's torso. Fearlessly, Raine stared into the blood red gaze of the monster. It needed to die. With a surge of fury, the old warrior stabbed wildly into the monster's neck, and as his blade cut out slices of white flesh, Raine screamed back to the archers.

"Now!" he bawled. "Don't worry about me! Fire!"

The archers looked to each other in apprehension, but amid their hesitation, Raine's unrelenting scream was still calling them to action. Finally, they set their aim on the giant. Raine fought desperately against the beast, madly stabbing and twisting his dagger, but the monster's powerful grip soon clenched around his neck and legs. As Raine's body crumpled under the weight of the monster's grip, the old warrior could feel his life being ripped from him. Still, the warrior was calling the archers to action. With a unified release, the archers fired their bows. The arrows flew through the downpour of blood, and just before they connected with their target, the beast violently hurtled Raine across the courtyard towards Odin and Galian's room. As each arrow struck the monster with perfect accuracy, Raine's body barrelled through the air towards certain death. Raine's eyes stared down his death with ferocity. Death, he decided, would meet him on his terms. However, just before impact, Raine's body halted in mid-air. Raine glanced around in confusion, twisting and contorting as he floated above the earth. As he finally looked through the window to Galian and Odin's quarters, he could see Galian's eyes locked onto his own. Galian's arms were outstretched as if to catch a large object. Then, as Galian lowered his arms, Raine's body descended out of the air and back down to the courtyard floor. Galian had managed to catch Raine's fall – a level of power that he had never before achieved. Haren looked to Galian in astonishment, and Raine too, as he allowed himself to regain his composure, offered Galian a thankful nod. Then, to Raine's left, the door to Galian and Odin's living-quarters kicked open, and Usis burst out and sprinted at the monster.

"Godammit!" Haren cursed. "Raine," she yelled, "stop him!"

Raine looked back to Haren in disagreement.

"Haren," he returned with regret. "We either all fight, or we all die."

Haren drew her hand to her forehead in deliberation. As she shook her head and looked back out into the hell storm, she elected the safest strategy.

"If Galian and Odin fight, they stay with the archers."

"Alright," Raine approved. "Now let's go!"

With no hesitation, the old warrior turned and sprinted back into the storm of falling blood.

Haren turned to the sons of Animus Letum, her words not asking, but pleading.

"You both heard Raine," she said. "You stay with the archers."

Galian and Odin both nodded, and after a look to each other they too dashed out into the fray.

The archers had riddled the beast with countless strikes of their arrows, but the monster was only slightly slowed by the onslaught. With a spear in hand, Raine rushed in and began a rampage on the beast's limbs. The giant's slower movement, as well as Raine's ability to read the timing of the chain lashes, allowed the warrior to cut methodically into the giant's flesh, slicing the tendons that were supporting its massive frame. However, the onslaught was barely inflicting damage. As Raine continued to scream and cut, Usis strategically stalked the beast from behind, hurtling his numerous daggers into the monster's back. The other monks followed Usis's lead, and as they began to fire projectile assaults at the beast, Odin and Galian quickly joined the archers. The twins added their strengths to the assault and began to fire arrows at the monster – Odin used a bow, and Galian, using his powers, launched entire quivers of arrows at the giant.

As the monks warred with the Blood Cael, Igallik began his descent from the High Temple. In his left hand he brandished the mighty staff of Serich that had crossed realms with Rhea fourteen years earlier.

Igallik began to yell at the monks below him.

"Brothers!" he screamed, "He won't die by our blades!"

Few monks heard, but of those who did was Galian. After Galian spotted the weapon in the head monk's hand, he immediately turned to his brother.

"Get close to the beast," he signed.

Odin was confused. "But Haren said to stay here."

Galian had to be clear.

"I will never lead you to failure," he promised. "Now is no exception. Trust me, we can kill it."

Odin conceded. And as he nodded his head in agreement, Galian's eyes lit up.

"Now, go!" he spurred.

With fervent speed, Odin turned on his heel and sprinted directly at the giant.

Raine had continued to dodge the chain lashes, but his repeated spear attacks had accomplished very little in defeating the beast. Then, with bravery but poor judgement, a young Torch who was barely eleven, rushed at the monster. The Torch failed in his anticipation of one of the chain attacks, and as the powerful swing of the monster's chains swept at his legs, the young monk fell heavily to the courtyard floor. Like a practiced hunter, the monstrous Blood Cael stalked the young monk. With emergency, Raine rushed to his aid. Raine managed to cut off the beast's path, but as he knelt over the Torch, he had no choice but to expose his back. The old warrior used what power he had left to hurry the Torch to safety, but as the young monk finally evaded the giant's range, the monster roared once more and violently crashed both its chains down against Raine's back. Raine crumpled instantly, and as he cried out in extreme pain, the giant crouched over the warrior's body, and then lifted him high into the air.

As Odin rushed into the human perimeter around the beast, he quickly grabbed Usis's attention.

"Get ready, we're about to go in."

"Go in?"

"Just keep your eyes on Galian. He'll let us know when it's time."

Trusting the sons of Animus Letum as his own brothers, Usis nodded and set his eyes on Galian. Galian was watching closely, hoping that Raine could last just a little longer in the monster's brutal grip.

After the head monk descended the final steps to the courtyard, Galian furiously motioned his arm to Usis and Odin, who immediately rushed at the beast. As they flanked the giant from the left, Igallik handed the mighty staff to Galian. Galian used his power to suspend the staff in front of him, and then his eyes to survey the battle for the proper timing.

As the monster's grip began to crush Raine's ribs, the old warrior's struggle began to falter. The monks, most of them trained by Raine, continued to fight, but as they fired their assaults at the beast, they could not escape the fear that Raine was about to die. Then, just as the last measure of Raine's air was being throttled from his lungs, Usis rushed into the giant's view. Usis whipped more of his daggers at the beast, none succeeding in slowing the giant. But as the monster's eyes met Usis's, it suddenly dropped Raine. Galian had found his moment, and he quickly used his power to hurtle Serich's mighty staff towards the giant. As the staff tore through the air, the monster had ceased the lashes of his chains and had stopped cold in front of Usis.

Usis stalled, but Odin did not.

He had locked his eyes on the staff, and as he dashed towards the monster from the rear, he used the heap of bodies to launch himself into the air. As Odin flew towards the giant's back, he caught the staff in midair, and then on his descent, he stabbed the bladed end of the staff into the back of the monster's neck. As the staff pierced effortlessly through the giant's neck, Odin used all his strength to drive the blade down into the monster's chest cavity. The monster let out a final scream, and as the bloody rainfall halted, the giant's body fell lifeless before Usis.

The chaos of the courtyard fell to silence, and as the surviving monks surveyed the aftermath, they, in mourning, held themselves in numbed silence. The Blood Cael had struck – its hands caked in the murder of one hundred and forty-six monks. No monk – not Igallik nor Haren – had words for the survivors. And so silence ensued. A massacre had been dealt, and the music of Death would play on.

14

Three days after the Blood Cael massacre, the monks of the Throne's Eye paid their final respects to the fallen. To pay the boatman, silver coins were placed over each of the murdered monks' eyes, and their bodies were ceremoniously burned to ash. The surviving monks struggled in their mourning. Some felt guilty – burdened by the mere fact of their own survival. Others simply shut down, paralyzed by the horror they had witnessed four days prior. However, in spite of the tragedy dealt unto them, the surviving monks of the Throne's Eye did have each other. Most allowed themselves that solace.

Usis did not.

His focus had been driven far beyond the chaos that had reigned within the walls of the Throne's Eye. He had promised his vengeance on the Metus Sane cult, and now, motivated by the spilled blood of his fallen brothers, he was intent to exact it. Determined to retaliate, Usis had elected to take a leave of absence from the monastery. To do so, Usis required the blessing of the Throne's Eye High Order of monks.

On the day of his hearing, Usis ascended the grand staircase to the High Temple. As he reached the summit, he could see Raine, who was standing guard in front the High Temple's massive bronze doors. As Usis approached, Raine made a pleading nod to his apprentice.

"Not too late to change your mind," he said.

"I have to do this," Usis answered.

"I know you do, mate."

Usis studied his mentor for a moment, reading the old warrior like a book.

"I can feel your fear, Raine," he said. "You know I'm never wrong about that."

Raine offered a sheepish smile. "Should have known you'd see that." For Usis, Raine tried to feign some composure. "It's nothing to worry about, mate," he said. "It's just tough to see you go."

Usis smiled at his mentor. "Don't worry, you taught me well."

The Aeris smiled, and as he began to draw open the Temple doors, he paused just before the doors were completely open. "Remember," he warned, "these boys can spot bullshit from fifty yards. Be honest."

"I will," Usis said.

Raine then drew the doors completely open, and after allowing Usis to enter, he closed the doors shut.

Usis approached the Order slowly, surveying the thrones for only the second time in his life. He had been present for a hearing only once – when the Order had voted to adopt him. As a child, the experience was frightening, but as Usis neared the front of the Temple, and Igallik offered a gentle nod, he realized that he was still in the presence of family.

Usis bowed to the crown of Animus Letum and then knelt in the foremost pew. As he stared quietly up at the thrones, the head monk recited the Order's pledge.

"Let it be understood," he said, "the verdict for this hearing will be final unless an exceptional force decrees otherwise. Because the verdict is final, the totems of the Order shall be permitted any length of time to make their verdict. However, if a totem is uncertain about a verdict – even in the least – he will defer his vote to another totem's speciality."

After the head monk made the pledge, he drew from his tobacco hookah and cast his eyes down onto Usis.

"And as for your request, Usis, I will reiterate that our verdict is final unless an exceptional force decrees otherwise."

Usis affirmed his understanding, and after Igallik motioned his hand, the hearing was opened to Usis's voice.

Usis rose from his pew to address the senior monks.

"Brothers, elders," he began, "upon this hearing, I will reserve no element of my intent. This is my vow, this is my word."

The Order monks nodded in respect, and then invited Usis's plea.

"My request belongs not entirely to myself," Usis said, "but also to the justice deserved of both my mother and father, and to the brothers we lost four days ago. As you are aware, all of these lives were stolen by the Metus Sane – the followers of Malum Ludus. Against these misfortunes, I now desire a leave of absence from our monastery to track, isolate, and destroy those affiliated by the Metus Sane."

"Is revenge your only motive?" Igallik probed. The head monk was well aware that the answer to his question was no.

"It is but one part," Usis said.

"What are the others?" Igallik asked.

"Answers," Usis declared. "Each witness to my role with the Blood Cael would no doubt acknowledge the beast's reaction to me.

It stopped cold when it met my eyes. Frankly, I will be neither content nor relieved until I understand why."

The Order monks, each paying Usis's appeal due respect, took time to deliberate. After an unusually short moment of deliberation, Igallik opened the floor to the other totems.

Raeman was first.

"Understand Usis," he said, "revenge is a destructive force. A man will always reap what he has sown. But in your case, I do believe you are entitled to your revenge. I see it as justice. You have my blessing."

Palis, the Mercy totem, concurred with Raeman.

"Yours was an undeserved fate," he said. "If you choose to follow your past, I too offer my blessing."

Usis bowed to Palis, and then awaited the judgement of the remaining Order monks. Nile offered only a silent nod of approval. But the Instinct totem, Bysin, seemed apprehensive, his eyes doing everything to avoid Usis's stare.

"You are apprehensive, Bysin?" Igallik asked.

Bysin nodded. "It is insignificant at this point," he said. "Three of us have voted: a majority. But let it be shown that it was not by my vote that Usis was awarded our permission."

Igallik paused for a moment as he examined Bysin. The Instinct totem's anxiety unsettled the head monk. Regardless, the Order had voted in majority. With a smile, the head monk returned his attention to Usis.

"Your permission is granted," he ruled. "We pray you truth and victory in your quest."

With another puff of his hookah, Igallik adjourned the hearing and allowed Usis and the Order monks to return to their quarters.

Bysin lingered in the High Temple until all but he and Igallik were remaining. Once alone, the Instinct totem approached the head monk.

"Dangerous move," he assessed of the Order's ruling.

"We are all aware of the implications," Igallik defended.

"If Usis looks in the wrong place," Bysin warned, "you know what he will find."

"Once again, Bysin, we are all aware of the implications. We trust that we raised him well. If he desires the truth, then he deserves the truth."

"What if the Order is wrong?" Bysin challenged.

Igallik inhaled deeply and then rested his hand on Bysin's shoulder.

"Let's pray we're not."

After his permission was granted, Usis was quick to collect the food, clothing, and weapons he would need to begin his quest. Only one day had passed before he was ready to set out.

As he, packed with his provisions, approached the Throne's Eye gate in departure, he was met by Odin, Galian, and Raine.

"I'm sorry, boys," Usis said to Odin and Galian.

"You still don't have to go," Odin reminded.

"Oh no," Usis said, "I'm going. I'm just sorry that you'll have to spend more time with Raine."

As Odin and Galian grinned, Raine threw a playful jab at Usis.

"Don't worry," he reassured. "The boys will benefit from a male influence."

Usis laughed, and then extended his hand to Raine.

"Thank you, brother, for everything."

Raine took Usis's hand, and after sliding a sleeve of golden coins into Usis's palm, he wrapped his arm around Usis's shoulders.

"It's been an honour thus far," he said. "Let's hope you return in the same spirit."

Usis smiled to Raine and then turned to Odin and Galian.

"Boys, you listen to Raine. He'll guide you through the next stage of your training."

Odin and Galian nodded.

"Always remember," Usis said, "there exists no storm you can't handle together. Use each other," he impelled. "When you lean your strengths against one another you become greater."

"You forget," Galian signed, "there are three of us leaning on each other."

Usis winked and pulled two silver coins from a pouch on his belt

"I'll never forget," he smiled.

Odin was shocked. "You joined the Forge?"

"The first chance I got," Usis replied. He then motioned to the path outside of the gates. "I promise you," he said, "I'll be back when you need me."

After swallowing back some emotion, Usis hugged Galian and Odin, and after thanking Raine again, Usis began his walk out of the Throne's Eye gates.

"I'll be back before you know it," he called back. "Take care of them, Raine."

"I thought princesses were supposed to curtsy before they left," Raine yelled as Usis departed. Without turning back, Usis raised his arm in a feminine wave.

Raine smiled and then turned to Odin and Galian. "Don't worry about him," he said. "He'll be more than fine."

After the three had watched Usis disappear from sight, Raine led the twins back to the heart of the monastery.

As they walked, they passed Igallik, who had watched the procession from afar. The head monk's eyes shifted between the gate and the twins.

The day of the Blood Cael had cut the Forge's numbers in half, and the trident of Odin, Galian, and Usis had been split.

Fate – the head monk prayed – would replenish the Forge.

Time – he hoped – would align the trident once more.

15

By their father's will, Galian and Odin had escaped from the afterlife.

I did not have the same fate.

Instead, I stood shackled in the wasteland that had become Animus Letum. Forneus had taken Serich's throne and Soul Cauldron, and like a disease, his malice had brought us an age of Hell. He had not only diseased the land, but he had infected the people. We had become shades of our former selves – purposefully broken from our hope. When the Lyrans had reigned, nature had prospered. There were cherry blossoms, sage, and bergamot. But under Forneus's rule, Animus Letum was in a bloom of decay. Our rivers had dried and our golden streets had charred to black. Nature had perished, and even our skies had darkened, blocking us from the stars and sun. Hell, we had learned, had a face.

I am not one to cast doubt upon Serich's sacrifice, but in the throes of Forneus's reign, one could sometimes wish that Serich had walked a different path. I must often remind myself that sacrifices, like the merits of one's life, are usually measured in hindsight. We were fated to endure the limbo existing between the great sacrifice's dusk and dawn. However, I do not speak for all left in the land of Animus Letum. I will not judge whom I am about to introduce – God knows not all souls have the courage to bleed as martyrs – but let it be understood that many in Serich's court found reason to abandon the true house of Animus Letum and serve the Serpent Messiah. To Forneus they became servants and officers, and to us they became traitors. To us, our former brothers and sisters became the enemy. If any mention was made of these traitors, it was in the past tense. They were dead to us. They became referred to as the Scale, and nothing more.

The great torture of Forneus's Hell was dealt onto our minds. With his every act he struck hard into our hope. If a person dare attack a Scale or Vayne, their families were killed. If one person even breathed the name Serich, one hundred people were killed in front of them. The Serpent made opposition to his throne too horrific to consider. Through fear, Forneus had destroyed the will of his enemies – the afterlife had become their prison. However, there were shadows in his land where heretics thought and spoke without censor. The shadows were few, but behind their dark sheath was a faction loyal to the Lyran House. The faction, in fear of undesired attention, did not even allow themselves a title. They chose to work as rogues, acting when necessary and meeting when imperative. Their actions and meetings were centered on one theme – the protection of information. There was in fact one crucial piece of information that they warred to protect: the faction knew that Odin and Galian were alive. The great value of this information was that Forneus did not have it. At least, not yet. The faction had been playing a shadow game with the king, but in the dark the Serpent saw clearer. On numerous occasions, the faction had scattered from a meeting only moments before the Scale and Vayne arrived. After regrouping, the faction often realized that they had left clues and evidence of Odin and Galian's existence. They were clues and evidence that a cunning mind could fit together. However, the Serpent was arrogant. Even though the sons had survived, the king believed that he had killed both of them. He knew – and could feel in his memories – how deeply he had cut Rhea's throat. The truth was that when Forneus hunted the faction, he was hunting for something other than the sons. The Serpent was searching for the crown of Animus Letum. When Serich sent Rhea to the first realm, he had sent the crown along with her. The crown held all powers of the Lyran Kings, and because the powers could be inherited from king to king, there was nothing Forneus desired more.

The crown had crossed realms with Rhea, and with the greatest measure of safeguard, it was stored in the High Temple of the Throne's Eye monastery. If any attempt were to be made to acquire the crown, the thieves would have to overcome the warrior army of Throne's Eye monks. Both the faction and the Throne's Eye – by oath to the name of Serich – vowed to suffer death if it meant separating Forneus from the crown's power.

On extremely rare occasion, the faction and Throne's Eye held audience with each other. Their discussions were always about protecting the secrets of Rhea and her sons' survival – any lesser cause was not worth the risk. Forneus had promised destruction on the souls found guilty of speaking with the first realm, and against that threat, the faction had to bow. The king was a lurking hunter that none had outmatched. Wisely, the faction lay low. After too many close calls, they placed a moratorium on speaking of the crown or Serich's heirs, resolving that only the gravest catastrophe could break their silence. The murders, massacres, and genocides of Forneus's kingdom passed before the faction's tearing eyes. Their burden was acknowledging that they could not help. Unless the crown or the sons were in jeopardy, the faction could not risk gaining attention.

Regrettably, I must report that jeopardy arose. In one instance, although it would lead to their end, the faction was left no choice but to send a message to the Throne's Eye. Eiydia, a woman in the faction, was the martyr of that message.

In your earth realm, Eiydia was a Deathrider. She possessed the unique talent of conversing with the souls that had passed into Animus Letum. However, with no guidance, her gift became a burden. As she matured, her ability became stronger, but when she spoke of Animus Letum, she was shunned. Her family believed that some form of madness had claimed her, and not knowing what else to do, they forced her into an insane asylum. As medication began to drown her gifts, one voice stayed afloat. The voice said its name was Serich, and through it all – through all of her suffering and isolation – he was there. Serich was the one voice who told her the truth – it was not madness that had claimed her, it was greatness. Eiydia did not learn who Serich was until after her death. Even worse, she never had a chance to thank him. When Eiydia crossed into Animus Letum, her guardian and voice of hope had just been murdered by the traitor Forneus. The faction soon found Eiydia, and when they explained who Serich was and what had happened to him, Eiydia was broken. Her greatest friend, the person who had loved her so dearly, was gone. As the pain settled, one thing was clear in Eiydia's mind – she would fight for him, just as he had fought for her. And so Eiydia took arms in the rebel faction.

Eiydia moved quickly up their ranks. She helped organize reconnaissance missions, and soon she was a scout herself. Her first assignment was to track a specific Scale member. Such assignments were rare and typically fruitless. However, this particular Scale had been observed making an abnormally high number of visits to Forneus's Throne Room. The faction knew that in Forneus's methodical reign, oddities were never coincidence. And so Eiydia became the Scale's shadow.

On the second night of Eiydia's vigil, her assignment proved pivotal.

As burning embers swirled through the streets of Animus Letum, blowing through the desolate corridors of Forneus's kingdom, the Scale descended from the Serpent's Throne Room. The roadways had been drowned in darkness, and as gloom painted over the golden streets, Eiydia's black hood joined her with the shadows. Moving like smoke over water, Eiydia crept through the blackness, following the oblivious Scale as he approached a broken down chapel on the bank of a depleted river. As the ignorant Scale disappeared behind the chapel's doors, Eiydia crept into the darkness, vanishing from the approaching Vayne and settling down at a poorly boarded window that overlooked the chapel's main room. As she crouched, Eiydia retrieved the pen and pad she carried at her waist and began to watch and jot down what she was seeing.

With torchlight colouring the inside of the chapel, the Scale sat down in the center pew. The chapel's altar and walls were charred from fire, and as the Scale sat, his green clothes seemed to glow brighter under the orange flames. After whispering to himself, the Scale pulled a red coin from a pouch, and with a snap of his fingers, he spun the coin on the top of the pew. As the coin whirled, it began to hum and drone much louder than it should have. The hum grew incredibly loud, and there was a sudden flash of red. In the very next instant, a massive figure stood ominously behind the blackened altar. As the giant figure nodded to the Scale, its features remained cloaked in the deep shadows of its burgundy cloak.

The monstrous figure began to speak.

"What is the word of your king?" he asked. His voice was hoarse and inhumanly deep.

"He finds your claim interesting," the Scale replied, his tone sparing of sentiment, "but I'm sure you would understand that a man in his position would desire proof. If an army is to be assembled on earth, your claim must be substantiated."

The figure remained motionless.

"Now, do not misinterpret the king's hesitation," the Scale said. "Our Lord is less than indifferent to the death of any residing in the first realm. However, he does detest the misuse of effort and time. What you have claimed would necessitate large investments of both. So again, the king demands proof. That, my friend, is your bargaining chip."

The figure, poised and brooding in the shadows, offered his rebuttal.

"My words are true," he said. "I can give your king the exact location of Serich's crown. All I ask is that when you claim your prize, you bring back mine."

Eiydia drew away from the window in fear.

"No," her mouth pled in whisper. However, as the massive figure's head tilted slowly towards the window, Eiydia forced her hands over her mouth.

The Scale, still oblivious to Eiydia, tried again to convince the giant.

"Be that as it may," he said, noting the figure's vow of honesty, "relying solely on your word is counterproductive to the terms of this negotiation. You desire our assistance in reclaiming your possession, and we desire tangible proof of your claim. Both of our needs can be met, but, my friend, give me proof. Give me something to bring back to my king."

Eiydia managed to compose herself, and acknowledging her responsibility, she tucked the piece of paper she had recorded on into a pouch on her belt and began to creep away from the window.

The figure's haunting voice seemed to follow her.

"If my words are not enough," he said, "I will give you another's voice – one you can bring to your king. My lady, if you would be kind enough to join us ..."

With a sound like wind through a cavern, the giant opened his hand to the boarded window. Fear pulsed throughout Eiydia's body. She knew the figure was referring to her, but somehow as much as she wanted to run, she couldn't move. By some power in his massive hand, the figure had frozen her strides.

The Scale, at first concerned by the third party, was quick to return to his imperial poise.

"It truly is discourteous to eavesdrop" he said. "In the interest of civility, I believe we are entitled to an introduction."

The Scale nodded to the figure, inviting his great power. "When you're ready."

The figure, still holding Eiydia in his invisible grasp, pulled his outstretched hand back towards his own torso. With a crash, Eiydia blasted through the wall, leaving a trail of stone and blood as she skidded helplessly across the floor. Feeling the figure's looming presence above her, Eiydia managed to crane her neck up. As her eyes focused onto the figure's ghastly face, fear struck through her very soul.

"No!" she cried. "It can't be!"

The Scale rose from his pew and drew his dagger to Eiydia's back.

"My dear," he coldly whispered, "let us be clear. Fear rather than doubt is restricting your senses. Take another look. This is a hard face to forget."

The Scale seized the paralyzed Eiydia by the hair on the back of her head and wrenched her neck back, leaving her no choice but to look up at the figure.

The figure's skin was blood red with glowing orange veins that bulged and pulsed from beneath his skin. Two jagged horns protruded from the figure's lower jaw, and his nose was badly disfigured. But the figure's most haunting feature was his eyes or, more precisely, the lack thereof. Two beady, vacant sockets glared out from where his eyes should be.

"Malum Ludus," Eiydia spat.

"I knew you'd remember the face," the Scale said as he dropped Eiydia to the ground. The Scale looked pompously back to the figure. "Your reputation goes before you Malum. It seems in your case, the architect precedes his work."

Malum was silent.

"Well, let us spare no time," the Scale said. "I will take our intruder to the king. You are sure she can vouch for your claim?"

As Malum continued to hold Eiydia in paralysis, he knelt over her and used his massive hand to lift her chin. With his vacant sockets staring into Eiydia's soul, Ludus turned the corners of his mouth into a callous grin.

"By her will or yours," he promised, "she will give you what you need."

As he watched Eiydia squirm, the Scale smiled, impressed with the measure of fear that Ludus commanded.

With a whistle, the Scale sauntered casually to the entrance of the chapel and summoned a small group of Vayne. As he returned, the Vayne seized Eiydia, and the Scale offered a small bow to the monster.

"You have proven quite useful," he applauded. "We will send word after the interrogation. Our deal is not dead."

With a snarl, Malum tossed the helpless Eiydia to the ground and began a slow march to the back of the chapel.

"Malum," the Scale called out, disrupting the giant figure's departure. "If you would be so kind, I'm sure our Vayne would appreciate a prisoner with live legs."

With a quick snapping gesture of his hand, Malum lifted Eiydia's paralysis.

"Is there anything else?" he growled.

With wide and alarmed eyes, the Scale shook his head no.

Ludus made a small grunt, and then retreated into the darkness at the back of the chapel. As he stepped into the shadow, a crimson red light flashed once around his giant frame, and in the next instant he was gone. It was as if in a single moment he had been seamlessly grafted into the shadow.

With Malum gone, the Scale returned his attention to Eiydia.

"I can promise you one thing, my dear," he said. "Our king is perhaps our most avid agent in interrogations of treason. When he looks into you, all that you know, whatever you have held dearest in this world, will belong to him. My advice for you? It would prove wise not to invoke his power."

As the Vayne dragged her, Eiydia wrestled against them, but her attempt at escape was easily neutralized.

The Scale moved assertively in front of her and issued his final warning.

"Your fate is set," he assured, "and it is not promising. However, I do intend to keep it on schedule. Do not test me again."

Eiydia met the Scale's eyes, studied him for a moment, and then spat in his face.

"You are a disgrace to this realm!" she scolded.

The Scale retrieved a piece of cloth from his belt and wiped the spit from his face. With a poised calm he placed the cloth back in his belt and then delivered a violent backhand to Eiydia's cheek. Eiydia was knocked unconscious by the impact, and as her body slumped into the Vayne's arms, the Scale adjusted the collar on his shirt and broke into a pompous smile.

"Sorry boys," he said. "I guess she won't be using her legs after all."

16

Word in Animus Letum has a way of travelling quickly. As soon as news broke of the Vayne escorting a rebel to the Throne Room, the streets leading to Forneus were lined with eager onlookers. The largest congregation of people was assembled at the base of the royal staircase. Trying his best to blend into the crowd was Shylam, the faction's unofficial leader. Shylam was kept aware of all activities being carried out by the agents in his faction, and when news reached him that a rebel had been captured, he was left with a regrettable task. He needed to narrow down the field of possibly captured agents and then deduce which one of his friends was about to be tortured and killed.

The field of possibly captured agents was narrowed down to Eiydia.

Shylam was joined on the streets by many of the faction, and as they lingered on the street, the weight of fear held them all in collective silence. They knew that Eiydia's soul, or any soul in the faction for that matter, posed no opposition to Forneus's strength. They knew that when Forneus looked onto Eiydia, she would tell him anything he wanted. The faction was well aware of Forneus's aptitude for interrogation. They knew that their existence was about to be compromised. They also knew that because of their actions, each one of their loved ones would be hunted and killed. It was the harshest of realities. The only question looming was how long? How long did the faction have until all its members were destroyed?

As Shylam and the faction continued to wait, they stood as one, all cognisant of one horrific truth. Eiydia would suffer first, and they would suffer second. The only gesture that seemed relevant was to be there – together. In their acknowledgment of the faction's terrible fate, they chose to stand as one, offering each other a small and knowing nod before hell swallowed their souls.

Soon, with the faction lining the roadway, a procession of Vayne approached from the east. It was Eiydia's convoy. When she came into view, the crowd's initial interest was replaced by a communal sense of pity. The Vayne had inflicted an even more violent beating on Eiydia than she suffered at the hands of Malum Ludus. As the Vayne dragged her bloody and torn flesh across the stone road, Eiydia was so broken she couldn't even manage a wail or yelp.

All together there were four Vayne and one Scale surrounding her. Two of the Vayne were behind Eiydia, holding spears at her back, and the other two were at her sides, dragging her and threatening any person who would think to come to her aid. The Scale walked in front of her, boasting of Eiydia's capture to the crowd.

"This is the fate of heretics!" he shouted. "Opposition to the Throne is futile! The Throne sees all!"

As Eiydia was dragged forward she seemed to suddenly realize that there was a crowd around her. Her body animated with a visible jolt of energy, and as she pulled herself into a crawl, her eyes began a furtive survey of the people in the crowd. Her eyes scoured the sides of the street desperately, darting and scanning until they locked intently onto Shylam. The look was beyond desperate. It was a raw, pleading stare, and it would not let him go. The faction leader was stunned. His body wanted to respond evasively, but his mind commanded him to hold strong. As the Vayne dragged Eiydia over the small expanse of dirt that separated the roadway from the beginning of the royal staircase, she nodded to Shylam and then fell flat against the earth. Shylam watched her hands work in rapid succession, but before he had time to decipher what Eiydia was doing, the Vayne violently pulled her back to her knees. With a massive gulp, Eiydia stared back at the Vayne, and as she glared into them, a giant mass – one too big to swallow – became visibly lodged in her throat.

"She's swallowed something!" the Scale yelled. "Hit her in the stomach! Don't let her die!"

With powerful strikes, the Vayne began to drive their fists into Eiydia's abdomen, and after a series of shots, a massive stone expelled from Eiydia's mouth. With her breath heaving out of her, the Vayne started to hit Eiydia again, but even amid the assault, her eyes remained locked on Shylam. As she held his attention, Eiydia used her finger to subtly point to a mound of dirt she had piled.

In the next second she was gone: dragged up the staircase to a certain death.

After Eiydia had disappeared from sight, most of the crowd dispersed. Shylam hung back for a moment, and after the commotion completely died, he made inquisitive strides to the mound of dirt that Eiydia had pointed to. As he reached the dirt, he knelt beside the mound, pretending to adjust his sandal, and after his eyes nervously scouted the surroundings, he quickly raked his hand through the dirt. His hand brushed against something that felt like paper, and with a

The Sons of Animus Letum

subtle grip he lifted the object out of the dirt and casually tucked inside his belt.

Shylam hurried his walk until he felt he was safe, and then retrieved the object from his belt. It seemed to be a page from a diary. As he looked it over, he recognized Eiydia's handwriting. The words scribbled at the bottom of the page, however, were of a truth he hoped to never recognize:

Get word to Throne's Eye: location of Serich's crown in jeopardy

As he swallowed his fear, Shylam knew that time was not on his side. Eiydia would soon tell Forneus anything he wanted to know. Word had to be sent to the Throne's Eye. They needed to be prepared. Shylam again tucked the paper into his belt, and with extreme worry he began a desperate sprint to the faction headquarters.

The battered Eiydia, by will of the Vayne escorting her, ascended the final step into the Throne Room. The condition of the Throne Room seemed to hold no memory of its previous reigns. It now belonged to Forneus. The pillars and columns surrounding the massive room had been left neglected and their once regal appearance had been overthrown by the twisting growth of snake like vines. Below the columns was a stone banister that surrounded the Throne Room. The banister had a deep groove carved into its top. During Serich's reign the groove had burned with an electric blue fire, but in Forneus's time of power the banister was overflowing with hundreds of slithering snakes. There were countless more Vayne standing guard in the Throne Room, and although their poses did not break, their yellow eyes all locked onto the new prisoner. At the back of the Throne Room was the Soul Cauldron, a massive cylinder with a slightly transparent shell. Its hue was like burning ember, and its fire-like texture cast the surrounding sky into a hellish orange. The sound of screaming voices rang out as white skeletons slashed around its inside. At the base of the Cauldron was Forneus's throne.

The king sat at rest in the carnage that surrounded him.

The Vayne dragged Eiydia to the foot of the throne and tossed her to Forneus's feet. Stricken with fear, Eiydia refused to look up. With pompous vigour, the Scale that had accompanied her from the Dark Pool informed the king of Eiydia's crime.

"My Lord, our barter with Ludus has revealed a new development," he said. "Ludus has assured us that this prisoner's mind holds the location of your crown."

The king nodded and then cast the Scale away with a motion of his hand. After rising slowly, the Serpent stepped silently forward, stalking the terrified Eiydia who was huddled before him. Forneus towered over her. His dark purple hood had drowned his features into black, but even in the gloom of their cover, Forneus's unmistakable eyes burned an unholy orange. Since the inception of his reign, none but the Scale and Vayne had looked upon the king. Rumours of his physical state had run rampant in Animus Letum. Some believed that he had become more serpent than man; others, acknowledging Forneus's ability to grow on pain, believed that with no opposition the king had taken to self-mutilation. But as Forneus stood and then removed the hood that covered his head and upper torso, Eiydia came to learn both rumours were true. Forneus's body was covered with hundreds of scars from self-inflicted knife wounds. His giant hands were calloused with mended lacerations, and his back had been mutilated by the lashes of a whip. But it was his skin that was most revolting. Forneus's once dark skin seemed to be rotting and peeling away to reveal black and green snake scales. His flesh and scales held to no pattern. His body said nothing of royalty. He had become a vision of rot.

As Forneus circled the frightened Eiydia, stalking her and preying on her fear, his calm, cold breathing announced no emotion, but also no mercy. Eiydia cowered in wait of her punishment, but the Serpent King only knelt beside her, whispering his words with accentuated sibilance.

"Understand," he hissed, "that through you, your brothers and sisters will suffer. Through you this land will submit its very soul to me. Through you," the Serpent promised, "I will send a message to all still loyal to Serich."

Forneus's voice invaded Eiydia's entirety. Her body wretched and recoiled against the Serpent's presence, but the wicked king only relished his power of tongue. Forneus again circled the pain-stricken Eiydia, until in an instant his true nature lashed out. Using his great power of mind, Forneus manipulated Eiydia first to her feet, and then cruelly suspended her in the air before him.

"Where is my crown?" his sadistic voice demanded.

Eiydia's body shuddered with fear, and as a shriek escaped her mouth, her body became wracked with incredible pain. She began to convulse and streams of blood ran from her nose and ears.

Forneus circled her once more, attacking Eiydia with his menacing tone. "I will not ask you again," he threatened. "You are certain to die today, and I am certain to attain what I desire. But if you speak now, you will save yourself great pain. Do not hold your tongue, my lady: it would prove quite unwise."

The Sons of Animus Letum

Eiydia, striving for defiance amidst her fear, could not miss this opportunity. The very devil of her land – the cancer of Animus Letum's soul – needed information she held. She would not give it to him. In the face of her death, Eiydia would honour the memory of her greatest friend. For Serich, Eiydia would be brave. With blood cascading down her face, Eiydia screamed through her pain.

"You are no king!" she wailed. "Your evil will pillage my soul. Your hands will deliver me to death, but you will never steal nor kill my heart. Do your worst!" she screamed. "Martyr my name!"

Forneus grinned in reply. "Martyrs die for their cause," he said coldly. "You will die for mine."

In an instant, Forneus lunged at the suspended Eiydia and used his left hand to dig deeply into the flesh surrounding her spine. As Eiydia shrieked in pain, the king's right hand clutched her face and began to crush her skull from temple to temple. As he held Eiydia in torment, Forneus's eyes began to burn a deeper orange. With a growl, his eyes ignited like fire, and then he, with his serpent talents, invaded Eiydia's mind. No matter how she tried, Eiydia was rendered a paralyzed witness. Using his great power, Forneus held and observed Eiydia's memories. He played them backwards in cruel mosaic, torturing his host with whispers of her futility. The serpent paraded Eiydia's memories back, step by step. He marched her to the foot of the royal staircase and observed as she buried her note and tried to attract Shylam's attention. As Eiydia felt and saw the depths of Forneus's talent, the king could sense her panic. Her terror pleased him, and desiring more of it, the Serpent King committed even greater force to his torment. He searched deep in Eiydia's mind, collecting her memories and tainting them with his slithering presence. As Forneus pushed deeper, at one image Eiydia screamed in protest.

The memory was of Eiydia standing outside a chapel. Shylam was approaching her, and as he approached he extended his hand and issued a welcome.

"Welcome to the faction," he said. Then, with a gentle smile he gestured to the chapel behind him. "And to headquarters."

Eiydia willed all of her power to somehow break Forneus's hold, but the serpent was too strong. The memories became more lucid, more vivid, and soon Forneus traced Eiydia's mind to the exact scene she was desperate to forget: Shylam was behind the altar in the faction headquarters. He was surrounded by many of the other high ranking faction members, but he was addressing Eiydia.

"You have overcome every trial we have presented you with," Shylam said proudly. "Your strength and wisdom have been humbling to observe."

In the memory, Eiydia nodded bashfully.

"I hope you can forgive the speed of this process," Shylam said, "but each trial was painstakingly designed to solicit our trust."

Shylam looked down the line of faction members and then spoke on their behalf. "I am proud to say that you have earned it. All we ask is that we have yours. Eiydia, we are asking you to approach our altar."

As Shylam invited Eiydia with his left hand, he used his right to quickly pull a blue curtain from behind the altar. Beneath the blue curtain was an empty glass cylinder with a tube sticking out from its inside.

"You know what we protect, and you know what we fight," Shylam said. "To be one of us is to forfeit any identity you now possess. If we are doing our job properly, we don't exist. However, now is your chance to take arms with us. Now is your chance to protect the hope of Animus Letum."

In the grip of Forneus's sinister embrace, Eiydia knew how her memory was about to unfold. She knew what she was about to say, and she knew what knowledge Forneus would soon possess. Forneus too could feel the gravity of the situation, and his delighted voice echoed in Eiydia's head.

"Rest easy, child. All is already lost."

Eiydia screamed in futility as the weight of the serpent's voice brought her to tears.

In the memory, Shylam had retrieved a ceremonial tobacco pipe, and after packing it and lighting the tobacco, he inhaled from the pipe and exhaled the smoke into the tube going into the cylinder.

"The smoke," he explained to Eiydia, "is one of the few elements that can cross back and forth between realms. Through it we can open a vision and, more importantly, a dialogue with anyone living or dead. It's like a séance. I would assume you know exactly whom we intend to reach."

Eiydia whimpered, pleading with the memory of herself.

"Don't say it. Please, god-damn-it, don't say it."

It was to no avail.

"The Throne's Eye," Eiydia said in the memory.

Shylam looked around to his colleagues with a proud smile.

An equally pleased Forneus was also present.

"The Throne's Eye," he repeated in revelation. "Serich's great secret."

His tone was dark and salivating, relishing the discovery.

Eiydia shuddered as she not only heard but felt the evil in his voice. She squirmed, praying for escape, but the Serpent was now completely invested in her memories, and the well of his hold only deepened.

In the vision, Shylam had exhaled more smoke into the cylinder. In the moments after, the smoke began to swirl into a column. Then, with a sudden green flash, the smoke exploded into what looked like a living plane, and a scene quickly emerged from within the smoke.

The scene was of the High Temple in the Throne's Eye monastery. Standing in the Temple was a very old man wearing a dark gray robe.

"Igallik," Shylam issued in welcome, "we bring you another loyal to the true throne of Animus Letum."

Igallik smiled heartily.

"Another?" he grinned. "We can always use another."

Shylam reached his hand out and invited Eiydia to the front of the cylinder.

"Igallik, meet Eiydia."

Igallik studied Eiydia for a moment. He seemed to hesitate before he spoke. Observing from her memory, Eiydia remembered what was about to happen. She was thankful for Igallik and his sight, but she now prayed for his timing. On the altar in the Throne's Eye Temple was the crown of Animus Letum. Forneus had yet to detect it. Somehow, someway, Eiydia remembered that Igallik was about to terminate the portal, but she didn't remember exactly when. She hoped it was soon enough.

In the memory, Igallik was still looking over Eiydia.

"She has passed the trials?" he asked suspiciously.

Eiydia's hope flickered.

"Every one," Shylam vouched. Shylam began to read Igallik's concern. "I assure you, she can be trusted."

Eiydia wanted to curse Shylam. She could feel Forneus's attention getting closer to the box. She could feel it and she wouldn't let it happen. Eiydia put the crown out of her mind, focusing all her attention on Igallik. It was no use – Forneus was too strong. As the crown found his attention, a sudden wave of cold – one that Forneus couldn't mask or control – shook through Eiydia's body.

"My crown!" his serpent voice growled.

The king was overcome with power lust and his evil mind delved even further into madness. But in the throes of his yearning, Eiydia could feel him relinquish some of his control over her.

In the vision, Igallik was still studying her. She remembered it was now that something got the head monk's attention. With Forneus's interests consumed by the crown, Eiydia began to scream at Igallik.

"Please," she shrieked, "Igallik! See it! Forneus is here!" As Eiydia cried for attention, she alerted Forneus, who quickly drew back into control. He instantly strengthened his grip, deepening Eiydia's torture tenfold.

"There is no help for you here," he promised. "He cannot hear you... no one can."

As Forneus's whispered voice seeped into her mind, Eiydia was powerless against the burden of his words. But in the memory, Igallik was suddenly taken with concern. He shouted a muffled order to his left, and then, just as Eiydia remembered but never understood, he turned his attention to the newest faction member.

"Eiydia, my dear, your worth will never prove greater than now. My child, I am so sorry ..."

With a quick wave of his hand, Igallik ended the vision.

Shylam and the other faction members were startled by the abrupt end to the conversation. They turned their attention to the equally confused Eiydia, but she too was at a loss for words.

The angry and lingering Forneus was not.

"Look at your friends," he hissed. "Appreciate their vitality, appreciate their presence, for neither you nor they will ever hold such company again."

Eiydia shed tears as she looked upon Shylam and the other faction members for the last time, and then in a violent snap, Eiydia's memory ended and she was back in the Throne Room. Forneus released his grip from Eiydia's head and back, and then slammed her against the marble base of his Throne Room. As the king stood over her, Eiydia battled against her incredible pain and managed to crawl to her knees. As her balance wavered, she screamed wildly at the Serpent Messiah.

"God damn you!" she cried. "This world will never bow to you! Hear me now, Serpent! Your rivers will run dry!"

Forneus knelt in front of the hysteric Eiydia and offered her a grim truth.

"That which grows on despair," he whispered, "will never run dry."

With a wild grin, Forneus stood, and as his eyes closed, he used his will to summon a great power. By command, the Soul Cauldron began to burn with greater heat. Its glow grew brighter until it painted the sky with a devilish amber. As the entire sky began to blush with the Cauldron's wicked orange, the skeleton figures in the Cauldron began to swirl with feverish anticipation. Forneus began to shake, and a deep and growling thunder started to sound from the Cauldron. Just before it seemed that the Cauldron would burst, Forneus's eyes exploded open and two waves of orange fire broke loose from the Cauldron. The flaming waves barreled outwards from the Cauldron like giant snakes, and then careened back, driving at Eiydia from her sides. As the streams of fire crashed simultaneously into Eiydia, a shockwave of flame and ember flew throughout the Throne Room. The streams of fire quickly merged into one, and as Eiydia screamed, the flames began to burn her so intensely that the layers of her skin bubbled and blistered. Amid the sound of Eiydia's shrieks and screams, the skeletons circled in wait, desperate to scavenge anything that was left. The snarling king would appease them. Forneus crossed his outstretched hands, and in an instant, the skeletons gorged upon Eiydia's frame. As Eiydia remained on her knees, the Cauldron's skeletons began to sear through her soul with hellfire. Her body burned orange, and as a white smoke emitted from her remaining pores, she screamed and convulsed under the weight of her terrible torture. The torment continued until the king again cast his powerful hands out to the skies. As the fire exploded out from Eiydia's skin, her body was ripped in half and the skeletons and flames retreated back to the Soul Cauldron.

Eiydia had been destroyed. She had ceased to exist.

As the Cauldron's glow died down, the satisfied Forneus took back to his throne. His gaze set out over his kingdom, hunting in the distance for the rebel faction.

As he reclined pompously in his throne, the king summoned the Scale who had brought Eiydia into the Throne Room.

"Assemble a unit of my Vayne," he ordered. "We have a faction to dismantle."

"And what of Ludus?" the Scale asked. "His end of the deal has been held."

"Ludus will remain blind," Forneus ruled. "Rivals I can allow – gods I cannot."

17

In the time of your earth realm that corresponded with Eiydia's demise, the sons of Animus Letum had reached their seventeenth year – they, and the Forge, were only eight years away from their predetermined death. At seventeen, both Odin's and Galian's powers had grown in great measure. Usis had still not returned from his quest for answers, but in his absence, Raine had helped build Odin into the indisputable champion of the Damns. Galian had also excelled in his vocation. With a strict discipline in the studies of Throne's Eye doctrine and practice, Galian was emerging with a power appropriate to his bloodline. In any realm, any parlour of the soul, Galian held a governance of sheer might. He was a giant among men.

The monks of the Throne's Eye knew that they were raising greatness. One could not dispute this fact. Each and every move the sons of Animus Letum made reflected the divinity in their veins. Their greatness was inarguable, and as a result, the Forge had grown stronger in numbers. After witnessing the twins' potential, most monks truly believed that Odin and Galian could defeat Forneus, and as such, the majority of eligible monks volunteered to be in their suicide army. However, even as the monastery acknowledged the staggering promise of Serich's kin, their great gesture was to treat Odin and Galian with no favour. Instead of applause and awe, the monks offered neutrality. Indeed, it was a gift. Within the walls of the Throne's Eye, Odin and Galian were normal – they could be normal. It was not easy to be the seeds of legend, nor was it easy to know where their paths were headed, but with the other monks' care and camaraderie, Odin and Galian at least felt like they had a home. While nearly all the monks treated Odin and Galian as equals, Haren could not. Haren respected the ways of the Throne's Eye, but she saw one distinct flaw in their methods: they adhered to the old and tried. Although she knew that there was purpose in the Throne's Eye's traditions, Haren also knew that the monastery had no precedent for raising Lyrans. The twins were exceptional entities within the Throne's Eye. Accordingly, Haren wanted them to be treated exceptionally. She refused to regard Galian's and Odin's talents as ordinary, and instead, her mind continuously sought the next step of the twins' development.

As morning peaked on the day of Eiydia's demise, Haren set her steps towards the High Temple to discuss that very subject. The ambitious Deathrider, believing that she had critical information, had made an emergency appeal to the Throne's Eye's High Order. Although Haren had had many disappointing hearings, this one, she believed, would be different.

The morning had carried a deep cold through the Throne's Eye monastery, and as Haren ascended the giant staircase that led to the High Temple, her breaths were calm, collected bursts of vapour. The Temple's bronze doors were unmanned as Haren reached the summit, and after looking skywards and tapping the bronze for luck, Haren passed through the twin doors.

All members of the Order were present as Haren approached, and after she had nodded to them, she moved quietly to the front of the Temple, bowed to the crown of Animus Letum that rested on the Temple altar, and then knelt at the foremost pew.

As was his ritual, Igallik puffed from a tobacco hookah, and as he exhaled, he commenced the hearing.

"Haren," he began, "you are not estranged from our customs, nor are you unfamiliar with this Order's practice. You have put forth an appeal. And you will speak. But understand that the respect we have shown you through our audience will be reciprocated in your respect of this Order's decision." Igallik paused a moment, allowing his words to resound their warning. "If you can agree to this," Igallik said, "the floor is yours."

Haren cleared her throat and stood up from the pew.

"My brothers, my elders, I am here with an ambition. Granted, measured against this Order, I am barely gifted in the meditative arts. But brothers, I beg you, recognize the potency of my heart. I am here to ask for your help. With due respect to this Order, I ask you for it now."

"What is your request?" Igallik asked.

Haren took in a deep breath.

"My request is that you educate Galian and Odin with *The Book of the Eterna*."

The elder monks surrounding Igallik immediately sounded their protest. *The Book of the Eterna* was the highest level text in the practice of the Throne's Eye monastery. It was as much a mirror of eternal life as it was a practice in the spiritual arts, and above all it was forbidden to any monk who was not part of the Order.

"The answer is simply no," Palis ruled.

The Order was quick to echo Palis's verdict.

"The notion is foolish," Nile agreed. "They are far too young."

Bysin and Raeman also disagreed, and after they signalled a no, the verdict had become a unanimous denial.

As Haren's head sunk, the head monk look sternly at her.

"You and I are both aware that this is not a request of whim," he said. "My sister, you have been allowed the privilege of our audience, use it wisely."

Haren could see she had tested Igallik's patience. After a anxious swallow, Haren came clean.

"I have received word from Animus Letum," she said.

The Order monks, Igallik in particular, were now paying close attention.

"What word?" Raeman asked.

"The location of Serich's crown, albeit not willingly, is believed to have been relayed to Forneus."

Igallik was silent amid the alarm that overtook his brothers. The Order monks continued to chatter in their anxiety, until Igallik hushed their panic. After they had quieted, Igallik turned to Haren with fear in his eyes.

"And what of the sons?" he asked. "Has their location been compromised?"

"At this time, it appears that Odin and Galian are safe," Haren said. "Forneus still believes that he has killed them."

A wave of small relief soothed the Order back into their stately reserve.

"This is manageable news" Igallik calculated. "In the defence of what we protect, we have lost a battle not a war."

The other Order monks nodded their agreement.

"Were you informed of the circumstances of this breach?" Igallik asked.

Haren nodded. "A priest – a woman named Eiydia – was captured amid a reconnaissance scout."

Igallik mouthed the name Eiydia. He seemed to remember the name.

"Apparently," Haren said, "she had learned of a prospective barter between Forneus's court and a second party for knowledge of the crown's location. She was able to warn the faction, allowing them to warn us, but she was taken to Forneus's court. It is believed the Serpent King interrogated her himself."

Igallik exhaled a deep and mournful sigh.

"Indeed, she was," he confirmed. "Eiydia is lost. But surely found is the gravity of our dilemma. Forneus is now certainly aware of our protection of the crown. This is a threat we must now fully consider."

As the Order again voiced their agreement, Igallik turned back to the violet-eyed Haren.

"I now see the mechanics of your logic," he said. "You believe that Forneus's discovery justifies your request."

Haren nodded.

"It is no secret that the twins are powerful," she said. "What is unknown is their potential. Igallik, I have watched over them since birth. Believe me when I say they are the greatest weapon we possess. With Forneus's knowledge of the crown's location, it is only a matter of time until he marches his faithful to our gates. The Scale of our realm will come." Haren left a long pause to allow the threat of attack to sink in. "With your permission to use the book," she campaigned, "Galian and Odin could be the weapon that would render our monastery unconquerable. I wish for you to teach them a power held specifically for their bloodline."

"You are delegating which powers to teach?" Igallik asked with some alarm.

Haren looked upon the Order monks with bold honesty. "Brothers, allow me to be candid. There is, in fact, one particular power that I want Odin and Galian to learn. I want them to be instructed in Vinculum Imletalis."

Without deliberation, Igallik made a quick and direct verdict.

"The answer is no."

"Will you not even consider?" Haren asked.

"No, I will not," Igallik ruled.

"If they could hone this power," Haren persisted, "they would be a great instrument of defence in any war we are to face."

Igallik could not believe he was listening to such a foolish request.

"They would die if they tried!" he finally yelled. "The bond of Vinculum Imletalis is barely conceivable for Aeris and Seraph."

As Igallik took his annoyed eyes off Haren, he looked to the other Order monks.

"In civility, I will open this issue to your vote. Such is the purpose of this Order. All in favour?"

None of the monks raised their hands. Before Igallik make the final ruling, Raeman voiced another concern.

"If I may ask, Haren," he said. "How exactly were you able to receive word from Animus Letum? None of us – even Bysin – were aware of any attempted communication."

Haren's posture became rigid. As the Order eyed her, the accusation became heavy, flushing her face with red.

Under the weight of the Order's stares, she finally threw up her hands.

"I Scoured," she said, her eyes already pleading for mercy. "But before you seek punishment," she begged, "please look at the result. It *was* necessary."

Raeman shrugged. "I am doubting that this was your first offence."

Haren could offer no argument. As she turned pleadingly to Igallik, the head monk returned a troubled stare. Although Haren's Scour had proved timely, the head monk also knew that Raeman would seek punishment.

On cue, the Justice totem raised his voice above the Order.

"I move that Haren is served five reeds," he announced. "Five is a light sentence for what I suspect to be multiple trespasses."

Palis immediately protested. "I move that she is served none," he argued. "Although Haren has faltered with our rules, she has done us a great service. There is a much larger picture here, brothers. May I remind you that Forneus now knows that we have the crown?"

Although Igallik was still irritated with the form of Haren's request, he agreed with the Mercy totem.

"I do not condone Haren's actions," he said. "But I also cannot condone five reeds. I believe that we can find another punishment."

With the Order standing at two-to-one, focus turned to Nile and Bysin.

Nile was first to speak.

"I see both sides of this coin," he said, "and both have their merits. Haren's actions have likely saved lives. But at the same time, we have built our rules with purpose. Because I cannot rightfully condone or condemn Haren, I am deferring my vote to Bysin's instinct."

Deferral was rare, and after its impact had set in, the entire High Temple looked to Bysin.

"The decision is yours," Igallik said.

"I fear you won't want it to be," Bysin replied. "I have sensed – and for a while – that Haren has been straying from our ways. I know no other recourse than to punish her."

As Haren looked up at Bysin, her eyes pleading for mercy, the Instinct totem tapped the arm of his living throne.

"My dear," he said, "yours is a heart that trusts few. Worse, it seems that you have lost trust in us. You are a brilliant woman, Haren. But a night full of stars shines brighter than a night with only one."

Haren's eyes were wet, but unflinching.

"Five reeds will not build more trust," she threatened.

"That is up to you," Bysin said. "I vote twice for the proposed punishment."

In defeat, Haren collapsed to her knees and pushed her fist against the bridge of her nose.

As Igallik watched her, he was burdened by his duty. Regardless, he took a puff from his hookah.

"Haren will be served five reeds at this evening's close," he ruled. "Today's verdict stands unless an exceptional force decrees otherwise. Brothers, we are officially adjourned. You may return to your quarters."

The totems rose, and as they began their exits, Palis tried to offer Haren some condolence. Bitterly, Haren waved him off, but before she left the Temple, Igallik's voice called her back.

Knowing no other option, Haren turned from the door and stormed back to the altar.

"If you could get the door," Igallik requested.

After a flippant wave, Haren obliged, and after shutting the giant bronze doors, she joined Igallik at the front of the Temple.

"You know I can't amend the punishment," he said. "As much as I want to."

Haren hated his honesty. "I guess I'll wait for an exceptional force," she said dryly.

"One would be unlikely to arrive," Igallik replied.

The words sunk Haren's posture even more, and as her eyes began to tear, she repeated the very words that she had said seventeen years earlier when Morello was killed.

"I will not be punished for this."

"You shouldn't be," Igallik replied, "but you will."

Haren cradled her head with both hands. "Am I to be forever the martyr?"

"Believe me," the head monk said as he patted her shoulder, "I know that question even better than you."

"Please," Haren shot back, "you couldn't imagine."

With calm eyes, Igallik removed the crown of Animus Letum from the top of the altar and then tapped the golden cloth beneath it.

"Remove the drapery," he instructed.

Haren met Igallik's eyes with a puzzled expression.

"The drapery," Igallik reiterated. "Remove it."

After wiping her eyes, Haren did as she was told.

As she pulled the thick golden cloth off from the top of the altar and revealed the glass container underneath it, her feet stumbled backwards. Inside the giant rectangular glass box were two massive red orbs. The red orbs seemed to have what looked like orange pulsating veins wrapped around their surface.

"These aren't ..." Haren stammered.

"The eyes of Malum Ludus?" Igallik said. "You'll never know how many times I've wished they weren't. Yet, here they are."

Haren waded even further back, raking her fingers though her thick hair as she searched for what to think or say. She quickly settled on the obvious.

"How?"

"The answer is sacrifice," Igallik replied.

Haren's confused eyes solicited more explanation.

"Pay close attention," Igallik said, "because I will neither repeat what I am about to say, nor will I ever again admit to sharing this conversation. Do you understand?"

Haren, still shocked by Malum Ludus's eyes, managed to nod her head.

"You recall, quite apparently, the story of Malum Ludus," Igallik said. "But please, in service to my curiosity, recount what you think you know."

After another look at the eyes, Haren managed to compose herself.

"From what I understand," she said, "Ludus was born of no mother nor father. His existence – the very inception of his breath – was conceived in the depths of human fear. He survives and thrives on the fear of souls in the second realm. It was understood that Ludus's eyes were the receptors by which he interpreted fear. If his eyes looked on another soul, he would immediately know what breeds its worst terror."

Haren hesitated a moment, waiting for Igallik's confirmation.

"Go on," the head monk said.

With a deep breath, Haren continued.

"Ludus had been an irritation to every king's reign in Animus Letum," she said. "His infamous indulgence was always torture. He constructed numerous labyrinths, using the fear of souls in the second realm as the inspiration for his designs. But because his great strength remained his ability to grow on and manipulate fear, his only weakness was the courage of his prey. For this reason, Malum Ludus was never a great opposition to the Lyran house. Their bravery proved his bane. A few details are still unclear, but it is understood that a Lyran king stopped Ludus before he could complete his master labyrinth – Ludus's eyes were torn right from his skull."

"An accurate portrait," Igallik said. "Most here at the Throne's Eye are unaware that it was Serich who tore out his eyes."

Haren acknowledged the small revelation while Igallik held to his reserve.

"Now," the head monk forewarned, "I am going to give you information that only the other Order monks have been privileged to."

Haren awarded all of her attention to the head monk. With careful hands, Igallik pulled the drapery back over the altar, placed the crown back down, and then scouted the rest of the Temple. After confirming their privacy, he turned to Haren.

"I brought Malum Ludus's eyes here," he said.

Haren was puzzled.

"That can't be," she argued. "Ludus was defeated nearly three hundred years ago… in Animus Letum"

"Actually," Igallik corrected matter-of-factly, "three hundred and nineteen years ago."

"That's impossible," Haren protested.

"Not quite," Igallik replied. "Nearly three hundred years ago, I performed a great favour to my king – a sacrifice. I, through Serich's great will, was able to cross realms and bring Ludus's eyes where he could never reach them."

Haren shook her head in confusion.

"How could that be true? How could you hide such an act?"

The head monk smiled. "It was intended to be hidden. Just like the queen bringing the crown, Malum Ludus's eyes needed to be escorted by a living soul. I was that soul."

"You're serious," Haren realized.

"These are Ludus's eyes," Igallik pointed out.

Haren began to understand.

"So that would mean you can never cross back. By law your soul can never again enter Animus Letum."

Igallik nodded again, this time with solemn eyes.

"That, Haren, is the weight of my sacrifice."

"But you remain immortal on earth?"

"Not immortal," Igallik said with a smile. "I would say, preserved by time. Death, for me, still remains an adversary."

Haren took in all the information she had been given. She was floored, speechless, even intimidated.

Seeing her tongue-tied, Igallik placed his hand on her shoulder.

"Do you know why I have told you this?" he asked.

Haren shook her head.

"Because," the head monk said, "I needed you to understand that sacrifice is the handmaiden of our victory. I need you to sacrifice tonight. I need you to sacrifice your pride."

Haren met Igallik's stare. "My pride?" she blurted. "The five reeds are an insult, not a sacrifice."

"Don't be petty," Igallik said. "If Forneus sends his army, many of our brothers will pay a far greater price than five reeds."

Haren lowered her gaze. "You know I don't mean to insult them," she said. "I would gladly give my life for our cause."

"I know, Haren. But I don't need you to. In truth, I need you to take your five reeds so that we can prepare you for something worse."

"Worse?" Haren faltered.

"As you requested at the beginning of the hearing," the head monk said, "I do recognize the potency of your heart. I have trust in you, and that faith is not merely given. It has been earned in the care you've shown for the twins."

Haren distrusted the moment. "Where are you going with this?" she asked.

"Towards a request," Igallik said. "We are all in agreement that Forneus's faithful will come for the crown. His followers are ruthless. They will bring violence and madness to our gates. At the first sign of war, I am asking that you and the twins withdraw here, to this Temple."

Haren eyed the head monk suspiciously.

"Is this the Order's will?" she asked.

Igallik shook his head. "This is mine. This is a plan I have thought on for seventeen years. I am not giving you a mere task, Haren: I am giving you an appointment. I am removing you from battle, because if we lose, I want you to survive. I want you and the boys to be able to escape."

"Lose?" she repeated. "Escape? To where?"

"To wherever you deem fit," Igallik replied. "I am asking you to be the boys' guardian. If the Throne's Eye is defeated, it is likely that you and the twins will be our last survivors. You will be our last hope of victory."

Haren turned away, remembering what Igallik had said about sacrifice.

"So I am to be the handmaiden," she said.

"Yes," Igallik said. "If we lose this battle, you will hear us die – each of us. The Scale will claim our home and our knowledge, and with it, they will become more powerful than is right. Your burden is that you must let them. And make no mistake, even if we destroy the Scale, they will come again. As long as we have the crown, the Scale will never stop testing us. If at any time we fail that test, you must flee with the twins. You will be fugitives in yet another world ruled by the Serpent King."

Haren tugged at her collar as she thought. "Why are you asking me?" she said finally.

"There are many reasons," Igallik said. "But there is one in particular. Do you remember what Serich's voice said when you were jailed in your village?"

Haren could never forget. "Follow the heron," she repeated.

Igallik offered a gentle smile. "We heard the very same message," he said, "though we don't believe that the Great King was talking about a bird."

The words were potent and heavy. Years earlier, in her village, Haren had known that a world awaited her. She just never believed that the world would demand so much.

"I'll be honest," she said, "this is becoming a heavy load to bear."

"Is it too heavy?" Igallik asked plainly.

Haren's eyes strayed from the head monk, searching the Temple for a moment before they landed on the crown of Animus Letum.

"I can think of heavier," she said.

"That is not an answer," the head monk replied.

Haren was quiet for a moment, an image of Galian and Odin flashing in her mind.

"If I must," she said, "I can carry this weight. I can for the men who are destined to carry more."

"So you will take your five reeds?"

"For them," Haren said, "I will."

"Then let us move as we should," Igallik said. "Tonight there will be reeds. But soon there will be war."

The words were imposing.

"How soon?" Haren asked.

"The first moment Forneus gets a chance."

As the head monk's grim prescience hung in the Temple, Igallik began to usher Haren to the door.

However, as they walked, their steps were disparate in spirit.

Igallik believed that he had solved a problem. Haren knew that it had become hers.

That night Haren was served her five reeds. Each left a long tear on her naked back. The first and second stung deep into the body, so deep that the remaining three seemed to strike the soul.

As Haren laid broken in the infirmary, her violet eyes caught a glimpse of a giant blue bird flying by. Strange, she thought, for a heron to fly by now. But just like so many years before, the bird seemed to spur something in Haren. And soon, Igallik's words began to echo through her mind.

"As long as we have the crown," he had said, "the Scale will never stop testing us."

Haren turned the words over and over, until suddenly it was clear.

Her pain had crystalized a thought.

Suddenly, a darker path had become the way.

18

In Animus Letum, a Scale ascended the royal staircase to the Throne Room. The Soul Cauldron burned its evil orange as the Scale reached the throne.

"Sire," the Scale said as he reached Forneus, "the faction has been dismantled."

From beneath his hood the Serpent hissed back his reply. "To what extent?"

"As you wished, my king: completely. The accused met their punishments. Their families – every soul bound by blood or amity – were gathered into the faction's headquarters, which we then burned in the audience of the traitors. As you requested we branded each traitor's body with your initial. They are now being held in our prison. They await your judgement."

"Very good," Forneus snarled.

With his eyes avoiding Forneus's stare, the Scale began to fumble nervously with his sleeve.

"There was one detail though, my Lord."

Forneus's emotionless eyes invited the news.

"We believe that the faction was able to send word to the Throne's Eye."

The Scale cowered, certain of his impending punishment.

The Serpent King only grinned. "The Throne's Eye," he mused, "Serich's great secret."

The Dark King stopped for a moment and then grinned again in contentment.

"Bring me one of our traitors," he ordered. "I will find for him a great purpose."

19

The Throne's Eye monks were bound by an unbreakable pledge. It was a vow that called them to fight for each other – even it cost them their lives. With Haren's news that Forneus had discovered the location of Serich's crown, the monks knew that their vow would be tested. There was no doubt that Forneus would come.

As the monks stood guard, tense in the preparation for war, many days soon passed. The monks knew that the curtain of battle would be drawn. But it seemed that only Forneus knew when. The Serpent had struck without striking, oozing a venom into the monastery that was draining more of the monks' energy each passing day. Even the mightiest of men will lose their vigour to time. In an attempt to revitalize his brothers, Igallik began to take advantage of the time that the monastery had been given. By the head monk's command, Raine led units of Torches out across the Throne's Eye acreage to set up scouting posts, while Raeman and other high ranking Sights set upon the task of helping junior monks receive word from Animus Letum.

In Raeman's unit, a young Sight named Symin eagerly took to the task of holding audience with the second realm. Symin was a tall and awkward boy with brown hair and freckles. He was highly intelligent, but generally unsure of himself. He, like so many of us, believed that he was only one event away from proving his worth. A grand feat – he knew – would earn his peers' respect.

Like the other Sights in his company, Symin had found only madness between the two realms. The sound was like one thousand fires burning all at once. But even with no success, Symin was committed. He, like all Sights, was well lessoned in the story of Haren. Because of her discovery of Rhea, Haren was endowed with a great level of respect and admiration by the monastery's junior monks. As the tale was recorded, Haren was barely at the age of seventeen when she found Rhea. Furthermore, she had come from an unexceptional background. These details now stood as inspiration to the Sights. In Symin's eyes, Haren was a living legend. She was the proof of a humble birth rising to greatness.

No words could argue Symin out of his admiration.

The very moment he was taught how to hail the afterlife, Symin swelled with hope. Holding tightly to Haren's legend, he launched himself into his task, hunting and hoping that the second realm would offer him a similar chance.

By Raeman's order, Symin and his company remained in a specific chapel while they attempted communication. The physical and mental stress that is caused by crossing realms is taxing. To cross the divide between earth and Animus Letum and then hold a line between both is like trying to focus your senses amid the cacophony of ten thousand screaming voices. And picking up a single word is like hearing a humming bird's wings amid a thunderstorm.

As midday bowed to dusk, the endurance of Symin's company gave way – first to rest, then to extended absence. But Symin would not deviate from what he believed to be a rare chance. As time passed, the number of Sights in Symin's chapel began slowly to decrease. It wasn't long until Symin was the only remaining monk. The sun was falling when Symin's stamina finally pled rest. The young Sight conceded, and after a deep exhalation, he tried to stretch off his fatigue. As he walked, flexing his lanky limbs upon every stride, the young Sight ambled slowly through the chapel. His eyes were looking, but his mind was not in the moment. As he continued to saunter, suddenly there was a loud hiss, and an orange glow overtook Symin's vision. The phenomenon snapped Symin back to alertness, and as the orange glow smouldered around him, he crouched, surveying the chapel with cautious eyes. Strangely, the light source was one of the stained glass windows. With a slow creep, Symin approached the window. The young Sight quickly realized that the window was a portrait of Serich; however, as he leaned in and examined the window's lines, a sudden realization startled him backwards. The lines on the glass were moving like a living plane, meandering on the glass surface like snakes through grass. As the lines slid and stretched, Symin leaned in, fascinated by the fire scene that was burning behind the image of Serich. Stunned but brave, Symin began to examine the window. As he inched forward, his skin began to singe, his hair fraying and hissing from the intense heat that was radiating off the window. Even so, he was undeterred. The young Sight approached even closer, watching as the fire scene took on the decipherable form of a figure sprawled over a giant stone. As Symin studied the flaming image, something about it seemed familiar. The heat was becoming unbearable, but with gritted teeth, Symin neared even closer. He knew he had seen the image. The trees, the stone, the branches overhead, the swaying grass – Symin didn't just recognize it, he knew that he had been there. Then, in a sudden flash, he placed it. It was the Sanctus Donum – the clearing where Haren had discovered Rhea. Certain that there was great purpose in the image, Symin withdrew none of his attention from the window. As the flames within the window swayed in eerie unison, the figure on the stone sat up in pain and seemed to be clutching something with both of his hands. As Symin tried to call out to the man, the fiery image in the window unexpectedly froze and a hollow whisper resounded from the glass.

"Serich's final gift..." the voice spoke.

With another hiss, a distinct cold swept through the chapel, and with a loud crash the stained-glass window cracked and exploded into one hundred fragments.

In an instant, the orange glow was gone and the room swept back into its previous solemnity.

Symin, however, could not.

"Serich's final gift," he repeated.

The possibility of a new discovery for the Throne's Eye was great. The young Sight's mind began to leap further and further to hope. As Symin's excitement grew, he seemed to forget the reason that he and the other Sights had been searching the second realm. With a boyish leap, he raced zealously out of the chapel, passing some other Sights who had been alerted by the sound of the crashing window.

"Symin!" one yelled. "Where are you going?"

"I'll be back!" Symin called back as he began his sprint to Sanctus Donum. "Tell Igallik I've made contact!"

Overtaken by blind ambition, Symin sliced his way through the forest on his way to the Sanctus Donum. As he neared, his thoughts raced with the great possibility that could befall him. This, for Symin, could be a discovery rivalling Haren's. It could be the moment that all Sights hope for. Finally, out of breath but high in hopes, Symin was within sight of the Sanctus Donum. In the distance, he could see a wavering and haunting orange glow at the entrance to the clearing. In fact he could hear it. The sinister crackle of fire became more and more audible as he closed in. As he drew within forty yards of the Sanctus Donum, he knew without a doubt that the clearing had been consumed with fire. As he reached the entrance, he peered fearlessly into the inferno. With his sleeve guarding his face from the intense heat, Symin searched desperately for the man he had seen in the window. As he stared into the blaze, he realized that there was only one part of the meadow that had not been touched by flame. Surrounded by the raging flames, there was a path of earth leading to center of the Sanctus Donum. The clearing was chaos. The meadow's grass was swirling in violent gusts of fire and the branched canopy roof was falling in pieces of smouldering ash, but amid the feral bursts of fiery bedlam, somehow, someway, there was still an untouched path. In one moment, in one break of the flurried blaze, Symin's eyes were able to follow the path to the center of the meadow. There, on the clearing's center stone was the man. His feet and hands were bound together, but between his hands he seemed to be clutching something.

"Serich's final gift," Symin prayed.

He knew he needed to save the man. He knew he needed to answer the call. After a deep breath, Symin drew the hood on his robe over his head, and without a second thought, he darted down the path.

As he delved deeper into the blaze, the flames slashed his frame with sporadic bursts of fire. However, there seemed to be a barrier around the path. As the young Sight cut determinedly down the untouched path, fending off the burning heat with his sleeve, it seemed that some power was holding the flames at bay. Symin's quick feet rapidly rushed him near the stone, and as he moved within range of the man, he leapt the final few yards and landed at the man's side. With focused eyes, the young Sight made a quick survey of the man's condition. His body was badly burned, leaving only strips of cloth to hide the many whip marks on his torso, and his hands and feet had been bound with a fine gold wire.

"I am here to help!" Symin shouted, as he reached for the man's shoulder. "I can get you out of here!"

With a scream, the man twisted away from Symin, doing his best to keep distance between them.

As Symin again reached for the man, he got a closer view of the man's bound legs and arms. The wire that surrounded them was cutting deeply and forcing a trail of blood down the man's limbs. Symin could also see that there was an orange orb wired into the man's hands.

"I can cut you loose!" Symin cried as he retrieved the dagger from his belt.

As Symin reached for the man's hands, the man wrenched them away.

The fire and smoke were growing more intense and Symin knew that the window of time was closing.

"Damn it!" he screamed. "You don't need to die!"

The man finally turned to face Symin. Cut in the center of his forehead was a gory letter F. More blood spilled from the man's mouth as his lips turned to a broken smile.

Whatever words he had intended were indecipherable. And as he leaned back onto the stone and his voice turned into a haunting laugh, his unintelligible speech was explained: his tongue had been cut entirely from his mouth. Symin was shaken by the man's unsettling laugh, but even so, he persisted.

"We're getting out of here!" he commanded.

With authority, Symin grabbed the man by his shoulders and tried to lift him to his feet, but the man would not assist in the rescue. Finally, Symin angrily grabbed the man by the ankles and began to drag him out of the fire. As Symin looked back, he could see that his path was beginning to close. As he tried harder to drag the man, the heat of the flames scorched his skin, and as he yelped, the man began a fit of relentless kicking and bucking.

"I am with Serich!" Symin finally yelled. "I was sent to find you!"

The man stopped in his tracks, his eyes bulging with terror. He began to swing his arms, shaking his head furiously as he screamed in protest. With even more vigour, the man began to buck away from Symin. The man's fierce struggle caused Symin to lose his grip on his ankles, and as Symin stumbled into a fall, the man bucked back towards the stone.

"For heaven's sake!" Symin shouted from the ground. "You don't need to die!"

As Symin climbed back to his feet, he guarded his face from the flames and tried to advance for another rescue.

This time the man screamed even more wildly, bucking and crawling desperately away from the young Sight.

As the man's wild screams continued to scold Symin, suddenly one name cut through the garble, and Symin halted his steps.

"Forneus?" Symin asked.

The man's eyes took to on intense urgency, and he began fervently to nod his head yes.

"What of Forneus?" Symin yelled against the ferocious flame.

The man rose to his knees and offered his bound hands to the young Sight. The man's eyes were trying to speak, but Symin could not understand.

"The orb?" he asked.

The man nodded his head yes as if he was in fever. However, before the man could offer any further explanation, a violent burst of fire rocked the canopy roof, and several large branches crashed heavily onto his back. The weight was immense, and within seconds the man was sprawled on the earth of the Sanctus Donum. Symin cried out to the man to catch his attention, but the man remained motionless. With a quick dive, Symin landed at the man's side, but as he shook his body, the man's limp torso and bloody ears confirmed his death.

With panic, Symin glanced around the burning clearing, each of his senses hissing with the effects of the wild blaze. The path was almost completely gone. As Symin glanced back to the man, he knew he couldn't let these events be in vain. He again drew his dagger, and with a quick cut, he sliced the wire around the man's lifeless hands. After cutting out the orange orb, Symin tucked it in a pouch on his belt and began his sprint out of the Sanctus Donum. The fire curled and slashed at his path, but the young Sight drew his hood even tighter and powerfully barrelled through the exploding flames. With a final lunge, Symin leapt out of the fire and tumbled back onto the path he had used to reach the Sanctus Donum.

Symin made a concentrated effort to catch his breath. He gazed once more into the fire, regretting the man's fate, but he determined nevertheless to deliver the orb to Igallik. Forcing himself up with his hands, Symin rose back to his feet, took a deep breath, and then raced back to the monastery.

As he reached the gates to the Throne's Eye, the Sights from his company were waiting.

"What did you find?" a Sight named Craine asked.

Symin broke from his sprint and hunched over, exhausted.

"This," he said as he held out the orange orb.

Craine and the other Sights leaned in to examine the discovery.

"What is it?" Craine asked.

"I don't know," Symin admitted. "But I'm sure Igallik will. Does he know I made contact?"

"I told him" Craine reported. "He's been in the High Temple ever since."

Symin nodded, and allowed himself to catch his breath fully. As he rose back up to full posture, he broke into a look of disbelief.

"You wouldn't believe what I had to go through to get this."

Craine grabbed Symin's wrist and raised his arm into the air.

"Behold brothers!" he joked. "Our fellow Sight, the noble and mighty Symin, puts us all to shame! Greatness has but one name to speak on this day," he cried to his laughing brothers. "And that name is Symin! Onward soldier! First to Igallik, and then to the pages of legend."

After Craine had released Symin, the other Sights patted Symin on the back, and in merry spirits they began their walk to the High Temple.

The news of Symin's discovery traveled quickly, and as the young Sight reached the base of the staircase to the High Temple, a congregation of monks formed around him. Symin calmly nodded to his brothers, and with a surge of confidence, he began his ascent to Igallik. As he reached the top of the staircase, he could see, through the open doors to the High Temple that Igallik and the monks of the Order had been waiting.

At first sight of Symin, Igallik hurriedly stepped out to meet him. Palis quickly followed.

Symin smiled proudly to them.

"I made contact," he announced. "And discovery."

The young Sight continued to beam, eagerly awaiting his due praise.

None would come.

"Was your discovery made in the Sanctus Donum?" Igallik asked sternly.

"It was, sir," Symin replied, confused with Igallik's tone.

The head monk and Palis looked very concerned.

"Of what condition was the Sanctus Donum when you arrived?" Palis asked.

"It was completely aflame" Symin answered. "I was able to make it to the stone. There was a man there, I tried to save…"

Palis stopped him there.

"Did the man have an *F* cut somewhere into his body?"

"Yes," Symin said, "on his forehead."

"Did he say anything to you?" Igallik asked.

"Well, no," Symin paused. "His tongue was cut out."

Igallik and Palis turned their backs to Symin and whispered to one another, but the young Sight didn't understand.

"I wasn't able to save him," he said, "and I'm deeply sorry for that. But I did manage to save this from the fire." Symin reached nervously into the pouch on his belt and presented the orb.

Palis and Igallik were barely paying attention. As Igallik finally turned back to the young Sight, and he saw what Symin was holding in his hands, his voice immediately sounded in panic.

"Throw it away, Symin!"

Palis turned back in alarm. He too, began to scream for Symin to get rid of it.

Symin was stunned. He froze. As Igallik and Palis continued to yell, Symin was too panicked to respond.

Suddenly, with a loud hiss, several small sharp needles shot out of the orb. With a yelp, Symin flinched from the pricks, the pain stinging him enough that he dropped the orb. After a few more winces and curses, the young Sight – not knowing what he had done wrong – tried to offer the Order monks an apology.

However, the Order monks were much more concerned with Symin's hand. Helpfully, Symin held up his hand so they could inspect the damage.

There were small punctures, but no cause for concern.

"I think its fine. I think I'm OK ..." Symin said.

As Symin began to calm himself, the veins in his right hand suddenly began to glow orange and pulse out of his skin. Symin looked on perplexed, until his hand, not by his will, reached for the dagger on his belt. Symin was confused at first, but as he realized what was happening, fear consumed his eyes.

"It's not me!" he shrieked. "Igallik! My hand! I'm not doing this! I'm not in control!"

"He's been hexed," Igallik yelled out. "Brothers! Hold him down!"

Igallik and Palis latched onto Symin's right hand, hoping to overpower whatever spell had possessed it, but they could not hold it back. In quick seconds, the Order monks arrived and tried to assist, but the dagger in Symin's hand was gripped too strongly. The dagger cut quickly through the piece of robe covering Symin's stomach, and then with wild arcs it began to slice rapidly at Symin's abdomen. The young Sight fell onto his back screaming, crying for help as the dagger cut numerous lacerations into his open flesh. As blood sprayed like a geyser, Igallik and the other Order monks tried to stop the dagger, but it seemed no use. Even with more Throne's Eye monks ascending the staircase to help, the dagger could not be stopped. As Symin writhed and cried, the dagger continued to cut maliciously into his skin.

Then, suddenly, the dagger rose up to Symin's throat.

"Please, no," Igallik pled.

"Igallik," Symin whimpered. "Please stop it! Please!"

Every monk within reach latched onto Symin's hand, hoping to save their young brother.

Their efforts were in vain.

With a quick and direct plunge, the dagger shot down into the center of Symin's throat. Amid bloody coughs and spit, Symin shook wildly. Igallik used his hands to try to stop the bleeding, but it was too late.

Symin's hand fell to his side, and the dagger dropped to the floor – Symin was dead.

With a yell, Igallik turned furiously from Symin's body, throwing his hands up in futility as he screamed and cursed the young Sight's fate. The other monks, Palis included, had never seen such anger in their head monk. Understanding Igallik's heavy guilt, they turned their heads away and began to bless Symin's deceased body. Igallik soon joined them, but the monks' minds were too scattered to bless Symin properly. No words or ritual could convey their apology. Symin never deserved such a fate. With grief, Igallik offered Symin's body a Throne's Eye prayer.

"The vow of time is not eternity. Nor is it a life without despair. Our promise is that in the opposition of pain we can hold moments greater than forever. Farewell Symin," the head monk said, "the vow was held."

With a slow hand, Igallik closed Symin's eyes and performed the final blessing over his body.

"Brothers," he whispered, "if you would, please bring our young Symin's body into the High Temple. We must prepare him for our final respects."

The monks surrounding Symin nodded in understanding, and after they lifted his bloody body into their arms, they began to carry him into the High Temple.

Igallik followed and was quickly joined by Palis.

"This is an unexpected and dangerous move," Palis whispered.

"Yes, it is," Igallik said angrily. "I fear Symin's misfortune is but a glimpse of what Forneus has planned."

The head monk paused to allow the monks carrying Symin to enter the High Temple.

"What I can't comprehend is what purpose lies in this attack," he said.

After entering the Temple, the Order monks stopped and observed for a moment while Symin's body was set down. With a grimace, Igallik watched as the other monks began to wash the blood from Symin's abdomen.

Palis shook his head in disbelief.

"There is barely a lesson here" he said in frustration. "What truth belongs to Symin's death? Why Symin?"

"I pray that time will unfold that mystery" Igallik said. "But for now we must concentrate on the task at hand. Evidently, Forneus knows our exact location."

"What can we do though?" Palis asked. "We have no idea when he'll come. Our waiting is his venom: the longer it persists the wearier we become."

Igallik nodded in regretful agreement.

"He will come," he assured. "We must be prepared."

As Igallik dropped his head, suddenly one of the monk's voices cried out from where Symin's body was placed at rest.

"Holy hell!" the monk shrieked.

Igallik and Palis immediately rushed to Symin's body.

As they arrived, and then looked down at the wounds on Symin's abdomen, a sick feeling grew in their guts.

"Damn you," Igallik cursed.

The blood from Symin's stomach wounds had been washed, and now only a series of methodical slashes were left. The slashes carved out a gory message:

         I COME TONIGHT –
         FORNEUS

20

The vileness of the Serpent King's message had been a mistake. Forneus had sent his message, but for it, he would pay. The Serpent sought to inspire fear. He had accomplished the opposite. Given Symin's ghastly fate, the Throne's Eye promised vengeance on Forneus's militia. Each and every brother committed himself to one purpose: they would crush Forneus's first realm Scale. In the swell of their determined vengeance, the monks had become deadly focused. War was the monastery's expert craft, and for Symin, they would showcase their mastery.

All but three monks from the Throne's Eye were to hold guard against the impending assault. The three exceptions were Haren, Odin, and Galian. As Igallik had planned, Haren and the boys would seek refuge in the High Temple. This strategy was met with great opposition by Odin, who begged Igallik to let him fight. In spite of Odin's spirit, Igallik resolved that the truth of Odin and Galian's asylum at the Throne's Eye could not be forfeited – the sons were simply too important.

With the hour of war suspended ominously over the monastery, Haren ushered Odin and Galian into the High Temple. Galian bobbed in with his usual walk, but Odin paced in dejectedly, his head sunk and his eyes brimming with anger. As they entered, Raine stood just inside the door, armed with his final instruction. Like nearly all of the monks, Raine was donned in his red and gold armor.

As the boys reached him, the old warrior tightened the front of his helmet up.

"Listen closely," he said. "The following three rules are for your protection. You must abide by them."

Raine paused and allowed his eyes to emphasize the critical importance of his order.

"First, at no point, circumstance, or emergency are you to unlock or open the doors to this Temple."

Galian nodded in understanding, but Odin ignored his mentor and began to pace at the back of the Temple.

"Odin," Raine finally barked, "you have no choice in this matter. At the very least, show some respect."

Odin cast back an irate stare. "What do you expect me to do?" he seared. "I need to fight. I need to help. You know I can help avenge Symin."

"You're damned right you could," Raine said. "But if the Scale realize who you are, every god-damned thing we've done to protect you and your brother is lost. Your father's sacrifice would be for nought. Use your head, Odin. You can't be in this one."

Odin halted his strides, and stabbed his hand wildly into the Temple air.

"You expect us to hide!" he yelled. "You expect us to hide while our brothers die!"

"The second rule," Raine said as he ignored Odin's ire, "is that Haren is in charge. You will do exactly what she says."

Exhaling with irritation, Odin paced again at the back of the Temple, throwing his arms up in frustration.

"And thirdly and most importantly," Raine said, "stay together. Do we understand the rules?"

Galian decided to answer for both him and Odin.

"We understand," he signed.

As Odin continued his tantrum, Galian tapped the old warrior's wrist.

"Don't worry," Galian signed. "I will calm him."

"Good to hear," Raine said as he projected his voice towards Odin. "I'm glad one of you can man up."

Odin cursed again, but Raine had already moved on. After tightening the strap on his helmet, the old warrior turned back to Haren who was waiting at the High Temple doors.

"It could be a long one," Raine forewarned. "Keep 'em safe, birdy."

"I will," Haren promised. "Godspeed, brother."

With a bow, Raine exited the Temple, and after he had left, Haren closed and locked the doors behind him. As she always did, Haren patted the giant bronze doors for luck, and after waiting to ensure that no one was seeking re-entry, she turned from the door and walked towards the center of the Temple.

"Buck up," she said to Odin. "It's not all bad. There happens to be a direct benefit to hiding in this Temple."

Calmly, Haren pulled a blue sheet of paper from under her robe.

"And that benefit," she said as she held up the sheet, "is privacy."

After seeing the paper, Galian hurried to Haren's side.

"*The Book of the Eterna*?" he asked.

"Yes, indeed," Haren answered. "Given the circumstances, I believe that some of Igallik's rules can be conceded to our gain."

Galian eyed Haren suspiciously. "Did you steal it?" he signed.

"I borrowed," Haren replied.

Galian thought for a moment.

"This can't be like Scour," he warned. "Death followed Scour."

"It won't," Haren promised. "In fact, this time we will prevent many deaths."

Galian was still eying the violet-eyed Haren. Something was off.

"What have you planned?" he signed.

"Something very powerful," she said.

With a wink, she tilted the blue page so that Galian could read the incantation.

Galian's eyes immediately lit up.

After Haren smiled back, she looked over to Odin, who had moved to a Temple window.

"You might as well join us," she said. "It will be worse if you can see the fight."

"I'm fine" Odin replied as he scanned the distance for Forneus's Scale. "I'm not a reader anyway."

Haren smiled, remembering what Raine had said to her years ago. "But you are a writer," she said. "You do intend to leave your mark on this realm."

Odin pointed to the courtyard. "Unless what you have gets me out there, I'm not interested."

"What I offer is a power that would never again demote you to being a witness of battle. What I offer you is a weapon – for this realm and the next."

Odin turned only faintly from the window, but Haren knew that she had stoked his interest.

"With what I can teach you," she said, "I promise that you will find your place on the frontlines of every future battle. Trust me this once," she solicited, "and reap the benefits for the rest of your life."

Odin looked back to Galian. Odin's greatest investment of trust had always been awarded to the quiet monk. And as Galian motioned for him to join, Odin was compelled to oblige.

"What is the power?" Odin asked as he approached the altar.

Haren presented the page.

"The power," she said, "is Vinculum Imletalis."

Outside of the High Temple, the threat of attack was imminent. Torch scouts had located a large caravan of vehicles and troops advancing on the Throne's Eye gates. With the caravan growing closer, the monks quickly armed themselves with spears, swords, and bows, and as they waited for the clash, Igallik took the reins of the moment. Unaware of Haren's trespass, the head monk stood at the base of the High Temple staircase, beating his chest as he yelled over the Throne's Eye monks.

"Brothers!" he bellowed out, "the moments defining our stand are not held in ambition or hope or prayer. Our victory is a decision we make now!"

The monks sounded their agreement in a communal war cry.

"Understand, my brothers!" Igallik cried. "An allegiance to Forneus is a death wish! Those belonging to his creed – those who seek his favour – do not fear their end! These foul souls will neither value our lives nor hesitate in our destruction! The Scale will go to any lengths to destroy us! But if it is death they seek," the head monk bawled, "we shall be gracious hosts!"

Again, the monks thundered their war cry throughout the monastery.

"For us!" Igallik screamed. "For Symin!" he roared. "And for the true house of Animus Letum!"

At that very moment, the two monks who were perched above the monastery gate yelled back into the courtyard.

"They're here! Prepare for attack!"

The monks immediately rushed to their battle positions. They would not be idle long.

With a loud hiss, two flaming flares pelted into the lookout monks, and as the two monks fell in a ball of flames, the crashing sound of hooves smashed against the Throne's Eye gate. With the monks holding back their arrows, the crashing amplified like massive metal drums, beating like thunder until the gate splintered and split. With a loud crack, the gate's hinges snapped, and three horse-drawn carriages blasted into the courtyard. The three carriages were more like large wooden platforms, and as they skidded into the center of the monastery, dozens of Scale flooded off the trailers. The militia's faces were painted with serpent-like black and green streaks, and over their bodies they wore soaked black robes.

Immediately, the archer monks released their arrows into the Scale, but strangely, the arrow assault only barely deterred the Scale's first wave. Many Scale fell, but many others, with wooden barbs sticking out of their flesh, sprinted wildly at the nearest monks and leapt onto them. The Throne's Eye archers immediately held their arrows and allowed the sword and spear wielding monks to rush in for a rescue. Even with the added manpower, the Scale militia was wrestling fiercely: they were spitting foam from their mouths as they clawed and ripped at the monks' flesh.

As Raine latched onto one of Forneus's Scale and began to rip him off, a strange smell coursed through his nostrils. Raine recognized the scent, but as he grappled with the Scale, he was confused about its significance. The pungent aroma was the exact stench of a flammable tar he had used in his childhood. As Raine's eyes instinctively checked back to the Throne's Eye gates, his eyes grew wide with panic. He suddenly understood the Scale's battle strategy. Standing at the gate there were thirty Scale archers, each armed with flaming arrows.

"Brothers!" Raine cried. "Their clothes! It's tar! They're going to light 'emselves up!"

Almost instantly, the Scale released their flaming arrows into their tar-soaked brethren. As the arrows all connected with great accuracy, the tar-doused Scale members exploded in flames. Even as the flames consumed the Scale and burned through their robes and skin, they refused to release their grip. In screaming pairings, the Scale and Throne's Eye monks were being burned to death. With screeches and shrills, the burning monks cried for help, but with more and more of Forneus's militia storming through the gates, none could be offered.

Instead, the Throne's Eye monastery delved even further into war.

Inside the High Temple, sheltered from the carnage outside, Haren had begun the preparations for Vinculum Imletalis.

"Galian knows this rite as well as I do," she said while placing candles around the altar. "But for your sake, Odin, I will explain. Essentially, Vinculum Imletalis can allow for the spiritual bond of two of the same blood."

After eyeing the candles curiously, Odin turned to Haren.

"What kind of bond?" he asked.

"If engaged properly," Haren said as she touched a match to a line of unlit wicks, "you and your brother's state of individual bodies would cease to exist. You would become a soul with one consciousness. You'd become one entity, a state of being we recognize simply as Daios."

"For how long?" Odin asked with some apprehension.

Without looking up, Haren made a few strange paces around the Temple.

"Not long," she reassured. "The power of two souls, even to the greatest degree, could only hold Daios for a short period of time. Ambitiously," Haren wagered, "I would think you and Galian could hold Daios for twenty minutes."

There was haste in Haren's voice – a rushing, almost panicked tinge in her instruction. As Haren arranged the ritual, Odin could sense it. The stress did not sit well. In fact, Haren's frenetic energy had begun to brew a ball of nerves in his gut.

"I'm not sure about this," he said finally. "I would rather wait."

Haren would not yield.

"Think, Odin," she campaigned, "you would have all of your own strength, but also all of Galian's as well. The two of you combined would be an awesome force. You would be like a god. Like your father."

Odin scratched the back of his head, still uncomfortable with the ritual.

"I still think I will wait until after the battle," he said.

Haren brought her hand to her forehead and let out a desperate exhalation. She was searching for an angle.

"Think of it this way," she said finally. "If we do this, Galian would inherit your strengths as well. He would feel what it is to run. He would be able to do all the things that birth robbed him of."

As Haren watched Odin's head rise up, she knew that she had hit the nerve that she had intended. Throughout the twins' lives, Odin had been excruciatingly aware of Galian's limitations. Odin was awed by Galian's power, but he was almost resentful of his weakness. Galian had never run. He had never even walked without pain. As was his character, Galian had never complained. He hid his grimaces and feigned comfort. It was in fact only Odin who knew the skill of his acting.

As Odin looked to his brother, he tried to maintain a neutral expression.

"You're sure about this?" he asked.

Galian smiled meekly. "I read about this rite when I won a day in the Ichor," he said. "I've waited for this chance ever since."

Odin shook his head. He had been beat. Knowing his brother as completely as he did, Odin knew he couldn't deny him.

"If you're sure," he decided. "I will do it."

"I'm sure," Galian signed.

After receiving both brothers' consent, Haren made a satisfied clap.

"If we are moving ahead," she said, "then we must be fast."

She rushed Odin and Galian to the positions that they would need to invoke Vinculum Imletalis, and then made a quick double-check of the ritual's layout. After affirming the precision of the arrangement, Haren's pace slowed and she turned to Galian.

"You remember how to focus the power?" she asked.

Galian touched his hand to his eyes.

"Eyes to soul," he signed.

"Very good," Haren said. "The majority of weight will fall on you," she warned. "You will be greatly drained afterwards, but remember that the further you can hold on now, the better you will stand after."

Galian nodded.

Haren made a minor correction to Odin's position and then gave the brothers their final counsel.

"Odin," she said, "although your brother is not practised in this art, he is well-read in similar rites. I am confident that he can instigate and hold the ritual. What I need you to do is maintain eye contact and allow yourself to feel. If you can do this, you will soon be aware of your brother's spiritual activity, and you too will be able to involve yourself."

Odin was confused. "How?"

"You'll know when it happens," Haren replied.

"Oh, thanks," Odin said sarcastically. "That was helpful."

Haren waved off his tone. "Trust me," she said. "And trust Galian."

After pulling out the blue Vinculum Imletalis page, Haren took a deep breath and stepped back from the twins.

"Alright, boys," she said. "Let's give it our best."

To begin, Galian accepted Odin's hand in his palm and then looked directly into Odin's eyes. It was a strange gaze – as if Galian were looking past him. As Galian seemed to settle in, Odin knew no other option but to hold the stare. With the boys in position, Haren began to recite from the incantation.

The words were strange, throaty sounds that Odin had never heard. The more the ritual progressed, the more skeptical he became. However, as he held Galian's stare, the quiet monk was clearly confident. There was a spark in Galian's eye that was telling him to be patient.

As Haren continued to read and Galian's eyes burned into him, Odin shuddered, keeling just a bit as he felt a strange sensation growing in his stomach. The feeling was bizarre – like something foreign moving inside him. As he jostled to recapture his composure, his back became rigid with the sudden realization that a breeze had manifested itself between him and Galian. The wind seemed to blow in surges, rippling the twins' clothes slowly, as if they were underwater. The experience was strange for Odin, but it was also exciting. As he held fast in the eerie unison, Haren continued to recite from the page, raising her voice and lowering it in direct time with the surging wind. As a bead of sweat rolled down his brow, Odin suddenly realized that the air was becoming incredibly hot, humid, and thick, and as Haren continued to chant, the rhythm of the incantation began to overwhelm him. A strange daze fell over his mind, and as he rocked slightly, a sudden snap of blue energy cracked from between him and Galian. The sight and sound felt good to Odin. Very good. The moment was dreamlike. Within seconds Odin felt another snap of energy, this one refusing to dissipate, humming and buzzing between him and his brother in the form of a bolt of lightning. The bolt, distinctly blue, began to grow thicker, and as it cracked and spat, the room began to pulse with light. The pulse was bright, and somehow, as the light rose and fell, the windows, golden pews, and even the Order thrones became cased in ice. As the ritual progressed, the Temple's sound, along with all of its warmth, became expelled from the room. Contrary to the sudden change in temperature, Odin felt extremely warm. His senses began to feel amazing. He felt more powerful than he had ever felt. More amazingly, somehow he could feel Galian in his mind. He could feel Galian guiding him, and it was exhilarating.

In the silence, the blue energy growing between Odin and Galian had begun to take on a form.

As Haren compelled all of herself into the last line of the incantation, the energy between Odin and Galian began to take on a human shape – a single spiritual force. As Haren eyed the blue form, she began to see the features of both twins emerging from within the energy.

Vinculum Imletalis was taking effect – Daios was emerging.

Aware of the great trespass she had committed by allowing the boys to initiate Vinculum Imletalis, Haren watched the boys with no regret. This, she had decided, was necessary.

As Vinculum Imletalis began to bloom, Odin became even more amazed. His sight was somehow not coming from his body. His vision and all other senses had become rooted in the blue energy between him and Galian. Odin was thrilled. Haren had said he and Galian would be a god. Haren was right. Odin felt beyond human. It was divinity. It was Daios. However, with Odin's sense of sight still rooted in the blue energy, he watched panic suddenly overtake Haren's face. Haren's arms flailed wildly, and she seemed to be shouting orders. Odin flexed his senses, but as he tried to read Haren, he began to feel incredibly sick. The feeling was vile, and somehow Odin could feel panic in his brother.

Then, as if Galian had sent the words into Odin's mind, one desperate phrase drowned Odin's consciousness:

"Brace yourself!"

As Odin tried to focus on Galian, the blue entity between them amplified into a blinding white flash, and with a sudden blast, the power between the twins erupted. The frozen pews and windows blew apart into shards of ice, and as the Temple's walls and roof rocked against the quake of the white surge, Odin, Galian, and Haren were blasted backwards into unconsciousness. Odin and Galian smashed into the side walls of the High Temple, and Haren was thrown into the Temple's bronze doors.

Vinculum Imletalis had failed.

Outside of the Temple, attempting to hold his own in the motions of war, Igallik's eyes and ears were hastily called to the blast originating from the High Temple. He immediately understood what had happened.

"No, Haren!" he cried.

In desperation, the head monk fought off each attacker in his way and rapidly cut a path backwards to the High Temple. As he ascended the Temple's staircase, Haren had begun to regain consciousness. The violet-eyed Deathrider fought to make herself alert, and then quickly set herself in motion.

First, she dragged Odin's and Galian's comatose bodies into hiding.

"Forgive me, brothers," she prayed.

Then, after affirming the degree of camouflage she had provided for the sons of Animus Letum, she advanced on Serich's crown. Her determined steps were interrupted with the fierce pounding of Igallik's fists on the Temple's bronze doors.

"Haren!" he screamed. "This was not the plan!"

Haren retrieved Serich's crown and walked calmly to the bronze doors.

"My brother," she said, "let us be clear: the plan was always yours. I have put something much greater into motion."

Igallik's fists beat against the bronze doors with even more panic.

"My plan was for the best, Haren! I beg you, please don't do this!"

"When these doors are opened," Haren said, "you will find me and the crown gone. Do not search for me," she warned. "You will only waste your time."

"For heaven's sake, Haren! You're risking everything! Please, don't do this!"

For minutes, Igallik's fists and pleading calls beat against the door.

No reply came. Haren was gone.

Igallik finally felt the sting of his fists against the door, and as he looked down at his swollen and bleeding hands, he had no choice but to acknowledge his failure. The motives of Haren's deceit were unclear, and the head monk had become rapt in their implications: so much so that he had become oblivious to the battle below. As he cast his eyes over the battlefield, he was instantly snapped back into alertness. Forneus's militia was overtaking a great majority of the Throne's Eye monks. The Torches and Aerises were effectively employing their great battle strengths, but the Sights were out of their element. They were battered and falling to the wild attacks of Forneus's devout. As Igallik observed from atop the staircase, he saw a sector of the militia breach the final defence line blocking the High Temple staircase. With only stairs in front of them, the Scale began a wild sprint up to the Temple door. A number of Aerises, including Raine, recognized the threat and leapt to the chase. Drawing from his dagger-laden belt, Raine ceased much of the militia's progress with the devastatingly accurate pitches of his blades, but despite his efforts, there was still a number of snake-faced assailants advancing on Igallik. As they reached the top, Igallik tried to fend off their growing numbers with his staff, but he could not manage long. Understanding Igallik's disadvantage, Raine rushed to the head monk's aid. As he reached the summit, he exploded into action. With the powerful slashes of his sword, Raine mercilessly spilled the blood of Igallik's attackers. Raine exploited the Scale's weakness of war with the mastery of his blade, and he cut their numbers down to none. As the final Scale fell, Raine scanned the staircase for any other approaching menace, but he quickly saw that his fellow Aerises had destroyed the threat.

Assured of his safety, Raine turned to Igallik.

"Are you hurt?" he asked.

"No," Igallik said as he brushed the crimson spatter from his hands and face. After wiping the last of the blood from his brow, he turned back to the bronze doors.

"They'll be fine," Raine assured.

Igallik's eyes fleeted back with tremendous worry.

"Haren's gone."

"What do you mean gone? She's with the boys."

"Not anymore," the head monk informed. "She has left and she has taken the crown."

"The crown?" Raine repeated. The old warrior was baffled.

"God damn it," Igallik cursed. "I trusted her. I trusted her and she has burned us."

Raine couldn't understand. "Birdy?" he whispered. "Why?"

"I don't know," Igallik replied.

Raine didn't know how to react. "What'll we do?" he asked.

Wrought with anxiety, Igallik could think of only one option.

"We win this battle," he answered. "If any of our ground is lost this night, we can't let it lead to this Temple."

Just as Igallik finished his order, two more horse-drawn carriages barrelled through the broken gates of the Throne's Eye. After the carts had entered completely into the monastery, the two Scale piloting the carriages careened into each other. As the six horses began to crash and trample over one another, the two weaving wagons flipped onto their sides and skidded across the courtyard's stone and earth. The carriages quickly ground to a stop; however, as numerous monks approached the broken carts, suddenly the two wagons burst into flames, and within seconds, they erupted in a massive explosion.

In an instant, dozens more of the Throne's Eye monks were dead.

Even atop the staircase, Igallik and Raine were rocked by the heat and impact of the blast. Raine quickly regained his wits and peered back over the battle, watching as dozens more of Forneus's militia hauled a massive black trailer into the courtyard.

"Stay on the outside of the battle," Raine said as he began to descend back into the courtyard. "We'll sort this out."

Igallik understood, and hoping to remove any and all attention from the High Temple, he too dashed down into the fray.

21

Inside the Temple, the thunderous blast had woken Odin. He was dazed in his first moments, and after realizing that there was a blanket draped over him, he pushed it off and stared blankly at his surroundings. He was in a small nook, and Galian was asleep beside him. As more wakefulness came, Odin examined the space, but as he leaned up, a sharp pain stung the left side of his face. Odin touched his hand to the pain, wincing as he traced a deep and bloody groove cut into his left cheek. After feeling out the length of the groove, Odin saw that Galian also had a scar, but Galian's was on the right side of his forehead. The scars confused him, and with a tinge of panic, Odin brought his fist to his chin and tried to replay his last hour. There was haze. But soon, an order of events fell into place. The Scale were coming. He and Galian were sent to the High Temple. Haren had a blue sheet. They had attempted Vinculum Imletalis. More haze.

As much as Odin tried, he couldn't recall how the ritual had ended. With a gingerly tap, Odin tried to wake Galian, but the quiet monk did not respond. As the tap graduated to a shake, Odin suddenly remembered that Haren had said Galian would be greatly drained by the ritual. Accordingly, Odin decided to let his brother rest and began to investigate the nook. Of the four sides of the nook, one had a golden drape covering it. Odin lightly swatted his hand into the drape, and after finding nothing behind, he drew the cloth to the side and exposed a small set of stairs that led up.

With a slight stagger, Odin followed the steps back into the main room of the High Temple.

"Haren," he called out as he reached the top. "Haren, I'm up."

There was no answer.

The Temple was in complete disarray. The pews and windows were smashed to pieces, and their fragments were sprawled over every inch of the Temple floor. The only items left untouched by the blast were the Order thrones and the Temple altar.

Through the broken windows, Odin could hear the clash of battle resounding from the Throne's Eye courtyard.

With slow steps, he approached one of the windows and peered down into the fray.

His hands turned to fists as he looked down. With a tight throat, he swallowed, sorry for the many dead monks he could see lying on the courtyard floor.

Odin scanned the Temple again.

"Haren!" he yelled.

Without Haren, Odin became increasingly tempted to unlock the Temple doors. He knew he could help in the battle. He knew he could prevent more deaths.

"For Symin," he whispered.

As the sounds of war sang to him, Odin put his back to the entrance wall and began to move towards the door, looking back into the Temple as he scanned for any sign of his violet-eyed minder. However, as his fingers reached the door's latch and he began to pull, his eyes suddenly fixed on something behind the altar.

There was a rope – a rope with one end bound to the altar and the other end hanging out of a Temple window. As his head tilted, analyzing the rope, Odin knew that the altar-end must have been tied first. As a series of thoughts and theories began to rush into his head, Odin's hand fell from the door latch.

Something was very wrong.

In quick seconds, Odin's training forced him to capture his nerves, and with fast and silent steps, Odin rushed to the back of the Temple. As he hung partway out of the window and looked down, he saw that the rope hung all the way to the ground behind the Temple. There was no one at the base, but as the moonlight crossed over the earth floor, Odin could see another rope hanging over the monastery's wall

In a flash, the rope, Haren's absence, and the fact that no one else could have entered the Temple, collided.

Haren had fled.

"Why?" Odin whispered.

It didn't make sense.

As the truth unsettled him, Odin rushed back into the heart of the Temple, and just as Raine had taught him, he began to take inventory of not just the events that had passed, but also of the items in the Temple.

As he stood at the Temple's center, scanning, surveying, and scrutinizing his memory, suddenly, at one object, Odin's mind halted.

"The crown..." he gasped.

Odin needed to prove himself wrong, and with wild paces he tore through the Temple, throwing and tossing the broken pews aside as he hunted for the golden relic. But minutes passed with no success. After scavenging the wrecked pews completely, Odin fell backwards against the wall, defeated by an inarguable truth.

The crown, and Haren, were gone.

As he pushed both of his hands backwards through his blonde hair, he let out a series of quick exhalations, his breath and mind taken by the moment.

"Why?" he repeated again and again. "Why?"

As his eyes burned forward, suddenly, a mass of broken debris caught his attention. Peeking out from the bottom of the pile was a corner of blue paper. It was Haren's page. It was the incantation.

Odin leapt up, stumbling forward as he rushed to the blue sheet. As he neared, he slid on his knees, skidding to the debris, until he hung over it. Quickly, he snatched the page, un-crumpled its corners, and began to read the golden scribble:

"Vinculum Imletalis: This sacred art belongs not to one. Nor does it belong to the weak. It belongs to two: two of the same blood, two of the highest measure. Vinculum Imletalis is a test of two, and if one fails, both do. Daios is round one corner, but Death is round the other. Beware brave souls: Death will claim the unworthy."

"Death?" Odin repeated in alarm.

His senses clenched. "Galian!"

With his heart pulsing like a metal drum, Odin threw the page to the floor, and sprinted back down into the nook. His feet slid down the steps, stumbling forward, as he catapulted to his brother. As he reached Galian, Odin gripped his shoulders, shaking him wildly as his voice shrilled throughout the nook.

"No, no, no," he stammered and begged. "Galian!" he shrieked. "Wake up!"

With a quick hand, Odin put his fingers to Galian's neck.

There was no pulse.

"Please, Galian," Odin cried. "Wake up! Galian, wake up!"

His brother was still.

Heavily, Odin fell backwards into the wall, rocking, as his hand covered his mouth and long throaty sounds expelled from his mouth.

"Got to be a way," he started rambling. "Got to be a way. Got to be a way."

Odin fearfully clasped his hands together, watching his motionless brother with horror in his heart. Suddenly, his eyes lit up with thought.

"Igallik!" he cried.

Odin turned on a heel and bolted out of the nook, leaping up the stairs with huge and flurried strides. In seconds, he was at the bronze doors. The sound of war was drowned out by Odin's panic, and ignoring Raine's first rule, Odin unlocked the latch and ripped the bronze doors open.

As the doors drew completely open, a wave of searing heat funnelled into the Temple, forcing Odin to guard his face. Peering from under his sleeve, Odin could see that pockets of flame burned in nearly every corner of the courtyard, and countless monks and Scale were strewn dead across the burning earth and stone. Amid the scene of death, the war was still raging. With the clashing sounds of steel blades, the monks and militia were trading blows, fighting fearlessly for the other's death.

Worrying about his brother, Odin slammed the bronze doors behind him, and then rushed to the edge of the staircase, scanning the war zone for any sign of Igallik.

It was Raine, however, who first detected Odin. After noticing Odin, Raine began to slash a brutal path through Forneus's militia, screaming wildly at his Lyran apprentice.

"Odin!" he screamed through the chaos. "Get back inside!"

Odin had to refuse.

With fervent slashes, Raine continued to fight to the staircase, but it would not be soon enough. Odin's eyes had found the head monk, and with frantic leaps and bounds, Odin flew down the stairway into the courtyard.

"Odin!" Raine cried again. "Get back!"

It was to no avail.

Before Raine could reach him, Odin hit the courtyard floor and took off in pursuit of the head monk.

With war spread out in front of him, Odin sprinted and weaved through the courtyard, tracking the head monk with perilous vigour.

Unaware that Odin was out of the Temple, Igallik stood at a corner wall, thrashing his staff against Forneus's devout. With a vicious arc, Igallik cracked a Scale into death; however, as the head monk turned emphatically to his next attacker, he did so too hastily. Igallik stumbled into a hoard of Forneus's militia, and as the whole of their numbers turned on him, the Scale claimed the battle advantage.

Seeing the head monk's blunder, Odin set his great skills into motion.

The Sons of Animus Letum

With a burst of strides, Odin exploded into an even faster sprint. As he ran, he leapt and hurdled over a series of fallen monks, retrieving idle daggers from their inert hands. After stocking himself with weapons, Odin's eyes narrowed on Igallik's attackers, planning their deaths before he would deal them. As he grew within range, Odin let go two precise and lethal whips of his hands, piercing the daggers into the necks of two Scale. Two were down, but three more were still hunting Igallik. Fearlessly, Odin tore even deeper into the fray, dodging and weaving around the monks and Scale; however, his strides had caught the attention of a tall and skinny Scale. As Odin sprinted, the Scale stalked him with slow steps, eying his prey, twisting his axe and timing his attack. With Odin's attention locked onto the head monk, the Lyran sped up, but as he began to call to Igallik, the Scale leapt out and swung his weapon into Odin's path. Odin's senses flushed – there was not enough time to defend. As Odin flinched and the axe careened inwards, suddenly, a monk leapt into the assault, accepting the axe blade into his own back. Odin and the Scale halted. As Odin looked down, Palis looked painfully up, the axe buried deep into his upper back. To Odin's surprise, Palis was not dead. Instead, the badly wounded monk tossed up a dagger, and as the Scale attempted to throw his fist at Odin, he parried it away and then thrust the blade into the attacker's throat. A burst of blood splashed from the Scale's neck, and with bulging eyes, Forneus's follower fell frantically to the floor, gasping and wheezing as his life bled out in front of him.

With the Scale dead, Odin tried to lift Palis to his feet, but the Mercy totem threw away Odin's hands.

"Just go," the Mercy totem begged.

Still shocked by the close call, Odin managed to nod his head, and with dagger in hand, he sprang back into action. The three remaining Scale that were battling with Igallik had cornered the disadvantaged head monk against the monastery's log wall. Igallik swung his staff in defence, but the onslaught of Scale attacks had pushed him flush against the wood. As one powerful attack removed Igallik of his weapon and a pending attack threatened his life, Odin arrived. He whipped his dagger into the closest Scale's heart, collapsing him to the earth. He then leapt at the Scale on Igallik's left, driving his right knee powerfully up into his jaw. As the Scale staggered back and fell, Odin snatched the head monk's staff from the ground, spun at the last Scale, and used his momentum to swing the wooden staff powerfully into his neck.

The immediate threat had been quelled.

When Igallik recognized Odin, his mind flurried in panic. Odin's presence, combined with Haren's deceit, spelled only disaster.

"Odin!" he cried. "What's happened?"

"It's Galian!" Odin yelled back. "He needs you now!"

Igallik's eyes grew wide.

"What's wrong?" he shouted.

"Galian's dead!" Odin cried. "He needs you!"

The words cut like a hot blade. As Igallik's greatest fear constricted his breath, he did his best to feign composure.

"Let's go!" he ordered.

Immediately, the two set off back to the Temple.

As they ran, Odin swung the staff forward, bowling through the battle as he stormed a path directly to the Temple stairs. As the militia's growing numbers continued to tilt the battle to the Scale's favour, many of the militia began to track Odin and Igallik.

Raine was first to detect the hunters, and as Odin and Igallik ran to the staircase, the old warrior called out orders to the remaining monks.

"Brothers!" he bawled. "Hold the stairs!"

Immediately, the monks of the Throne's Eye retreated from the core of the courtyard and began to form a phalanx at the base of the Temple's stairway. As Odin and Igallik grew near to the stairs, Raine cut behind them, driving a powerful shoulder into three of the stalking Scale. The militia members were tossed airborne, and as they crashed back to the earth, Raine swiftly executed each of them with his blade. With blood staining his sword, the old warrior's eyes fleeted back to the stairs, his pulse raging like one hundred drums. Nimbly, Odin and Igallik had cut behind the last line of monks, sliding past them as they assembled their phalanx. After cutting another flurry of his blade into the Scale, Raine sprinted over to join the formation, but strangely, only some of Forneus's militia were challenging the human wall. Most of the Scale had retreated to the massive trailer that been had hauled in after the two carts had exploded.

As the monks assumed the final stage of their phalanx, Raine was wary of the militia's sudden change in strategy. With authority, he yelled back to Igallik and Odin.

"Get him inside!" he cried. "Lock the doors!"

With panic ringing through his soul, Igallik tried his best to comply.

Raine quickly settled into the formation, but as he looked back over the courtyard, he could see increased movement at the militia's trailer.

"Steady, boys!" he called to his brothers. "Impulse breaks us!"

However, in one moment, Raine realized his battle flaw. Storming out from behind their giant trailer came one hundred Scale, each armed with a bow. As Raine's gut turned, the militia ignited their arrow tips and drew them back.

"Take cover!" Raine screamed.

With a unified yell, the militia released their flaming arrows. Odin and Igallik had just reached the giant bronze doors. As Igallik turned back and recognized the threat, he knew that there was no time. The fiery arrows lit up the dark sky like a hellish rain, and as they began to arc down, Igallik quickly pulled Odin to the ground and then threw himself over Odin's body.

The entire Throne's Eye population winced in wait.

As their fates fell in the form of flaming arrows, suddenly the bronze doors of the High Temple exploded open. Bearing his scar from the failed attempt at Vinculum Imletalis, Galian erupted out of the Temple in a furious limp. As the flaming barbs flew in for the strike, Galian bowed his head and then launched his arms out against the oncoming arrows. Immediately, a howling wind burst from Galian's frame, and as the quiet monk stormed forward, the hundreds of arrows froze in mid-air. The monks of the Throne's Eye looked skywards, dumbfounded, as the flaming arrows floated only ten feet above them. In even greater display, Galian reached his right hand high into the air, and as the wind screamed around the monastery, he drove his palm into the stone beneath him and used his power to launch the flaming arrows violently back to their senders.

In an instant, the battle had been won.

The Scale that were not dead were badly wounded.

Igallik and the other monks looked back to the young Galian in silence. They, like the militia, had never seen such power displayed in the first realm.

The astounded hush ensued until Igallik managed to grab the reins.

"Brothers," he called out. "You know what to do."

Raine understood, and he quickly ordered his brothers to destroy the surviving Scale and then deliver all wounded monks to the Throne's Eye infirmary.

"And Raine," Igallik said as the old warrior began his descent of the stairs, "leave one alive."

Raine nodded and then followed his brothers down into the courtyard.

With clasped hands, Igallik approached Galian, but as he reached him and placed his hand on Galian's shoulder, he immediately withdrew.

"Galian," he winced. "You're burning hot."

Galian nodded and signed the hand gesture for water. As Igallik rushed into the High Temple, Galian walked slowly to his brother, wrapped his hands in the excess fabric of his brown robe, and lifted Odin to his feet.

Odin met Galian's eyes with relief. "I thought you were dead," he confessed.

"Probably should be," Galian said. "I owe you an apology."

"Apology?" Odin repeated. "You saved us."

Even with Odin's forgiveness, there was an element of Galian's soul that would carry guilt for the rest of his life. He knew exactly why Odin agreed to attempt Vinculum Imletalis.

"It was selfish of me to involve you," Galian said. "It was beyond us ... beyond me."

With heavy eyes, Galian traced his hand over the scar that Vinculum Imletalis had left on Odin's left cheek.

"We're lucky to be alive," he said.

Odin could see that the toll of Galian's shame was heavy.

"My scar will look great in a couple of days," he said with a smile. "Yours, however, is going to look like hell."

Galian smiled. "It's okay. I was getting tired of being the good-looking one."

Odin turned his ear to his brother. "I'm sorry, I didn't hear that. Could you speak up?"

As Galian threw a jesting jab at his brother, Odin deflected it and then motioned to the courtyard.

"You left it a little late," he said of Galian's feat.

"Oh?" Galian said. "Would you have preferred not at all?"

Before Odin could reply, Igallik returned with a glass of water and handed it to Galian.

"You will come with me," he said to Galian. "We have something very important to discuss. And Odin, find Raine and assist him. I need to speak with Galian alone."

The absence of levity in Igallik's voice conveyed the absence of choice in Odin's and Galian's next moves.

"Now, boys," Igallik ordered.

As Galian followed Igallik back into the High Temple, he shot a wry smile back at his brother.

"It's busy being great," he signed. "Someday I'll tell you about it."

Odin grinned. "I'll be too busy to listen."

22

Just as Igallik had instructed, the monks in the courtyard left only one member of the Scale alive. Odin accompanied Raine and two more Torches as they dragged the wounded and wildly thrashing Scale to his prison cell.

As Raine and Odin stood back, the two Torches threw the prisoner into lockup. Madly, the Scale screamed in protest, tossing his arms as he thrust himself repeatedly against the steel bars.

As the Scale bucked and smashed, Odin watched him with interest.

"Why would Igallik want him alive?" he asked Raine.

"Of that, I'm not sure," Raine answered. "But Igallik tends to be about four or five steps ahead of us bruisers."

Odin nodded with a smile. But as he turned back to the cell, the Scale leapt close to the steel, wrapping his fingers around the bars as he scolded Odin with a stare.

"Something you like, boy?" he spat.

Odin looked right back, mocking the Scale with feigned fear.

"Oh, you're brave," the Scale laughed. "Too brave to be left alive."

Odin shrugged. "Are you almost done?" he asked.

"No, but you are," the Scale shot back. "You know," he boasted, "the snake is a cunning creature. It can slither through walls and borders thought to be impenetrable. The Throne's Eye is such a wall," he seethed. "You have a traitor in your ranks, boy, and his grip is strong."

Raine rolled his eyes and approached the prison cell.

"There is a serpent here," he said as he stopped in front of the cell. "But I'm not concerned about his grip."

"And why's that?" the prisoner sneered.

With a quick strike, Raine hammered the butt end of his sword into the Scale's fingers.

"His fingers are broken," the old warrior smiled.

After squealing and bounding wildly around the cell, the Scale spat at Raine and began to leap into the steel bars.

"You too, will fall!" he screamed. "Each one of you!"

"More than likely," Raine agreed. "But not by your hand."

With a firm grip, Raine put his hand on Odin's shoulder.

"Time to leave," he said. "We'll save this one for Igallik."

As Raine and Odin emerged back into the courtyard, they were immediately met by Igallik and Galian.

Igallik quickly called Raine aside, and as the two walked out of earshot, Odin leaned into his brother.

"What did Igallik say?" he asked.

"Something good," Galian signed. "He's asked me to attempt the Descent trial."

Odin was startled, his posture becoming rigid with alarm.

Descent was the most daunting task in existence. It was the ritual that turned Sight into Seraph. To accept the Descent trial was to accept hell. And because it involved the excruciating split of body and soul, it had always terrified Odin. The torture of Descent was most often deadly – a fact that Odin could never dismiss.

"You're not ready," Odin argued. "You need to wait."

"Igallik believes this is my chance," Galian replied. "With all the confusion here today, he believes my soul can enter and leave the afterlife without detection."

"That's why he left one prisoner alive," Odin realized.

"Yes," Galian said. "He's my ride for Descent."

Odin shook his head, trying his best to keep composed. Ever since Galian had become a Sight, Odin had been afraid of this moment.

"I don't want you to do it," he said. "You're not ready."

Galian's posture sank. Of anyone, he thought Odin would be the most supportive.

"Odin," he assured, "I can do this."

"I've always believed you could," Odin said. "But this is sudden. Too sudden. Twelve monks have been successful. Twelve out of hundreds. The rest died."

Galian knew the statistics. He also knew himself better than anyone.

"Lucky thirteen," he predicted with a smile.

Galian's confidence angered Odin. Descent was a hellish trial, and the quiet monk seemed to be laughing it off.

"I have protected you our entire lives," Odin said sternly. "And I always will. But right now I have to protect you from this decision. You can't do this, Galian. You're going to get yourself killed. Please, you need to listen to me."

Galian beat his hand against his heart. "I listen to myself," he said angrily. "And I *am* strong enough."

Odin tried to grab Galian's shoulders, but Galian shrugged away.

"Don't do this," Odin begged. "You're not ready. For me, please, don't do this."

"You don't get it," Galian signed. "It's not your choice. It's mine. I am doing it. We are supposed to die in eight years, Odin. I am doing this for *our* future – to seize more power for *us*."

Odin tilted his head back, eying his brother skeptically.

"For us?" he repeated. "Or for you?"

"I thought you'd be proud," Galian said, "not afraid and small."

"Small?" Odin repeated. "I'm looking out for *you*. Your ego almost killed us in the Temple. Your arrogance almost cost us our lives. You were elected as the heir, Galian. Does that mean nothing to you? You're not allowed to gamble with your life. Just wait until you're stronger. Please."

"What do you know about strength?" Galian shot back. "You are a body. Nothing more."

Odin was hurt. He made a few frantic nods, flexing his neck as he tried to swallow back the emotion closing his throat.

"Good luck with Descent," he forced out. "It'd be a shame if your ego cost you your life."

Galian's words had cut both brothers, but as the quiet monk tried to apologize, Odin dismissed him and stormed angrily back to his quarters.

As Odin sped off, Igallik and Raine broke from their discussion and returned to Galian's side.

"Raine has agreed to hold his part," Igallik said.

As Galian signed his thanks to Raine, Igallik put his hand on Galian's shoulder.

"I will only ask you this once more," the head monk said. "Are you sure you want to do this? This will be the first Descent without a Lyran on the throne. This will bring many more complications."

Galian's eyes fleeted back to Odin. He wished Odin would see that there was a bigger picture than the two of them. There was more than Odin's feelings in the balance – there was an entire world.

"I will attempt," Galian said.

"Alright," Igallik agreed. "We will proceed with Descent in one hour."

As Igallik turned towards the High Temple to prepare for the ritual, Raine's eyes shifted between the twins.

"Is your brother alright?" he asked.

"He's being childish," Galian said.

Raine shrugged. "Childish is thinking about only yourself," he said. "I overheard him. He's worried about you."

"There's a bigger picture than me," Galian replied.

"Not to him," Raine said.

Galian shook his head. "That's his problem. I'm wrestling with bigger ones."

After one hour had passed, Igallik, Raine, Galian, and the sole remaining Scale moved into the High Temple. The Temple was still in disarray from Odin and Galian's failed attempt at Vinculum Imletalis. The pews and windows were broken to pieces, and their fragments littered the entirety of the floor. The only items in the Temple that had been untouched by the blast were the totem thrones and the Temple altar.

With contemplative strides, Igallik stepped around the broken pews and busted glass, arranging candles as he finalized the ritual's layout.

Although Raine had silenced the Scale with a cloth and rope, the Scale refused to accept his fate. He tried to wrestle himself away from the old warrior, bucking and kicking against his captor. As the Scale thrashed desperately for freedom, Raine began to reprimand his efforts with breath-robbing shots to the abdomen.

In the aftermath of his feat in the courtyard and at the dawn of Descent, Galian was calm. Although his mind was dwelling on his brother, his heart was committed to becoming the thirteenth Seraph in the Throne's Eye history. Galian's motive was honest. This enormous undertaking was as much for the monastery as it was for him. Seraphs were the masters of soul, and by their power, the world and all in the Seraph's favour gained great reward. Each Seraph who had returned from the afterlife had emerged with a fantastic power. Some returned with the ability to heal ailments, and one was even able to slow time. The twelve Seraphs were the proof that gods could walk among men. The promise of the undertaking excited Galian. He only wished that Odin felt the same way.

Soon, as a crisp air breezed through the open Temple windows, Igallik declared that the moment had arrived.

"You will sit here," he said to Galian.

With a suspicious eye, Igallik leaned over the quiet monk.

"If I were to hazard a guess," he said, "I would think that Haren has given you instruction in this art?"

An ashamed Galian nodded his head.

"Unburden your heart," Igallik said. "The fault was not yours."

Galian managed a small bow of thanks.

"Now if you will," Igallik said, "please take your seat. We will begin in a moment."

The quiet monk obliged, and as he took his seat, Igallik turned and invited Raine to play his role in the ritual. Raine had only been a part of one previous Descent ritual, but as he gripped his massive hands around the prisoner's ankles, he remembered clearly what his responsibilities were. With a powerful heave, Raine dragged the panicked and thrashing prisoner to the Temple altar, strapped him to the table, and prepared to deal him into death.

As Raine bound the Scale, the candles that Igallik had prepared drowned the table with a deep orange glow. It was a strange radiance – a surreal aura that made the ritual seem haunting and grim.

After binding the Scale completely, Raine nodded to Igallik, who then turned to Galian.

"If not now," Igallik said, "then never."

Galian understood. "It is now," he signed.

To begin, the quiet monk concentrated all of his will into meditation. Spiritually, he allowed himself to loosen all stressors, and with deliberate breaths, he quickly arrived in the relaxed state of mind that was necessary for Descent. Igallik acknowledged Galian's progress, and then, inviting the next step of the ritual, he handed a double-pronged dagger to Raine. The width between each blade of the stiletto disclosed the dagger's exact purpose. They were separated enough so that in one stab, the two ends would pierce both lungs of its victim. Raine raised the dagger over the pleading eyes of the Scale, and as he suspended the dagger, Igallik began to recite slowly from *The Book of the Eterna*. As Igallik spoke the ancient words of Descent into the Temple air, the candles began to burn with greater intensity. Their flames began to elongate, stretching even longer than the candles. As the flames flickered, there was a strange stillness to the room. It was a dense feeling, like moving underwater. As the heaviness drowned the Temple, the candlewicks began to sizzle, echoing somehow, like fire falling down a well. Soon, the candles began to burn a translucent blue, but strangely, instead of heat, the candles were producing a distinct cold. As the chill filled the Temple, the flames began to pulse in a slow rhythm, becoming brighter and brighter, until, in the blue afterglow, Igallik reached a critical point of the ritual. After commanding authority into the ritual's final words, he called on Raine to complete his stage of the sacred art. Raine assented, and with the indifference of duty, he plunged the dagger into the prisoner's chest, piercing the Scale's lungs in one stab. As blood leaked from the Scale's chest, he let out a muffled scream – one that deflated quickly, fading in exact time with his punctured lungs. Small moments – seconds that were still heavy and thick – passed with only the faint gasping of the prisoner breaking the silence. As the cloth muzzled over the Scale's mouth started to be stained red with the blood surging from his air passage, it was clear that death was close. As expected, the prisoner took his last gasp, and as his airy breath whispered into the air, an orange mist began to seep slowly from the puncture holes in his chest. After seeing the mist, Galian rose slowly to his feet and approached. The mist bled into the Temple air like dust in a faint wind. And as the orange mist swirled and twisted, Galian reached out his hands and cupped the orange matter with one smooth arc. After collecting the mist, Galian drew his hands to his eyes. The head monk nodded to affirm Galian's method and form, and after receiving the head monk's confirmation, Galian slowly pressed the orange mist into his own eyes. This was the stage of Descent that allowed Galian's soul to bond with the prisoner's soul.

The moment the orange mist completely penetrated Galian's eyes, the prisoner went limp in death. Galian's body did the same. As Galian toppled, Raine lunged and managed to catch the quiet monk before he crashed to the floor. With Galian hung in Raine's arms, suddenly every candle in the Temple extinguished. However, the Temple was not without a light source. Galian's and the prisoner's bodies both pulsed with light – glowing as if the raging orange flames were swelling from beneath their skin. The glow slowly died, and as Raine continued to brace Galian, Igallik leaned in and examined Galian's eyes.

"Galian," he shouted as he studied the quiet monk.

There was no answer.

"He's gone," Igallik confirmed. "There is not much else we can do. A battle of wills has begun."

"Where should he lie?" Raine asked.

"His quarters should be suitable," Igallik replied.

Raine nodded, and after lifting Galian over his shoulder, he and Igallik walked calmly out of the High Temple.

23

Raine carried the comatose Galian into his room, and he was caught by surprise as Odin's silhouette, cast from the lone candle in Galian's room, appeared against the wall.

"Help me a bit," Raine called to Odin. "He's a little heavier than he looks."

Odin quickly leapt to Raine's side.

"Did it work?" he asked as he helped Raine place Galian down on the bed.

"Igallik thinks so."

"He'll be alright, though?" Odin tried to confirm.

"He should be," Igallik answered as he entered the room. "But he is going to need all of our help."

After eyeing the unconscious Galian, Igallik reached into a pouch on his belt and pulled out a large hourglass. The hourglass was crafted with a light blue glass and thick white ivory, and the sand grains within it were noticeably larger than what was typical.

"This will be a long fight," the head monk said as he set the hourglass down on the room's lone table. "It could last days, even weeks. Our task is to be as vigilant in this realm as Galian must be in the next."

Odin nodded, not even knowing what Igallik meant. Even though he had not agreed with the trial, he was eager to help his brother in any way he could.

"How do I help?" he asked.

"You watch," Igallik said as he pointed to the hourglass.

"Watch?" Odin repeated.

"In anticipation of Descent," Igallik explained, "your brother and I linked his soul to this hourglass. The purpose of that rite was to create a totem that allows us to clearly observe when Galian's soul will return to this realm."

Odin was still confused. "So, when the sand runs out, it means he's returning?"

"Quite the opposite," Igallik said. "If the sand runs out, it means he is never returning. It means time has run out on your brother. The sand in the hourglass represents Galian, and the hourglass's upper and lower bulbs represent our world and Animus Letum. If all the sand falls, it means your brother has died. It means he has completely fallen into the afterlife."

Odin had always known that time was the villain for all monks attempting Descent – the body cannot survive long without the soul – but to have a tangible measurement of Galian's life unnerved him.

As Odin fell silent, Raine tried his best to be Odin's voice.

"So what are we watching for?" he asked. "I mean, how do we know when he's coming back?"

"We are looking for a reversal of the fall," Igallik replied. "There is no doubt that sand will fall in Galian's fight – the hourglass will drain. Depending on his condition in the second realm, it may drain very quickly. However, the moment Galian's soul begins to return to our realm, the sand will stop falling and float back up into the upper bulb. The floating sand represents Galian's soul emerging back into our realm. It represents resurrection."

"So we just wait and watch?" Raine asked, suddenly understanding the powerlessness Odin was feeling.

Igallik nodded.

"I will take first watch," Odin volunteered.

Igallik was not surprised.

"I figured you would. If you are to watch him, I should inform you that there are a few severe but common side effects of Descent. Firstly, tremors and seizures indicate the separation of body and soul. They will look painful, but they are common. Secondly, blisters, heavy sweating, and the loss of Galian's skin pigment will occur. These symptoms will carry on for a few weeks, but as Galian's soul begins to return to this realm they will stop."

Igallik stroked his beard for a moment.

"I believe that is all. Anything else would be irregular."

Odin looked back to his brother, his fingers drumming an anxious beat against Galian's bed.

"He didn't rush into this, did he?" he asked. "He should be fine?"

"I'm sure your brother will return soon," Igallik said. "I have seen many monks attempt Descent. And I have seen a few become Seraphs. Odin, believe me when I say that your brother is the strongest monk to have ever attempted this trial."

With an airy breath, Odin let some of his anxiety dissipate.

"In these hours," Igallik continued, "Galian will be greatly tested. But I believe he should pass this test with relative ease."

Igallik looked to the hourglass and then brushed his hand through his beard.

"That being said, if at any point you think he is in grave danger, alert me as soon as possible. I will be in the High Temple."

"I will," Odin affirmed.

"Very well," Igallik said.

After another look to Galian, the head monk began to back towards the door.

"I will return at daybreak," he announced. "Let's hope for a good night."

Igallik seemed to bow, and after a slow turn, he disappeared into the night.

With the head monk gone, Raine leaned over Galian, examined the scar over his right eyebrow, and then turned back to Odin.

"I think he's going to be fine," he said. "You boys could wrestle greatness out of a shit pile."

Odin looked to the floor, and after shaking his head, he chose to confide in Raine.

"I don't feel good about this one," he confessed. "He's leapt into it, and to be honest, I've never felt further from him."

"Well, he is in Animus Letum," Raine pointed out.

"Not like that, Raine. He didn't even care that I asked him not to do it. He brushed me off like I didn't have a say."

"And you think you should," Raine realized.

"It's always been he and I," Odin said. "Always."

With a sigh, Odin's eyes fell to the floor. "It's not his fault, Raine. He wanted this for our entire lives, and I..."

Odin went silent. Dutifully, Raine lowered his own gaze and tried to catch his apprentice's eye.

"You what?"

"He told me that I was nothing more than a body," Odin said.

"He was heated," Raine replied.

Odin shook his head. "He was right. He amazes everyone, Raine. He is *the* Lyran. You saw what he did to the Scale. Galian grows stronger and wiser every day, and I don't. I do the same thing. I brawl in the Damns. I feel like he's leaving me behind – like he doesn't need me."

Raine scratched his temple as he thought.

"I get it," he said finally. "Probably more than most."

"Then what am I missing?" Odin asked. "How do I fix this?"

"With people like Galian," Raine said, "we have to concede a lot of ourselves. Stars like him, they don't know how to stop shining.

It's their nature. It's all they know. They brighten every place they go, and although they don't intend it, their brilliance casts us in the shadow."

Odin let out a deep breath. "That's how it feels," he said. "Like with or without me, he'd be doing exactly the same as he does. Like he doesn't need me."

"It hurts to think that way," Raine said, "but it's probably true. And it's not his fault, either. God built him to shine."

Odin was silent for a moment.

"So what do I do?" he asked. "I have to do something. I won't let myself resent him."

Raine shrugged – a shrug that said there was only one option. "We dig through the shit, Odin. It's the price we pay for being that close to greatness. Galian will shine – no matter what. But for him, we dig through the shit. It's our duty. Darkness will hunt him. They will try to make him suffer for no other reason than the way he was born. But for him, we fight. We wage the wars that the stars should not. We dig in the shit because a soul like Galian's shouldn't have to."

Odin slumped. "That's all?" he asked dejectedly.

"That's all," Raine confirmed. "But it *is* enough. Our job and duty – the one we must never abandon – is to let them shine. We take the hits for them. We take the beating. Trust me, Odin, even when we watch from the marsh, we get a pretty great view of the stars."

There was noticeable hurt in Raine's voice.

"You sound like you're remembering," Odin said.

"I am, mate."

Before Odin could reply, Raine bumped him with his shoulder and rose to his feet.

"I'd love to stay here with you," he said. "But a hell of a day deserves a hell of a night's rest. Take care of your brother, Odin. I'll be back tomorrow."

Odin nodded. "I will," he said. "I'll see you in the morning."

"Morning?" Raine said with a wry smile. "I intend to sleep past lunch."

"Don't worry, I'll send a wakeup call."

"You do," Raine said as he held up his fist, "and I'll brick you in the pouch."

"No wakeup call," Odin decided.

With a laugh, Raine patted Odin's shoulder and then left Galian's quarters.

With only Odin and Galian left, Odin sat and settled in for a long night.

As the night progressed, Odin kept very close watch over Galian's body and the hourglass. At times, Galian's arms would release a spastic punch, but otherwise, it seemed like a serene calm had encompassed the quiet monk. Similarly, the pace of the hourglass's sand-fall was incredibly slow and without change. Judging by the speed of the hourglass, it appeared that Galian had an abundance of time to complete Descent. As he acknowledged the hourglass's pace, Odin became less and less anxious about Descent. In fact, an excitement began to grow. Odin knew that the bounty of Descent was great, and the prospect of Galian inheriting a great power fascinated him. However, as Odin dreamt of Descent's reward, suddenly the pace of the hourglass surged, and with a violent jolt, Galian's body seized and began to showcase the great price of splitting body and soul. Galian's body, as if it were fighting suffocation, began to thrash into violent, painfully contorting bucks. Seeing blood leaking from Galian's ears, Odin quickly latched onto his brother and tried to outmuscle the seizures, but the fits were nearly impossible to wrestle. Instead, as Odin struggled to control Galian, he was repeatedly struck by the spastic releases of Galian's flailing limbs. As the welts began to amass on Odin's face, he began to yell furiously for help. In quick moments, three torches, and then Igallik and Raine, rushed into Galian's quarters. Even with their added strength, Galian could not be contained. Instead, the monks' attendance only added more witnesses to Galian's suffering. They were powerless – paralyzed by Galian's growing spasms and fading hourglass. Without entertaining any other course, the monks stayed with Galian all night. In hopes that it might better his condition, Igallik called on Wylak the herbalist. Wylak soaked Galian's body with potions and herbs, but it was to no avail. The seizures and sweating continued. Although refusing to say it aloud, the monks were in unanimous agreement that Galian was enduring hell.

Fortunately, hell seemed to prefer night. As the sun began to rise, the sand-fall of Galian's hourglass slowed, and a gentle breeze and calm returned to the monastery.

However, the weather would not argue the monks out of what they had seen. After have being rendered bystanders, Odin and the monks of the Throne's Eye could only acknowledge one truth: the first night of Galian's battle was an excruciating loss.

It would be the first night of many.

The Sons of Animus Letum

As days passed with Galian's body enduring Descent, the hourglass spoke nothing of resurrection. Instead, there were painful repetitions of the first night. Each day, after sunfall, the hourglass drained and Galian's body suffered. Morning brought ease from Galian's hell – his body and hourglass slowed – but any hope that daybreak instilled was thieved by dusk. For Galian, and all who tended to him, nighttime had become torture. Odin, who was at his brother's side each night, was the most distraught. The days of Galian's torment turned into weeks, and soon after, marked by the half-empty hourglass, the torture reached a month. Although never doubting his strength, the monks of the Throne's Eye began to fear for Galian. The quiet monk had already endured Descent longer than any other monk in the monastery's history.

Taken with worry and holding new information, Igallik called Odin to the High Temple. Odin was not ignorant of the monk's concern, nor did he resent it. He wished only that it would prove false. Gripping to hope and stubborn against his worry, Odin began his march to the High Temple.

Odin ascended the staircase and pushed through the massive bronze doors. Igallik was alone inside, and with his hand he invited Odin to join him at the Temple's front pew.

"How are you doing?" Igallik asked as Odin sat down.

Odin fidgeted in his seat. "I'm fine."

"This is a difficult time," Igallik said, "one where truth can be painful. But honesty should never be compromised."

"Okay," Odin said. "I'm afraid."

Igallik nodded. "I understand. And I wish I had good news for you. I wish I could lie to you now, but if I fail to give you the complete truth, you can never honestly weigh the situation. Do you understand?"

"I do."

"Let me begin by assuming you know that time is not on your brother's side."

"I am aware," Odin said.

"Then I will speak no more of it. But there is another matter I feel should reach your attention. A new voice has emerged from the second realm – a voice faithful to your father."

Odin was shocked. "My father?" he repeated. "I was told that those faithful to my father were being hunted in Animus Letum."

"That is true," Igallik said. "This voice, however, is operating in deep secrecy. As a name he has only offered us the letter V."

"Why is this important?" Odin asked.

"Because V has given us word about your brother."

Odin immediately turned his full attention to Igallik.

"What word?"

"V believes there is a specific reason your brother has not returned. It appears that Galian is using all his might to avoid the detection of Forneus."

Odin's posture crumpled, and as he exhaled deeply, the accompanying sound was more emotion than breath.

"Odin," the head monk solemnly reported, "V believes that Forneus is getting very close."

Futilely, Odin tried to argue against Igallik's news.

"It can't be like this," he started to ramble. "This is Galian we're talking about. *Galian*," he repeated. "He doesn't lose."

"Odin," the head monk said. "V is certain."

Odin keeled over. His brother's peril was the realization of his greatest fear. Descent had ripped Galian from his reach, and for the first time Odin was unable to protect him. Igallik tried to place his hand on Odin's shoulder, but Odin quickly shrugged it off and stood up from the pew.

"This was *your* plan," he scolded as he began to pace. "You asked him to do it. You should have known!" Odin yelled. "You should have known he wasn't ready!"

"You are right," Igallik said. "The blame is mine to bear. But there is hope. V suspects Forneus is still unaware of you and your brother's survival. It appears the Serpent only detects a relic of your father, not his actual son."

"What do you expect me to take from that?" Odin complained. "That's not hope."

"It's what we have," Igallik campaigned. "V has committed all efforts to return Galian to this realm. This is something we can hold onto."

"Forgive me if I'm skeptical," Odin said dryly. "You've given me next to nothing."

"You need to trust this, Odin. Fate doesn't roll dice. I believe we can rely on V."

Odin turned briskly to the door. "Is there anything else?"

"Yes," Igallik said sternly. "I'm ordering you to take the night off from Galian's side. You need rest."

"I don't and I won't," Odin said.

"You do and you will," Igallik countered. "I will watch Galian tonight. You will go and find Raine. Just rest until tomorrow."

The Sons of Animus Letum

Odin was not foolish enough to argue with the head monk. But with his anger still dominating his mind, he made a mocking bow and then stormed out of the Temple.

As Igallik watched Odin's departure, the head monk lingered in the High Temple for a long moment.

"V," he whispered, "we're counting on you."

As morning broke the next day, the weather was peaceful. The sky was clear and a light breeze gusted through the monastery. Odin awoke early and immediately set his steps to Galian's quarters.

Igallik was just exiting as Odin arrived.

"It was a bad night," the head monk said, "but a good morning, thus far."

The morning had not washed away Odin's anger.

"Alright," he said curtly. "I will watch him for the rest of the day."

"Very well," Igallik agreed. "For now, I will be found in the infirmary."

Odin paused for a moment. "Why's that?" he asked, remembering that every time Igallik had finished a watch, he had immediately set his steps to the High Temple.

Igallik momentarily reserved his answer, conceding it to a regretful shake of his head.

"I have an idea," he said finally. "It's one that I'm not entirely set on, but give me a few days."

With tension still lingering between them, Odin nodded to the head monk, and the two went their separate ways.

Odin surveyed his brother's body as he entered the room. Galian's body was badly blistered, and the pigment of his skin appeared as if it had been drained to a pale white. Although he hated the painful routine, Odin leaned over and investigated the hourglass. The night had stolen even more time from Galian. The hourglass's upper bulb was less than a sixth full. With the surges of sand-fall it was impossible to determine exactly how much time Galian had, but if the established pace continued, the hourglass would be empty in roughly six days.

With his mind burdened by that truth, Odin watched Galian until midday. Odin's thoughts were heavy with the conversation he had had with Raine a month prior. Raine had said that for the stars we must often take a beating. For them to shine, we must wrestle in the dirt. Odin had believed the fight was waged with weapons. He didn't realize that they were waged with a heart.

Struggling in such a battle, Odin found himself at his brother's side knelt in prayer – not to one god, but to the kings of the Lyran House.

"I am not one to beg," he began as he looked skywards, "and I pray that makes me more worthy of your help. But this," he argued of Galian's suffering, "leaves me no option but bent knee. I am told that you are great. I am told that you are gods. My adopted home bombards me with the legends and stories of our bloodline. To be honest, I don't really care for the stories. It is very difficult for me to take pride in triumphs that I had no hand in. It is very hard for me to feel a connection to men that I have never met. That being said, I do not doubt the might of the Lyrans. I have witnessed it. I believe in our bloodline because of Galian. Surely, you see yourselves in his greatness. He proves to me that you existed. But now, I need more... from you. I am not offering to barter. I am offering a sacrifice. I am begging you: steal all powers of my life, even breath, and with them aid my brother's battle. Damn me," Odin begged. "Throw me to the wolves. I will suffer the darkness of one thousand years, as long as a star can hang high once more. Please, if ever there was a time, prove to me that the Lyrans are just."

As Odin's hands – in fear of unworthy appeal – refused to unfasten from their plea, a familiar voice sounded from the door to Galian's quarters.

"If both of you fall comatose," the voice said, "I really won't have any reason to be here."

As Odin turned, he was met with a set of strikingly dark eyes.

"Usis!" Odin cried.

"Good to see you, too," Usis grinned.

Odin quickly rose to his feet and offered his hand in welcome.

"A handshake?" Usis marvelled. "You have grown up."

As Odin grinned, Usis ushered Odin's hand away, and then wrapped his arm around Odin's shoulder.

"It's been a long time, brother. A handshake simply won't do."

"Perhaps," Odin replied as he grabbed Usis's wrist, "you'd prefer this."

With abrupt torque, Odin wrenched Usis's arm back.

"And the skills are sharp," Usis smiled. "But not sharp enough."

With a quick twist, Usis reversed Odin's grip, and sent his old friend tumbling to the floor.

"Not too bad," Usis said as Odin collected himself. "Just not better than me."

Odin, still the student, shed a respectful nod to Usis and then rose to his feet.

"When did you return?" he asked

"Only moments ago," Usis replied.

"Have you met with Igallik?"

"Just briefly," Usis answered. "He informed me of Galian's condition."

"It's been over a month," Odin reported. "It was supposed to be a few weeks at most."

Usis and Odin took a seat at Galian's bed.

"Don't be afraid," Usis said. "Fear is seldom rational and almost always a behaviour. Praying, as you just were, is a far better habit."

"You almost sound wise," Odin joked.

"I've learned a lot. The last three years have been the gravest of my life. But in pain and in loss, I have found new purpose."

"So the mission was a success?" Odin asked.

"It was a good start. But my work is far from over."

Usis leaned over Galian and studied the scar that had been left from Vinculum Imletalis.

"I heard whispers of Haren's treachery," he said. "Many in certain circles believe she was turned."

"And what do you believe?" Odin asked.

Usis traced his hand over Galian's scar and then examined Odin's.

"It is hard to condone the danger she put you two in. I strongly doubt she was an agent of Forneus. But if the question is raised of whether her mind had been corrupted, I offer no more evidence than your two scars."

"There has been no sign of her since," Odin informed, "no path to follow, not even a trace of my father's crown."

"Whatever Haren has done was accomplished with no lack of foresight," Usis said. "We will hear nothing of her, until she decides it is time. But I trust," Usis predicted, "that we will hear from her again."

Odin nodded.

As the two continued to talk until dusk, Usis regaled Odin with tales of his adventure, and with ease, the great amity between them was recovered. After a couple of days, however, Usis's presence in Galian's quarters became less and less frequent. For the most part

Usis remained in his old quarters. It was unusual, but Odin chose not to encroach on the time and space that Usis had made for himself.

With Galian gone, Odin was just happy that a brother was near.

24

After Usis's return, Galian's physical condition had neither improved nor degraded. The only measure of change was the ominous hourglass. If the hourglass's sand-fall remained consistent, it promised a haunting deadline: Galian had two days. Unrelentlessly, Odin had been at his brother's side for each moment. At the close of a particularly bad night for Galian, fatigue stole Odin from his wakefulness, and the young monk fell asleep.

When he woke, the sun was emerging on the horizon, and Igallik and Palis, the Order monk who had saved Odin during the Scale battle, sat quietly next to him.

"I must have dozed off," Odin apologized as he wiped his eyes.

"No need to apologize," Igallik said. "Take a moment to wake, and let us know when you're focused. Palis and I have something important to discuss with you."

Odin nodded in understanding, and then rose to his feet and shook and stretched off the sleep. After a few moments he sat back down, and invited the Order monks' counsel.

"Let me not mince words," Igallik started. "This issue is best served directly. We have received more word from V: more word on your brother."

"What word?" Odin asked.

"As V first suspected, Forneus was only aware of an energy in Animus Letum similar to your father's. Forneus, at this point, is still unaware that you and your brother exist. He does not recognize your brother's energy as anything more than a relic of your father's reign."

"He hasn't investigated?" Odin asked.

"As of yet, no." Igallik answered. "But I will not underestimate the Serpent King's curiosity. He will investigate, very soon."

Odin's eyes lowered. But his moment of grieving would be short. He understood the urgency of the dilemma and could not condone wasted time.

"So what do we do?" he asked.

"It's not what *we* do," Palis stepped in. "It's what I do."

Odin failed to understand the implication, and he looked at Palis quizzically.

"But you're wounded."

"Not just wounded," Palis corrected, "dying."

"I don't understand," Odin confessed.

Palis smiled. "Allow me to explain. Our advantage in this situation is that Forneus is unaware of its gravity. If an actual relic of your father's, like the mighty staff your mother brought to this realm, could enter the afterlife, we could buy your brother more time. The staff is an energy Forneus would instantly recognize, and using it, we could lead Forneus's attention away from your brother."

"How, though?" Odin wondered.

"Like I said, Odin, I'm dying. What I am saying is that I will gladly surrender my last few days, for an earlier and more purposeful death. I will die and complete this deed. I will take the staff with me to the afterlife and lead Forneus's attention away from your brother."

Odin shook his head in disbelief of Palis's proposal.

"You'd do that?" he challenged, "understanding what Forneus will do to you if he finds you with the staff?"

Palis smiled again. "Do you know what position I hold in the Order?" he asked.

Odin nodded. "You are the Mercy totem."

"Very much so," Palis said. "It is my speciality. I have delved very far into its truth, further than most go in any direction."

Odin didn't follow. "What are you saying?" he asked.

"I am saying," Palis said, "that I understand much about mercy. And my greatest discovery about its power is that mercy is not just an act, it is a state of mind. It is not just an event. It is a way to see the world."

"And what are you seeing?" Odin asked.

"A chance to prevent innumerable deaths," Palis replied. "A chance to be merciful to the souls that haven't even suffered yet. I am volunteering to get your brother back, because I expect that one day, you and the Forge will reclaim the throne. I am doing this so we will have a chance."

The words were daunting, but even with their gravity, Odin was compelled to address a pressing issue.

"What I don't understand is why you have come to me like this," he said. "If you are sure, then that is enough for me."

Igallik was first to speak. "There is one hitch to this plan, Odin, one that I feel you need to be aware of. If the staff crosses back and Forneus were to claim it, the Serpent King's power would grow immensely. His malice would delve even deeper into the afterlife, and there would be even greater suffering for the people of Animus Letum. That," Igallik forewarned, "is the risk we run."

Odin rested his head in his palm, taking time to weigh the consequences of Palis's proposed sacrifice.

"And you expect me to make this choice," he realized.

Palis spoke solemnly. "Odin, I need no one but you to make this call. This is a choice that affects your destiny more than anyone's. I just ask that you remember what I have said. Remember that a great part of mercy is extending it to the people who haven't even suffered yet. Mercy is a foresight, Odin. People are going to suffer regardless of which decision you make. The point is, you can decide if the suffering ends."

Palis then pointed to the hourglass. "Time is ticking," he said. "If I were you, I'd make this call as soon as possible. I have learned, my friend, that you must never miss an opportunity to kick dirt in the devil's eyes. Now is as great a chance as any."

With a smile, Palis rose from his seat. He was quickly joined by Igallik. As Palis limped to the exit, Igallik offered Odin a final counsel.

"Believe me, Odin, I understand the weight on your mind. I will give you the day to consider. Think it over and know that whatever your decision may be, we will stand behind you."

Odin managed a nod, and after the Order monks had left, he sat quiet and alone at his brother's side.

He would do so all morning.

As he watched Galian, he knew he needed him back. But how could he justify the price of Galian's resurrection when its cost carried the potential of the harming millions? As the sun rose to midday, Odin left Galian's quarters. There was no agenda to his departure, but without realizing it, Odin's steps soon led him to Usis's door. Odin knocked and waited for Usis in the hopes that his old friend would have some insight. But minutes passed with no answer. Resolving to wait, Odin leaned his back against Usis's door and used the solitude to deliberate. However, even as the hours passed with Odin's debate, there was no sign of Usis.

As evening fell on the monastery, Odin, drained but decided from a day of consideration, elected to take his verdict to the High Temple. As much as he hated it, Odin had his answer for Palis and Igallik.

The staff would not cross back.

Just as Odin began his ascent of the High Temple staircase, a firm hand fell across his shoulder.

"You're in a daze, mate," Raine joked. "I thought I'd taught you to be more aware than that. You ought to have seen me coming from thirty yards."

"Sorry, Raine," Odin said. "I just have a lot on my mind."

"I know you do, mate," Raine said. "The Order monks let me know what they've asked of you. And I'd guess with you heading up these stairs, you've made your decision."

"The staff is not crossing back," Odin said. "Galian would make the same call."

Raine thought about it for a moment. "He might, but then again he might not."

Odin shook his head.

"I need him back. As much as I want anything, I want Palis to do this. But I can't justify what it brings. The hourglass still says two days. Galian can still do this without sending the staff back."

"Can I tell you what I'd do?" Raine asked.

"Please."

"I'd send the staff back," Raine said. "And let me tell you why: first and foremost, your dad sacrificed himself for you and your brother. And do you think the wisest king of the afterlife didn't know Animus Letum would fall on hard times because of it. I'm telling you, Odin, you owe your dad this one."

"One life is not worth millions," Odin argued.

"What if that one life could save millions more?" Raine asked. "We've talked about this," the old warrior reminded him. "This is the time when we have to dig through the shit."

Odin slumped. "I figured you meant in battle, with swords and shields."

"I did mean a battle," Raine said, "the fiercest one there is: the battle inside you. People are going to suffer because of what you do today – either way. If you send the staff back, people are going to be broken beyond repair. Worse still, if Forneus claims the staff and grows in power, every soul that he tortures will be a weight upon your soul. It is a truth that should not be avoided. The weight of hell will be on you. And it makes sense that it should be. The price of digging in the shit is that we get dirty – a filth beyond physical."

"Why would I choose that?" Odin asked. "Why would I surrender my soul to that?"

"For your brother," Raine replied. "You'll dirty your soul with countless deaths, so that Galian can shine once more."

As Odin's head sunk, Raine remained assertive.

"You have a chance to be the catalyst," he said, "the soul who would not break – even under the weight of hell. Animus Letum is going to bleed regardless of what you do. But with your brother, you can stop the bleeding. You're destined to, Odin. With Galian and the Forge you can salvage the afterlife."

"What if I can't stop the bleeding?" Odin asked. "What if the best I can offer is to limit Forneus's power?"

Raine looked sternly at Odin. "You're wrong to assume that's your best."

Odin began to run his hands through his blonde hair, and then, with a defeated exhalation, he stood and looked up to the High Temple.

"Well?" Raine prodded.

"There's still two days." Odin said.

"So you're not going to let Palis do it? After all that?"

"Still thinking," Odin said.

With another deep breath, Odin turned and began his ascent of the stairs.

"You better make your call!" Raine shouted after him.

As Odin ascended out of earshot, Raine shook his head.

"Do the right thing, mate. You're too important to be selfless."

With one thousand thoughts weighing him down, Odin reached the High Temple. He slipped quietly through the bronze doors, and as he sauntered into the Temple, he remained unnoticed by Palis and Igallik who were at the altar.

Palis had removed the top of his robe, and Igallik was re-bandaging the wound on Palis's back.

Seeing the Order monks in such a private moment, Odin sat back and chose not to interrupt.

Palis's wound was grave.

"How long do you think?" Palis asked the head monk.

"Optimistically?" Igallik said. "Two weeks. This wound will kill you very soon."

"We all must go sometime," Palis said with a strange smile.

As Igallik pulled the bandage tight around his back, Palis's face wrenched into a grimace.

"You know," he grunted, "this isn't a fair fight."

"In what sense?" Igallik asked.

"All odds are against us. Doesn't that worry you?"

"Of course," Igallik said. "But the truth is, our team still holds the most powerful piece. You must realize that Odin has no idea how powerful he and his brother are. They are a hurricane, Palis."

"A hurricane?" Palis repeated.

Igallik smiled, the great wisdom in his eyes beaming just a little brighter.

"Under the right pressure and circumstance," he said, "they will grow to be unstoppable. Together, they will crush even Forneus."

Palis laughed. "I'd love to watch."

But with a sigh, Palis's smile left his face. "Odin needs to trust this," he said. "If he says no and this wound kills me, I will die with only regret."

"There will be no need," Odin said from the back.

Palis and the head monk turned back to Odin.

"You've reached your verdict?" Palis presumed.

"I have," Odin replied.

Igallik tilted his gaze. "And?"

"Let's kick some dirt in the devil's eyes," Odin said. "Whenever you're ready."

25

After Odin's decision, Igallik went quickly to work on preparing what was needed for Palis's sacrifice. As two fervent hours passed, Galian's fading hourglass suggested that about only one day remained. Acknowledging the time, Igallik hurried himself, *The Book of the Eterna*, and the mighty staff of Serich into Galian's quarters.

Palis, Odin, and Raine were waiting.

"The moment has arrived," Igallik announced as he entered the room.

Palis nodded.

"I trust you were able to reach V?" he asked.

"I was," Igallik answered. "V will keep Forneus busy for a while, but our window is not large."

"I'm a small man," Palis joked. "Even a small window will suffice."

Exhaling deeply, Palis seemed to collect himself, and after a series of small nods, he rose and walked into the center of the candles that had been set up for the rite.

Odin quickly leapt up and grabbed Palis's arm.

"You will never be forgotten," Odin said. "Our fates have been bound forever. Whatever I accomplish is built on what you do now."

Palis bowed to the young monk.

"Let my last words to you be these," he said. "Courage and faith. If you can possess these rare graces, no victory will ever evade you."

Palis smiled to Odin for the last time, and then turned to Raine, letting the old warrior know that the time had come.

"Alright, mate," Raine said as he drew his sword.

Igallik glanced quickly at the emptying hourglass. He handed the mighty staff to Palis and then began to search for a particular page in *The Book of the Eterna*. After he had reached the page, Igallik nodded to the Mercy totem, and the small Order monk dropped to a knee.

As Palis held the mighty staff and prepared himself for the sacrifice, Igallik began to recite from *The Book of the Eterna*. The words were very much like the words Haren had recited during Vinculum Imletalis – they were throaty and seemed somehow ancient. As the rite proceeded, Odin was unsure what to expect. With the three senior monks committed to the sacrifice, he imagined that a great amount of energy would encompass the room. He imagined that the sounds and sights would rival Vinculum Imletalis. Strangely though, except for the delivery of Igallik's words into the night air, there was no perceivable change in the state of Galian's quarters.

With a sibilant whisper, Igallik's versing came to a halt, and the head monk smiled to Palis.

"Godspeed, brother," he said.

Palis nodded to his old friend, and as he took in a deep breath, he hugged his arms around the mighty staff. As Palis's face winced, complete silence overtook Galian's room. Odin could hear nothing – not Igallik, not Raine, not even his own breath. It was a haunting quiet. As the Lyran relied on his vision, he watched Palis's chest relax, and as the Mercy totem let out his breath, it blew out of him like a morning breeze. With no audible sounds, the curtains and candles began to dance against the wind, and with a flare of fire, violet flames sprang from the base of the staff. The fire wrapped around the weapon like a purple snake. Palis bowed his head, and the fire began to spread around his small frame too. With the rope of purple flame burning around the Mercy totem, Igallik caught Raine's attention and gave the old warrior an affirming nod. Raine nodded back, and with precision, he drew his blade back like a bow and then launched his sword forward, piercing through Palis's spine with one powerful stab. As Odin watched the eerily quiet rite, he had to block his eyes as the fiery rope flared into a blinding flash. As Odin lowered his sleeve, the fire had extinguished, and there were plumes of spiralling smoke lingering in the exact form of Palis's silhouette. Igallik approached. He wafted his hand through the clouds, and after a few swings, the smoke spread and dissipated, leaving no trace of Palis nor the staff.

Sound returned to Galian's quarters, but in honour of the Mercy totem, Odin, Igallik, and Raine chose to remain in silence.

Finally, after a long moment, Igallik spoke.

"It is done."

"Is there any way to know if it is working?" Odin asked.

"Once again, we can only watch the hourglass. It is the sole window into Galian's condition."

Raine shook his head in frustration. "This waiting game is killing me."

"I know," Igallik said, "but it is the only one we can play."

Raine turned to Odin, but before he spoke, he saw that Odin was already seated next to his brother, intently surveying the hourglass. The image hurt the old warrior's heart, but as he began to seat himself, Igallik cancelled Raine's action with a shake of his head.

"Leave them be," the head monk whispered.

After a final survey of Odin and Galian, Raine nodded and joined Igallik in departure.

Throughout the night, Odin's eyes did not break away from the hourglass. The only piece of Odin not present in Galian's room was the pleading and bleeding prayer he had sent to the fallen kings of the Lyran House. In his desperation, Odin had sought a covenant from any deity he could imagine. He had pledged his soul if it meant his brother would return. However, as night began to bow to morning, nothing had changed: the hourglass and the heart of its closest observer were still fading. In care and curiosity, nearly every monk of the Throne's Eye deliberately passed by Galian's room. Their gesture, although small, was to be present if needed. The sentiment was held by all.

One monk, whose heart was invested more than most, soon arrived in Galian's quarters. As Usis entered the room and caught Odin's attention, he was instantly under fire.

"Where have you been?" Odin demanded.

"I've been busy," Usis defended himself.

It was a futile defence.

Odin's eyes scolded his old friend. "Galian is dying." He seared. "I'm terrified. And you were busy?"

"I'm here now," Usis said. "Trust me, I came when I could."

"For the finale?" Odin cried. "You came too late, Usis. Galian is losing."

Usis quickly recognized Odin's fatigue.

"You're weary from watching this hourglass," he said. "Do not add undue fear to this dilemma."

Tears had begun to well in Odin's eyes. "There is barely a chance," he wept. "Usis, I'm breaking..."

Usis's eyes looked sternly at Odin's.

"You know Galian's heart greater than anyone does," he reminded. "Do not sully that privilege with fear. This is Galian: he does not lose."

"You don't think I'm holding to that?" Odin replied. "Every piece of my heart believes he can rise. But my eyes and mind are tortured by that hourglass."

"There is still time," Usis said. "Do not give up on your brother. Believe in him."

"I can't endure this," Odin said weakly. "I can't watch anymore. I can't watch my brother die."

"You won't have to," Usis promised. "Trust me, he will return."

Odin dropped his head and wiped the tears from his eyes.

"I'd be lost without him," he said. "You know I'd be lost."

"We all would," Usis said. "But we are not going to mourn a death that has not happened. We must be patient now. We must watch and pray."

Odin was ashamed of his own weakness. As he looked up through his tears, his body was shaking, trembling with the fear of losing his best friend.

However, even after the two month fray, Usis knew that Odin was not empty. Usis knew that within Odin, there was one last, invincible strand of faith that could never surrender his brother.

"Odin," he said sternly, "there are few times in our lives when one choice can define us forever. Now is such a time. Whether your heart beats bravely or with fear – whether you master fate or become a victim to it – is a choice you make in this moment. You choose courage now," Usis promised, "and you choose courage for eternity. I beg you, announce your heart to this worst of hells. Believe in your brother… believe for both of you."

Odin was even more ashamed. It felt more so than ever that he was forsaking Galian. But Usis was right – there was a piece of Odin that would never surrender his brother.

After a few slow strides, Odin seated himself next to Galian.

"Till the end," he said as he looked back to Usis. "I'll fight till the end."

Usis smiled. "Hope suits you much better," he said.

With a very composed breath, Usis sat himself on the other side of Galian's bed.

"As for you," he whispered as he patted Galian's chest, "we all know this realm suits you much better. It's time to come home."

With their hearts hanging in the balance, Usis and Odin became quiet, sitting still as they prayed for a resurrection.

However, time was a callous villain. Like blood dripping from a fatal wound, the sand of Galian's hourglass fell with an agenda of death. Excruciating seconds turned to torturous hours, and as the hourglass dwindled to its last minutes, Odin had been reduced to sheer panic. He could not stay still. His fear had robbed him of any calmness, and in his frenzy, he paced wildly throughout Galian's quarters. In small repeated breaks, Odin halted his feverish gait and invited an update from Usis. In each instance, Usis reported no change to the hourglass, and Odin's strides returned to frenetic pacing.

Amid the uneasy sound of Odin's footsteps, Usis remained calm. However, as his eyes remained fixed on the hourglass, he became pained by an inarguable truth: one that he was burdened to report.

"There's one minute left," he announced.

Odin's steps were instantly halted. His breath became punishing, and he keeled over as if his air was being throttled from him.

"Deep breaths," Usis coached. "Come on, Odin, power through."

Against his great distress, Odin knew Usis was right. He could not abandon Galian. With a defiant surge, Odin composed his wheezing gasps, and as he regained his breath, he knelt next to his dying brother.

Only seconds remained.

"Galian," he promised. "I will never desert you. Please, don't desert me. Please, finish this. Come back…"

As Odin clutched desperately to his last hopes, his eyes looked pleadingly to the hourglass. And in that moment, in that devastating fragment of time, Odin's heart was ripped to pieces.

The last grain of sand had fallen from the hourglass's upper bulb.

Odin and Usis were rapt in heartbreak. Words meant nothing. Actions were useless. Instead, Galian's room was drowned in the painful, soundless score of tragedy. As Odin finally spoke, it was as if his soul were being expelled in one torturous, repeating phrase.

"I'm lost," he wept. "I'm lost."

Usis knew there was no consolation for Odin. He looked scornfully back to the hourglass, but suddenly his heart flared with hope.

"Odin!" he shouted. "Look!"

As Odin immediately turned to Galian's hourglass and he surveyed the timepiece, his eyes grew wide in astonishment. The last grain had not touched down. It was floating in the hourglass's lower bulb just barely above the hill of fallen sand.

It was disputing with nature. Slowly, it started to rise.

"He's done it!" Usis cried. "He's coming back! He's won!"

With only joy, Odin's head fell hard into his palm.

"Thank you," he whispered to Palis, the Lyrans, and any who aided in Galian's victory.

Galian was returning.

As the sand in Galian's hourglass began to ascend quickly into the upper bulb, word of Galian's triumph flooded throughout the monastery. The monks of the Throne's Eye were overjoyed. A Seraph was arriving.

As one more day passed, Galian's state became recognizably improved. The blisters on his skin healed, his breathing was calm and without distress, and his body was regaining its proper mass. Even the weather was indicative of Galian's victory.

In the warm sun and calm wind that bathed the monastery, the monks could not help but to stoke the flames of a burning question: what strength would Galian awaken with? It was a fact that each monk having returned from Descent had awoken with a great power. Acknowledging Galian's already formidable strength, the monks of the Throne's Eye could not guess but only wait to see what power would emerge with Galian's resurrection.

Midnight passed on the following day, and as a heavy fog settled onto the monastery, some of the Throne's Eye monks sat around a burning fire pit. After a few failed attempts, the monks finally convinced Odin to leave Galian's side and join them at the pit.

"Just for a moment," Odin had said. "I want to be with him when he wakes."

As Odin sat down at the fire, Galian's amounting triumph and, more specifically, what power he would reap in his resurrection were under discussion.

Raeman, the only Order monk present, was advocating what he believed would be Galian's new power.

"Healing," he declared.

In good fun, a few monks waved off the notion.

"We want something bigger," one of them laughed.

Raeman broke into a smile. "Bigger? I don't know if Galian could manage much bigger. We all saw what he did to the Scale."

Craine, a Torch monk who helped with the rearing of the monastery's horses, saw it differently.

"Healings been done before," he said. "I bet it's flight."

"Now that would be something," Raeman smiled.

With curiosity, Craine turned to Odin.

"What do you figure?" he asked.

Odin angled his head for a moment and then broke into a smile.

"I just wish he'd be able to talk."

Craine and the other monks laughed, but it was clear to them that Odin only wished for his brother to wake up.

The small group of monks continued on into the early hours of the morning. As the moon shone its dim light through the quickly moving clouds, and as the fog moved through the courtyard, an eerie cold shook Raeman. He was about to dismiss it, but a figure suddenly emerged into the firelight and flooded the burning fire with a bucket of water. The monks surrounding the fire hurriedly turned in alertness to the figure, but were shocked when they saw his face.

Odin gasped. "Galian?"

Galian quickly looked each of the monks in their eyes and drew his index finger to his lips to encourage their silence. The stunned monks managed to quiet themselves, and then watched, baffled, as Galian spread his hand over the smoke emitting from the doused fire. By Galian's will, the smoke from the coals spread in thickness and in range until a wall of smoke surrounded the monks. All visibility beyond six feet was lost. As the monks all began to wonder aloud about what was happening, Galian was quick to quiet them. Using the smoke to blend into the courtyard fog, Galian led the small congregation against the corner of two walls running adjacent to Throne's Eye front gates. Galian used his power to shape the smoke into a slightly transparent wall in front of him and the other monks.

For a long moment, Galian held the monks there in suspense. Finally, Odin whispered to his brother.

"What's happening?"

"There's an attack coming," Galian replied.

"How do you know?"

Each of the monks watched eagerly for Galian's answer.

"Because," Galian revealed, "I can see the future."

26

As the monks waited, Galian handed Odin a small leather-bound book.

"What's this for?" Odin whispered.

Galian placed his hand over Odin's heart. "Place it here."

Odin did as he was told and tucked the book into his breast pocket. As the monks held their silence, they were soon able to hear the sound of footsteps outside the Throne's Eye front gates.

"Sounds like fifteen to twenty men," Odin assessed in a softened voice.

"But they'll need someone to let them in," Raeman whispered back.

"Just wait," Galian signed.

The monks were deadly silent until Galian pointed his hand to the center of the Throne's Eye courtyard.

"There."

The monks watched transfixed as the silhouette of a monk appeared through the smoke screen. The tall and slender silhouette moved slowly through the courtyard, striding calmly toward the Throne's Eye gate.

"A traitor," Craine gasped.

The silhouette reached the gates and began to speak with the men on the other side.

"Remember the plan," the silhouette advised. "No added casualties. We take what we came for, and we only kill the targets."

Odin knew the voice but refused to place it.

After receiving the acknowledgment of the men outside the monastery walls, the silhouette unlocked the gates and began to draw them open. With one motion of his hand, Galian dispersed the smoke around him and the other monks and left the traitor and his partners robbed of their desired stealth.

"Usis!" Raeman growled.

Usis turned in alarm, his hand already wrapped around the hilt of his sword.

Odin was numb.

As Odin watched Usis's men draw their weapons, he was frozen. Odin fought to ready himself for a fray, but seeing Usis as a threat had thrown him off.

"Put the blades down!" Usis ordered his accomplices. "There is no need for bloodshed."

The men refused.

"God damn it!" Usis yelled. "Put the blades down!"

Odin needed to be answered.

"Usis," he cried, "what is this?"

"Shut up, Odin," Usis snapped. "This has nothing to do with you."

"How does it not?"

Uninterested in their leader's squabble with Odin, Usis's men tried to draw the monks into open combat.

"We'll kill them all," they shouted.

Usis, however, was steadfast in his mission.

"We only kill the targets," he commanded.

With a threatening eye, Usis turned his attention back to the Throne's Eye monks.

"There is only one target here."

"And which one of us is that?" Raeman demanded.

Usis looked at the Order monk with cold eyes.

"You, Raeman."

Raeman was shocked. "After what I… what we, your brothers, have given you?"

"It's not what was given to me," Usis shot back. "It's what was taken."

A heartbroken Odin looked back to his brother. Galian expressed a woeful and understanding nod, but with sharp eye movements, he encouraged Odin to look to the ground at his foot. Odin glanced down and saw a small blade floating at his ankle.

"You're mad!" Raeman yelled at Usis.

Usis's eyes and voice turned irate.

"Do not feign your ignorance!" he raged. "You know god damn well what was taken from me!"

"And you'll kill us all? Each of us who acted that day?"

"Yes I will," Usis said coldly. "Right now."

With his men behind him, Usis began to advance on Raeman.

Galian looked to Odin to affirm the timing; Odin nodded, and Galian used his power to float the small blade up into Odin's grip. As Usis walked in front of him, Odin sliced the blade in front of Usis's face, and then held it pointed to his throat.

"God damn it, Odin," Usis cursed. "I do not want to hurt you."

"Nor do I," Odin fired back. "But another of your steps promises my action."

Odin tightened his grip on the dagger.

Unimpressed, Usis stared into Odin's eyes.

"You're forcing my hand, brother," he said.

"No, Usis," Odin mourned. "You have forced mine."

Usis hated that Odin was present. His worlds had collided. Nevertheless, Usis could not allow Odin to stop him. He was too close.

"I do not believe you will act," Usis said as he pressed his neck into Odin's blade.

"Try me," Odin invited.

Usis continued to advance on the blade until blood ran down the side of his neck.

With tears welling, Odin's eyes were begging Usis to yield, but Usis would not comply.

"I'm sorry," Usis said. "You shouldn't have been here."

With a quick swat, Usis displaced the blade from his neck and turned Odin's arm back. As Usis held Odin in submission, he ordered his men into action.

The men quickly sprang upon the monks of the Throne's Eye. Galian used his power to elevate five of Usis's men into the air and then slam them powerfully into the Throne's Eye wall. Even with Galian's added strength, the monks were heavily disadvantaged. Bravely, they employed their skills in Raeman's defence. But their disadvantage proved too much, and each monk, including Galian, was quickly subdued. With hate brimming in his dark eyes, Usis handed Odin to one of his men and approached Raeman.

The Justice totem, alone and at the mercy of Usis, would prove to be no match for the traitor. Raeman cried in agony as Usis rained down ferocious blows onto his head and torso. Even as the helpless and beaten Raeman fell to the courtyard floor, Usis refused to relent.

"He is your brother, goddammit!" Odin screamed.

Usis ignored Odin's cries, and with ferocity he continued to thrash the Justice totem.

Finally, satisfied with the damage he had dealt, Usis drew a dagger from his belt.

Raeman managed to wipe the blood from his battered face and look up at Usis.

"You're lost," he wept. "You're lost and you don't even see it.'

"That's a matter of perspective," Usis asserted. "Not all of us see by the Throne's Eye."

With a salivating grin, Usis drew the dagger back to strike Raeman down. However, with a desperate shove, Odin broke free from his captor and charged his shoulder into Usis's back. As Usis jolted from the force, he dropped the dagger, and with a quick stab, Odin snatched the dagger from mid-air. After altering his grip, Odin cocked back the blade and poised himself into a defensive position.

The man who had been holding Odin tried to reclaim his grip, but Usis's eyes shot down his ambition.

"I will handle this," Usis said sternly.

With arrogance, the traitor turned his eye to Odin

"Heroic," he assessed of Odin's actions, "but futile."

With his eyes locked onto Odin's, Usis wrapped his hands around Raeman's skull, pulled back his head, and then snapped his neck.

"No!" Odin screamed.

As Raeman's lifeless body fell to the courtyard floor, Odin began to scream even more wildly.

"God damn it, Usis! Look at what you've done! We can never go back!"

Usis's stride turned to a fervent pace.

"You don't know what I know!" he yelled back.

Usis was trying to hold to his composure, but his voice began to break with emotion.

"You weren't supposed to be here," he cried. "I'm not the villain."

"The blood is on your hands," Odin ruled. "You did this."

Usis's pacing came to an abrupt halt.

"No!" he screamed at Odin. "The Throne's Eye did this!"

Odin shook his head in disbelief.

"You *are* mad. You've lost it."

"You're wrong, Odin," Usis said coldly. "You don't know what this monastery has done to me."

"What could it have done to justify this?" Odin screamed. "You tell me!"

"They killed my parents!" Usis cried.

Odin's neck craned backwards. "I don't believe that," he said. "We protect, we don't destroy. The Metus Sane killed your parents. You heard the story just as I did."

"I heard," Usis agreed. "My mistake was that I believed. It was the Throne's Eye monks who killed my parents."

"That's a lie," Odin yelled.

Usis shook his head in frustration.

"I don't care what you believe. We are done."

"You don't mean that," Odin said.

"Continue to hold that dagger," Usis promised, "and my indifference to you will be proven quite clear."

"This dagger," Odin coaxed as he held the blade in the air. "Oh no, Usis, this one's staying with me."

"Fine," Usis decided.

Usis promptly drew another dagger from his belt and launched it at the dagger in Odin's hand. The aim was to displace the weapon from Odin's grip, but in the commotion, Usis's usually deadly accurate pitch missed its mark. The dagger pierced Odin's chest, and Odin fell hard to the courtyard floor.

Usis's eyes could not hide his alarm.

"Odin!" he screamed.

His panicked eyes scanned for any movement in Odin's body, but there was none.

The men with Usis began to sense the panic in their leader.

"Somethin' special 'bout that one," one of them said sarcastically. "You need a moment?"

Usis had to quickly make clear his allegiance. He couldn't go back. With tears in his eyes, he turned emphatically to the remaining Throne's Eye monks.

"Let us be quite clear," he raged. "I am the death of the Throne's Eye. Who of you will rise to stop me?"

There was silence in the courtyard until a voice broke from the heart of the monastery.

"I'll take that challenge, mate."

Usis, his men, and the monks of the Throne's Eye turned back to see Raine, Igallik, and fifty monks standing in the center of the courtyard; twenty of the monks were armed with bows.

"A little late," Usis ridiculed his old mentor. "Two are already down."

"Not quite," Odin corrected as he rose to his feet and pulled the dagger from the book Galian had given him.

Usis frustratingly looked to Odin, and then back to Raine.

"You'll not win the war," he vowed to all the monks within earshot. "I will deliver you all to dust. This night is but one leading to your ultimate demise."

"Oh," Raine taunted, "you're leaving?"

"There will be another time for us to settle this," Usis pledged to his old mentor.

The Sons of Animus Letum

"Oh, no," Raine corrected. "We," he said as he motioned to the fifty monks behind him, "intend to finish this tonight."

With deadly eyes, Raine raised his hand into the air, and the archers drew back their arrows.

"Your advantage is only in numbers," Usis asserted. "Sleight of foot belongs to me."

"I still like our odds," Raine replied.

With that, the Aeris dropped his hand, and the archers released their arrows into their targets. In quick succession, each of Usis's remaining men were fatally pierced by the arrows. Usis managed to dodge the arrows directed at him, but as the arrow attack ceased and Raine gave the order for the archers to reload, Usis had no choice but to recognize his defeat.

"You best tuck that tail between your legs," Raine yelled as Usis backed himself towards the Throne's Eye gate. "Sleight of foot won't stop this next wave."

"Take your consolation," Usis reiterated. "You only prolong the inevitable."

Raine again dropped his hand and the archers released their arrows. Usis darted to avoid the arrows, and within seconds he had disappeared behind the monastery gates.

Igallik quickly called out an order to all the monks present.

"Follow him! And when you catch him, kill him!"

Immediately, forty monks sprinted in pursuit of the traitor. After the hunters filtered out of the gate, Igallik and Raine made their way to the sons of Animus Letum.

Igallik turned first to Galian.

"Welcome back, Seraph. Superb timing, I must say."

"I agree," Galian smiled.

"How did you know?" the head monk asked.

"The reward of my resurrection is to see the future," Galian said. "It allowed me to know the truth about Usis."

Igallik was shocked.

"There is more," Galian divulged. "When you get a moment, we should talk."

Igallik agreed and with his hands on his hips he looked over the courtyard. His posture sank when he noticed Raine and Odin standing over Raeman's body.

"Your brother," Igallik asked, "will he be alright?"

"He will be," Galian affirmed. "But it is time for him to know what we know."

Igallik's eyes shifted in deliberation.

"If you're sure," he finally consented, "bring both him and yourself to the High Temple in one hour."

"I will," Galian agreed.

As the true weight of the night hit him, Igallik gazed across the horizon. His studied gaze was that of a man looking for answers. But instead, as the head monk's eyes fell back onto Raeman's dead body, he had only a question.

"This was inevitable, wasn't it?"

"There are many factors," Galian answered. "Though, I am certain it was inevitable tonight."

Igallik exhaled deeply.

"One hour," he reminded as he patted Galian's shoulder.

After another mournful shake of his head, Igallik turned and began a slow and contemplative walk towards the High Temple. Galian watched the head monk for a moment and then walked calmly to Raine and Odin. As Galian came within ear shot, he could hear the pain in his brother's voice.

"It doesn't make sense. He was my friend… my brother."

"I don't know what to say, mate," Raine admitted. "It breaks your heart…"

Galian arrived between the two monks and turned first to Raine.

"If you could, Raine, we need to prepare Raeman for his final respects."

A tearful Raine was thankful for the interruption.

"Will do, mate."

Galian then turned to Odin.

"It will make sense soon. It will still hurt, but it will make sense."

"What do you mean?"

"We need to talk," Galian said. "We'll clean you up, then we'll go to High Temple."

Odin nodded, but then shook his head again.

"I can't believe it," he whispered.

"Neither could I," Galian confessed. "But it is done. Come, let's go clean you up."

Odin seemed to concede, and after Galian wrapped an arm around him, the two brothers began the kind of walk that destiny required of them – a walk dependent on each other.

27

One hour later, Galian led Odin into the High Temple. Igallik was sitting on his totem throne, and at first sight of the twins, he motioned for them to join him at the front.

"First, let me apologize to you both," Igallik said as Odin and Galian sat down. "Today should have never happened."

"If you are apologizing on behalf of Usis," Odin said plainly, "there is no need. It was Usis, and Usis alone, who killed Raeman."

Igallik dropped his head. "But I did play a part in Raeman's murder," he said. "I withheld information from Usis. From almost everyone. When Usis left on his quest three years ago, I sent him off without the complete truth." Igallik tugged on his beard for a moment. "Odin," he said, "the worst is true of what Usis said we did to his parents. We did kill them."

Odin could not remain silent.

"But why? There had to be a reason."

"There was, Odin," Igallik said. "Please believe that."

Igallik shook his head, battling his guilt as he replayed the events that had led to Raeman's murder.

"Do you remember the story Usis told of how his parents died?" he asked.

"I do," Odin said. "The Metus Sane killed them. They had intended to kill Usis, because they believed that he was the spiritual vessel of Malum Ludus, but they only managed to kill his parents."

"This is almost true," Igallik revealed. "The Metus Sane were going to kill Usis. But, the whole truth is that Usis's parents were the leaders of the Metus Sane. They were going to sacrifice Usis on his fourth birthday – his own parents were going to kill him."

Odin was speechless.

"What were we to do?" Igallik said. "We had to intervene. Raine, Raeman, and a few other monks arrived in time to act. And they did."

The head monk stroked his beard, his eyes shooting around the room as he tried vainly to swallow his regret.

"We should have told him. Tonight could have been prevented."

"So he found out the truth during his quest?" Odin asked.

"It would appear so," Igallik concluded. "But someone or something has twisted the truth to suit their needs."

"Something?" Odin repeated.

Igallik nodded. "Did you ever wonder how Usis was able to know when you were afraid?"

"All the time," Odin said.

"You see," the head monk said, "the Metus Sane weren't far off in their assessment of Usis."

Odin flexed back. "You mean he actually is a vessel of Malum Ludus?"

"He is," Igallik answered sombrely. "For a long time I had to fight the evidence. And believe me, Odin, I fought. But my efforts were based on hope, not truth. It was on the day of the Blood Cael that I could not deny it anymore."

Odin had thought a lot about that day.

"Because the Blood Cael stopped when it saw Usis," he remembered.

"It didn't just stop, Odin: it was about to bow."

"Bow?"

"Yes. The Cael recognized Usis as its master. In the afterlife, the Blood Cael was Malum Ludus's bodyguard. In fact, when Ludus was at his most powerful there were eight such beasts labouring under his protection."

"So Usis was born this way?" Odin asked. "This was inevitable?"

"Is it inevitable that the Lyrans reclaim Animus Letum?" Igallik asked. "No. Such a task requires choice and effort. Usis is no different. Unfortunately, he has contributed a large effort to a poor choice, and as we stand he has decided to become Malum Ludus's apprentice."

Odin was hurt. It would have stung less if Usis were dead.

"So what do we do?"

"Our first act is to track Usis," Igallik replied. "We need to find him."

"We will fail," Galian signed. "He evades us."

Initially, Igallik was stunned by Galian's statement, but after realizing he had never encountered a phenomenon like Galian's new power, he became curious about its lengths.

"I must ask, Galian, how far can you see into the future?"

"I have not investigated fully. But I can judge by milestones. And there is no sign of Usis all the way until Odin and I are twenty years old."

Igallik's eyes grew wide in disbelief.

"Galian, that is in three years."

Galian smiled. "Hell of a gift, right?"

"My God," the head monk marvelled. "That is truly amazing."

"Three years?" Odin said. "And no Usis?"

"There's even worse news," Galian signed.

Odin turned to his brother in alarm.

"What news?"

"In three years," Galian said, "you're still an idiot."

Odin fought against the smile surfacing on his face, but he eventually broke.

"Should have left you in the coma," he muttered.

The head monk looked skywards, sighing as he let his shoulders slump in defeat.

"For heaven's sakes," he said, "couldn't they just say they missed each other?"

Neither Odin nor Galian would admit it.

Igallik shook his head. "Dumb *and* stubborn," he said. "You can both leave. It has been a hell of a day, and having two idiots at my side offers me no advantage in deciding our next move."

Odin was the first to break. He rose quickly to his feet and turned towards the exit. As he looked back, Galian was still seated.

"Go ahead," Galian encouraged. "I just had a two-month sleep."

"It didn't look peaceful," Odin said wryly.

Galian met Odin's eyes. "I need a couple of minutes with Igallik," he said. "I'll meet you in my quarters."

Odin scratched his temple for a moment.

"Seraph stuff?" he presumed.

"Very much so," Galian signed.

After another nod, Odin turned and ambled out of the High Temple.

The moment Odin disappeared behind the Temple doors, Galian turned his attention back to the head monk. A grave look had taken over the quiet monk's face.

"I need you to know something," he said. "I lied to you. I have determined how far I can see into the future."

"And how far is that?" Igallik asked.

"Three years," Galian restated. "But that is only my sight."

"I don't understand," Igallik said. "What else is there?"

Galian did his best to explain. "There are two elements to my ability: the first is sight, but the second is feel. I can feel the energy in what I see. I feel happiness in some visions, in others I feel pain. I feel beyond three years," Galian signed. "And what I feel brings great concern."

"Why? What do you feel?"

"I feel excruciating pain, like being tortured... and then nothing."

"Nothing?" Igallik repeated.

"I assume it is death."

Igallik swept his hand through his long gray beard.

"Tell me this," he enquired. "What is the very last thing you can actually see from the future?"

"I see Odin enter an old white carriage before a mercenary mission."

"And you can only feel pain beyond that image?"

Galian nodded.

"To be honest," Igallik said, "I don't know what the pain could be caused by. Fortunately, we do have the luxury of three years to find out. I promise you, Galian, I will do my best to uncover the source of this anguish."

"Thank you," Galian said. "But I must insist on one thing."

"As you please."

"Odin is not to know of this. I have put him through enough."

"If that is your will," the head monk said, "then it shall remain between us."

"It is my will," Galian said.

"I will comply," Igallik agreed. "But I must warn you, secrets have sharp edges. One such as this will likely cut both of you."

"I am aware," Galian signed.

"Very well," Igallik said. "Is there anything else?"

Galian shook his head.

"Then you should go tend to your brother," the head monk said. "Descent hurt him just as badly as it hurt you."

"Did he suffer?" Galian asked.

"Very much so," Igallik replied.

Galian swallowed a heft of guilt. "On my way," he signed.

The moon was still high as Galian bobbed to his quarters. From a distance, he could see Odin waiting at the door. As Galian approached and reached a grinning Odin, the quiet monk threw his arm around Odin's shoulder.

"I missed you," he signed. "I'm not sure you know how much."

"I think I can imagine."

"Perhaps," Galian said. "Come, we must talk."

Odin nodded and then followed Galian inside. As they sat, Galian first gave Odin an appreciative nod.

"Thank you for your decision with Palis. He saved my life."

"Do you know what happened to him?" Odin asked.

"No," Galian said. "I saw him for only a moment. It is likely that Forneus found him."

"Did you see Forneus?" Odin asked.

"No, but I felt him."

Odin's eyes looked intently at his brother, expecting a description, but Galian was eerily still.

"Well?" Odin finally prodded.

Galian fidgeted for a moment, his fingers tapping anxiously against his leg.

"He is the most evil adversary I can imagine," he said finally. "I searched for his presence. I regret that I found it. His aura is so cold it paralyzed my mind. But in the paralysis, Forneus overwhelmed my consciousness. His thoughts became my thoughts."

To see the fear in Galian's eye made Odin shudder.

"It took all of my strength to get away," Galian said. "But the scary thing is, I wasn't even in his sights. If he had committed his full focus onto me, I would not be here."

Odin was reminded of why Palis agreed to take the staff back to the afterlife.

"Knowing what you know now," he said, "do you think we can reclaim the afterlife? Do you think that we and the Forge are capable?"

"There are a lot of factors to consider," Galian answered.

Odin looked flatly at his brother.

"Is that your real answer?"

Galian exhaled deeply, and then met Odin's stare with complete seriousness.

"The truth is, we must. That realm is Hell. But you must understand that Hell is not a place, it is a condition. It is a pressure so cruel that good men surrender their morality. The state and power of Hell is fear. People will forfeit many virtues when they are afraid. They surrender to fear, and worse, they become its partner. The victims become the assailants. The afterlife is a raging river of fear, Odin. And even the strongest souls choose to ride the current. It is horrid, but it is survival."

"So what do we do?" Odin asked. "What can we do?"

"We train," Galian answered. "We honour our parents, we honour this monastery. We have eight years until we meet our destiny – eight years until we face Forneus. Every day that separates us from that destiny cannot be wasted. Tomorrow, we begin. No excuses."

Odin knew the seriousness in his brother's eyes.

"I am with you," he vowed.

"Alright," Galian signed. "First, we must take a trip outside the monastery walls."

"To where?" Odin asked.

"Northton," Galian replied. "We have an appointment."

"Should I bring weapons?" Odin asked.

"No," Galian said. "It is just a small meeting."

"Easy enough," Odin said.

Galian eyes lowered – it was clear that he knew something different.

"Take the rest of night to rest," he encouraged. "But tomorrow, at daybreak, we set out."

Odin slumped a little – he had waited two months for his brother to come back and now he was being told to leave.

Galian read Odin's heart as if it were written on a page.

"We will talk tomorrow," Galian signed. "I need you to be rested. I promise, we will have time tomorrow."

Odin swallowed his hurt. "As you wish."

As he exited, he stopped at the door, resting his hand against the doorframe.

"It's good to have you back," he said. "I missed you."

"I know," Galian replied.

Galian angled his head as he studied his brother.

"I'm sorry about Usis," he said.

"It's fine," Odin lied. "He only proved that he wasn't our brother."

"You will see him again," Galian promised. "Be prepared for that."

"We'll get prepared tomorrow," Odin decided. "Tonight, I may choose to sulk."

Galian nodded. "Tomorrow, then."

After tapping the wooden doorframe, Odin forced a weak smile and then left Galian alone.

Galian would stay awake all night.

He now knew the challenge ahead and vowed – at any cost – to secure a victory for the Lyran House. Forneus was greatly powerful. The Serpent Messiah had become a deity of evil. When the sun rose the next day, Galian and Odin would partner in the daunting task of deicide. Forneus – the Serpent God – needed to die.

However, having seen the future, only Galian knew the price of such a destiny.

28

The next morning, Odin woke at daybreak. It was only minutes before he was out of his room, and as he emerged into the courtyard in his full black attire, he was met by Galian lounging on the half wall next to his quarters. Galian was wearing his customary brown robe.

"Morning," Galian said.

Odin craned his neck towards the clear skies. "A good one," he replied.

Odin's eyes shifted back down, and he examined the red leather bag that was hanging from Galian's hand.

"What's with the bag?" he asked.

"Supplies," Galian said.

"Food?"

"No. Nature will feed us. These are just a few things we need."

Odin nodded. "Shall we set out?"

"We shall," Galian said.

With that, Galian rose, and the sons of Animus Letum began what would be a two day trek.

While they walked, no topic was off limits. They strolled down a rock path surrounded by two sides of mighty forest, talking about Usis, the Forge, and nearly every other factor that was related to their destiny. They even explored the lengths of Galian's new power.

"Heads or tails?" Odin asked.

"Tails," Galian signed.

Odin flipped his coin, and after it had landed back into his palm, he slapped it on to the backside of his hand.

The result was as expected.

"Tails it is," Odin said. "That's eighty-five in a row."

Galian smiled. "I could go all day."

"And do you?" Odin asked, testing his brother's new power.

Galian smiled again. "Watch this."

The quiet monk dropped to a knee, picked up a large stone from the pathway, and then pulled a dagger from the leather bag that he was carrying. As he inhaled and closed his eyes, Galian shifted the rock in his palm, weighing it as if his hand were a scale. After confirming its weight, Galian underhanded the rock into the bush, and just before the stone crashed down, he lobbed his dagger up into a perfect arc. With a thwack, the stone hit a branch, and as the sound echoed back to the roadway, a small hare bounded out of the shrubs. As the hare leapt across the stone path, the perfectly timed dagger arced down and plummeted blade first into the hare's back.

Odin's eyes were wide with marvel. "That was impossible."

"Obviously not," Galian smirked.

"So what did you see?" Odin asked. "I mean, which part of that event did you know would happen?"

"All of it."

"So you don't even choose what you do?" Odin said. "You follow a script?"

"I have a choice," Galian said. "My choice was to throw the rock or not."

"And what if you didn't?"

"Our entire lives would change," Galian replied.

Odin eyed his brother for a moment. "Our entire lives?" he repeated. With a laugh, Odin waved off the notion. "There's no way," he said. "It was an insignificant moment."

"Perhaps," Galian said. "But without it, we would not have had this conversation. Or the next. Or the next. It doesn't change where we are going, just how we get there."

"So it changed our timing?" Odin asked.

"Forever," Galian said.

Odin's head tilted.

"Do you like this power?" he asked. "It seems like a lot."

"It is a lot to manage," Galian said. "But it does give us an advantage."

"You didn't answer my question," Odin said.

The quiet monk exhaled with a shake of his head. "The future hurts," he signed. "My burden is that I feel it already."

Before Odin could reply, Galian pointed to the hare.

"Can you grab that?" he asked. "That's our dinner."

Odin took the cue. "How long until we camp?" he asked as he retrieved the impaled rabbit.

"Not long," Galian said. "Our site is only a few hours away."

As Galian held out his bag, Odin dropped the hare into it and patted his brother's shoulder.

"I know I'll never understand your power," he said. "But if you ever need a crutch, you should know that I can bear the weight."

"I know," Galian said, "even more than you."

A few hours later, Galian and Odin were seated around a campfire. The sky was clear, and under the blanket of stars, Odin was cooking the hare.

"I think she's almost ready," Odin said, as he rotated a makeshift spit.

Galian made a half-interested nod as he used his power to form different shapes out of the fire's floating embers. The quiet monk had been reserved for hours, giving only small nods for affirmation.

"Is there something wrong?" Odin asked.

"Not yet," Galian replied.

"Not yet?" Odin said. "What's going on with you?"

Galian used his power to extinguish all of the embers.

"Do you ever think about Cole?" he asked.

"About how I killed him?" Odin said.

"Yes."

"I don't regret it if that's what you mean."

"I know you don't." Galian said. "But do you wonder if you halted his destiny: if by killing him, you took more than his life – you took his future."

Odin shrugged. "You tell me," he said. "The future seems to be your specialty."

"I didn't agree with your killing Cole," Galian admitted. "It bothered me for many years."

"You're speaking in the past tense," Odin remarked.

"I am," Galian agreed. "After being in Animus Letum, I see death in a different way. Something in me has changed."

"For the better?" Odin asked.

"Time will tell," Galian replied.

The quiet monk began to play with the embers again.

"Tomorrow will be difficult for you," he said, "but I need you to trust me."

"You know I do," Odin said.

Galian smiled weakly. "One day you might not want to."

With a shake of his head, Galian let himself fall flat against the earth.

"I'll wake you in the morning," he signed.

Odin stopped turning the spit, puzzled by Galian's resignation.

"You're not going to eat?" he asked.

Galian shrugged. "Not hungry."

Exhaling, the quiet monk turned his back to the fire and balled up inside his brown robe.

Odin rotated the spit a few more times, watching his brother as a mass of anxiety grew in his gut.

"What do you see?" he whispered to himself.

As promised, Galian woke Odin at daybreak. Galian had already gathered some berries from the surrounding forest, and as Odin sat up, wiping the sleep from his eyes, Galian presented him with breakfast.

"Eat up," Galian said. "We need your muscle today."

Odin nodded his head lazily. "I thought you said it was just a small meeting."

"I did," Galian said. "And it is."

Odin took a handful of berries and stuffed them into his mouth, filling both of his cheeks until they swelled out of the sides of his face.

"I need a minute," he mumbled.

"You have five," Galian replied.

Five minutes later, the sons of Animus Letum were on the road again.

Odin was still trying to capture his wakefulness, and as he laboured forward, he stared down the long road with weighted eyelids.

"How far to Northton?" he asked.

"We are fairly close," Galian said. "We will be there before noon."

"Will it matter if we're late?"

"Yes. But we won't be."

"Are you sure about that?" Odin taunted. "What if I change our timing? What if I fall right here and go back to sleep."

"You don't."

"Don't what?"

"Fall asleep."

"Just watch me," Odin said.

With a mocking yawn, Odin knelt down and then laid on the stone path.

"You see," he said as he reclined awkwardly over the road. "You were wrong. I just changed our timing."

"I didn't say you wouldn't lie down," Galian replied. "I said you wouldn't fall asleep."

With a quick jerk of his hand, Galian used his power to start dragging Odin across the stones.

As Odin slid sideways across the pathway, he tried stubbornly to ignore the rocks sticking to and scraping his back, but after a half minute, the young Lyran leapt back to his feet.

"Fine," he said as he picked stones from his clothes. "I'll stay up."

"I thought you might."

With a smile, Odin shoved his brother off balance.

"Your vision is a strength," he said, "but I believe your body is still a weakness."

"Don't do it," Galian said.

Odin started to dance in front of his brother, throwing jabs into the air.

"Oh," he taunted, "you've seen what I am about to do?"

"I recommend against it," Galian signed.

"I bet you do."

With a quick release, Odin jabbed at Galian's shoulder.

Gracefully, Galian weaved back, and the punch sailed harmlessly past him.

Odin's eyes lit up. The challenge was on.

In quick combination, Odin threw a flurry of fists and feet at his brother, but with the very same grace, Galian ducked and weaved away from each of them. It was like trying to punch the wind.

As Odin's hands fell back to his sides, he offered his surrender.

"Fine," he said dejectedly. "You win."

"Not yet," Galian replied.

With a confident smile, the quiet monk closed his eyes and nodded. Instantly, twenty stones lifted off the roadway, careened inwards and pelted Odin's hunched up body.

"Alright, alright," Odin cried. "I'll shut up and walk."

"Wise choice," Galian said.

It was just before noon when the twins arrived in Northton. The township was an older one, and the bulk of its center was entirely surrounded by steep hills of dense forest. The town's stone structures were built on the low ground, nestled in the center of the rising wall of trees. The layout made Northton appear like it had been built at the bottom of a crater – albeit a very green one.

The sun fell upon Northton magnificently. Because of the surrounding wall of forest, a shadow was almost always painted over the town, and as the accents of light and dark swept over the town structures, Northton appeared as if it had a restless soul – it was in a constant motion of light and shadow.

From atop the wall of forest, Galian and Odin watched the town for a long while.

"Better than looking at a log wall," Odin said.

Galian nodded. "Without question."

The two continued to take in the view, choosing to leave a long silence between them.

"Do you see our destination?" Odin said finally.

"I do."

"Is the timing right?" Odin asked.

"Almost," Galian replied. "You see that farmer?" he asked as he pointed down into the township.

Odin peered over the grids of green farmland. "On the left?"

"Yes. As soon as he goes inside the barn, we will walk down."

"Alright," Odin agreed.

Galian tapped his hand gingerly against Odin's shoulder and then pointed a few times at the path in front of them.

"Pretty steep," he said.

"I'd say," Odin agreed.

Galian offered a sheepish smile. "You mind giving me a lift?"

Odin laughed. "Do you already know if I do?"

"Yes."

"Then what's the point of asking."

"Manners," Galian replied. "If you prefer, next time I will just jump on your back."

Odin shook his head and dropped to a knee.

"Climb up," he said.

After Galian hobbled next to his brother, he climbed clumsily onto Odin's back.

"Is the farmer gone?" Odin asked as he rose to full posture.

Galian pointed in affirmation.

"Then hold on," Odin said. "You're a lot fatter than you used to be."

Adeptly, Odin carried his brother down the steep slope of forest and quickly arrived on the grounds of Northton. After climbing off Odin, Galian took the lead. He led Odin around the town's outer edge for ten minutes and then announced that they had reached their destination.

Even with the limited information that he had been given, Odin was confused by the details of the meeting. Strangely, he and Galian were standing near a mineshaft, shrouding themselves with a bulk of bushes as they watched a group of twelve men saunter around the mineshaft's lift.

Galian was still carrying the red leather bag.

"We're meeting with them?" Odin asked.

"One of them," Galian replied.

Odin shook his head. "This is very bizarre," he said. "Why these guys?"

"I need them," Galian replied.

"Why?"

"Be patient," Galian signed.

As Odin watched from the bush, eleven of the twelve men entered the lift. The men varied in age. The youngest – who didn't enter the lift – was a boy of around fifteen. The rest appeared to be thirty or over. The men on the lift wore dark overalls with no shirt underneath, and they were all carrying large picks and hammers. As the sun glinted over their frames, it was clear that each of them shared the same ginger hair and white skin. The similarity was enough to safely assume that they were all related by blood.

After the eleven men had settled on the lift, the boy gave them a nod and began to crank a series of levers and gears that lowered them down into the mineshaft.

"Are they bad men?" Odin asked as he watched.

"No," Galian said. "I am counting on them being very good."

Before Odin could reply, Galian pushed through the bushes, limping forward on a direct path to the boy operating the gears.

The boy looked up almost immediately, his eyes squinting through the beating sun.

As Odin and Galian reached within earshot, the boy relinquished one hand from the lever and offered the twins a salute.

"Throne's Eye, eh?"

As Odin hustled up to his brother, he nodded back to the boy. "How'd you know?"

"The clothes," the boy replied. "You guys dress the part."

"The part?" Odin said

"Oh, no offence, eh," the boy said. "Your skills are legend round here. The Godmen," he laughed.

The boy had a contagious charm.

"And what are your skills?" Odin asked.

"Us?" the boy said. "We're the Minin' McEnrow," he said. "Family's been minin' for 'bout a century. We're damn good, too."

Galian nodded with a strange smile and then walked around the shaft, inspecting the descending lift with a studied focus.

"What's with him?" the boy asked as he nodded to Galian. "Doesn't look like most of the Throne's Eye that come through."

Odin conceded the point. "No, he doesn't," he agreed. "But looks can be deceiving. Would you believe that he's the strongest monk we have?"

"I'd need proof," the boy laughed. "He ain't got much to him."

Odin knelt and picked up a stone. "Ask and you shall receive."

With a slow lob, Odin tossed the stone across the mineshaft towards Galian. As the stone arced over the shaft, Galian snapped his fingers and the stone exploded into dust.

"Holy shit, eh," the boy chuckled. "That's a trick!"

As an amused Odin looked over the shaft to Galian, the quiet monk communicated to him in sign.

"He don't talk?" the boy guessed.

"He is unable," Odin said.

"So what's he sayin?" the boy asked.

"He wants to know how deep the shaft is."

"'Bout six hundred feet," the boy said. "But she spreads under us for miles."

The information seemed to satisfy Galian, and after a nod he bobbed back to the boy's side. Once he was next to him, Galian signed another message to Odin.

"Now what's he sayin?" the boy laughed.

Odin was still trying to understand the message himself. "It was a message for you," Odin said. "You and your family."

"Well," the boy prodded, "what was it?"

Odin watched Galian for a moment, and then turned to the boy.

"He says 'sorry'."

In a flash, Galian pulled the dagger from his leather bag, sliced the cable that was supporting the lift, and then leapt at the boy, tackling him down as he stabbed wildly into his neck. As blood splashed and sprayed, Galian hacked into the boy's throat, plunging his blade repeatedly into the boy's windpipe.

Odin froze.

"Galian!" he cried finally. "Galian, stop!"

As the boy went limp, Galian pulled the blade from his throat. Before Odin could say anything, Galian silenced him with his finger.

As screams and then a massive bang echoed up the mineshaft, Galian nodded, and with an eerie calm, he rolled off the boy and began to wipe the blood from his face and hands.

29

Silence followed the murders.

Galian remained his customary quiet self, and Odin, in complete shock, was keeled over, watching his brother with horror churning in his gut.

"Not you," Odin began to ramble. "Not you. Not you..."

Suddenly, Odin's voice erupted into a hoarse yell.

"God damn it!" he screamed. "Not you, Galian! Not you! You are the star! Don't you get that? You are the star!"

Galian looked painfully up at his brother, blood still splattered on his face and hands.

"I had to," he signed.

"Why?" Odin demanded as he pointed furiously at the boy. "Why this? You're the light! You're the one we follow! God damn it, Galian, you've ruined yourself!"

"I had to," Galian repeated.

Odin buried his face in his hands, screaming wildly into his palms.

"You don't get it!" he cried through his fingers. "I lied to you! I lied to you about Cole! He haunts me every god-damned day! I'm damned by his ghost! I would never want that for you!"

With a hard swallow, Odin's voice turned to barely a whisper. "I ended him, Galian. Cole should have had a chance... a chance to choose who he was supposed to be. I took that from him..."

"I know," Galian said. "I just took the same choice from the McEnrows."

Odin turned away, craning his neck as he looked helplessly to the heavens.

"Why?" he demanded. "Why would you do this? Why would you damn yourself?"

"It had to be done," Galian said.

Odin's hands clenched into fists. "That's it?" he cried. "*It had to be done?* That's all you'll give me?"

"That's all," Galian said. "Give up trying to understand. I can never tell you more. The sooner you realize that, the better."

"After everything we've been through," Odin seared, "You're choosing this? You're choosing secrets? I'm warning you, Galian, this is not a path for two."

"I know," Galian said.

Odin exhaled furiously. "I need a moment away from you..."

After another hard swallow, Odin turned from his brother, and with curses spilling from his mouth, he stormed away.

Odin did not return for nearly half an hour.

As he came back to the mineshaft, he could see that Galian had used his power to raise the lift. All twelve bodies were lined next to each other, and Galian had placed silver coins over each one of the McEnrow's dead eyes.

"What's next?" Odin asked as he grew close. His voice was devoid of any and all affect. It was flat and even, like a man who has banished his own emotions in the name of duty. Galian, after all, was his duty.

The change in Odin's tone had no effect on Galian.

"We burn them," he said.

The quiet monk reached into his leather bag and pulled out a book of wooden matches and a vile of flammable tar.

Odin eyed the items for a moment.

"Can you manage?" he asked. "Or shall I?"

"I've come this far," Galian replied.

Ten minutes later, the sons of Animus Letum were leaving Northton, a funnel of black smoke rising behind them.

Their walk back home was quiet and heavy. There was an argument looming between the brothers, but as they walked, it seemed that neither of them wanted to make the first move.

So instead, they kept on, each knowing that something had changed between them.

Choosing to forfeit a night's rest, the twins made it back to the Throne's Eye in only one day. The two walked through the gates and parted ways without a word.

As Odin walked away, he prayed for rain. He prayed for a thunderstorm to wreak its havoc over the Throne's Eye. Odin needed to see the chaos. He needed to watch the rage. He needed something to reflect his state of mind – something he could stare into so that he didn't feel alone.

No storm came.

Instead, two days after the McEnrows were burned to ash, the twins were called to the High Temple. Odin knew exactly why. Odin was still angry with his brother, but he also believed that Galian would set things right. Surely, in front of the hallowed Order, Galian would explain himself: he would give his reason why, and in doing so, he would vindicate himself to the Order and, more importantly, to Odin.

The sun was just rising when Odin got the call.

After collecting himself, Odin walked slowly out of his quarters. The morning was bleak and dreary. The sky was painted over with thick gray clouds, and the earth was damp and intoxicating.

Odin forced himself up the Temple staircase, and as he passed slowly through the Temple doors, he moved like a man expecting release. There was a heaviness to his walk, but there was also a small bounce of hope – an expectation that Galian was about to ease his soul. For two days, Odin had been carrying the burden of Galian's actions, and as he dragged the ball and chain towards the altar, he fully expected that he would be released from its shackle.

Inside the Temple, Galian was already seated at the foremost pew, and in front of him, all five totems were seated in their thrones. There were two new totems in the Order. A tall and lanky white man named Jeston had replaced Palis as the Mercy totem. Jeston was a middle-aged Sight who spent a lot of his time in the Spine. He was lessoned extensively in world history, and it was with little reservation that he was appointed into the Order. The other new appointment was Raine. After Raeman was murdered by Usis, the Order considered its options, and ultimately, they voted unanimously to appoint the monastery's strongest warrior into the role of Justice totem. Odin was ecstatic when Raine's appointment was given, but now, as he sat with his brother in the foremost pew, he could only manage a sparing look at his mentor – he was a little embarrassed that their relationship required this chapter.

After taking a quick draw from his hookah, Igallik commenced the hearing. There was a shortness in his voice – an anger that was just barely contained by his sense of decorum.

"Let it be understood," he said sternly, "the verdict for this hearing will be final unless an exceptional force decrees otherwise. Because the verdict is final, the totems of the Order shall be permitted any length of time to make their verdict. However, if a totem is uncertain about a verdict – even in the least – he will defer his vote to another totem's speciality."

The Order totems each gave a nod of affirmation.

Igallik took another short puff from his hookah.

"It is pledged," he said as he exhaled.

As the smoke spread out into the Temple air, Igallik glared down at the twins, his stare cutting angrily through the billows.

"Take a trip recently?" he asked curtly.

Odin turned to his brother, expecting Galian's explanation, but somehow, Galian seemed quieter than ever.

Igallik sat further back into his throne. "We had visitors last night," he informed. "A group from Northton arrived."

Odin tried to spur Galian's explanation with a small knock to the shoulder, but Galian seemed uninterested.

As he watched, Igallik was beginning to sense the rift between the brothers.

With a loud clap, the head monk continued. "It turns out the visitors wanted our help," he said. "A family of miners was murdered, and they've asked our monastery to hunt down the killers and bring them to justice."

Still, Galian would not speak.

Igallik eyed Odin for a moment. "Anything to say, Odin?" he asked.

With his heart torn between loyalties, Odin looked back and forth between Galian and the head monk.

"No," he said after a long pause. "Nothing to say."

Igallik nodded, and after pulling a sleeve of coins from a pouch on his throne he lobbed a handful of twenty-four silver coins onto the floor between the twins.

"Shouldn't be too hard to find the killers," Igallik said as the coins sprawled across the floor. "Some pretty familiar looking coins, wouldn't you say."

It was as if both brothers had been born mute.

The head monk turned to the Logic totem, Nile.

"You've seen these coins before, haven't you, Nile?"

Nile adjusted his glasses for a moment. "I have," he replied. "They are a one of a kind silver."

"One of a kind, you say?" the head monk said. "Why is that, Nile?"

"They are minted here at the Throne's Eye," the Logic totem said.

"I *did* think they looked familiar," Igallik agreed.

After another look at the twins, the head monk turned to Raine. The old warrior had been purposely keeping his gaze down and away from Odin and Galian.

"Were you aware of any Torches or Aerises leaving our monastery two days ago?" Igallik asked.

"No," Raine said. "There were no scheduled departures."

"But you did see two monks leave, correct?"

"I did," Raine confirmed. "I watched Odin and Galian leave early in the morning."

"Curious," Igallik said.

Igallik turned back to the boys and left a small moment of silence. The silence began to build and become uncomfortable, until, suddenly, Igallik slammed his fists against the arms of his throne and the charade was over.

"Why would you do this?" he demanded. "What right did you have? You better have a hell of a good reason!"

It was only Galian who knew the reason, and he wasn't telling.

"Silence?" Igallik yelled. "You are choosing silence?"

The twins answered with more quiet.

"Fine," Igallik said sternly. "The punishment for the murder of any innocent citizen outside our walls is three reeds. You two have killed twelve citizens; therefore, I move that the thirty-six reeds are divided evenly between you."

Igallik looked to the totems on his left and right. "All in favour of eighteen reeds served to each brother?"

Odin's eyes bulged with panic. He hadn't considered the punishment. As Odin's face flushed with red, his heart began to beat throughout his entire body, thumping his consciousness with unarguable truth: eighteen reeds would *kill* Galian. He couldn't allow it.

"I did it!" Odin blurted before the Order could rule. "I killed them. Galian tried to stop me, but I wouldn't let him."

Igallik's eyes narrowed in on Odin. "Why, Odin?" he demanded. "Why would you do this?"

Odin tried to hide his grief under a heft of attitude.

"I wouldn't expect you to understand," he replied defiantly. "You're not a Lyran."

Igallik returned a piercing stare. "No Lyran ever killed an innocent," he said sternly. "Your father would be ashamed."

The words stung, but after a hard swallow, Odin shook them off.

"My father's dead," he said. "I doubt he cares."

After keeping his eyes down for most of the hearing, Raine raised his head and looked pleadingly to his apprentice.

"Were they bad men, Odin?" he asked. "Do you know something we don't?"

Odin looked fleetingly at his brother and chose to repeat the exact sentiment that Galian had given him.

"Give up trying to understand," Odin said to the Order. "I can never tell you more."

Raine's hands fell to his sides.

"If you won't give us a reason," he said, "we cannot amend the punishment. It is that simple. By your own admission, you are courting thirty-six reeds. That is greatly more than we have ever dealt. Thirty-six will wreck you."

"I am aware," Odin replied.

Raine let out a deep sigh. "Thirty-six it is," he said. "Any other thoughts, brothers?"

Bysin and Nile indicated no, but Jeston, the new Mercy totem, was eyeing Odin with suspicion.

"I get the impression that it is *you* who is being merciful," he said. "Am I wrong to assume this?"

"I don't know what you mean," Odin said shortly.

"This is your last chance," Jeston said. "This is your last chance to seek our mercy. You are in the power-seat, Odin. Not us."

Odin shrugged. "We both know that's not true."

With an irritated huff, Igallik grabbed for his hookah.

"Very well," he said firmly. "Odin will incur the punishment of thirty-six reeds. They will be served at this evening's close."

The head monk took a puff of his tobacco.

"Brothers," he said, "we are officially adjourned."

Odin and Galian stood immediately, but before Galian could grab his brother's arm, Odin turned on a heel and stormed out of the High Temple.

As Galian stood in the center aisle and watched his brother, the Order monks rose and filtered past him. They seemed intent not to address him. It was as if each of them suspected they had been given only half the truth – Bysin more than anyone.

As Galian managed to catch the Instinct totem's eyes, Bysin's return look was somewhat scornful.

"I hope you know what you're doing," he said as he passed by. "Even love can die if you beat it long enough."

Galian met Bysin's eyes dead-on. "If you only knew."

That evening, the storm that Odin had been waiting for swept over the monastery. Lightning and thunder laid claim to the night, and the wind was so fierce that the rain blew sideways across the courtyard. Trees were bending like weeds, swaying wildly as their leaves howled like a pack of mourning hounds.

It was a fitting scene for thirty-six reeds.

Amid the tempest, Odin had been locked into a wooden stockade. Typically, the punishment of reeds was dealt to a person hanging over a post, but because Odin was supposed to be served thirty-six, he was confined to the stocks to ensure that he did not crumple.

The only monks present were Igallik, Raine, and Odin. No rational monk would ever choose to see or hear the pain that Odin was scheduled to suffer – especially Galian.

As the rain poured down over Odin's bare back, a flash of sheet-lightning overtook the sky, painting Odin's soaked flesh – if only for a moment – with the white flare of storm-light. As the light faded, Raine wound back his oak reed, and as the thunder roared mightily from above, the old warrior struck his weapon against Odin's naked back.

Odin's cries were drowned out by the storm.

After five reeds, Odin's skin had torn away, the blood on his back channeling down his spine like a crimson creek. After ten reeds, Odin's body trembled and wavered in the stocks, convulsing more and more with each ensuing reed. After the twentieth reed, six of Odin's ribs had cracked and he was limp, whimpering weakly as he hung helplessly in the stockades.

With Odin's blood spattered over his own face and hands, Raine looked pleadingly to Igallik.

"No more," he begged. "He can't take no more."

"Sixteen more," the head monk ordered. "I will permit half force."

The old warrior nodded regretfully and stood back for a moment as he wiped his massive hand through the rain and tears on his face.

"I'm sorry, mate," he whispered.

The beating continued.

As Raine cracked the thirtieth reed onto Odin's back, he felt and heard Odin's spine shift.

"I won't do no more!" he yelled through the storm. "I'm done, Igallik! He'll die if I hit him again!"

"Alright, Raine, alright," Igallik conceded. "Take him down."

With a puddle of blood encircling the base of the stockades, Raine quickly unlocked the wooden trap and cradled Odin's unconscious body to the courtyard floor.

As lightning lit the scene and Raine's frame flashed in the light, the head monk stumbled back – every line in Raine's face was growling at him.

"If I have killed him," Raine threatened, "you'll be next. I promise you that. You should have called it!" Raine yelled. "This is not us! We are not monsters!"

Igallik reclaimed his poise. "Does he have a pulse?"

Raine gritted his teeth as he put his fingers to Odin's neck.

"It's faint," he said begrudgingly.

Igallik nodded and then turned back into the heart of the monastery.

"Wylak!" he yelled. "We need you! Bring your chest!"

The herbalist quickly arrived and was soon followed by another twenty monks. As Wylak began to administer herbs, Raine and the other monks lifted Odin's limp body and began to carry him to his room.

Odin did not regain consciousness for three days.

When he finally woke, he did so screaming. Each breath shifted his broken ribs, and as he lay in a body splint, nearly every move he made was torture.

Galian was seated next to him.

As Odin gasped and wheezed, Wylak sped into the room, and after kneeling next to Odin's bed, he poured a vial of crystal blue liquid down Odin's throat.

"For the pain," Wylak said. "Just hold on, Odin. It will take effect in a minute."

With gritted teeth, Odin's limbs locked and clenched into paralysis as he grunted through a minute of hell.

Finally, the tension released, and Odin began to pant heavily, letting his lungs fill without the strain of his broken ribs.

"Better?" Wylak asked.

"Better," Odin grumbled.

"I'll be just outside the door," Wylak said. "Call if you need anything."

Odin managed a nod, and with an exhausted breath, he let his head fall against the bed. He had purposely turned his head away from Galian.

For an entire hour, not one word was spoken. Both brothers knew what was at hand.

As Odin finally turned to his brother, his eyes were heavy.

"You knew I would take the reeds," he presumed. "You saw it before it happened."

"I did," Galian signed.

"Maybe I should rephrase that," Odin said. "You knew you'd *let* me take the reeds."

"I did."

"And you still won't tell me why?"

"No."

Odin nodded. "Then I assume you know what I am about to say?"

As Odin met his brother's eyes and he saw the pain in Galian's face, Odin's throat began to tighten – it was the only time that Odin had seen Galian cry.

"I not only know what you're about to say," Galian said. "I've seen it in practice."

Odin swallowed. "Well, just so I can hear it, I'm going to say it anyway. We will never be the same, Galian. I have lost the trust that was between us. It was knocked out of me thirty times."

Tears began to roll down Odin's face. "You used me," he said. "You knew I would take the reeds. You knew and you still went ahead."

"There is a bigger picture," Galian tried to argue.

"Not to me!" Odin yelled. The force of his voice immediately cost him. As he winced and gasped, it was as if he channeled the pain into his eyes.

"Not to me," he repeated with a cold stare. "Was it like the hare?" he asked.

Galian would not answer

"Yes or no, Galian. Did you have a choice?"

Galian wiped the tears from his eyes. "Yes."

The answer hurt more because it was expected.

With tears streaming down his cheeks, Odin took a long and meditative breath through his nose. "Take a walk, Galian. And don't come back."

"I don't blame you for being angry," Galian signed.

"Angry?" Odin shouted. "I'm not angry, Galian. I'm ashamed. Mostly of myself. I was foolish to think that I mattered more to you. I asked you not to attempt Descent. You did. I want to know why you killed the miners. You won't answer. It's clear that you only need me when it's convenient. I am telling you now, that this year, when we have the Forge meeting, I will be resigning my name. You're the heir, I am the spare. You'll do just fine without me."

"You can't," Galian protested.

"I will," Odin replied coldly. "I wasn't given a choice in the first place," he seared. "I think it's only right that I have one now. I am tired of carrying you."

"I have never asked you to carry me," Galian asserted.

"That's exactly right," Odin fired back. "You just expect me to. You expect me to take the hits for you. Like Cole, like the miners. I am done. You take the glory, Galian. I'll take the hits."

Before Galian could reply, Odin pointed to the door.

"Go," he ordered. "Before I hate you even more."

Galian took one pace, but stopped and turned back to his brother. As pain wrenched his face, Galian clenched his fists, and with red flushing his face, suddenly, a sound forced through his throat.

Even amid his pain, Odin's eyes grew wide – it was the first time that Galian had made a sound.

With tears welling, Galian tried again, but after a moment of strain, it was clear that there would be no second sound.

"I'm sorry," he signed. "And I'll be sorry forever."

Ashamed, the quiet monk hid his face from his brother and limped away.

I have told you once that the scythe can hurt less than breathing. I remind you of this now, on behalf of Odin and Galian. As Galian shuffled away, both brothers had been broken.

Although Odin would heal from his wounds, his heart would not mend fully. I regret that something in Odin had changed.

That year, amid wild protest, Odin removed his name from the Forge.

30

In the years after Odin's thirty-six reeds, the Throne's Eye was free of any attack on its soil. Galian's power of sight had allowed the monks to eliminate all threats against the monastery long before they reached their gates. In that safety, Odin's and Galian's skills had grown immensely. Unfortunately, the twins had also grown apart. After he had been served his reeds, Odin made good on his word. He had removed himself from the Forge and only spoke to Galian when it was necessary. For the most part he avoided his twin at all costs. Galian tried extensively to mend their broken bond, but his efforts were repeatedly thwarted by an unmoved Odin. The rift had affected the entire monastery. It was a slow poison that forced monks to censor themselves and, even worse, pick sides. Many members of the Forge began to worry about their mission. Without Odin, the army was far weaker. The Forge's mass suicide grew closer every day, and understanding this, many monks attempted to force a reconciliation between the twins. But Odin was unflinching. Trying not to offend Odin, the Order monks had given him his space. They believed – and hoped – that Odin was simply showing his youth and that maturity would eventually help him come to his senses. However, they may have given him too much space. Many seasons soon passed upon Odin's stubbornness – seasons that spanned nearly three years.

In those years, Odin dedicated himself to his craft – more so than ever. Not believing he had a role in the afterlife, Odin switched his focus to the first realm. The Damns became his salvation. From dawn until dusk, Odin applied himself in the martial arts, and soon, his calloused fists and undefeated record announced him as the Throne's Eye battle god. His instincts and skillset in combat – measured against any who had contested him – had grown without equal. Without reservation, Odin was awarded the privilege to attend the Throne's Eye mercenary missions. There were even rumours that he would be given the rank of Aeris, a fitting title for the greatest fighter that your realm has even known. The mighty Odin!

Allow me now to praise the great Galian. No flattery of word will ever truly convey his greatness. But allow me to make one truth clear: he was the most powerful entity to ever set foot in your realm. His weakness was non-existent. Galian's sight, wisdom, and work ethic were equally matched by his humility, compassion, and understanding. The mission that Galian had chosen as a child had been achieved – he had become a worthy Lyran.

Although their paths had breached, the sons of Animus Letum had become the two strongest members of the Throne's Eye monastery. Much good came from this truth. Galian had become powerful enough to read the pain in other people, and with the lengths of knowledge and instruction Igallik offered, Galian learned how to heal the physical ailments of others. At the same time, Odin had become a pivotal piece in the mercenary excursions that Raine orchestrated. However, it was soon becoming apparent – even as Odin's humility fought it – that Raine's missions would be far more successful if Odin attended them alone.

Five months after Odin and Galian's twentieth birthday, and at the completion of one of Raine's missions, Odin made his way back to the Throne's Eye gates. His convoy had been away for nine weeks. The sun was setting as they arrived home, and as the gates unlocked, the fatigued monks nodded to each other in acknowledgement of a successful mission, and then, seeking to heal their wounds, they lined up at the door to Galian's quarters.

As the line grew, Odin slinked away. He always did. Stubbornly, he chose to suffer pain rather than to ask for Galian's help.

As Odin broke away from the pack, a heavy arm fell across his shoulders.

"Well, my friend," Raine said, "another wrong has been righted, the world is a little more at peace, and I want a drink. Shall I pour two?"

"If you're hurting," Odin replied, "you should stay in line."

Raine shrugged. "A beer should do just fine."

"You don't have to tend to me," Odin said flatly. "I'm alright."

"I know," Raine said. "But I like beer."

With a firm grip, Raine began to steer Odin towards the library.

"One drink," he said. "You owe me that much."

Odin conceded. "One drink."

After the two had settled down in the Spine, one drink quickly turned to ten.

As Raine nursed his tenth beer, he kicked out his legs and reclined back in the library chair.

"Good to be back," he said as he stretched his arms. "Much nicer pace here."

"What?" Odin prodded with a smile, "the missions getting too fast?"

"Aw shit, Odin," Raine complained. "They're way too quick."

Odin laughed and then watched his mentor for a moment.

"You know," he said finally, "you've trained us all pretty damn well. You don't need to come out as often."

Raine dropped his head a little, muttering before he took another swig of his beer.

"Go on, then. I know what you got on your mind."

"Let's be quite clear, Raine. I don't want to do this."

"So it's your burden, is it?"

"It's my responsibility" Odin said firmly. "I have not and never will doubt your judgement in the field. You weigh all factors of war with a great wisdom. But now you have to be honest about your own abilities. Raine, you know you hurt us on that mission."

Raine was visibly offended, but it was not an offense rooted in surprise. He knew that this conversation was looming.

"I've known for a while," he admitted. "My mind still has a leg up. But my body's 'bout three steps behind."

"There's no shame in that," Odin said with a smile. "Realistically, you've been the best fighter in the world for thirty years."

Raine laughed. "I guess that is a hell of a run."

"So you'll not fight this?" Odin said. "You'll stay back a little more often?"

"Shit, Odin, what else can I do?"

"I didn't mean to corner you like this," Odin apologized.

"It's alright, Odin. It had to be done. Though, I suppose it does lead into something we need to talk about."

Odin was caught by surprise. "What's that?"

"Like I said, mate, I knew my time was closing. What I needed to make it official was Igallik's blessing. And I got it before we left on that last mission."

Odin was confused. "You needed Igallik to okay your retirement?"

"No," Raine said. "I needed him to give me the okay on electing the next Aeris. Odin, we've elected you. You're our new Aeris."

"I'm an Aeris?" Odin repeated in disbelief.

Although he had always wanted the title, Odin was tentative about accepting it.

"Are you sure?" he said. "There are other candidates – monks with far more experience."

"More experience, maybe," Raine said. "But more talent? Not a chance. We've all known this was coming," Raine said. "It was written in the stars, mate. We figured with the possibility of me stepping down, it'd make sense to have you step up."

Odin couldn't wipe the smile from his face.

"You carry the torch now," Raine said as he raised his beer. "It's never been in better hands."

Odin raised his drink too. "To the torch, and to all the hands that have brought it to me."

After their bottles clinked, Raine winced and gripped his shoulder.

"Bloody hell," he groaned. "That one hurts."

"You should go to Galian," Odin said.

"Maybe I should," Raine said. "Maybe you should, too."

"You know I can't," Odin replied.

"Why?" Raine challenged. "'Cause he killed those miners and let you get your back smashed up?"

The drink had obviously loosened Raine's nerves. But even still, his abruptness made Odin flex back.

"You knew?" Odin asked.

"We all did, mate."

"And you let it happen?"

"If my memory serves, so did you."

Odin looked for any way out of the conversation.

"I think you've had too much," he said as he tapped his beer. "We can talk about this another time."

"You gotta bury the hatchet, mate. A brother is a terrible thing to lose. Especially if you can choose to get him back. We only got about five years before you boys and the Forge go back. You need to use those years for all they have. The Forge needs you."

"They have Galian," Odin said plainly.

Raine shook his head. "Is your pride really that hurt?"

After Odin took another swig of his beer, his eyes fell to the floor.

"Time will tell," he said curtly.

After studying his apprentice for a moment, Raine was a little ashamed of his actions.

"I didn't mean to ruin your moment," he said. "Come on, mate. Be happy. You're an Aeris now."

As Raine held up his beer for another toast, he examined it for a moment, frowning at what he considered to be an insufficient amount of beer.

"We'll each have one more," he said. "We'll end this night the right way."

Odin managed a nod. "One more."

The eleventh beer hit Raine harder than expected, and it was only minutes before the old warrior was passed out in his chair.

Choosing to leave his mentor in peace, Odin ambled out of the library. He too was feeling the effect of the alcohol, and as he sauntered clumsily around the monastery, he soaked in a great sense of achievement. He was an Aeris! Without even realizing it, his steps began to lead him to Galian's door. Some part of him – some piece of his soul that sought to forgive his brother – wanted to share the news. When Odin suddenly realized where he was headed, he halted mid-step.

The new Aeris paused for a long moment, his posture wavering from the beer. After a few staggers, he reclaimed his balance.

"I'm an Aeris now," he whispered towards Galian's room. "But you probably already know that ..."

With a discouraged exhalation, Odin kicked against the courtyard floor and then turned back to his own room.

As he rounded the corner into his room, he could see that someone had left a gift on his side table. There was a small black bracelet with a hand-written note folded over top of it. Odin retrieved the note, but as he looked at the handwriting, he immediately crushed the paper in his hand.

It was Galian's cursive.

"A little late for gifts," Odin muttered.

After slapping the bracelet off the end table, Odin collapsed onto his bed.

He would need the rest.

The next day, his life would change forever.

31

The next morning came early for Odin. He awoke to the abnormally busy sound of the Throne's Eye courtyard. Odin stretched off the sleep, and feeling a little rough from the night before, he laboured out into the commotion. As he exited his quarters, he could see that there were eleven large, black carriages and one old, white carriage parked just inside the monastery's gate. In addition to the many carts in the courtyard, there were also at least thirty darkly robed women of varying age. The majority of them were outside one of the Throne's Eye temples, but a few were wandering by themselves.

Odin scanned the courtyard. He eventually saw Craine lounging next to the monastery stables. With a wave, Odin crossed the courtyard to join him. Craine was an Indian Sight of about Odin's age, and after the rift had grown between the twins, Odin had often found himself in Craine's company.

"What's all this about?" Odin asked as he sided up to Craine.

"The Sisterhood," Craine replied. "I think they need our help."

As Odin looked across to the largest congregation of women, he watched Igallik and a woman in red exit one of the temples in the heart of the monastery. The head monk called Raine, and after adding him to their numbers, the three re-entered the temple.

"The woman in red," Odin recalled, "she has only been within our walls twice, and both times she was asking for big favours."

Craine nodded. "This is true," he said.

As Odin wondered what today's favour might be, Craine returned his attention to one of the mares in the stable. The horse was a monstrous, jet black mustang that Craine had found and named Desia. Craine had been training Desia for two years, and because of her incredible brawn, the Sight had expected great things. However, Desia's previous owner had abandoned her, and as a result, the horse was easily spooked and did not give its trust freely.

"How is she?" Odin asked.

"I'm working on her," Craine said. "I think she's almost ready to be saddled."

"You're not giving up on this one, are you?"

Craine reserved his answer for a moment. "I see something in her," he said finally, "something that shouldn't be given up on."

"What do you see?" Odin asked.

"Something you'd probably recognize," Craine replied.

"Why would I recognize it?"

"Desia's a marvel of power," Craine said, "but she's focused on the wrong part of her makeup. She doesn't realize where her strength lies."

Odin flexed back a little. "That's pretty vague," he said.

"Maybe. But the way I see it, Desia's fate is being ruled by her weakness and not her strength. I'm hoping something is going to startle her, you know? I'm hoping she needs to react to something that is bigger than her own problems. She'll run then, I'm sure of it. A lot like you and your brother."

Odin rolled his eyes. "I just got up," he said. "And I was drinking last night. It's a little too early for this conversation."

Craine shrugged. "Better too early than too late."

Before Odin could reply, Raine exited the temple and called to him from across the courtyard.

"Hey, mate!" he shouted. "We need you over here!"

Odin nodded, and as he began to jog across the courtyard, he gave Craine a sarcastic grin.

"Who knows? Maybe I'm about to be startled."

After Odin had reached the temple, Raine slapped him on the shoulder.

"Feeling alright?" he asked.

"No worse for wear. You?"

"Like hammered shit," Raine laughed. "I had a few too many."

"That's alright," Odin grinned. "You're retired now."

"That I am," Raine said. "But you, my friend, are not."

Raine pointed behind him to the temple. "There's a job waiting for you through those doors."

"I'd expect nothing less," Odin said.

"Figured."

With another slap to the shoulder, Raine ushered Odin into the temple.

Igallik and the woman in red were waiting. The old warrior directed Odin into the pew directly across from Igallik, and almost immediately the head monk spoke.

"We had hoped that our newest Aeris would receive more than a day off, but duty has called."

Odin smiled at the head monk and then awaited the briefing.

"It would seem," Igallik explained, "that three young women of the Sisterhood have been kidnapped."

"Three particular women," the woman in red added. "It is nice to meet you, Odin," she said as she extended her hand. "My name is Evelyn, and I hold the post of the Sisterhood's chancellor."

Odin accepted Evelyn's hand, and then quickly returned to the matter at hand.

"What is so particular about these women?" he asked.

"Each was set to begin a ritual that would allow us to recognize them as adults within our circle," Evelyn answered.

Evelyn then nodded to Raine, who promptly handed Odin a letter.

Odin began to read as Igallik further explained the situation.

"What really sets this abduction apart," he said, "is those who have claimed responsibility for the kidnapping."

Odin shook his head and then looked to Igallik as he finished reading the letter.

"This is gibberish. It's nonsense."

"Not quite," Igallik said.

Igallik handed Odin a small mirror and instructed him to angle it so that the letter would appear in its reflection.

Odin did so, and after re-reading the letter, his posture slumped a little.

"It's the Scale," he realized. "Forneus's faithful have done this."

"Yes," Igallik confirmed. "Our adversary has targeted the Sisterhood. We are unsure why, but we do know that we have until midnight to neutralize their intentions for the three girls."

Odin was still examining the note. "What is this black mark?" he asked as he pointed to a symbol at the bottom of the letter.

"We're not sure, Odin," Igallik said. "It is being looked into. We can only act on what we know, and what we know is that the three girls are in jeopardy."

"Okay, what's the plan?"

"Your brother," Evelyn informed, "has divined an exact location in the city for where the girls are being held. I have no previous experience with Galian's fortune-telling, but if you are willing to trust his hunch, we will get you to that location before midnight."

Odin seemed to swallow back some emotion. "If Galian says the girls are there," he said, "then they are there. It would prove stupid to ignore his sight."

"We have a deal then," Evelyn agreed. "Prepare yourself," she said as she rose from the pew. "Your transportation will be leaving in fifteen minutes."

After shaking Igallik's hand, Evelyn exited the temple and left the monks of the Throne's Eye to speak among themselves.

"If not made already clear," Igallik said to Odin, "this mission will be operated solely by you."

"That's fine," Odin affirmed.

"Alright, Aeris," Igallik said, "do what you do best."

As Igallik rose, he patted Odin's shoulder and left Raine and Odin to discuss the mission's particulars.

"What do you figure?" Odin asked pertaining to weaponry. "Loaded up or stripped down?"

"I figure Sleipnir will do," Raine said.

The old warrior paused to think. "Actually," he corrected, "you better make that Sleipnir and a handful of stitchers."

"A man of taste," Odin grinned.

"First and foremost," Raine replied.

Understanding that time was not a luxury, Odin speedily dressed himself in his black battle attire and made his way to the Throne's Eye armoury. He quickly retrieved Sleipnir – his bow staff – and six long daggers that the Torch monks called stitchers.

Sleipnir was a small gray cylinder with a button located in its center. When the button was pressed, the two ends of the bow staff either extended out to a combined length of six feet, or retracted in to a length of about one foot.

After testing Sleipnir's action a few times, Odin emerged out into the courtyard, and it was only minutes before Evelyn's white carriage was ready to leave.

Raine was next to the carriage with his final counsel.

"I'd shadow-game it," he said to Odin. "No need to get public."

"I'll assess the threat level," Odin replied. "But it is the Scale after all. I might want to show off."

Raine narrowed his gaze. "You better make sure the girls are safe first."

"Will do,"

"Alright, Aeris," Raine said, "make us proud."

After the two had shaken hands, Odin stepped one foot into the cab's rear door. As he stepped up, and hung halfway out, Galian emerged into his line of sight. The two brothers held eyes for a long moment. There was something in Galian's gaze that seemed different

– almost vulnerable. As the stare held, Galian offered a farewell wave, but with an air of dismissal, Odin ignored it and tucked himself into the carriage.

Moments later, the carriage was on the move.

As Galian watched the white carriage leave through the Throne's Eye gates, Igallik walked next to him.

"It's now, isn't it?" he said.

"Yes," Galian answered. "My sight is now gone."

Igallik watched the departing carriage for a moment.

"Are you sure you shouldn't have told Odin?"

Galian's posture slumped. "I have lost him, Igallik. He wouldn't care."

"I think you underestimate him," the head monk replied.

"I wish that were true. I wish he wanted to be my brother again."

Igallik brushed his hand through his long beard. "Do you still feel only pain in the future?"

"Hell is very close," Galian confirmed.

"What do you want me to do?"

"I'm not sure. It seems like fate is in charge now."

Igallik looked skywards for a moment. "I have learned that fate can succumb to prayer."

"Then pray I must," Galian decided, "because I am no match for Hell."

32

Odin held himself mostly in silence as Evelyn's white carriage delivered him to the location of the three abducted girls. In his cart was the driver, one young woman of the sisterhood, and the crimson-attired Evelyn. The carriage occupants' only exchange of words was brief. As the young woman noticed the storm clouds in the distance, she began to weep. Evelyn was quick to console her.

"It's not like last time, Chloe," she assured. "I promise you, it's not happening again."

"What's not happening again?" Odin asked.

Evelyn, who was exceptionally protective of her girls, became uncharacteristically candid.

"Chloe has a unique sense," she said, "one that has proven quite accurate. She is actually able to feel death."

"She feels it now?" Odin asked with some apprehension.

Chloe wiped her eyes and clenched her hands around Odin's.

"I feel it very strongly," she whispered. "From the moment I saw the letter, I knew Death was coming. Odin, Death is wrapped in that letter."

Odin did his best to console her.

"Tonight I will more than likely be an agent of death," he said. "But, trust me, the men I strike down are bad men. They deserve to die."

"No, Odin," Chloe sobbed. "Tonight, someone very good is going to die."

Her voice was too certain, so much so that the hairs on Odin's neck stood up.

After a small pause, Odin tried to offer some comfort to Chloe.

"I'm sure it will be okay," he said.

But words could not stop Chloe's tears.

Instead, the carriage again fell into silence, and Odin found himself suddenly wary of the distant storm clouds.

33

Shortly after Odin's departure, Igallik led Galian into the High Temple. The head monk's hope was that the hallowed Temple would repel whatever evil was coming for Galian. Aside from the distant and approaching thunder, the Temple was solemnly quiet. Galian had elected to meditate, and Igallik, in both anxiety and initiative, had resolved to do the same. The two meditated for three hours, but as the thunder started to roll over top of the monastery, Galian broke from his meditation and began to pace. The frenzied sound of Galian's footsteps quickly alerted the head monk.

"What's wrong?" Igallik asked as he broke from his trance.

Galian shook his head in confusion.

"I don't know. I've never felt this way. There is something about the thunder."

"Is your breathing okay?" the head monk asked.

"Erratic," Galian replied.

Igallik looked around the Temple. "Please," he said as he grabbed a stool, "sit down."

"I can't," Galian signed. "Something is very wrong. I feel it."

As a worried Igallik scoured his own mind for answers, the sound of crows echoed from outside the Temple doors.

"That's strange," the head monk whispered to himself.

"What?" Galian asked.

"The crows," Igallik said. "They never fly here. The eagles in our forest keep them far from our monastery."

As his curiosity rose, the head monk made his way to the Temple doors. However, as he pulled the giant doors open and peered over the monastery, his arms fell limp and the bronze door flung out of his control. Hundreds of crows were circling the monastery, swooping and cawing over the courtyard like black tornadoes.

"Holy heaven" Igallik gasped.

As the sound drowned out his own thoughts, the head monk turned back to Galian.

"Something is very wrong," he said. "Get back into the Temple."

Galian nodded, but as he turned, an astoundingly loud crash of thunder filled the monastery. Thinking that lightning had struck the monastery, Igallik turned fearfully back to the courtyard, but as he surveyed the monastery, there was no sign to indicate lightning had touched down.

Nervously, Igallik began to wring his hands. Not knowing what else to do, the head monk closed the Temple's bronze doors shut. However, as they slammed closed, a loud and very dull thud echoed from behind him.

As Igallik turned to the sound, he stumbled clumsily back into the door.

Galian was sprawled on the Temple floor.

"Galian!" the head monk screamed.

There was no answer.

With speed he hadn't used in years, Igallik rushed to Galian's side and began to shake him. There was no response. Instead, as the head monk tried desperately to wake Galian, blood began to seep from Galian's ears. In his panic, Igallik threw the Temple doors back open and began to scream furiously for Raine.

Only short moments later, the old warrior rushed up the Temple staircase.

"What's the problem?" he yelled in worry. As he stormed into the Temple, the problem was clear.

"What's wrong with him?" Raine asked as he knelt down to brace Galian's neck.

"I don't know," Igallik admitted. The head monk's panic seemed to cut through the air.

"Come on, Igallik, you gotta know."

"I don't," Igallik painfully repeated.

"What do we do?" Raine asked.

Igallik ran his hands through his gray hair in frustration.

"You're to go get Odin," he decided.

"Right now? During the mission?"

"Yes. Grab Craine and tell him the situation. Tell him to rig a carriage and get you there as fast as possible."

"You're sure?" Raine checked again. "The boys aren't even on speaking terms."

"It won't matter now," Igallik said, "not when Galian's like this."

Raine nodded, and with panic controlling his pulse, he turned and sprinted out of the Temple.

In Raine's absence, Igallik checked Galian's pulse.

It was faint and fading.

Once again, time was not an ally of the great Galian.

34

Night and heavy rain were falling as Evelyn's white carriage reached its destination in the town's outer district. Through the rain-soaked windows, Odin could see an old run-down church. The church, long forgotten by the hands of beauty, seemed to fade into the weathered backdrop of the town's dark corner. Next to the church, a gothic clock tower lurked. Odin exited the car and glanced up at the time: 10:36. It was accurate. There was still over an hour before the Scale's threat would come to pass.

As Odin looked over the old church, Evelyn spoke to him from inside her carriage.

"We will wait here," she said. "Please, Odin, bring our girls out safe."

Odin nodded. "I won't be long."

After another look at the clock, Odin turned and entered the church doors.

As he breached the door, the sound of rain faded to a faint patter. The ground floor of the church was eerily dark. In the limited light, it appeared that this floor was the chapel segment. As Odin skulked slowly through the broken pews, he could hear footsteps echoing down from the church's upper floor. He assumed that the girls were upstairs, but in adherence to his training, he first began a quiet sweep of the first floor. Attached to the chapel, there were four rooms. As Odin crept slowly through the darkness, he found that the first three rooms were vacant of both people and objects of interest. However, as Odin neared the final room, he could hear two voices. Using the shadows as his ally, Odin armed both of his hands with a stitcher, and then, like a spectre, he floated inaudibly through the dark doorway. As he gained his vantage point, he observed that there were two Scale labouring in front of a large basin. The two were in the midst of what seemed like a ritual, and they were executing their gruesome rite with industrial precision. To begin, the Scale on the left would reach into a barrel, and after retrieving a live snake, he would subsequently cut off its head and then hand it to the Scale on the right. Once the headless snake was passed to him, the second Scale would use his hands to squeeze the serpent from tail to head, using the force of his grip to push the snake's blood down into a jar.

"Is that fifty?" the Scale on the left asked.

"Shite, I thought you were counting."

The first shook his head and tapped his finger against an open leather book resting on the side of the sink.

"It has to be fifty," he said. "No more, no less. Death must be precise."

"In that respect, I think we actually agree," Odin said as he emerged from the shadows.

As the two Scale turned back, Odin offered a pompous grin, and then pitched his daggers powerfully into each of their throats. The impact knocked both of them backwards into the sink, and as the two thrashed and gasped, Odin drew back into the shadows and waited for Death to claim his victims. As he waited, Odin armed himself again and crouched in the darkness, poised to kill any Scale that would come rushing in. After an anxious moment of silence, the two Scale went limp in death and it appeared that Odin's stealth was still intact. Flowing with the quiet, the Aeris approached the basin. As he looked over it and saw the dozens of dead snakes, the rancid smell forced him to withdraw his head. However, in his quick glance, he had noticed that one of the Scale had knocked the leather book into the sink. Suspecting that the text could explain the Scale's earlier rite, Odin again approached the basin, and after covering his nose with his cuff, he snatched the large leather book. As a few steps sounded from above him, the Aeris paused once more in the silence, breathing slowly and evenly as he held his pose like an alert cat. The steps passed, and after a small nod, Odin laid the book on a table away from the sink and investigated the page it was left open to. The top of the page had been smeared with some of the Scale's blood, obscuring most of the text. However, on the bottom of the page was the exact symbol that Odin had seen on the letter claiming responsibility for the abduction of the girls. Below the symbol were the words: *The Reaper's Covenant*. As Odin continued to read the page, it seemed that the text was a list of ingredients. The ingredients were strange. One measurement was for the blood of fifty snakes.

In spite of what he had found, the new Aeris resolved that securing the girls' safety remained his primary objective, and the implications of the symbol needed to wait.

After finishing his survey of the church's first floor, Odin crept quietly up the church's spiralling stairwell. As he ascended to the second floor, dozens of lit torches flared into his vision. With a few quick steps, he tucked into a corner and allowed his senses to adjust, and after regaining his vision, he began a furtive assessment of his surroundings. The second floor was centered by a long crimson red hallway that was lined with more lit torches. The flames of the torches were swaying a little, and it took Odin a moment to detect that there was an air current blowing down the hall. There were a few doors lining the hall, but as Odin studied the hallway, he suspected that the air current was coming from two gothic doors set at the hall's end. As he crouched and attuned his ears, Odin could hear many voices behind the doorway. Most of the voices sounded male, but among the different murmurs, Odin thought he could decipher higher pitched, and likely female, voices. Believing the girls were captive behind the doors, Odin sided against the hallway's wall and began to move towards the end of the hall. As he crept, one of the torches cast a moving shadow on the door at the end.

For a moment, Odin considered Raine's advice.

"Shadow-game it," the old warrior had said.

"Not this time," Odin grinned.

As the shadow at the end of the hall materialized into a hooded figure, Odin tapped his dagger against the side of the wall, letting the sound of his blade echo down the hallway. Like an owl, the hooded Scale turned his neck to the sound.

By his own volition, Odin's stealth was gone.

The Scale stared down the hallway; he slowly drew his hood back, allowing the torch light to reveal the snake scales painted on his face. As Odin eyed his foe, the Scale sounded a loud hiss, pulled a very long knife from his belt, and lashed his forked tongue across the end of the blade.

Odin was unimpressed.

"You shouldn't play with knives," he warned. "It'd be a shame if you cut yourself."

As six more Scale emerged from the end of the hall, the initial Scale shot back his retort.

"There are greater shames than a cut," he spat. "Your failure to save the girls, for instance, will be hard to live with." With another hiss, the Scale drew back his knife. "Fortunately, you won't have to live long with that burden…"

With a wild pitch, the Scale hurled the blade down the corridor. Contrary to instinct, Odin sprinted towards the barrelling blade. As he darted down the hall, he lunged onto the wall on his right. After three propelling strides off of the wall, Odin swiftly caught the thrown knife by the blade, and as he spun off the wall, he hurtled the knife back down the hallway. The knife scorched back down the corridor, and, like a harpoon, it speared its owner in the forehead. As Odin rose to his combat stance, he retrieved Sleipnir from his belt and pressed her center button to extend her two ends into a bow staff. Five of the remaining six Scale members advanced on Odin, but the Aeris quickly and precisely destroyed their efforts. The last of the Scale was at the end of the hallway trying to unlock the twin doors, fumbling nervously with the keys. Seeing his foe's back, Odin erupted into a sprint. As he closed in on the last Scale, he used Sleipnir to vault himself into the air, and once airborne, Odin delivered a flying kick into the Scale's spine. With a crack, the door splintered open, and the Scale's lifeless body launched into the next room.

Odin calmly entered the locked room and began a quick assessment of the situation. The room was quite massive. At the far end, the hard rain fell outside of a huge, mostly broken window that revealed a direct view of the clock tower's face. Massive gold torches circled the outer ring of the room, and at the center the three sisterhood girls were bound with rope to one of the room's supporting beams. In the room there were twelve Scale members wearing dark hoods and one very large member who, by his distinct red hood, seemed to be a leader. The red-hooded Scale had a large python wrapped on his shoulders, and on the floor in front of him there seemed to be a six-foot-wide pool of crimson blood.

The leader turned directly to Odin.

"Welcome, Throne's Eye!" he bellowed. "To the year of the serpent! To the year of your demise! I, Sykos, am your gracious host!"

As the three girls saw Odin, they began to squirm and scream for help. The Aeris quickly caught their eyes, and after nodding to give them some hope, he turned back to Sykos.

"I am giving you one last chance to let them go," he said. "You should take it. If you don't, tonight will end very poorly for you."

"Arrogance," the leader spat.

"Truth," Odin countered.

"Oh, no," a familiar voice said from room's rear shadow, "we are definitely dealing with arrogance."

After ordering the Scale to stand down, the source of the voice emerged into the torch light.

"Usis," Odin snarled.

"Well hello, Odin," Usis greeted.

"You're not much," Odin said, "but stooping to the level of Scale is below even you."

"Please," Usis laughed. "I am no Scale. You know the expression: the enemy of my enemy is my friend."

"I think you got shortchanged," Odin said.

Usis smirked in amusement.

"I love the climb you've made! You've made yourself a man! You should be proud of your ascent, especially now, because you're really going to hate the fall."

"Sorry, Usis, today is not that day."

"I beg to differ," Usis grinned. "The letter was delivered, was it not?"

Chloe's prophecy flashed in Odin's mind.

"What about the letter?" he demanded.

Usis laughed again. "Your brother is dead! The great Galian has met the scythe."

Odin's mind immediately recalled the leather book.

"The symbol on the letter," he said. "You used the Reaper's Covenant."

"Very good, Odin. You're a sleuth!"

Suddenly, thirty-six reeds didn't matter.

Suddenly, Odin's greatest fire returned.

"You've just died," he promised Usis. "You just don't know it yet."

"Really?" Usis scoffed. "By your hand?"

Odin's returning stare was a sufficient answer.

"You should have never involved Galian," he said. "You should have stayed focused on me. After everything, how could you send Death to him?"

"It was actually quite easy," Usis explained. "Death, like any great hunter, is thrilled by the prospect of big game. Besides, I hear you two don't even get along anymore."

Odin's deadly eyes locked onto the traitor.

"He is always my brother," he seared. "He is not like you."

"Well then you can join him in death," Usis laughed.

With an arrogant wave of his hand, Usis turned to the thirteen Scale members present.

"Your part of the bargain is held," he said. "You may kill him now."

As Usis backed up to watch, each Scale but Sykos advanced on Odin.

As his minions charged Odin, Sykos's python slid onto his outstretched arm, and the leader began to recite from a scorched scroll. The members of the Scale, armed with spears and swords, wildly converged on Odin, but Odin's mastery of combat began to quickly suppress their attack. Odin swung Sleipnir with deadly precision, and within moments, half of the Scale were dead.

As Odin engaged the remaining Scale, Sykos finished reciting from his scroll and then threw the parchment into the deep pool of blood before him. The blood instantly began to boil, and after calmly removing his crimson hood, Sykos pulled a large dagger from his belt. The python, apparently in tune with the rite, wrapped its head around the dagger, and in the next instant, Sykos plunged the dagger deep into his own abdomen and fell into the pool of boiling blood. Odin, engaged with the Scale, noted Sykos's actions, but failed to comprehend their significance. The confusion did not sit well with him. Unpredictability was an enemy of strategy. Odin resolved that the quarrel needed to end. He began to swing Sleipnir in methodical, devastating, death-driven arcs, and within another minute the remaining Scale were no more.

The sound of clapping, cold and slow, came from the broken window.

"Well done," Usis said as he emerged from the shadows. "Perhaps," he goaded while tapping the end of his sword, "you'd prefer a higher calibre of sparring."

"Higher calibre?" Odin repeated. "Usis, you're not ready for this."

"Indulge me," Usis replied.

"As you wish," Odin said. "But first, we let the girls go. They serve you no purpose."

"Fair enough," Usis agreed. "Cut them down."

While keeping a close eye on Usis, Odin backed towards the girls and drew one of his daggers. Odin addressed the girls as they cried in gratitude.

"When I cut you down," he instructed, "you leave immediately. Do not look back. Just get to Evelyn outside."

The girls nodded in understanding.

While carefully watching Usis, Odin released the first girl. She immediately left. After another glance over his shoulder, Odin released the second girl, but as he began to reach for the rope binding the third girl's hands, the second girl hysterically latched onto him. The moment was all Usis needed. In a matter of seconds, Usis had pitched three blades at Odin's back. While holding the second girl, Odin manipulated himself into a roll that just narrowly evaded the projectile daggers. As Odin looked back and realized Usis was advancing on him, he lifted the girl to her feet and then sternly spurred her out of the room. Odin watched to confirm the girl's departure, and as he turned, he instinctively parried a combination of Usis's sword attacks.

With the clash of their weapons still ringing in the air, the two foes backed off to size each other up.

"You're not playing nice," Odin jested.

Usis offered a pompous grin. "I've learned that mean usually wins."

"Let's test that theory," Odin decided.

Odin speedily drove the left end of Sleipnir into Usis's right shin, and as Usis lowered his sword to guard his legs, Odin drove the opposite end of Sleipnir into Usis's throat. Usis stumbled back, coughing as he grabbed his own neck.

"Too mean?" Odin taunted.

Usis brought his sleeve to his mouth, and after observing the blood on his cuff, he began to circle Odin.

"The speed is commendable," he said, "but I'm sure the defence is not."

With ferocious speed, Usis sliced a combination of five swords attacks at Odin's legs and core. Odin parried the first four away, and as he lunged outside the range of the fifth, he swung Sleipnir back and connected her hard into Usis's ribs.

"Range," Odin stressed. "It makes a hell of a difference."

"Good point," Usis agreed.

With a quick release, Usis hurtled one of his daggers at Odin's heart. Odin reacted in time to deflect it, but Usis was quickly on him. The exchange of attack and parry quickly hit double digits. Usis managed to graze one of his attacks against Odin's shoulder, but Odin rebounded with a kick that severely disabled Usis's ankle, followed by a shoulder thrust that sent Usis tumbling to the floor.

"Face it, Usis, I am better than you. You've stagnated."

Usis tried to stand, but his injured ankle would not allow it. Understanding his vulnerability, he began a desperate crawl to the open window. However, Odin's stalking steps had remained close on his trail. As Odin towered over him, Usis snarled and spat a grim promise at his old friend.

"You may have won today," he conceded. "But I promise you, your victory will be short lived. Hell is nigh, Odin. And she will destroy you."

"Enough of your games," Odin threatened as he put Sleipnir to Usis's throat. "Speak truth or die."

Usis grinned menacingly. "That which befell the father," he said, "has come to befall the sons."

"What have you done?" Odin demanded.

"Just a little exchange of information," Usis laughed. "Forneus now knows who, what, and where you are. You, Odin, are a dead man walking."

For Odin, it was not panic, or fear, that responded to Usis's words. It was rage.

Usis had become prey.

Odin smashed Sleipnir into Usis's injured ankle and then furiously stomped on Usis's abdomen. As Usis bucked from the impact and held his stomach, Odin speedily locked Sleipnir against the front of his throat, and then drove his own knee into the back of Usis's neck. Odin was relentless, but as Usis's life began to dwindle, the pool of blood that Sykos had fallen into began to boil. Odin quickly assessed the situation. Every fibre in his body was driven to kill Usis, but there was still one of the girls bound to the room's supporting beam. As Odin pressed unremittingly into Usis's neck, Sykos emerged slowly out of the blood pool, his body soaked with a coat of crimson. His eyes, which now burned orange like hot coals, seemed to be hunting through the room. The seeking embers quickly passed Odin and Usis and landed on the final Sisterhood girl. Like a rolling boulder, Sykos began to march towards the captive girl. Seeing the threat, Odin relinquished one hand from Sleipnir and hurriedly drew one of his belt's remaining daggers. With practiced accuracy, he launched the dagger into the rope that was binding the final girl's hands. The rope, despite Odin's efforts, only partially disbanded, and the girl was left terrifyingly still at the end-length of Sykos's warpath. Odin could feel Usis dying, but despite his own desire for revenge, the traitor's death did not outweigh the importance of the girl's life. With a furious breath, Odin released Usis from the choke and darted across the room to engage Sykos.

As Sykos came within an arm's length of the screaming girl, he stabbed his hands at her neck. However, after an urgent leap, Odin smacked Sleipnir down onto Sykos's forearms, and the Scale's hands immediately recoiled. Before Sykos could react, Odin threw an elbow at his jaw, and as he staggered, Odin swung a strong roundhouse kick into his back. The impact knocked Sykos airborne, and with a heavy thud his body tumbled clumsily across the floor. Speedily, Odin tried to release the final girl, but in a matter of seconds, the Scale leader sprung quickly back to his feet.

"My master has a message!" he growled.

Furiously, Sykos wrapped his hands around one of the room's massive gold torches. The torch must have weighed close to three hundred pounds, but Sykos inhumanly lifted it into the air. Odin watched perplexed as Sykos, by some inheritance of the earlier rite, began to swing the torch as if it were the weight of a regular sword. Amid Sykos's screams and swings, Odin's mind began to search for a strategy. As he took inventory of the room, he first realized that the giant vacant window was a great asset. He subsequently realized that Usis was gone. Odin cursed Usis's escape, but it was a frustration that needed to wait. Instead, Odin quickly calculated the risk and range of the giant torch, and he immediately led Sykos's attention away from the bound girl. Sykos took the bait. However, as Odin used his agility to evade the Scale leader's wild torch attacks, Sykos's feral assaults began to smash the church into disarray. Sykos had smashed all other torches to the ground, and atop the cracked and splintered floorboards, fire had begun to consume the giant room. With flames slashing between them, Odin leapt away from another attack, and as Sykos's weapon lodged into the floor, Odin weaved backwards towards the gaping window. With his foe falling into the trap, Odin danced away from another attack and left Sykos standing precariously in front of the open space. However, Odin remained uncertain of the limits of Sykos's new power. He needed to test the boundaries. As the torch sailed past him in a wild arc, Odin lunged within close proximity of the Scale leader, and with their eyes only a foot apart, Odin hacked Sleipnir into the back of Sykos's knees. Although the force caused Sykos's knees to buckle, his reaction was not indicative of the strength Odin had used. Seeking any advantage he could, Odin methodically speared Sleipnir into one of Sykos's fiery eyes. As the attack caused Sykos to stagger within feet of the broken window, the Scale leader began to scream, keeling over as an orange mist began to seep out of his eye socket. As the mist bled out, Sykos seemed to have greater difficulty brandishing the giant torch.

Odin would play his hunch.

As Sykos regained his poise and pointed the lit end of the torch at Odin's head, Odin's hand slid for his dagger.

"Throne's Eye!" he roared. "Heroism has become your downfall."

Amid the screaming, Odin tightened his fingers around one of his remaining daggers and began to unsheathe it from his belt.

"Watch now," the oblivious Scale leader spat, "as I become more of my master! I am going to destroy…"

With a lightning quick whip, Odin launched his dagger directly into the leader's eye. As Sykos stumbled back, Odin used his great speed to pitch another blade into his other eye. With a painful wail, the Scale leader began to stumble clumsily in front of the broken window. As the entirety of the orange mist left his eyes, Odin sensed his opportunity, and with fire spread over the ground between them, Odin charged at his foe. As he grew close, Odin again used Sleipnir to vault himself into the air, and while airborne, he delivered a heavy kick to Sykos's chest. The impact was devastating, launching the Scale leader helplessly out the window to his death.

With the Scale destroyed, Odin turned back to the last Sisterhood girl. The swaying fire was encroaching around her, but Odin calculated that the risk of harm was low. As he calmly approached, hoping to lessen the great trauma she had been through, suddenly she began to scream hysterically and point behind him. As Odin turned, the leader's python lunged out of the blood, but with a timely reflex, Odin adjusted his step and promptly crushed the snake's skull with his boot.

With the entirety of the Scale destroyed, Odin reached the last girl, and after cutting the rope around her wrists, he wrapped a caring arm around her shoulder.

"It's over," he assured. "You're okay."

The girl's head fell hard on Odin's chest, and as she cried with relief, Odin cut around the fire and led her out of the church.

Calmly, Odin emerged back onto the street in front of the church. Evelyn's carriage as well as one of the Throne's Eye carts was waiting. Odin delivered the last girl to Evelyn, and after receiving numerous hugs and words of gratitude, he made his way to the Throne's Eye buggy.

As he grew close to the cart, the curtain in the back window slid open, Odin was shocked to see who was sitting in the back seat.

"Get in, mate," Raine requested.

Odin obliged.

As Odin sat down, Raine quickly turned to the driver. "Take us home, Craine, and make it quick."

Craine nodded, reined the horses, and then whipped them back onto the road.

"Onward, Desia!" he shouted.

Weighing both Raine's presence and Usis's earlier boast, Odin knew something was wrong.

"It's Galian, isn't it?"

"Yeah, mate," Raine somberly answered. "He's pretty sick."

Odin shook his head in disbelief.

"What happened?"

"Igallik's not sure," Raine said. "Your brother collapsed in the High Temple. It was weird. There were hundreds of crows circling the monastery, and I'm telling you Odin, there was something in that thunder."

Odin's mind immediately identified the culprit.

"It was Usis," he said.

Upon hearing the name, Raine's interest became intently focused.

"What about Usis?" he demanded.

Odin's eyes were deadly. "He was at the church," he said. "Not only has he sent Death to my brother, he has given Forneus every detail concerning me and Galian."

Raine's expression turned irate.

"That prick," he cursed. "What a god-damned waste."

Odin simply nodded. His fury had already settled into focus.

"We have to find the letter the Scale sent," he began to strategize. "The symbol on the letter is the emblem of the Reaper's Covenant. If we can destroy the letter, I bet the covenant will break."

Still incensed by Usis's actions, Raine composed himself enough to agree.

"And Craine," Odin calmly added to the driver, "if Desia can run, I think now is the time to show off."

35

It was early morning when Odin's carriage reached the Throne's Eye gates. A wind storm had ransacked the last hours of the trek, and as the gates were drawn, it was clear the wind would not relent. The trees within the monastery were flexing and bending against the wind, rustling madly as their leaves howled like one thousand whistles. Amid the whirlwind, the tornado of crows still spiralled above.

After he had breached the gate, Craine quickly drove the horses as close to Galian's room as he could, and after the carriage had come to a stop, Odin and Raine burst out. As Odin and his mentor rushed across the red stone, they ran headlong into pressing winds, their clothing rippling as they fought to make it to Galian's quarters.

The majority of the crows as well as the majority of the Throne's Eye monks were waiting. Odin sliced through the crowd and slid to Galian's side. Igallik and the other monks of the High Order were next to the bed. There were many lit candles in the room, and Wylak had administered countless acupuncture needles to Galian's body.

As Odin rushed in, Igallik seemed too distraught to notice.

"Igallik!" Odin shouted as he grasped the head monk's shoulders. "I'm here!"

Igallik immediately swung back into attentiveness.

"Odin," he realized. "You're here."

"The letter the Scale sent, where is it?"

Igallik searched his mind for the answer.

"It's on the altar – the altar of the temple where we met with Evelyn."

Odin looked back to Raine to confirm that the old warrior had heard.

"Got it," Raine affirmed.

In seconds, Raine had sped across the courtyard to find the letter. As Raine began his search, Odin knelt beside Galian's bed, and after surveying his brother, he turned to the head monk.

"How is he?"

"Not good," Igallik answered. "More of him is stolen each moment."

Igallik was visibly exhausted. As the head monk began to massage his temples, Odin's first question seemed to fully register.

"What do you want with the letter?" he asked.

"The symbol at the bottom is the seal of the Reaper's Covenant." Odin said. "Usis used the letter to make a pact with Death."

"Usis?" Igallik repeated. "He is with the Scale?"

"No, he used them to get to us."

Igallik let out a deep sigh.

"I've often thought it was a mistake not telling Usis about his parents," he said. "I will suffer no more in that anguish. The mistake was not letting Usis's parents kill him."

Odin would not argue.

"At least we know what has become of your brother," Igallik said.

"If we destroy the letter, can we save Galian?" Odin asked.

"I believe so."

As Odin glanced back across the courtyard, he saw Raine sprinting back from the temple with the letter in hand.

It was going to work.

However, as Odin watched his mentor, it suddenly seemed like the old warrior's pace had slowed. Odin couldn't understand why Raine would slow. Time was not an ally. As Odin continued to watch, he suddenly realized that even the leaves, in spite of the roaring winds, had slowed down. Something sinister was moving within the courtyard – something Odin could feel.

"Come on," he whispered as he watched his mentor. "Twenty more yards."

As Raine laboured across the yard, the old warrior's face appeared anguished. His face was wrenched in pain, and with every step it seemed to be getting worse. Then, just as Raine let out a strained cry, there was a ghostly hush, and the old warrior's movement was frozen in mid-stride. As Odin turned to alert Igallik, he began to feel incredibly cold, and pins and needles began to strike everywhere on his body. Desperately, Odin reached for Igallik's shoulder, but mid-reach, Odin's movement became completely halted. Somehow, against their will, Odin, Igallik, and the other monks had become deadly still. The monks were still aware – their senses and thoughts remained engaged – but they had been robbed of action. They had become statues. The only movement in the monastery was the circling and squawking crows.

While the monks fought futilely against the paralysis, suddenly the candles in Galian's room started to flicker and spark. Their light cast every monk's shadow onto the wall. Odin could see Galian's,

Igallik's, and his own inert silhouette framed against the wall in front of him – it was as if he were watching a play of shadows.

Frozen as they were, the monks' thoughts had become imprisoned in their motionless bodies, feeding them with a claustrophobia that was worsening with every second. All of the monks' powers – all of their discipline and strength – had been rendered useless. Some foreign power had defeated them before they had even realized they were in a fight.

As the paralysis continued, paranoia and fear began to grow. When the mind cannot see its enemy, it can stretch many lengths. Fear begins to make demons out of dust. Many times, the imagination can build greater terrors than those that are found in reality.

This was not such a time.

As sweat began to bead down every monk's brow, suddenly, without anyone entering the room, another shadow began to emerge onto the wall. The shadow, seemingly coming from no source, began to unfold and grow to an inhuman height. With every monk watching, the shadow arched its back and two massive wings stretched across the wall. As the figure's wingspan spread completely open, the figure reached its boney hand into the darkness of its own shadow and began to pull out a giant scythe.

Odin's voice was loud in his own head, screaming and roaring at the shadow. But no sound came from his mouth. The shadow was stalking its prey, and there was nothing Odin could do but watch.

After ten slow steps – ones that creaked hauntingly throughout the silent room – the shadow stood ominously over Galian.

As he watched, one tortured phrase was repeating itself in Odin's mind.

"Not like this… Not like this…"

The words were more like a whimper, and as the shadow drew back its scythe, three years of silence burned through Odin's heart.

"Not like this!" Odin screamed. "I can't lose him like this! Please, God! Not like this!"

The prayer would not be answered.

Mercilessly, the giant shadow slammed down its scythe and plunged the blade powerfully into Galian's core. The Seraph's abdomen exploded open, and as his body bucked violently, the gory puncture wound began to spit out Galian's blood and guts.

Helplessly, Odin and the other monks watched Galian's blood and a dense blue mist start to pour from the wound. As the mist flooded into the air, it began to take on a human form. The vision was horrifying – it was a disgusting scene, forcing every monk present to watch Galian die. As the mist completely flooded from Galian's body, it resembled his exact form – it was his soul. It even had Galian's scar from Vinculum Imletalis.

With his face gritted in pain, Galian's soul squirmed and reached out for his brother, but as his hand stabbed desperately for Odin, the giant shadow cocked back its weapon and then speared the end of his scythe into Galian's soul. The scythe began to heave backward, dragging Galian deep into the shadow – towing him to death.

As Galian clawed for escape, suddenly there was stillness. The scene that the monks had been forced to watch froze like ice.

"Please..." Odin begged. "Please, let him go."

Death would not assent.

With a crack, thunder boomed over the monastery, and then, for an entire devastating minute, darkness overwhelmed Galian's quarters. There was nothing to see but the shadow of Death's cloak.

In the darkness, Odin was broken. For three years he had chosen to speak no words to his brother, but now, in this one heartbreaking moment, he begged God to let him speak only two.

"I'm sorry..."

As the darkness fell away, the re-emergence of light proved Galian's soul gone – its absence made hauntingly clear by Galian's body lying dead and destroyed on the crimson-soaked bed. With a sudden and powerful wave of cold, the monastery was rocked back into real time.

Every monk but the distraught Odin was knocked to the ground.

As Odin screamed in horror and collapsed over Galian's broken body, the head monk rose furiously to his feet and began a deadly focused march to the High Temple. Odin clenched Galian's dead hand, pleading with God to undo the devastation, but in spite of that demand, no miracle was awarded. Instead, by some power of the Reaper's scythe, Galian's body began disintegrate into ash, and Odin's heart and hands were left to sift through his dead brother's ashes. Death had been merciless – stealing Galian's soul and leaving no body for Throne's Eye final respects.

As Igallik rushed out of Galian's quarters, Raine finished the last leg of his duty and arrived at Galian's door with the letter in hand.

He quickly read the monk's eyes. "It's too late," he realized.

"Nothing could have been done," Igallik said.

Regardless of the pardon, Raine felt responsible.

"What happened?" he cried.

"Not sure," Igallik answered as he sped towards the High Temple.

Raine looked through the doorway and saw the heart-broken Odin.

"Aw, hell," the old warrior cursed. "It can't be like this."

Raine fell hard into the doorframe, his hands shaking as he heard the screams from Odin's mouth. Raine recognized the sound – it was the horror that cried out of him when he lost Ruscai. He would never wish such a pain on anyone.

The memories quickly became too much, and the old warrior launched himself after the departing head monk.

"What do we do?" he yelled. "How do we act?"

"Give me twenty minutes," Igallik yelled back. "Twenty minutes, and then assemble the Order and bring them to the High Temple."

Raine managed a nod of understanding. Out of necessity he took a moment to regain his composure, but as his breath began to slow, Odin burst out of Galian's quarters.

Odin's strides were wild and erratic like a wounded animal.

"Igallik!" he screamed hysterically. "Igallik! Get back here!"

Raine quickly positioned his massive frame across Odin's path.

"Not now, Raine!" Odin screamed as he tried to push through the old warrior.

Raine used both his body and voice to restrain Odin.

"You need to trust me, mate. Let him be for now."

"He's the only one who knows!" Odin cried. "He knows what happened! Igallik!" Odin screamed again. "Tell me what happened!"

"You're right, Odin," Raine said. "He knows. And you know in your head that he needs to be the one to understand. Give him some time," Raine said. "Just give him some time."

Odin's head collapsed onto Raine's chest, and his entire body began to tremble as tears streamed down his face.

"What do I do?" he began to sob. "I can't... I can't... not without him..."

Raine didn't have an answer. The only thing that he knew to do was to wrap his arms around Odin.

After a minute passed with Odin collapsed on Raine's chest, Craine emerged from Galian's quarters.

"Craine," Raine said quietly, "get the rest of the Order monks and bring them to the High Temple. Tell Igallik, I'm sitting this one out."

Craine nodded, and he quickly began his task. As Craine left, Raine wrapped his arm around Odin's shoulder.

"C'mon, mate. We'll take a walk, and then we'll go speak with Igallik."

Odin shook his head with a sniffle. "I need to be alone for a minute," he said weakly. "I just need a minute."

Raine patted Odin's back. "I can give you that," he said quietly. "If you need anything, just ask."

Odin nodded, and after wiping his nose with his sleeve, he fell away from the old warrior.

Staggering away, Odin's mind was replaying the scene of his brother's death – every piece of it. It was gruesome and wrenching, but Odin did so because he needed something, some image of his brother that he could hold on to. Many in your realm do the same then they lose someone. They search their memories for pieces of their loved ones.

Galian must have anticipated the search because he had left Odin something more tangible than a memory.

He had left him a letter – the one Odin had discarded the night he became an Aeris.

As Odin paced away, he suddenly recalled this, and as his posture jolted, he wiped his eyes again and sped towards his own quarters.

36

Upon Igallik's request, the Order assembled in the High Temple twenty minutes after Galian's demise. Instead of joining the Order, Raine chose to remove himself from the hearing in case Odin needed him.

For a half hour, Raine gave Odin time to himself. But finally, with his nerves balled in his gut, the old warrior went in search of his apprentice. He finally found him at the top of the Temple staircase.

"Waiting?" Raine asked as he ascended the final few steps.

"Have to," Odin replied.

Odin's face was pale white and his voice was low and hoarse as if he hadn't slept in weeks.

As Raine sat himself on the step next to Odin, he began to hear the voices of the Order monks echoing from inside the Temple. The monks' words were indecipherable, but their emotions were not. There was great anger and even greater worry.

"You're trying to listen to that?" Raine asked.

"Trying to," Odin said. "Can't manage much focus."

"I can shut up, if you want," Raine said.

"I think I'd rather talk," Odin replied.

"Okay. What about?"

"Galian left me a letter," Odin said, "a final message."

"What'd it say?" Raine asked.

Odin pulled the letter from his belt. "See for yourself."

The old warrior watched Odin for a moment.

"You sure you want me to read this?"

"I would appreciate it," Odin said.

"Okay, mate," Raine consented. "I'll give it a read."

With careful hands, the old warrior unfolded the page and set his eyes onto Galian's cursive.

> *Odin,*
>
> *I know I have lost you. My actions broke us. My heart knows this pain even more than yours. I took a hammer to the diamond that we were, and now we are apart – scattered in the pebbles of something that should have been grand.*
>
> *Three years is long to be without your soul. That is what I've been. You were, and forever will be, my greatest friend. I robbed myself of you, and for that, I am damned. I wish I could explain what I did. I wish I could show you*

why. But the future requires my silence. Our destiny – if it can ever be recovered – requires us to dance alone.

I write this letter because I have no idea if it will ever reach you. Hell stalks me, Odin. I wish I could face my future with you. I want nothing more than to be at your side when I face my greatest foe. But from what I have seen, I am alone when I meet my end. Fate has me believe that I will never be your brother again. Fate tells me that I die with you still hating me. I have never carried a pain like that. I have never suffered more.

This is my goodbye, Odin.

This is me saying that I hate myself for what I have done.

Our love – our great mighty roar – should have crushed Hell. We were the ones! The might sons of Animus Letum! We were kings.

I robbed us of that ...

My death is coming, Odin. Of this, I am sure. And the only thing I want is to have you back in my life. As I look towards my death, I realize the last three years of my life have been wasted. All I want is for us to reclaim the greatness we were.

But I killed that chance.

I pray you remember us, the way we were supposed to be – as kings.

Live strong my brother. And think of me when you become the hero that I know you are.

Forever your friend, forever your brother,

Galian.

Raine wiped his eyes, a small tremble sounding in his voice.

"I'm sorry, Odin," he said. "It should never have been like this."

Odin swallowed, and with his throat still tight, his voice whispered weakly from his mouth.

"He died thinking I hate him," he said. "I never did. I never did... I just... God damn it, Raine. He's gone! He died without me. I should have protected him!"

"It's not your fault," Raine said.

"But it was!" Odin yelled. "I chose to leave him! He was the star! And I left him. I should have protected him. It was my job! My one job!"

Odin's face fell hard into his palms, his head shaking as he sobbed through his fingers. Raine patted Odin's back, doing anything to offer condolence, but the pain in Odin's voice made it clear that the only sympathy Raine could offer was a caring quiet. So the two sat in sorrowed silence – grieving a man who had never spoken a word.

Another fifteen minutes passed before the High Temple's bronze doors were drawn open. Igallik exited first, followed by the other members of the Order. Odin leapt to his feet immediately, awaiting anything from his brothers, but the Order monks seemed intent not to address him. Instead, each Order monk was thanked by Igallik, and after they offered Odin an apologetic bow, Nile, Bysin, and Jeston descended the Temple's long staircase.

Unsure of the implication, Odin turned his eyes to Raine, and then to Igallik.

"Come inside," Igallik said as he retreated back through the bronze doors. "Both of you."

The two Aerises quickly followed, and as they entered the High Temple, Igallik sat quickly back on his throne and grabbed for his tobacco hookah. After Raine and Odin had seated themselves in the foremost pew, Igallik took a series of small puffs from his hookah, exhaled, and addressed Odin.

"I would imagine you have many questions," the head monk said. "If you can be patient with me, I will try to answer them now."

Odin did not hesitate.

"What's happened to Galian?" he demanded.

"Your brother is dead by the Reaper's Covenant," Igallik said. "His soul has been taken to Animus Letum."

"Why couldn't he see this coming?" Odin asked. "How come he couldn't prevent it?"

"Galian did know this was coming," Igallik said. "For the last three years he and I have been on a mission to prevent the events of today. Obviously, we failed. It would appear that Forneus has played his master hand. I doubt you will take any solace from this," Igallik added after a pause, "but you should know that Usis was merely a pawn in this game. He was the marionette to Forneus as puppet master."

Odin couldn't care less. "He chose to be a pawn," he said bitterly.

"I suppose you're right," Igallik said.

With disdain, Odin shook off all thoughts of Usis and returned his focus to Galian.

"So if Galian is in Animus Letum, he should be fine, right?" he asked. "We can get V to find him and hide him from Forneus."

Igallik shook his head, deeply apologetic for what would be his honest answer.

"V will be unable to help," he said gravely. "Your brother has been taken to Forneus's Soul Cauldron. And the power of ten thousand souls now binds your brother in torment."

The head monk inhaled deeply. "I hate to tell you this, Odin, but in this tragic time I must be forthright. The Cauldron is a prison of virtually no escape. Galian will likely die under its weight."

Odin keeled over. "No!" he yelled. "It can't be! He can't…"

Raine rested his arm over Odin's shoulders, and looked pleadingly to the head monk.

"There's got to be some hope," he said. "You said there is barely a chance. That is better than none."

As Igallik saw the hope in the two Aerises, he regretted that he had to dash it.

"Galian's only hope is to break the Cauldron," he said. "And the only way to break the Cauldron is to kill the king. If Forneus were to be defeated, Galian could be freed. But in that plan lies two impossible tasks. Firstly, someone would need to kill Forneus. And as if that were not enough, Galian would also need to endure the pressure of the Cauldron for an unprecedented amount of time."

"What about V?" Raine asked in desperation. "There's got to be some move there?"

"I have tried everything I can to contact V," the head monk said. "He is nowhere to be found."

"We need to do something," Raine cried. "We can't surrender. You have to think, Igallik."

The head monk raked his fingers through his hair. "I'm at a loss…" he said finally. "I don't know what to do."

After collapsing in his throne, the head monk wrung the air with his hands and repeated himself.

"I don't know what to do…"

"I do," Odin declared as he stocked his hand with a dagger from his belt.

"Odin," Igallik cautioned as he saw the dagger, "please, rest your mind. This is not a time for impulse."

Odin looked the head monk straight on, his eyes full of sorrow, but his face steeled with determination.

"Galian died thinking that he had lost me," he said sternly. "He died thinking I hated him. I will die to show him he was wrong. I will die to save him. Brothers, this is goodbye."

"Odin!" Igallik cried. "No!"

It was too late. Odin's heart had made up his mind. The mighty Odin, against all odds, looked once more upon the earth realm, and with a furious exhalation, he stabbed the dagger deep into his own chest.

The moment the dagger pierced Odin's heart, the entire environment morphed into a different world. Odin had been broken from his flesh. He had become only his soul. Odin was still in the Temple, but the Temple was not of its earthly structure. The golden walls and roof of the Temple had turned into a giant piece of black coal that was being rapidly torn apart by the world's raging winds. Even Raine's and Igallik's forms had transformed and were being blown to ash.

In moments, the Temple and all in it were no more, and Odin stood defiantly alone at the summit of the monastery's giant staircase. As Odin craned his neck up, he witnessed the crimson red sky, its deep hue playing host to a hundred crows, and blowing wildly with black ash.

As Odin watched, suddenly, he felt a pull in his core, and as if the feeling were towing him, he marched slowly to the mouth of the giant staircase.

As he looked down, there, standing with ominous intent, was Death.

The great Reaper's skeletal face was waiting under its dark hood, and as its hollow eyes gazed up, it measured its prey like a practiced hunter. No act would stop it from claiming the second son of Animus Letum.

Odin stood unafraid.

He would use the Reaper, regardless of the scythe's allegiance, as his great ally.

"Claim your prize!" he roared.

Death would assent.

Death slammed its scythe into the courtyard, and as the weapon ignited with purple flames, the Reaper stretched out its massive fifteen foot wingspan. After a moment of stillness, the Reaper made a few powerful flaps, and after ascending effortlessly into the air, Death began to climb the staircase in flight. With its flaming scythe dragging behind it, the Reaper soared directly at its prey. As the haunting Reaper flew at him, Odin tried to brace himself for impact. I regret that there exists no adequate preparation. As Death reached the staircase's summit and it swung its burning scythe forward into Odin's abdomen, Odin was struck with a pain he could never have imagined. Odin squirmed and screamed. The Reaper dragged him across the stone floor, bouncing and skipping his body hard against the ground. After thirty yards, Death slowed its pace, and as its black wings swung in haunting symmetry, it raised its scythe and peered callously into Odin's eyes.

Odin's face and body wretched from the incredible pain that the scythe had delivered to him, but he still managed to stare back into Death.

"Play your part," he seared.

A devious smile turned on the Reaper's skeletal face. And in the next moment darkness of not just sight but of mind and soul fell over Odin. There was nothing. It was a horrifying torture. Void of all awareness but pain, Odin slowly faded.

Seconds passed until all consciousness was gone.

Odin had died.

37

In the Temple, after Odin had driven the dagger into his own chest, Raine and Igallik tried desperately to revive the young Aeris.

As minutes passed, Igallik painfully recognized the truth.

"He's gone. Both of them…" he said with tearing eyes, "gone."

Raine threw his hands up in futility.

"Did we fail? Did we ruin this?"

"I pray the answer is no, Raine. Not after everything… not after everything we've been through."

"What'll we do?" Raine brooded. "What can we do?"

Igallik hated to acknowledge his decision. He was torn. His mind was sure of the next step, but his heart was reluctant to take it.

"First, we must honour Odin's body," he said finally. "If Odin is to succeed, there is an individual in the afterlife whom we must pay a toll. Secondly, we must prepare the Forge."

Raine shook his head, at odds with both the speed and gravity of their dilemma.

"Igallik, be honest with me," he said. "What are Odin's chances? I mean, even with the Forge?"

"Not good," the head monk replied. "But if he is to have any, we have to hold to our end of the deal. I need you to bring his body to the altar."

Raine shook his head. "I can't. Not like this."

"Raine, we must," Igallik said. "Please, I need your help. If Odin is to have any chance, we must act quickly."

After a furious breath, Raine conceded. "Fine," he said. "For Odin."

As Raine heaved Odin's dead body up over his shoulder, Igallik made his way to one of the Temple's cabinets and retrieved two silver coins. Igallik then unlatched an unlit torch from the Temple wall and brought the torch and coins to where Raine had laid down Odin.

"The coins should ensure safe travel," Igallik said as he placed them over Odin's eyes. "And the torch will sever Odin completely from our realm."

After moving the torch over a lit candle, it ignited in flames.

As Raine again shook his head in deep regret, he reached down and patted Odin's chest.

"You'll do great, mate," he tearfully bid. "Make us proud."

The Sons of Animus Letum

Igallik, too, allowed himself a farewell.

"Tragedy brought you to us, and now tragedy takes you away. But in between, we were witness to a king. It is time to honour your father's sacrifice. Take back your birthright, Odin. Be the miracle we have waited for."

After a solemn breath, Igallik touched the lit end of the torch down onto Odin's body, and the Aeris's body was slowly set aflame.

In silence, Igallik and Raine watched Odin's body disintegrate to ash.

The second son of Animus Letum, only hours after the first, had vanished from the first realm.

After the burning had completed, Igallik patted Raine's back.

"Come," he said, "we must prepare the Forge."

Raine nodded; however, as he and the head monk began to walk towards the Temple doors, they began to hear screams and cries echoing from the monastery courtyard.

Hastily, Raine swung the doors open.

The sight was horrifying. Dozens of monks lay dead on the courtyard floor.

"No…" Igallik protested. "It can't be…"

38

In Animus Letum, the Serpent sat on his throne. The king's orange eyes burned intently at the Scale entering his Throne Room.

The Scale, proud and certain his news would appease his king, slowly approached the Serpent Messiah.

"My Lord," he boasted as he grew close, "your plan has come to pass. The sons of Animus Letum, both the mute and the warrior, have passed into our realm."

"And the people?" Forneus growled.

"It would seem that any faithful to Serich remain completely unaware of the mute brother's presence in your Cauldron."

"Send my serpents to the Boatman," the Dark King ordered.

"If I may," the Scale said, "are we not overestimating this warrior? Is he not the weaker of the two?"

"A master is never unprepared," Forneus said. "It was in fact Serich who underestimated me. Scale," he coldly repeated, "send my serpents."

The Scale nodded and quickly left to carry out his orders.

With a grin, Forneus, the great predator, set his hunting eyes upon the far reaches of the horizon.

"Come," he snarled to the second son of Animus Letum, "face your villain."

39

Once Odin had died and arrived in my realm, it was his ears that first woke to consciousness. The sound they heard was like a serene water bank. However, the sound quickly evaporated, and Odin began to wince as the strident pitch of one hundred thousand screaming voices cut through the dense air. Odin's thoughts began to return to him slowly, and as the echoes of the first realm surfaced in his memory, he was instantly reminded of his actions. He was dead by his own hand and was now in Animus Letum. Odin fought to open his eyes, but as he strained, he startled himself with the realization that his eyes were open. He was blind. Instinctively, Odin brought his hands to his face, and as he pressed into his eyes, he could feel a thin metal coin lodged into each of his eye sockets. Odin attempted to remove the coins, but even after committing his full strength, the two coins remained intact. Confused but driven, Odin began to feel out his surroundings. Odin ran his hands over his clothes and soon realized that he was in the same battle attire he had worn when he died. Even Sleipnir and his four daggers remained locked to his belt. With calm, even breaths, Odin quickly detected the rocky earth beneath him.

The ground, although Odin could not see it, was barren and black. And the skies above were scorched with slashes of orange and purple cloud. As Odin began to move, he collided with numerous other walking bodies. Odin could hear the mournful cries of what seemed to be millions of other sightless souls walking the rocky ground.

The others, unlike him, had no coins in their eyes.

Odin was on the Isle of the Lost. It was the barren rock where every poor soul, not given the Boatman burial rite, was doomed to walk blind for eternity. Screams of panic and pleas for help screeched through the air as the millions of people wandered in blind hysteria. Odin tried his best to keep his composure, and then, using his hands, he began to navigate through the myriad of terrified bodies. As the mass of damned souls screamed and fought futilely against their blindness, Odin wandered through them for a half hour. His lack of sight combined with the persistent terror of the many voices was beginning to unreel his calm. The sound was madness. But as Odin, in an attempt to break from the auditory burden, knelt down to the black rock, a new and very strange voice moved by his ears.

"No eyes on you," the strangled voice declared. "You either. You'll have to stay."

Odin quickly began to track the voice. The voice continued to make his rulings, until, as Odin grew close, Odin nearly trampled him.

"Step back!" the annoyed voice threatened as he turned back to the Lyran.

However, after seeing the coins in Odin's eyes, the creature's tone turned to an excited squeal.

"I got one!" he cheered. "You'll come with me."

With a quick stab, the creature wrapped his bony hand around Odin's arm and began eagerly to drag Odin through the maze of bodies.

Soon, Odin could again hear the soft sound of waves hitting the shore. As the creature, who was my small servant Zyled, led Odin to my dock and boat, I remained unaware of the situation's gravity.

"Zyled," I called in welcome. "Do we have one?"

"Oh yes, Boatman, sir," Zyled answered as he dragged Odin closer. "We've got one."

"It's been a while," I joked to Zyled.

"Over forty moons," Zyled agreed.

"Well, bring him here then."

As Zyled brought Odin to me, I retrieved four small gems from my waist pouch.

"For your work," I said as I placed the gems into Zyled's small hands. "I trust you can find another."

"Of course," Zyled smiled as he dropped the gems into his pouch on his belt.

"Off with you then," I spurred.

As Zyled quickly left, my attention turned to my guest.

"You're a man of a lost offering," I said with a laugh. "No one pays the Boatman anymore. What's your name?"

Still blind to his surroundings, Odin donned a complimentary smile and answered.

"Well, Odin," I said, "if you can hold still, I'll fix those eyes of yours."

After he had consented, I reached my right hand over his head and cupped my left in front of his eyes. After a firm knock to the back of his skull, the two silver coins fell easily out of Odin's eyes and into my left hand. As the coins fell, Odin was rewarded with his vision. He rubbed his eyes and became reacquainted with sight. He watched me turn from him and bring the coins back to my boat. On my right ankle there was a shackle that tethered me to the boat's bow. After dropping both coins into a slot on the boat, two more chain links were pushed out from the boat's insides.

With welcome, I looked on the added length to my chain.

"Your burial must have been nice," I said. "Those were some fine silvers. You wouldn't happen to be from the Throne's…"

However, before I could finish, my breath, in great awe, was taken from me.

"Dear, God," I gasped as I saw the colour of Odin's eyes. "Your eyes: they're blue!"

"Yes, they always have been," Odin said with a calm nod.

With a puzzled look, the Lyran leaned over and investigated my eyes.

"Your eyes," he said as he pointed to my pupil-less green hue. "Why are they like that?"

"In that question lays an important answer," I said. "But in your blues, my great friend, lies the grandest answer."

Trying to rein my excitement, I pointed Odin to the water. "Take a new look at yourself."

Odin obliged, and after leaning over the water, he was astonished to see his reflection. His eyes were a solid electric blue with no pupil or iris.

Odin was confused. "I don't understand. Why are my eyes like this?"

"In your earth realm," I explained, "there is an expression that the eyes are the window to the soul. In Animus Letum, that expression is exactly true. The colour of anyone's eyes here in the second realm is in effect a measurement of that person's soul."

"And blue eyes? What do they mean?"

I smiled. "They mean, Odin, that you are royalty."

Odin was instantly guarded – he knew who reigned in my realm. As his hand moved to his dagger, I was quick to calm his suspicion.

"Grab an oar," I said. "I am no enemy."

Odin was not convinced of my allegiance.

"I strongly recommend you get in the boat," I said as I stocked my hand with an oar. "The sooner we get you across these waters, the better."

"And if I don't?" Odin tested.

"Son of Serich, trust me now. Your short attendance in this realm has already ensured that hunters are on your trail. Allow me to serve the true house of Animus Letum. Please, get in the boat."

Odin did not have the advantage of choice. Time, or rather the lack thereof, was his brother's enemy. Finally, Odin elected speed, and as he eyed me cautiously, he stepped into the boat.

"And pull your hood over those eyes," I said as Odin grabbed an oar. "If we hide those blues we may get across unnoticed."

"And if we're noticed?" Odin asked as he set his oar into the water.

"Then we," I predicted as I pushed off the dock, "will be in for a bumpy ride."

40

Understanding the great danger that Odin was in, I held myself in silence as I rowed fervently to the mainland of Animus Letum. Although my mind was racing with the great implications of Odin's appearance, my priority and great responsibility was to ensure Odin's safe travel.

However, after twenty minutes of rowing, my fears became realized.

After I cursed fate, the arcs of my oar ceased and Odin looked at me in alarm.

"What is it?" he asked.

"The ride just got bumpy," I said.

As Odin immediately stood, searching the seas for signs of danger, I altered the grip on my oar from tool to weapon. There was an eerie silence as we searched, but it would not last long. With a dull thud, my boat's base suddenly jolted and the water at the port and starboard began to swell.

"Arm yourself!" I yelled at Odin. "They're not after me."

On cue, two massive serpents, one green and one red, began to rise from the water. As the orange sky glowed off of the serpents' scales, the two snakes hissed and snapped their massive jaws, spewing their venom as they rose twenty feet out of the water.

As the massive serpents coiled and flexed their bodies, Odin quickly armed each of his hands with a dagger. I began to swing my oar in Odin's defence, but the serpents paid no heed to my efforts. Their eyes were set on the bigger game.

Unfortunately, for the serpents, the game would prove too big.

As the green serpent stretched back its neck and prepared to strike, Odin launched himself off the boat and plunged his daggers into the snake's neck. With furious stabs, Odin drove each of his daggers into the serpent's scales, and as green blood exploded from each wound, Odin climbed the snake like a ladder. As the serpent began to thrash, Odin's body slammed from side to side, but the serpent's efforts would not be effective. The numerous knife punctures quickly took their toll, and as the serpent's bucks slowed, Odin climbed his way to the snake's crown.

With my oar, I had kept the red serpent at bay, but as it sensed the wounded hisses expelled from its counterpart, it quickly set its yellow eyes onto Odin. Odin was aware. As he met the red serpent's eyes, he drove his daggers deep into the green serpent's skull and then altered the grip on his weapons so that he could control the serpent's movement. With a seething hiss, the red serpent coiled back like a catapult, but as it launched itself over the boat, Odin twisted his own body and manipulated the green serpent's head directly into the assault. With a wet crunch, the red serpent's jagged teeth snapped powerfully into the green serpent's skull, crushing its bones like a twig. As the green serpent began to sink, the red serpent bucked frantically to unlock its bite, but it was no use. Odin retrieved two more of his daggers, and as the red serpent bit even deeper into green one, Odin plunged his blades deep between the red serpent's eyes. Odin twisted the blades, roaring his voice as a yellow puss burst from the snake's eyes. With a final dagger twist, life left the snake's body, and its massive jaw released.

Eerily, both serpents fell back beneath the sea.

Standing poised atop the sinking green serpent, Odin allowed the serpent's crown to sink to sea level and then stepped confidently off the snake's skull back into my boat.

I could not hold back my awe. "If there was any doubt that you were of Serich's blood, let it be quelled now. That, Odin, was near godly."

Odin nodded and then reached for his oar.

I could not miss my opportunity.

"I think it would be wise of you to allow me to give you what you need," I said.

"What I need is a hand," Odin replied. "Grab your oar, Boatman. Time is not on my brother's side."

"Your brother?" I blurted, unaware of Galian's demise. "He is with us? He is in Animus Letum?"

Odin nodded. There was fury in his eyes.

"Galian's soul was robbed from the first realm," he said. "He was taken to the Cauldron."

"The Cauldron?" I cried with even more surprise. "Forneus must have been waiting for him."

Odin's sombre eyes affirmed my assumption.

"You're going to face him," I realized. "You're going to face Forneus."

"I am going to face him," Odin said. "And I am going to kill him.

My eyes grew wide in the acknowledgment of Odin's nearly impossible task. I knew and had always known that Serich's sacrifice would lead to this moment. But mountains always seem more conquerable from afar. I, beside the determined Odin, now stood at the base of a giant. However, in tribute to the great Serich, my heart would honour no choice but to become a partner in Odin's climb.

"If you are to embark on this challenge," I said, "you will need what I offer."

"I need to cross this sea," Odin repeated. "My brother fades more with every moment."

"Forneus will not send more of his serpents," I predicted. "In that mistake, I will arm you with what you need. Trust me, you need all the help you can get."

Acknowledging his monumental challenge, Odin understood the truth in my words.

"What do you offer?" he asked.

"This chain," I said as I pointed to my shackle, "is not by choice. In your father's reign, I was somewhat of a specialized historian. But when Forneus's rule was instated, my talent was not needed. And instead, Forneus chained me here and demanded my service."

"What is your talent?" Odin asked.

"I have the ability not only to hold but also to transfer exact moments of time," I said. "And my mind holds the entire history of Animus Letum."

Odin looked at me inquisitively.

"And you intend to show me what?"

"What you need to see," I said. "The fall of Forneus."

41

After taking a moment to consider, Odin eventually nodded his assent.

"Be quick, Boatman," he said. "I will not allow any time to be wasted."

"As you wish," I consented.

I then removed my long coat in preparation.

"How does your power work?" Odin asked.

"You will see," I said. "Do you prefer sitting or standing?"

"Standing," Odin replied. "Why?"

I smiled as I stretched my hands. "Just brace yourself. This will feel like nothing you've ever experienced." I then placed my hand on Odin's shoulder, and allowed my green eyes to employ the great mastery of my craft.

In the very next instant, Odin and I were standing in the Throne Room of Animus Letum, witnessing an event that had taken place twenty years prior.

In front of Odin and me were the mighty Serich and his then faithful general Forneus. Serich was seated on his throne. His powerful frame, shaded blue by the luminous Soul Cauldron behind him, was the inarguable proof of his deity.

"That's my father?" Odin marvelled.

"Quite a sight," I agreed.

"Can he see us?" Odin asked.

"No," I answered. "What we see are exact moments in the past. Our attendance is limited to the role of witnesses. We can neither interact with nor influence these moments. We can only observe."

In the vision, Forneus had begun to argue with the king.

"I don't understand," he complained. "I can be of much more use to you."

Forneus's solid purple eyes pled with the king, but Serich could not yield.

"My friend, I need my best at the Dark Pool," he said. "Those at the Dark Pool have made clear their ambition. They brood in disgracing my throne. Rhea is not safe. My unborn sons are not safe. This greatest of errands can only be fulfilled by your hands. I send you because I expect victory."

Forneus could not argue against the king's reason: Forneus was the most fit.

"For you, my king, I will concede. If it is great for the throne, then it is great for me."

"Farewell, Forneus," the king said. "I await your glorious return."

"I will not disappoint," Forneus pledged.

As Forneus bowed and began to leave the Throne Room, Serich didn't realize that he would never see his friend again.

As Odin and I watched Forneus stride towards the Dark Pool, I had to look away.

"It's still tough to look at," I confessed. "Those steps lead a brave heart to its death."

Odin's eyes were locked intently on the departing Forneus.

"He was a good man," Odin realized. "My father trusted him."

"The unsurpassed measure of Forneus's loyalty is why the serpents took such great interest in him. The Dark Pool brought both petty and grand evils on your father. Destroying his best friend was their grandest feat. If you will allow me, I would like to show you the depths of that accomplishment."

"As you wish," Odin said.

After flexing my hands once more, I traced my mind to the next necessary scene, and in a flash I delivered Odin and myself into its heart.

There before us was Forneus standing on the sinister bank of the Dark Pool. It was not the sight but the sound of the Dark Pool that was most haunting. The sound was like a thousand serpents hissing in unnerving unison. The actual structure of the Dark Pool was a massive hollow cavern located against the sea that surrounds Animus Letum. The Cavern had no roof and very little rock face surrounding its sides. It was almost like a massive rock tent. The waves of the sea crashed against the Dark Pool's sides, capping over the cavern's rock barriers. And although there was water of substantial depth inside the Pool, the appearance of surging waves was actually created by the movement of thousands and thousands of slithering snakes.

The Pool was the haven of Animus Letum's worst conspirators. Behind the Dark Pool's strident and wicked hiss lay the motive of every evil act ever committed in Animus Letum. It was the Hell of the afterlife.

There were always many Vayne brooding in the sinister effluence of the Dark Pool, but in the moment I had brought Odin to, the only Vayne present were the dozen dead at Forneus's feet.

In the vision, Forneus sheathed his bloody sword and then drew a leather bound book from a satchel pouch.

"What's with the book?" Odin asked me.

"The book is Forneus's journal," I said. I then pulled out five sheets of paper that were tucked into my belt. "And these are the entries from that journal."

"These are from Forneus's journal?" Odin asked.

"Exact copies," I replied. "He actually only made the five entries."

"You've carried them all of this time?"

My reply was honest. "I've prepared for this moment for twenty years," I said. "Both I and this land have waited a long time to meet you."

Odin seemed aware of what I was saying. However, his acknowledging smile conveyed a great lack of scope with regard to the situation. He thought he was here to save his brother; I knew he was here to save all of us.

"Just read," I said. "Begin to understand."

Odin nodded and then set his eyes onto Forneus's first journal entry:

> I stand here. I stand true: the elected foe of the afterlife's perdition. Serich has endowed me with a great honour and trust. I will not fail my king. The Dark Pool will fall by my hand. I have only been here for weeks, but in that time an even more lethal ambition has grown in my heart. I hear the Pool. I almost hear words. And that unsettling realization has strengthened my desire for conquest. This evil should not be allowed to exist. I am beginning to understand the serpent's arsenal. Few men stand a chance against these whispers and against that hard truth I know I must conquer – for Serich, for me, for all. It appears quite clear that I must find the Pool's source. Every fibre in my body believes the source to be deep in the Dark Pool. However, I still have not found the courage to dive in. Time, I hope, will grant me that audacity. Fortunately, for king and country, time I have.

In the vision, Forneus closed his journal and retreated into a shack that he had built near the Dark Pool's bank. The moment Forneus disappeared behind the door, numerous serpents slithered out from the base of his shack. The thirty serpents, with their devilish tongues flickering across their mouths, scaled up the exterior of the shack, and once atop, they coiled their bodies up. This position was held for a long moment. It seemed to make no sense. But I again, and Odin for the first time, both winced as we witnessed the reason for the serpents' behavior. The hiss of the Dark Pool, like a baleful whisper, was amplified tenfold and was directly channelled at Forneus's shack.

"That sound," Odin shuddered, "it's what Galian told me about."

"He was here?" I asked.

"No," Odin answered, "but he once spoke of Hell. That sound is what he described."

"What did he say?" I wondered.

"He said that Hell is a condition that will lead good men to surrender their morality. I see now why that's true."

"Apt assessment," I agreed. "Now imagine half a year of this."

"Is that how long Forneus lasted?"

"Almost exactly. Disregarding the outcome, I think the amount of time he withstood this place is almost inhuman."

Although impressed, Odin felt no need to compliment the man who killed his parents.

"When was the second entry recorded?" he asked.

"Allow me to show you."

Odin agreed, and then, in barely a moment, I transported Odin and myself to the next necessary scene.

Again, the initial impact of the vision was delivered by the hiss of the Dark Pool.

"It's louder," Odin noted.

"That's all that it gets," I replied. "It amplifies."

After Odin adjusted his ears to the sound, he began to scan the scene with his eyes.

"There," I pointed in assistance.

Odin turned his eyes and found Forneus walking on the very edge of the Dark Pool. Forneus was noticeably slimmer, seemingly frantic, and pacing in front of the Pool.

"What's he doing?" Odin asked.

"You'll see in one second," I replied.

As Odin watched intently, Forneus shook his head wildly, took a deep breath, and then dove headlong into the Dark Pool.

A deep hush, one that seemed almost more powerful than the hiss, ensued. Two eerily silent minutes passed before Forneus's thrashing body surfaced. As his head rose out of the Pool, he began to cough painfully and vomit out a black liquid. In desperation, he began to thrash a path to the shore. As his feet finally trudged back onto land, he flung numerous snakes off his body and then collapsed on the shore.

With his body sprawled on the bank, Forneus took only deep, exhausted breaths. However, as he strove desperately for composure, five Vayne emerged from over a near ridge and set their hunting eyes on him.

Even though fatigued, Forneus managed to rise to his feet and draw his sword.

The Vayne converged quickly on the king's friend, and although Forneus was an astoundingly adept warrior, his great lack of energy had tilted the fray in the Vayne's favour. The Vayne's initial attacks were just narrowly parried, but the subsequent assaults began to land onto Forneus's frame. Understanding the great gravity of his situation, Forneus quickly resolved that the passivity of his defence was not an ally. So instead, he threw his skills into a blitz of offensive ferocity. Forneus lunged at the nearest Vayne, and after stabbing it repeatedly in the neck, he grasped the spear from its dead hand and launched the weapon into the chest of another Vayne. With two down, Forneus, contrary to his exceptional fatigue, seemed to grow in his rage. He swung his sword into another blaze of attacks and very quickly struck down the last three attackers.

However, the slashes of his blade did not cease with their deaths. Forneus hacked his sword repeatedly into the Vayne corpses until his hands, body, and face were caked in crimson spatter.

His fit of madness endured for quite some time.

When his sword came to a halt, whatever had become him did so too. As Forneus's eyes seemed to lift from an iniquitous spell and he surveyed the aftermath, the king's friend was taken by a genuine fear. His expression was of true horror, and as he began to shake his head against his actions, his heart beat in shameful rhythm. Forneus began to wildly wipe the blood from his face and hands, and the breaks of his voice were more emotion than word. Erratically, he turned in a panic and rushed into his shack.

As Forneus finally emerged, his body had been washed clean of the blood, and he was holding his journal. Forneus's purple eyes were set hard into the distance, but behind their amethyst hue was a pain of very close proximity. Forneus, deeply ashamed of his actions, held his gaze for minutes, but when he finally broke, he collapsed on his stoop and opened his journal.

"Read," I instructed.

Odin obliged.

> *I am an ashamed man. Victory is earned, not by prayer nor hope nor barter. It is won with an unflinching conviction that loses nothing to its bane. I, for a moment's trespass, strayed from that conviction. Victory was robbed of me today. And I know the culprit. I, having now submerged myself in the Dark Pool, know Hell's voice. It was like all my past anxieties — each and every rational or paranoid fear — had never been conquered or overcome, but rather cast into the Dark Pool to stew in longing of a resurrection. They were resurrected. I must confess that while deep in the Pool I was afraid. But the fear felt altered — as if someone or something was manipulating my fear. This inexplicable second party has stoked my paranoia. I hate to report that while submerged, it felt as though my heart unwillingly admitted my fears to the Pool. My foolishness would have me believe that fate would not allow such a forfeit. But I know the fears were received. I could feel it. My hope fights but stumbles against that truth. And instead I breathe heavily, terrifyingly aware of the haunting degree to which the Pool now knows my heart. However, there was an even greater horror in my plunge — as the Pool saw into my heart, so too did I see into its. My mind, not initially, but quickly by emotion, was corrupted — to this, the five disgraced corpses of the Vayne lie as a bloody testament. In the throes of my despicable violence I was neither repulsed nor restrained. I was a demon born of no mother but wrath. My king once lessoned me in truth. He said you must provoke all thoughts and feelings until they break or prove sustained. The thoughts that hold unshakable to challenge, he said, do so because they are truth. Since my plunge in the Dark Pool, I have been stricken with an ill thought. I have tried to attack this dark poison in my mind. I have locked my sights on this demon, and through my aim launched all my virtue. But still my conscience is shaded with guilt. The thought, this thorn refusing to break from my mind, is that I enjoyed the madness. The truth of this revelation, even against my vigorous challenge, is that there was great power in the*

> *bedlam: an invincibility that I crave. As I struck down the Vayne, I was fearless. I was godly. I cannot yet tell whether my affinity for this power is genuine of myself or is another seed planted by the Dark Pool. Either way I must hold strong in the conviction never again to enter the Pool. My objective of destroying the Dark Pool's source seems more daunting with each passing breath. In the wake of the madness I endured, I am indecisive about remaining here. It is clear to me, especially after being inside, that any and all weakness is exploited by the Dark Pool. My pride begs me to endure this hell to its worst degree, to prove myself untouchable to this evil. But my reason thinks otherwise. Retreat – a notion never having been chosen by my heart – has arisen in very strong form. But I must also realize that I am better positioned now than anyone has ever been in defeating the Dark Pool. For my king, I am electing to endure, though time may soon find my steps scampered in retreat.*

With a deep exhalation, Forneus closed his journal and withdrew back into his shack.

"His heart is fading," Odin recognized.

I nodded. "The serpents drove lethally at his faith. They needed him to doubt."

Odin almost felt sorry for his adversary. "This is a pillaging," he admitted. "He stood no chance."

"And this devolution," I reminded, "was only after one plunge."

"Does he make another?"

"Yes," I answered, "just one more."

"Does an entry coincide with it?"

"Actually, two do: one immediately before the plunge and one immediately after."

Odin nodded. "Okay, Boatman, take us there."

Again, I agreed, and in the next moment Odin and I were standing at the scene of Forneus's third and fourth journal entries. In the vision, Forneus was seated on the ridge of one of the Dark Pool's rock barriers. His muscle mass was greatly degraded from its original form, and his purple eyes seemed dimmed of their earlier brightness. Simply put, he looked ill.

As he sat, he pulled his journal out from his pouch.

"This is the first of his two entries," I said. "Pay close attention."

Odin nodded, and then turned his eyes onto the third page of Forneus's journal.

> *I have been here too long. The Pool is relentless. I fear I am becoming something worse than indifferent to these serpents. I can feel myself drifting. And worse, I have succumbed to a sickness that seems to carry words onto the Pool's hiss. One word repeats: coward. My heart, at first defiantly strong against this label, has now realized its truth. I am a coward; not because I haven't tried to win, but because I have begun to take counsel from my fears. I am terrified of the Dark Pool. I know I must destroy it, I know I must reach its source, but my fear has kept me at bay. I remember well the mayhem that overtook my head and heart after my only plunge. And I am afraid of that madness. Its memory has begun to haunt each of my breathing moments, and it is a pain that has struck hard at my pride. The Pool challenged me, and I have cowered... I am a coward. I feel as if Serich has trusted me with a task too great. I truly believe only he can reap a victory from this hell. But I will not concede my defeat. I, against the serpents' insult, will dive once more into the Pool. If I fall, I will fall valiantly. By either victory or death I will show my king that I was committed to his reign. Serich deserves nothing less.*

Forneus's pen stopped, and after he tucked the journal back into his pouch, he threw the bag back onto the shore. As he rose and surveyed the Pool from his elevated position, he looked skywards in pleading.

"Use me, fate," he prayed. "Before it is too late."

With a deep breath, Forneus poised himself on the rock and then dove once more into the Dark Pool.

Again, a silent hush overtook the cavern. As Forneus's second plunge endured to an inhuman four minutes, the hush began to feel threatening. The hush had a silent energy that although invisible to the senses, brought a sickness to the soul. As both the hush and Forneus's submersion refused to relent, dozens of Vayne began to appear on the bank of the Dark Pool. Their yellow eyes remained fixed on the Pool, searching the serpent waters for Forneus to surface. Then, after his fateful second plunge into hell, Forneus's head emerged at the center of the Dark Pool. In contrast with his first dive, Forneus was considerably more calm. Instead of panic, there seemed to be a relishing and invigorated flare in his eyes. As his feet found the bank of the Dark Pool, his final strides onto the shore were devilishly poised. Once he had completely emerged onto the bank, strangely, the Vayne on the shore did not attack him – nor did Forneus challenge them. Instead, some form of stalemate had nullified their quarrel. As Forneus eyed the Vayne, he began to exhale deeply – not with an exhausted respiration, but rather an exhilarated breath, thrilled in the throes of his re-emerging madness. His purple eyes shot around the bank until he found the pouch that he had thrown to the shore only minutes before.

As the exhilaration and madness quickly grew, Forneus's desires were dominated by the craving to write another entry. And then, defenceless against his own spellbound mind, Forneus pulled his journal from the pouch, and in a hellfire of madness, he scorched his possessed pen onto its parchment.

I am awake. I am at the dawn of myself. I am alive. My heart, for as long as it has beat, has suffocated. Not by pain, but by ignorance. But now, I am breathing. Now, my mind races with the gales of a higher creed. Now, I am aware. The power that reigns in me now is unstoppable. I have fought against this might, I have driven my will against it, but it persists. It thrives. Serich lessoned me in the unshakable. And this is that. This thrilling, thirsting, throne-worthy force screams of truth. My ears are attuned. My soul is amazed. Even Serich, a great deity, would envy this most becoming of bedlams. But Serich will not have it. His fate was given to him. His fate was inherited. Mine is earned. And by my earning I shall be over all and beneath only the crown on my head. One mere deed divides me from that destiny. Tonight, I pledge, my truth and terror shall begin their reign.

As Forneus's pen stopped, he beat his chest and yelled wildly over to the Vayne in front of him

"Rest yourselves," he called, "for your fight has now become mine. The dawn of your victory is fulfilled through me. Your messiah is born today!"

The Vayne raised their right hands, pledging their allegiance as a wicked hiss sounded from their mouths.

With a callous smile, Forneus cast his eyes into the far distance. He had only one promise for the far off king.

"Serich," he seethed, "tonight I take your throne."

In anticipation of the most unholy of sacraments, Forneus turned and retreated into his shack.

Odin's eyes were locked onto his every step.

"He spoke of tonight. What happens?"

"A baptism," I replied. "This night he forges a bond between his own mind and the heart of the Dark Pool."

"Is that where the final entry is made?"

"Yes," I answered.

Odin nodded, inviting me to invoke the final vision.

"Brace yourself," I warned, "this vision is perhaps the most grisly."

Odin nodded again, and after I had employed my power, Odin and I stood at the scene of Forneus's final journal entry.

Again, we were at the Dark Pool.

The skies were painted with a devilish dark orange, and the roaring winds tore through the cavern like a hellish swarm of locusts. The sea that surrounded the Dark Pool crashed mightily against the cavern's barrier, but strangely, the water within the Dark Pool was of an eerie calm. There were even more Vayne present at the Pool than in the previous vision, and at the forefront of the Dark Pool's bank, Forneus stood with his journal in hand.

Only three sentences would be written.

It is time now to rid the crown of the weakness it rests upon. I now bind my fate to the destiny of the Dark Pool. Great malice, give unto me all of your power.

With an arrogant wave, Forneus threw his journal to the bank and declared his intention with a furious scream.

"Dark Pool!" he commanded. "Embrace your messiah!"

Instantly, heavy pelts of rain began to assault the Dark Pool. As the rain pattered over the Dark Pool like metal drums, orange lightning cracked on the bank, lighting the scene with a haunting orange glow.

Bathed by the eerie glow, the serpents in the middle of the Pool began to part from its center. It was strange to see. It was as if nature had choreographed the moment many moons ago.

In rhythm with the serpent's rite, Forneus dropped to his knees and waited intently for his prize.

Within seconds, a pure black serpent with glowing orange eyes surfaced at the center of the Dark Pool. The serpent was the great master of the Pool's madness – its source and conspirator.

As the snake's four foot long body waded in lateral arcs towards the bank, Forneus snarled in content and drew one of his daggers. Slowly, the snake approached, and as its tongue darted in and out of its mouth, Forneus lowered his dagger onto the mud of the bank. As the snake slithered close and the rain gleamed off its black scales, Forneus hissed, and the snake began to coil itself around the waiting dagger.

Staring at his prize, Forneus caressed the snake and then touched the blade of the dagger to his other forearm. With a grimace, he began to saw, carving a slow and gruesome incision across his left forearm. As the blood cascaded down to his wrist, Forneus began to laugh maniacally, and as he cackled into the storm, he guided the black snake to the mouth of his open gash. The snake flicked its double-pronged tongue against Forneus's seeping blood, tasted the crimson flow, uncoiled from the dagger, and then slid itself into the open cut. As the snake slithered gruesomely through the depths of the gash and its body bulged under Forneus's dark skin, the traitor began to convulse from the great pain.

In his madness, he seemed to be enjoying it.

The snake was sliding purposefully to Forneus's spine.

As Forneus laughed and stared madly into the horizon, the snake reached its destination. Almost instantly, the wicked bond of serpent and man began to take effect. Forneus arched backwards, and with his spine bending impossibly, he bellowed hoarsely into the night, embracing the moment as the lightning, rain, and thunder swelled into a tempest of godly rage.

At the next crash of thunder, Forneus's arms struck out to the heavens, and his eyes opened.

They were completely orange.

The goodness and loyalty of Forneus's purple eyes had surrendered to the evil, infinite hollow of the amber hue.

Forneus was gone; the Serpent Messiah had arrived.

The new incarnation rose furiously to his feet. He turned his orange eyes to the distant blue glow of Serich's Soul Cauldron.

With a snarl, the wicked Serpent King elected war.

Sensing their Messiah's aim, the Vayne on the shore as well the many emerging from the Dark Pool began to follow the Serpent King, shadowing him on what would be his merciless march.

"This was never a fair fight," Odin said as he watched Forneus's army assemble. "No one could stand against this onslaught."

"You've greatly underestimated your father," I said.

"He was really that strong?" Odin asked, his tone based more in hope than scepticism.

"Odin," I said, "your father was a god. He was beyond the power of a hundred of Forneus's armies."

Odin was proud, astounded by the father he could never meet.

"Your father's might is something you really need to have seen to believe," I said. "It would be my honour to grant you that privilege."

"Okay," Odin said. "Whenever you're ready."

After a deep breath, I concentrated the power of my green eyes onto the next scene, and in an instant Odin and I were standing in Serich's Throne Room.

I was actually present twice in the vision. I was observing with Odin, but I was also a character who played in the events of the scene. My past self stood with the queen, watching as the Serpent Messiah arrived to face the king.

Backed by his Vayne, the serpent screamed his bile at the heart-broken king.

"Destiny awaits a new king, sire," he seethed.

In the next instant, war erupted in the Throne Room.

As Serich's body exploded into blue flame and he tore through the Vayne, Odin could not withhold his astonishment.

"He's incredible."

"He truly was," I agreed.

Odin and I watched each sequence of the fateful battle. We watched Forneus order his Vayne to kill the queen. We watched the king quarrel with Forneus's twin dragons. And we watched Forneus slice his blade across the pregnant queen's throat.

"His only weakness was his family," Odin said as Serich caught the wounded queen. "Forneus exploited his heart."

"That was the only way to hurt him," I replied.

In the vision, Serich had cast a thick swell of blue energy across the Throne Room, and in its protection, he was tending to his queen. Wildly, Forneus slashed his blade through the energy, and as the queen was elevated in the blue fire, Serich smiled at her.

It was then that the villain struck. The king collapsed, and as his blue energy evaporated, the queen and the blue fire surrounding her suddenly imploded into nothingness.

Even though I knew how it would end, I was still heartbroken when the great Serich's body disintegrated to ash.

In that moment my past self was apprehended by Forneus's Vayne, and the Serpent Messiah decreed my banishment.

"Your king may be dead," he boasted to me, "but your service to the throne is not. You, Charon, have inherited a new role. My Vayne," he ordered, "bind our friend to the boat."

With a grin, Forneus then pointed to my right ankle – the bleeding ankle that he had pierced with his dagger.

"Chain that ankle," he said to his Vayne. "Our new Boatman will live with the pain of his failure."

The Vayne followed their king's order, and as I kicked and cursed, they dragged me out of the Throne Room.

In the aftermath of his conquest, the Serpent Messiah had set his orange eyes onto the throne. As he approached Serich's seat, his eyes demonically surveyed the prize of his victory. Proudly, he climbed onto the throne, but to take his seat as the succeeding king of Animus Letum, he still needed to perform one last deed.

At the length of each of the throne's arms was a button. When pushed, the buttons released sharp blades that served as the divining rods of each new reign. The Serpent pressed the buttons, and then he slid his palms slowly over the blades. As his blood began to leak down a channel towards the Soul Cauldron, the Serpent King reclined arrogantly on his throne and awaited the true inception of his reign.

The moment the blood reached the base of the Cauldron, the Throne Room began to tremble. Orange sparks began to flare out of the blue Cauldron, and as a tornado of hellfire started turning in the Cauldron's base, the blue light of Serich's reign started to expel violently into the night sky. As the tornado burned, its orange hue started to overwhelm the entire Throne Room. Then, with a series of cracks and hums, the cyclone of hellfire stabilized.

The new Cauldron – and the new reign – were born.

As the orange Cauldron seared its glow onto the Throne Room, the hundreds of Vayne dropped to their knees.

"It is in this moment that Hell begins its reign," I said. "It has been a long twenty years – longer than you may know."

"Has no one contested his reign since?" Odin asked.

"A few have, but their attempts were foolhardy. Forneus is simply too powerful to attack. Instead, other means of battle have been employed."

"What means?" Odin wondered.

"Means I hope you will utilize," I said. "I have shown you all you need to see. What is now important is that we get you the help you need when you reach the mainland. There is a faction, an army…"

"Boatman," Odin interjected, "I don't have time to seek an army. Each passing second drives my brother's soul even further into jeopardy. I must face Forneus."

"Believe me," I said, "I know yours is a hurried hourglass. But, Odin, I am honest when I say you cannot win this battle alone. There is a soul on the mainland named V. You must find her."

Odin looked surprised. "V's a woman?"

"Yes," I answered. "You've heard of her?"

"A few times," Odin replied. "She actually helped my brother complete the Descent trial."

"Well, now you need her to help you. She can arm you with the weapons and soldiers you need to win this fight. Trust me, without V your mission is impossible."

One of Galian's sermons instantly arose in Odin's mind.

"My brother once said that the heart does not know impossible. I realize that I aim at the unlikely, but if I fail, I will fail because Forneus has killed me, not because time has run out. My brother – my best friend – is dying. Trust me when I say there has never been a more powerful motivation."

Odin's eyes looked sternly to mine.

"If you are to know anything about me, Boatman, it is not that I am Serich's heir. It is that I am Galian's brother. And not Hell, nor time, nor fate is going to stop me from saving him. I don't need an army," Odin said. "When my brother is in danger, my heart swells beyond human. I become the army."

As I listened to Odin, I was awed by the ferocity of his spirit. It was in those moments that I saw Serich in his eyes – that I saw a worthy king.

Satisfied with the man I saw before me, I ended the sequence of visions.

Quickly, I grabbed my oar, and before I set into the water, I used it to point to a blue blanket draped over one of the corners of my boat.

"You'll find a great treasure beneath that drape," I said. "I think you'll find it fits quite nicely."

Odin looked quizzically at me as if I had spoken in riddle, but as I again motioned to the blanket, he eventually removed the blue cloth.

Lying under the blue blanket was a suit of Lyran armour. The armour was crafted with gold, and it included leg guards, arm plates, swords, two golden hatchets, and a burgundy cape that fell backwards off the detailed chest plate.

Odin marvelled at the golden armour.

"Go on," I said. "Try it on."

"Whose is it?" Odin asked.

"Think of it as your family crest," I said. "This armour will bond to you, and only to you. I guarantee you that this armour will move and flex with you in a way you've never experienced. It is as strong as steel, but moves and sounds like fabric."

As Odin inspected the golden mail, he could not deny its strengths. It was flawlessly crafted, and he knew simply by studying it that the armour would be an advantage in any fray he found on the mainland.

"I am a Lyran," he said with a smile. "It is only right that I look the part."

"Then suit up," I said as I cut my oar into the water, "because we're about twenty minutes out."

42

Given the severity of Odin's situation, not one stroke of my oar was sculled in leisure. Odin and I reached the mainland as rapidly as we could, and as I docked my boat, Odin had donned the Lyran armour. I looked him over, thinking the past had never seemed so close.

I was staring at a king.

Odin was quick to leap to the black earth of the shore.

"It fits," I judged. "Damned well, I must say."

Odin agreed. "I thank you, Boatman. You were a great help."

"It was a privilege," I replied, allowing myself a bow.

Odin, slightly confused by my bow, nodded back to the Isle of the Lost.

"I think it might be best to head back," he said. "I expect the Forge will be coming."

"The Forge?" I repeated.

"My army," Odin said. "Two hundred monks who have sworn to help me reclaim the afterlife."

The news was promising. "I will be able to sense if they cross into Animus Letum," I said. "If they do I will give them transport. You intend to wait for them?"

Odin shook his head. "I can't," he replied. "Not with Galian still in the Cauldron. The Forge will be my reinforcement, but they can't be my strategy."

"I will attune my senses for their arrival," I said. "If they cross I will find them."

Odin smiled. "And in the meantime?"

I managed a hopeful nod. "I want to be close if heaven returns," I said. "I think I'll stay on the mainland."

Odin smiled again. "Don't go too far."

"This damned chain," I smiled back, "it's a real drag."

"Thanks," Odin repeated, "I hope to see you again."

"As do I. However, in that hope, I am compelled to offer a final counsel."

Odin nodded. "As you wish."

"When your brother spoke of hell," I said, "when he explained that hell is a condition so cruel that good men are driven to surrender their morality, he was more accurate than you know."

"I saw the Dark Pool," Odin reminded me. "I am ready for this."

"You saw it for only moments," I said, "not years. The Pool has spread a sickness over this land for two decades. Some have resisted its darkness, but most have become its partner. What I am saying is that good men have become nearly extinct in the afterlife. You are entering Hell, Odin. And I implore you to trust no one."

"Even V?" Odin challenged.

"You're not stupid, Odin. I trust you can distinguish between help and harm. My point was that you've entered a land where you're basically a fugitive. And if the last twenty years have taught me anything, it is that people will go to great lengths to appease a king they're afraid of. As for V," I said, "she has been a loyal servant to your house, even when it was in rubble. She is worth finding."

"I can't promise I will seek her out," Odin said, "but I do trust your judgement. If it happens that V can assist me, I will accept her as a friend."

After pushing the hair from his eyes, Odin turned and set his eyes towards the distant orange glow of Forneus's kingdom.

"Tonight," he pledged, "I will win or I will die."

"My prayers are with you," I said. "Farewell, son of Animus Letum. Heaven is on your side."

Odin nodded and then began his march into the heart of Hell.

"And, Odin," I called as he forged into the shadow, "hide those blues as best you can. They will garner more attention than you need."

"I will," Odin called back.

Then, beneath the hellish orange and purple sky of Animus Letum, Odin disappeared from my sight.

Odin kept himself to the shadows as he traversed the dark earth of Animus Letum. In his desire for stealth, the dark skies proved a valuable ally. The skies were cut with slashes of orange and purple cloud that cast a dark gloom over the land. Under the clouds' dark shadow, nature had perished. The earth was black as coal, and the thousands of trees and shrubs appeared as if they had been burnt to cinders. As Odin sprinted through the array of lifeless nature, brutal winds scorched his path, gusting against his frame with surges of ash and ember. As the wind howled like a demon hound, it seemed to burst from all directions. Odin sprinted against the hellish winds for what seemed like miles. His hair and clothes became singed by the pelting embers, but against the swirls of orange wind-fire, Odin's contrasting blue eyes crusaded towards his destiny.

As he pushed a steady pace through the barren outskirts of Animus Letum, he soon arrived at a large hill. Odin used the hill as a momentary cover from the scorching winds, and after composing himself, he scaled to its top. As he reached its summit, he was awarded with a view of Forneus's kingdom. The entire land of Animus Letum lay before him.

Odin used his vantage to survey the core of the afterlife. Even against the ash and amber streaked winds, Odin's eyes immediately identified Forneus's glaring Soul Cauldron. The orange Cauldron was atop a distant mountain, and its glow covered the entire kingdom with its devilish hue. It was a hellish sight. As Odin studied the landscape, attempting to claim any advantage from the living map, he noted that there was a massive staircase that led up the mountain to the Soul Cauldron. He then observed that below and at the front of the Cauldron's mountain were thousands of stone structures. The structures, many with golden roofs, stretched further across the horizon than Odin could see. He wagered that the majority were living quarters, while a smaller portion, he assumed, were chapels. From his distance and elevation, Odin was at the advantage of seeing most of the kingdom's roads and alleyways. Odin could clearly see the most obvious path to his destination. However, heeding my warning, he began to trace an indirect route for his blue eyes. Once satisfied with his plot, Odin drew his hood even further over his head and began his descent into the core of Animus Letum.

Only minutes passed before Odin's steps found the roadways of Animus Letum. The streets were littered with atrocities. There were hundreds of rotting corpses lining the alleyways and countless more serpents sliding in and out of the dark corridors. The disgraced bodies of men, women, and children served as the inarguable proof that Odin was in Hell.

As he forged further into the kingdom, Odin employed great deceptive strategy in the pace and lines of his walk. However, before long, he began to hear the screaming voices and panicked steps of others in the kingdom. Choosing to trust no one, Odin kept his presence guised in stealth. He stuck to the shadows and held his strides to a deliberate quiet.

As Odin's path converged on an intersection of road centered by an dilapidated statue of his father, a large commotion of oncoming bodies began to tread into his path. With his stealth in jeopardy, Odin was left no option but to backtrack and lunge into the open doorway of an adjacent building. Odin hid in the darkness of the corridor for a long moment, but as the terrified voices began to grow closer and louder, he realized he was in a vulnerable position. In an attempt to reassess his situation, Odin crept carefully to one of the room's gaping windows and began to survey the intersection of roads. As the screams became louder, suddenly numerous children, women, and men came running into view. The hues of the crowd's eyes varied from green to purple, and against the dark backdrop of Animus Letum, they were a scope of brilliant colour. However, the crowd's wild pace and terrified shrills were a testament to true panic. As they fled across the intersection, Odin was unsure what they were running from. But, as they came even further into view, a barrage of screaming arrows exploded from the corridor behind them, causing each runner to fall upon the cobblestone roadway. The majority of the crowd was dead. The few wounded survivors cried in pain, but their whimpers only alerted the bowmen, who promptly approached to complete their murders.

As the attackers came into view, Odin became rapt with shock. The assailants were monks of the Throne's Eye. They were Odin's brothers.

As the five yellow-eyed monks pulled out their daggers to execute the survivors – some of whom were children – Odin knew he could not remain idle. He leapt out the window and roared his censure onto the fallen monks.

"Lay down your blades or lay down your lives!" he threatened. "The choice is yours."

The monks turned immediately to Odin and became perplexed by his blue eyes. They held their baffled pause until a voice sounded from the shadows behind them.

"The mighty Odin," the voice welcomed. "What an honour to meet you here."

Slowly, the source of the voice emerged completely into view.

"Raeman?" Odin blurted.

"Good to see your memory is still intact," Raeman said with a smile.

"What madness is this?" Odin demanded. "These are children, not enemies."

Raeman sneered.

"Save your righteous dribble. We are in Hell, Odin. Morals are nothing more than shackles here."

"That is your defence?" Odin cried. "You'll kill children because this realm demands it?"

"No," Raeman replied, "I will do it because my king demands it."

Odin was horrified.

"You serve Forneus?"

"We do," Raeman answered coldly. "Our ambition is self-preservation. I trust you can see the reasoning in that. If we must side with someone in this battle, we believe it is wise to side with the one that will win."

"That is not wise," Odin scolded. "It is gutless."

Raeman offered a pompous grin.

"I'm not interested in your opinion, Odin. Your presence, however, is of great interest. I must say, you have given us a very lucrative opportunity."

With an emotionless wave of his hand, Raeman motioned to the crowd that his brothers had littered with arrows.

"There was a bounty on their heads," he said. "Forneus has ordered that all associates of V be killed. To be honest, the pay is good. We enjoy some spoils, and Forneus allows us some freedom. But we are not dogs, Odin. We do not prosper under a master."

"I do not feel sorry for you, Raeman. You are a ghost of your former self."

"Not a ghost," Raeman corrected, "an adaptation. I was once the Justice totem of our home," he laughed. "What a fool I was! I dedicated my life to seeking justice. I thought it to be the highest order of our earth realm. And what I did get in return?" he asked. "I got killed by the very man I saved from death. I suppose I should thank Usis," Raeman chuckled. "He showed me the folly of my ways. There is no justice, Odin: it is a construct of feeble minds. There is only survival." Raeman made a grand sweeping gesture to the blackened world around him. "I have built myself around the hell I live in," he said. "I now look to better my own plight, not those of others. And with you, Odin, I can vastly better my plight."

"I am not in your service," Odin declared.

"I doubted you would be. In fact, I expect you to greatly contest my next move."

"And why's that?"

"Because I am going to take your head. Like I said, we have not prospered under a master. We desire more freedom. But like anything in this world, we must barter for it."

Raeman looked callously at Serich's heir. "We are going to kill you, Odin. And after we cut your head from your neck and toss it before our king, we are going to receive great recompense: freedom."

Odin looked confidently at the fallen monk and smirked.

"Take my head? If your ambition truly is self-preservation, it would prove wise not to test me."

"You are outnumbered, Odin: by my count, six to one. You don't stand a chance."

Odin unlocked Sleipnir from his belt and pressed her center button. As she extended into a bow staff, Odin offered his former brothers an ultimatum.

"I am going to make this very simple: if you do not back down and leave immediately, I will kill you. I will cut you down with the same malice you intended on those children. Whether you live or die is a choice you make now."

Raeman grinned in amusement.

"Your ego is impressive," he granted. "But ultimately, egos need to be humbled. Brothers, kill him."

At Raeman's command, the five other monks instantly converged on Odin. As the first monk lunged at him, trying to spear him with a dagger, Odin evaded the attack and then swung Sleipnir so powerfully into his throat that the impact shattered his wind passage. As the next two monks attacked from Odin's left and right, Odin fell backwards onto his hands, and after the two monks crossed in front of him, Odin sprang back to his feet and smacked Sleipnir hard across both of their jaws. With three down, Odin amplified the ferocity of his assault. He drew one of his daggers, and as the next monk came within range, Odin leapt at him and stabbed the dagger repeatedly into the side of his neck. Odin then pulled the dagger from the monk's fatal wound and hurtled the blade directly into the next attacker's heart.

Only Raeman remained.

The former Justice totem was not experienced in combat, and as Odin stalked him, he sought only evasion.

"You think you've won?" Raeman scolded as he darted around the statue of Serich. "There is no winning in this realm, only survival. We live because Forneus allows it."

"You'll die just the same," Odin promised. "Tell me, Raeman, where is your king now?"

Raeman seemed to fret, but after a moment, he broke into a pompous smile and pointed to the corridor behind Odin.

"He's right on time."

Odin instantly turned, and as he peered down the alleyway, three armed Vayne marched into view.

"He's here!" Raeman cried to the Vayne. "Serich's heir, ready for slaughter!"

As the Vayne neared, Raeman paraded confidently out from behind the statue.

"You're a dead man, Odin," he said with a laugh. "You should have known this was inevitable."

As his arrogance began to swell, Raeman leaned in to offer Odin a final insult. However, once Raeman was within an arm's length, Odin drove Sleipnir forcefully into his ankle and then quickly wrapped his arm around Raeman's throat. As Raeman struggled to escape, Odin stopped him with an even stronger chokehold. With his unremitting vigour, Odin had made sure that the traitor's last moments would be spent listening.

"You were a monk of the Throne's Eye," Odin seared into Raeman's ear. "You were of our highest Order. Brave were your mind and heart. But now, in this hell, you have disgraced yourself."

As the three Vayne began to circle him, Odin raised his dagger to Raeman's neck and whispered coldly into the fallen monk's ear.

"Consider this a gift."

With a violent cut, Odin slit Raeman's throat clean through. In a heap, Raeman's lifeless body fell to the roadway. Odin eyed the crumpled mass and then spit onto it in disdain. Raeman's treason had brought a great rage to Odin's eyes, and as the three Vayne prepared to attack, they would be the first to bear its brunt.

Odin lunged first to the serpent on his left, and after evading an anticipated punch, Odin locked Sleipnir around the Vayne's throat and violently snapped its neck. As the next Vayne sprinted at Odin and threw a wild punch, Odin retrieved one of his remaining daggers and drove the blade precisely into the center of the serpent's oncoming fist. The Vayne reeled back clutching its hand. Odin used Sleipnir to vault into the air, and while airborne, he delivered a powerful kick into his assailant's skull. As Odin descended back down from the fatal blow, he used his momentum to tumble into a grounded somersault. And as he rolled out, he speared his shoulder into the final Vayne. After heaving it onto his shoulder, Odin wrapped his left arm around its neck and slammed the Vayne down onto his own knee.

The final Vayne expelled a painful wheeze and then fell agonizingly into death.

Odin surveyed the dead, and in anticipation of another battle, he collected each of his used daggers.

As he gathered his blades, he was startled as the sounds of crying echoed from behind him. As he turned, Odin realized the cries were from the survivors of the monks' arrow assault. There were three survivors: two violet-eyed girls and a young green-eyed woman.

The two girls were kneeling beside the lifeless body of a man, shaking him and pleading for him to come back. As they screamed and beat their terrified fists against his chest, Odin averted his eyes. Their pain was a vignette of Hell, a torturous vista into Forneus's rule. As Odin looked to the final survivor, he realized the young woman had her eyes locked intently onto him.

"Is it true?" the young woman asked.

"Is what true?" Odin replied.

"What Raeman said – are you Odin?"

"What difference does it make?"

"If the answer is yes," the woman said, "then it makes a world of difference."

Odin, unsure of what response he could allow, paused for a moment. As Odin stood in the quiet, suddenly, a series of bloody coughs broke the silence, abruptly calling Odin and the young woman's attention to where the two girls were crouched. The young woman quickly rushed to the children, and as she arrived at their side, she realized that the man they had been mourning had come back to consciousness.

"Azean!" the woman cried, "you're alive!"

As more blood spilled from Azean's mouth, he painfully sat up and then wrapped his arms around the two small girls.

"My girls," he wept as they latched hysterically onto him. "It's okay, it's okay."

Azean held the girls for a long moment. After their tears had slowed, he turned to the young woman.

"Adara," he said, "the ship will not make it back to port."

Azean then drew out an old parchment from under his clothes.

"I hope this works for you," he said as he handed it to Adara. "We have been too long without him."

Adara's emerald green eyes dimmed considerably as she accepted the scroll. After she had tucked the scroll under her robe, Azean looked up to her with a final request.

"I ask only that the ship sink admirably," he said. "I want it to be remembered for its strength, not its weakness. I should also like a word with blue."

As Adara wiped her tears, she turned to Odin, and somehow, without speaking, her words began to resound telepathically in his mind.

"Azean is speaking in code," she said. "His wounds are grave, and he is not going to live. He has asked that his daughters be spared from watching him die. He has also requested to speak with you."

Odin was stunned by Adara's ability, but tentative about Azean's request. However, as the battered Azean began to motion for Odin to join him, Odin found it hard to refuse. Adara quickly called the girls away, and once they were out of earshot, Odin knelt next to the badly wounded Azean. The dying man grabbed Odin by the arm and began to speak between intervals of coughs and bloody spits.

"Before you attempt to convince me otherwise," he started, "let me be quite clear: I know who you are. I've waited a long twenty years for you, Odin, and I'm not going to spend my last moments pretending you're someone else. I'm not going to die in charade."

Odin recognized the urgency in Azean's voice. It was the very same grit that had compelled him to follow Galian into the afterlife. The parallel hit Odin in such a way that he chose to forfeit any and all disguise.

"What can I do for you?" Odin asked.

"It is not what you can do for me," Azean replied. "My time is done. It is what you can do for my daughters. They've had a father, Odin. They've never had a king. I want them to know heaven – just as I did when your father was on the throne."

"I hope the same for them, but I am not here to –"

"I do not have the time for debate," Azean asserted. "Odin, you are the heir to the throne. I am asking you to take back your birthright. I am asking you to get to V, and with her redeem this vile land."

Odin shook his head, regretful that he couldn't comply.

"I can't," he apologized. "You don't understand why I'm here. I can't waste time finding V."

"My girls can take you," Azean promised.

As Azean's grip became even stronger around Odin's wrist, the sound of numerous footsteps echoed from down one of the streets.

"It's the Vayne," Azean said with panic. "Only they travel in packs that large."

Odin began to draw Sleipnir from his belt, but Azean quickly arrested his efforts.

"There are at least thirty of them," he informed. "You can't win that fight. Please," Azean begged, "take my girls away from here.

Take them to V. I will buy you enough time. Please, Odin, get them to safety."

As Azean's tearing eyes pled for Odin's help, Odin knew he had to agree, not only for Azean and the girls, but on behalf of the Throne's Eye. It was a matter of heart. Hell had claimed Raeman and his troop, breaking their hearts and then rebuilding them with malice. Against the very same pressure, Odin needed to prove that Hell couldn't claim him. He needed to be a testament to his adopted home – proof that even in Hell, he could honour what was right.

"I will take them," Odin agreed.

"You must go now," Azean impelled. "I can hold off the Vayne, but not for long."

As Azean looked to his daughters, more tears welled in his eyes.

"Tell them I died a hero… tell them I died so they could know heaven."

Odin was humbled: so much so that he had no worthy reply. As the Vayne's footsteps grew louder, Odin realized that the only way he could honour Azean was through action. He needed to get the girls to safety.

"Now, go," Azean spurred. "Remind this land of its former greatness."

Odin nodded and then rose quickly to his feet.

"Your daughters will know," he promised. "You have my word."

As the Vayne's shadows advanced even closer towards the intersection, Odin gave a final nod to Azean, and then turned and sprinted to Adara and the girls.

"We have to go," he announced as he reached the three.

Odin instinctively glanced over his shoulder and saw that the first of the Vayne had emerged into the intersection. Odin turned urgently back to the girls.

"We have to go now," he urged. "We need to run."

Adara quickly understood, but the girls refused to abandon their father. Although he regretted it, Odin knew he had to lie to them. Feigning calm, Odin positioned the girls so that their backs were to their father, and then knelt coolly between them.

"Your dad's an old friend of mine," he said in a softened voice. "And you know what he always told me? He always said that his girls were like navigators. Do you know what a navigator is?"

As the girls shook their heads, Odin could see that behind them, the battered and dying Azean had laboured painfully to his feet to face the Vayne. As the first wave of Vayne began to surround Azean, Odin's eyes fleeted back to the girls.

"A navigator is someone who can always find her way home," he said. "Your dad told me you girls can do it blindfolded. I didn't believe him. But he said you could do it right now. What do you think? Could you find your way home from here?"

One of the girls nodded, but as Azean's voice screamed furiously from behind them, the second girl turned immediately back to her father. The entirety of the thirty Vayne had arrived in the intersection, and it was clear that Azean was doing anything to keep their attention on him.

"I'm here you bastards!" he raged as he brandished two daggers. "Taste my blades!"

As the callous Vayne converged on Azean, his daughters began to scream in panic. Their attempt at stealth was gone. The Vayne identified the girls and immediately began a deadly pursuit.

As Odin began to search for a strategy, Adara's voice echoed once more in his head.

"Run!"

Odin agreed, and with great speed, he and Adara each grabbed a girl, lifted them into their arms, and began a desperate sprint away from the Vayne.

As they ran, Odin could feel Adara's voice calling out directions in his mind.

"We need to get to the main road!" her voice resounded.

Unable to reply psychically, Odin yelled back his reply. "Why the main road?"

"Because that's where our codes are."

Odin didn't understand, but there was a confidence in Adara's voice that compelled him to follow.

With the Vayne on their trail, Adara made a combination of rights and lefts, and within thirty seconds, she had led Odin onto the main roadway of Animus Letum. It was the grand promenade of the afterlife – the path to the throne. The street was based with golden stones, and thousands of torches lined the side of the laneway. As Adara and Odin sprinted over the golden floor, Odin could see Forneus's orange Soul Cauldron in the far distance. However, the present peril was at his back, and as Odin and Adara ran, the five Vayne had closed the distance between them to twenty yards.

"Look for an L!" Adara cried. "It's the start of our code! It will lead us to V!"

"Where do I look?" Odin called back.

As Adara realized the Vayne were closing in, her voice filled with panic.

"Everywhere!" she yelled.

Odin didn't have time for confusion. He was at a deadly crossroads. He was unsure of the code, but certain that Adara and the girls were in jeopardy. If he engaged the five Vayne, he knew he could defeat them. He also knew that if it turned into a brawl, he wouldn't be able to protect the girls fully. Their survival would be a coin toss. So, siding with the girls' best odds, Odin took Adara's instruction and hunted the laneway for an L.

As he ran, Odin fervently scanned the street and adjacent buildings. The buildings were battered and broken down with boards nailed over their many doors and windows. There was no prominent L in the laneway, and as Odin continued to search, he could hear the Vayne's footsteps growing closer. Odin's understanding of the code was basic at best, but as he scanned the buildings ahead of him, one of the boarded windows caught his eye. It was painted blue. As he grew closer he saw that it was in next to an alley and, more importantly, that the boards were nailed together to form an L.

"Adara!" Odin yelled as he pointed to the window. "There! Is that it?"

Adara's eyes followed Odin's pointing finger, and after recognizing the L, she immediately confirmed Odin's suspicion.

"That's it!" she called back. "Take the alley!"

While still carrying the small girls, Odin and Adara dashed off the main road and cut down the narrow corridor marked with an L.

As Odin allowed Adara to take the lead, it was clear that the chase had begun to drain her. As she carried the small girl, her strides became more and more laborious. Odin quickly calculated the risk. With the Vayne's pace and Adara's fatigue, the threat of attack was imminent. The strategy needed to change. As he searched his mind and surroundings for an advantage, Odin quickly noted that the alley, unlike the main road, was narrow enough to engage all five Vayne without putting the girls in danger.

He just needed Adara's cooperation.

"Adara!" he yelled. "You need to take the girls!"

Adara refused. "No, Odin! We're stronger together!"

"I'll catch up!" Odin promised. "Let the girls run! You can't last much longer at this pace!"

Adara could not argue. Her fatigue had become a liability. As she looked back and realized that the Vayne were within striking distance, she had to agree.

The Sons of Animus Letum

"Okay," she consented. "Put them down in three."

A countdown then sounded in Odin's mind. "Three... two... one..."

In unison, Odin and Adara landed the girls onto their feet, and as Adara became relieved of the added weight, she found a resurgence of energy. With the girls at her sides, Adara began a desperate sprint down the alleyway.

As the girls fled, Odin did the opposite. He quickly unlocked Sleipnir from his belt, pressed her center button, and then leapt into a half axel. As Odin spun aerially to face the Vayne, Sleipnir extended to her full length, and after altering his grip, Odin swung Sleipnir into the closest Vayne's neck. As the first Vayne collapsed and the remaining Vayne spread out in front of him, Odin's blue eyes glanced back to Adara and the girls. They were getting away.

As the three sped down the backstreet, Adara managed to relay critical information to Odin's mind.

"The code spells LYRAN," she said.

Odin allowed the code to register, and as the Vayne began to attack, Odin set his skills into a blaze of offensive fury. Within seconds, he had cut down the five Vayne. As the last of Forneus's henchman fell lifelessly to the floor, Odin's senses clenched in panic as the sound of screaming girls echoed from behind him. He was certain it was Azean's daughters. With furious speed, Odin turned and then bolted down the alley. As he tore determinedly down the backstreet, Odin was uncertain if Adara and the girls had made it to the next letter in the code. His action hinged on that information. As he neared an intersection of roadways, he saw that one of the paths was marked with a pitchfork missing its center prong. He was tentative to identify the sign as a Y. What if it wasn't the code and he made a wrong turn? What if it was the Y and he bypassed it? The stakes were incredibly high. The only sense that seemed relevant was instinct, and as Odin reached the intersection, he relied on his gut and made a turn down the pitchfork-marked roadway. As the lane turned into a tunnel, Odin could hear more of the girls' screaming reverberate through the roofed underpass. He was on the right path. As he neared a stairwell that led down into a courtyard, he quickly realized why the girls were screaming.

Adara had been captured.

Two Scale members had apprehended her and were holding their daggers poised to her neck. The Scale also seemed to be aware that Odin was coming. They stood behind Adara, screaming threats down the dark tunnel.

"Son of Serich," they wailed as they held their daggers to her neck, "Cease your madness or we will embark on our own."

Unfortunately for the Scale, Odin was in no mood for negotiation. As his electric blue eyes emerged into the stone courtyard, he leapt powerfully off the top of the stairwell and began to descend on Adara's captors. Before the two Scale even had a chance to react, Odin soared over Adara's head and crashed his knees heavily into the two Scale's skulls.

The Scale were instantly dead.

The attack was so quick that even Adara hadn't processed what had happened. As Odin began an urgent survey of the stone courtyard, she seemed in a daze.

"Where is the R?" Odin asked. "I don't see an R."

Adara shook her head to snap herself out of her stupor.

"I don't know," she said. "There are literally hundreds of LYRAN paths. I have never taken this one."

The great dilemma of the stone courtyard was that there was a stairwell at each of its corners. Omitting the tunnel they had arrived in, there were three viable paths. In addition, there was extensive graffiti plastered on the wall. There were phrases and symbols, but, to Odin's chagrin, no obvious R.

Odin turned to the girls. "Have you taken this path?" he asked.

The girls shook their heads.

"Okay," Odin said, "everyone look for an R. We must be very quick,"

Adara and the girls instantly undertook the assignment. As they scanned, Odin instinctively checked the four stairwells. If one thing had been made clear during his time in the afterlife, it was that danger was always close. As Odin alternated between scouting and searching for the code, it became apparent that the R was expertly hidden. The code could only be found with a creative eye. So, with an abstract eye, Odin made a repeat survey of the walls, but as the fruitless search continued, the sound of numerous footsteps began to echo from two of the corner corridors. Odin knew, and feared, that if the Vayne or Scale converged into the courtyard from multiple angles, he, Adara, and the girls were as good as dead. But then, as shadows began to move down the two corridors, Adara pointed to one of the stairwells in revelation.

"There!" she alerted.

Odin followed her eyes, and after he saw a question painted next to the stairwell he understood.

The question was "Are we doomed?" but the word *Are* was painted in blue. As Adara looked to Odin for consensus, Odin knew he needed to make a quick ruling.

It was their best chance.

"That's got to be it," he said. "Let's go!"

With the Vayne still seconds behind them, Adara and Odin each grabbed a girl and sped up the stairwell. It seemed that they would escape undetected. However, as they fled from the stone courtyard, the scroll Azean had given Adara jostled out from under her clothes and fell down a crack in the stairwell.

Adara was instantly aware.

"Dammit!" she cursed. "Odin! I need to go back!"

"No!" Odin yelled. "It's too late!"

"You don't understand!" Adara cried. "I need that scroll!"

Odin tried to argue, but Adara had made up her mind. She quickly put down the girl she was carrying and dashed back into the courtyard. As she reached the stairwell, she immediately identified the narrow crack the parchment had fallen through. In a desperate attempt to retrieve the scroll, Adara knelt down and stabbed her arm repeatedly into the crevice. Each attempt failed – the parchment was just out of her reach. As the seconds passed in her futile attempt to claim it, the Vayne had grown dangerously close.

As Odin watched Adara's frantic efforts, he knew the parchment had to be important. But regardless of its worth, Adara was risking a great deal to retrieve it.

"Adara!" he finally yelled. "There is no time! Let it go!"

"I almost have it!" Adara yelled back. "Two more seconds!"

Odin had to refuse.

As Adara tried again to claim the scroll, Odin grabbed her by the arm and lifted her sternly to her feet.

"We have a priority," he said as he motioned to the girls. "Azean's actions will not be in vain."

Adara was compelled to argue, but as she looked on Azean's daughters, she knew Odin was right. After a conceding nod, she abandoned the scroll and began to follow Odin out of the courtyard. As she fled, Adara took a fleeting look back in an attempt to make a mental map of the parchment's location. However, the moment she glanced back, her emerald eyes immediately locked onto the yellow eyes of Forneus's hunters.

"No!" she shrieked to Odin. "They saw us!"

"How many?" Odin yelled back.

"At least twenty!"

There was only one option.

"Run!" Odin ordered.

With the Vayne close on their trail, Odin and Adara tore desperately down the corridor. The laneway was short and narrow, and as Odin and Adara reached its end, they spilled out into a massive garden. There were dozens of towering statues and fountains that, even after being left untended for years, granted the court an impressive royal class.

As Odin and Adara pushed into the garden's center, Adara realized she had been there before.

"I know this place," she said into Odin's mind. "There are other LYRAN paths that converge here."

"Do you know where the A is?" Odin yelled.

Adara nodded. "The statue of your mother points to it! Look for her! She will be holding a purple staff!"

Odin understood, and as he sprinted through the massive garden, his eyes scavenged the stone structures for his queen mother. As Odin intently surveyed the garden, he realized that there were too many statues to inspect. The layout of the garden was a maze of stone and earth, and nearly every path looked like the one before it.

"Adara!" he finally yelled. "I can't lead! This place is a labyrinth!"

Within the vast garden, Adara's past experience would prove timely.

"Follow me!" she instructed. "I know where to go!"

Adara bolted ahead, and as she led Odin through the myriad of massive statues, the trailing Vayne began to fall further into the distance. After five sequential turns, Adara pointed to a statue and allowed her voice to echo in Odin's head.

"That's it!" she said.

The statue was of Rhea, and the purple staff in her hand pointed directly to an A-shaped archway. With the entirety of the Vayne left searching the garden, Adara led Odin under the arch and down into a wide laneway. As they ran, Odin noted the Vayne's failed search, and after angling himself, the girls, and Adara into the roadway's shadow, he allowed himself to decelerate into a jog.

"Is the N close?" he asked.

"Very," Adara replied as she put Azean's daughter down.

After a deep breath, she nodded to a broken-down building at the end of the road. The building had barn-style doors, and the white wood panelling on the doors formed a perfect N.

Odin and Adara continued to use the shadows as their ally, and after a short run, they arrived at the barn doors. Once Adara had confirmed that there were no Scale or Vayne on the roadway, she knocked her fist into the door in a specific rhythm. Almost immediately, a slot opened on the door, revealing the studying eyes of a guard on the other side.

"Twice down?" the guard asked.

"Thrice up," Adara replied.

"It appears that you have company," the guard said.

Although it was protocol, Adara became instantly irritated with the guard's questions.

"For god sakes, Dahnus, Azean's daughters are out here. Open the god-damned door."

After a small moment of silence, the slot closed and the barn doors separated enough for entry.

Odin allowed the girls and Adara to enter, and after a making a final survey of Animus Letum's barren streets, he stepped through the doors and entered into V's inner sanctum.

43

After Odin had entered through the barn doors, Adara and the girls began to lead him deeper into the structure. However, as Odin tried to follow, he was immediately confronted by four armed guards. As the guards drew their weapons on him, Odin quickly raised his hands in a sign of goodwill.

Though he had expressed his passivity, Odin's eyes had instantly earned the guard's contempt.

"Blue is quite a colour to be walking around with," the lead guard Dahnus said. "What magic is this? You mock our kings?"

"There is no magic," Adara promised. "I assure you. These blue eyes were inherited."

Dahnus and his troop were not convinced. As they continued to hold their weapons against Odin, Adara's tone took a drastic change.

"Gentleman, if you truly do serve the Lyran house, a bow would be much more appropriate than a brawl. And frankly, after seeing him in action, a bow would be the wiser choice."

Dahnus looked Adara over and then returned his examining eyes to Odin.

"If you truly are a Serich Son," he said, "then you should have no difficulty with this."

Wildly, Dahnus threw his fist at Odin's jaw. As Odin managed instinctively to weave away from the assault, the other three guards began to attack. The guards were considerably weaker opponents than the Vayne, and with non-lethal force, Odin resolved the conflict in a matter of seconds. Three of the guards were sprawled on the floor, and Dahnus was pinned against the wall with one of Odin's daggers.

Although humiliated, Dahnus voiced his judgment.

"A Serich Son you are," he decreed.

Adara shook her head.

"You're wasting our time Dahnus. Just give us a torch so we can get to V."

After Dahnus unpinned himself from the wall, he handed the dagger back to Odin and handed Adara one of the many lit torches that were mounted behind him.

"I trust you know the way."

"I do," Adara affirmed. "However, I require a favour from one of your guards."

"What favour?" Dahnus asked.

"Azean's daughters need an escort. Their mother lives in the south district, and Odin and I are headed to the east."

"As you wish," Dahnus consented.

With a wave of his hand, he nominated one of his underlings, and shortly after, the guard led Azean's daughters down a dark tunnel that went to the south.

There were three tunnels inside the barn. The tunnels were narrow, allowing for no more than three people at a time, and each one of them was drowned in darkness.

As Odin eyed the three burrows, Adara reached for his arm, and with torch in hand, she began to lead him down the eastern tunnel.

"You better brush up on those skills," she called back to Dahnus. "They may matter someday."

"I was beaten by a Lyran!" Dahnus said in excuse. "There's no shame in that!"

As Adara's laugh echoed back from the tunnel, Dahnus smirked, and with a sense of hope flaring in his soul, he watched the amber glow of Adara's torch disappear into the darkness.

Odin and Adara maintained a brisk pace as they moved through the tunnel. The speed of their travel had not allowed for conversation, but as Adara's body finally pled for rest, she keeled over, and after a moment of heavy breathing, she leaned against the rock wall of the tunnel.

As Odin stopped and Adara began to regain her breath, Adara felt the need to excuse Dahnus's behaviour.

"I'm sorry about the guards at the doorway," she said. "Dahnus is charged with protecting a great deal. These tunnels are our lifeline. They are the haven and home to every soul who refuses Forneus's rule."

"How many of you are there?" Odin asked as he and Adara began to walk.

"Thousands," Adara replied. "We are basically a settlement. When your father was murdered, the wisest of us retreated. We roamed the far lengths of this realm until these tunnels were built. And for the last few years, we have expanded them and made them our home."

Something clicked in Odin's head.

"When were these tunnels built?" he asked.

Adara thought for a moment. "Time works differently here in the afterlife," she said. "But if I had to guess, I'd say these tunnels were started about three years ago in your earth time."

Odin's posture slumped. "Three years…" he whispered.

"About that," Adara said.

A small smile began to surface on her face. "That's when the Minin' McEnrow arrived," she said. "At least that's what they call themselves. They're strange ones," she laughed, "but they're good people."

Odin's pulse started to thump throughout his entire body. The truth was what he had feared. As tears began to well in his eyes, Odin's breath became short and he stumbled against the rock wall.

Adara quickly braced him.

"Odin," she cried, "are you alright?"

With sweat beading everywhere on his skin, Odin shook his head clumsily.

Adara felt Odin's forehead. "What's wrong?" she asked.

"Me," Odin said. "Just me…"

As Odin covered his mouth and his breath became a struggle, he tried to force out a question. However, in his pain, he couldn't find his voice. Finally, through his wheezes, he formed the question that he knew would break his heart.

"Would you still be alive without these tunnels?" he asked.

Adara was confused by Odin's behaviour. "No," she answered. "Without them we would have been crushed."

Odin fell even further back against the wall, dropping into a crouch. As he raked his fingers through his hair, he began to ramble.

"I knew it…" he whispered. "I always knew it. Fool!" he cursed himself. "You damned fool!"

"Odin!" Adara shouted. "What's going on with you?"

There was a long silence, but eventually, Odin wiped his eyes and stood up defiantly.

"It's just added motivation," he said firmly. "Let's move."

As Adara stared at him, she was expecting an explanation, but Odin had already started to march farther down the tunnel.

Frantically, Adara jogged next to him.

"Are you going to explain that?" she asked.

"No," Odin said.

His voice and walk were prompt and driven.

"Why were you on the surface?" he asked.

"Oh, so you can ask questions," Adara said sharply.

"Please, Adara. I cannot not explain myself… not yet."

After another long silence, Adara threw her hands up in surrender.

"We were looking for Azean and his daughters," she said. "They had gone missing. The only clue we had was a letter that Azean had left. It said that he had found a way to free my father and that he needed to bring his daughters."

"Your father, is he in the Cauldron?"

"He might as well be," Adara answered. "You've likely met him. He has a giant boat tethered to his ankle."

"Your father is the Boatman?"

"Yes," Adara confirmed. "But more importantly, he is one of the few people brilliant enough to out-think Forneus. My father has thousands of years of history stored in his mind. He knows every flaw and strength in this land, and if we are to have any advantage in this battle, we need him at the helm."

Odin was confused by their dilemma. "Why haven't you already freed him?" he asked.

"The laws of this land won't allow it," Adara replied. "Because a king banished him to the boat, only a king can free him. That was, until Azean found a way. Unfortunately, the scroll I dropped down the stairwell detailed the method Azean had discovered."

Odin offered Adara a sympathetic nod.

"It was almost perfect," Adara lamented, "but, alas, not meant to be. The more I see, the more it seems that fate doesn't have a moral compass."

"My brother would likely argue against that point," Odin said. "He believes in will over fate."

"Then he'd get along with V," Adara said.

Odin offered a simple nod. As Adara turned to look at him in the torchlight, suddenly Odin's presence fully registered and she became shocked that she hadn't asked an obvious question.

"Why are you here?" she blurted. "I mean, why have you died?"

"The simple answer is that I had to," Odin replied. "My brother Galian went before me, and by suicide, I came after."

Adara was surprised. "Your brother has passed too?"

"He has," Odin answered. "That's the reason I'm here. I killed myself so I could save him – so I could free him from Forneus's Soul Cauldron."

Adara was silent for a moment. Regrettably, even after witnessing Odin's skill, she was doubtful that Odin could beat Forneus on his own.

Although, despite her doubt, Adara knew that hope was a weapon.

"If your aim is to defeat Forneus," she said, "then it is appropriate we are going to V. She can organize an army around you."

As Adara imagined V's army with Odin at the helm, her green eyes seemed to flicker with promise.

"You can lead us," she said. "You can be our advantage."

Odin shook his head. "I will meet with V," he said, "but I cannot wait for her to marshal an army. I can't even wait for my own army. I promised Azean I would get his daughters to safety, and I have done that. My priority has returned to freeing Galian. And he needs me immediately."

As Adara's posture slumped slightly in dejection, Odin knew he had to be honest.

"I understand what I represent to you," he said, "and I understand that this land is suffering. But my immediate duty is to save my brother. Trust me, I know the pain of this land. I know how it feels to be good when evil is winning. But if I am to have any impact in this realm, I can't forfeit my heart. And if Galian falls twice into death, my heart will follow. I am no one without him."

"You are mistaken to think that our battle is between good and evil," Adara said. "In Animus Letum, the fight is between fear and hope. Raeman and the monks you struck down are the proof. They were not evil, Odin: they were afraid. They were afraid that no matter what they did, this hell would persist – that this atrocious world could never break, and that they would be forever its victims. It was fear, and not evil, that twisted them into hell's partner. They sided with darkness because they forgot that there was light."

Odin shook his head. "That doesn't excuse them."

"I am not offering an excuse, Odin. I am offering the reason. This world is awful. And when the fear that it can never change turns into the belief that it can never change, hearts fade and hell grows. The only thing that separates me, or V, or any of our faction from Raeman, is that we have hope."

"What hope?" Odin asked.

"Hope that one day this hell will end," Adara said. "Hope that you and your brother will return."

Odin was struck by both the content and delivery of Adara's words. He was speechless. He had been muted by emotion.

As he fumbled in the quiet, it was Adara who finally broke the silence.

"That's V," she said, pointing to a flickering torch down the tunnel. "That's her church."

The golden torch was mounted next to a large, red-studded door. In the torchlight, Odin could see very little. However, as Odin and Adara arrived at the red door, he saw the letter V branded above the doorframe.

"This door has a slightly different code," Adara said as she handed Odin her torch.

She then knocked on the door in a different rhythm than the barn doors, and shortly after a circular slot opened where the doorknob should have been. Adara pushed her hand through the hole, and once it had arrived on the door's other side, she manipulated her fingers into a sequence of seven different hand signs. After Adara withdrew her hand, there was a small moment of silence, but after a loud creak, the red doors opened.

As Odin followed Adara inside, he was surprised to see that the inside of V's church was decked in almost royal tailor. Gold trim covered the walls, pews, and torches of the hall, and the altar was crafted with massive, perfectly cut bronze blocks. There were at least sixty members of the parish in the large church, and as Odin scanned their numbers, Adara called for their leader.

"V!" she shouted. "You have a visitor!"

The sixty people in the church turned inquisitively, but then became completely rapt by the sight of Odin's blue eyes. As the fascinated crowd stared in disbelief, a small boy caught Odin's attention. The boy had no eyes and something about him seemed very familiar.

Then, a slender, purple-eyed and red-robed woman emerged at the front.

"Haren?" Odin blurted.

"Odin?" Haren gasped. "How?" she asked as shock overtook his face. "This is far too soon! Why are you here? How has this happened?"

Odin was equally shocked. "You? You're V?"

"Yes," Haren hastily answered. "But why are you here? Where is your brother?"

"I thought you would have heard," Odin said. "Galian died. He was thrown into the Cauldron."

"The Cauldron?" Haren stammered. "That can't be. Forneus would have had to claim him directly."

"He did," Odin reported. "He used the Reaper's Covenant."

As the news registered, Haren cursed and then slammed her hands furiously onto the bronze altar.

"How long has it been?" she asked. "How long since he was taken?"

"I'm not sure." Odin confessed. "I came immediately after him. It's been two days at most."

"Were you killed in the Metus Sane assault?" Haren asked.

"The Metus Sane?" Odin repeated. "They never attacked us. I killed myself."

Haren's tone became deeply apologetic. "Odin, the Throne's Eye is in rubble. Usis and his Metus Sane burned it to the ground. Most of our brothers were killed. I had assumed that you and Galian had gotten away."

"There's no way," Odin tried to argue. "I practically broke Usis's ankle in half. He was in no shape to overtake our brothers."

"I don't know what to tell you, Odin. I wish I was wrong. I wish it with all my heart. But I assure you, our home is burned. Our brothers are dead."

"Even Raine?" Odin asked, his voice breaking with emotion.

"I don't know," Haren replied. "But it is likely that he is dead."

Haren's harsh truth towed another in its wake.

"And the Forge?" Odin asked.

Haren shook her head. "I don't think they're coming. I doubt Usis would have given any of them the Boatman rite."

"But they would have had their coins on them," Odin argued. "Every member of the Forge was supposed to carry the coins."

"It wouldn't matter, Odin," Haren said. "The coins need to be placed over the eyes."

As Odin's eyes went blank in shock, Haren allowed her brother a moment of mourning. However, acknowledging the immediate danger, Haren knew she had to return to the more important point.

"You're sure Galian was taken to the Cauldron?" she asked. "Because, honestly, information of that magnitude should have found me."

"I don't know," Odin faltered. "Igallik thought so."

"Well, let's be certain," Haren said.

With authority, Haren turned to her parish.

"We are in need of a Green Eye!" she shouted over them. "We believe a Lyran is in the Cauldron, and we need someone to take a look!"

Including Adara, only five of the sixty parishioners had green eyes. The ability incumbent on Green Eyes was that they could instigate a Shamance, a rite that would allow them to look into the Cauldron.

Rysan, the only male with green eyes, could not hold back his alarm.

"Look in the Cauldron?" he cried. "Are you mad? You know what that would mean. It would announce our church to this entire realm. Not only would our tunnels be found, but every one of us would be put in serious danger."

Lilas, another woman with green eyes, added to the concern.

"Not only that, whoever instigates the Shamance is exposed completely to the Cauldron. They bear its entire weight. V, we can't entertain this. It is stupidity and not courage that would choose this. None of us are foolish enough try a Shamance with the Cauldron."

"I am," Adara volunteered.

Rysan immediately objected. "You can't be serious, Adara. This is folly. It would be the end of us. You're not seeing the risk."

"I'm seeing a chance, Rysan," Adara replied, "or, at least, the closest semblance to one we've had in two decades. I can't live like this anymore. Whether I'm in the Cauldron or not, I have become Forneus's prisoner. I've got nothing to lose."

Rysan shook his head in disbelief. "Yes, you do! I can't believe we are having this argument. If we look into the Cauldron, it will undoubtedly look back. Our entire safeguard – our entire network of stealth – would be in jeopardy. You're talking about suicide, Adara."

"I'm talking about hope," Adara said firmly.

"You don't realize what you're saying," Rysan said mournfully. "If you do this, you're sacrificing more than yourself. You'll risk everything we have."

"Everything we have?" Adara blurted. "For God's sake, Rysan, are you listening to yourself? All we *have* is fear. All we are doing is waiting to die."

"This is whim," Rysan replied. "I am not going to debate this nonsense. If this is truly what we have been waiting for…"

"Rysan!" Haren interrupted. "I'm having difficulty understanding why you think you have a say. I have asked for a Green Eye, and I have found one. We are moving forward."

Rysan looked pleadingly at Haren. "We can't do this. This is…"

"My church," Haren asserted. "If you have a problem with my decision, you are welcome to leave. In fact, Dahnus had been asking for a replacement for years."

As Rysan sank reluctantly back into silence, Haren turned to Adara.

"This is your last chance to say no," she said. "But if you are willing to move forward, we will do so immediately."

Adara looked to Odin, and after a deep breath, she made her choice.

"I will do it," she said. "Just let me grab my tools."

Haren nodded, and after Adara turned to gather her tools, Haren led Odin into a small room behind the massive bronze altar. The room was oval, and in its center was large empty glass cylinder with a small tube sticking out from its inside.

As Adara continued to hunt down her utensils, Haren used the small moment to issue an overdue apology.

"I am sorry about that scar," she said as she inspected the mark below Odin's right eye. "But, believe me, there was great purpose in instructing you and Galian in Vinculum Imletalis. It was not just a ploy to take your father's crown."

"You almost killed us," Odin said. "I find it hard to believe you were acting on our behalf."

"Can't you see that I was preparing you?" Haren said. "I was anticipating this exact moment. Everything I've done has been on your behalf."

"Then why did you take the crown?" Odin asked. "You should have known we would defeat the Scale that night."

"I didn't doubt it, Odin: I was counting on it. Taking the crown was pure strategy. Forneus knew that the crown was in the first realm. So I took it to the last place he would think to look: right here, right under his nose."

"That was reckless."

"It was, but it appears to have worked."

"But why go by V?" Odin asked. "Why the disguise?"

"To protect you," Haren answered. "I needed to be someone with no connection to you and your brother – someone whom Forneus wouldn't look for. I had the crown, Odin; I couldn't allow myself to be caught."

Odin's head sunk a bit. "I'm sorry Haren. There seems to be a lot I don't know."

Haren nodded sombrely. "The McEnrow?" she presumed.

"Galian should have told me," Odin cried. "It would have changed everything. It would have given us another three years."

"He couldn't tell you, Odin. Even if he had wanted to."

"But why? Why couldn't he tell me?"

"When Galian attempted Descent, I was already here in Animus Letum. Galian found me and came up with the plan to kill the McEnrow. Our pact was that we couldn't allow you or anyone else to die with that information. If you had passed and Forneus had found you, Forneus would have picked your brain as if it were seeds in a bowl. Our entire safeguard would have been compromised."

Odin wiped his eyes again. "I can't let it end like this."

Gently, Haren placed her hand on Odin's shoulder.

"I've worked my whole life to protect you and Galian," she said. "I've sacrificed a great deal to ensure your legacy. And now, when it matters most, I must give you my best. And in this moment, my best comes as counsel."

"What counsel?"

"I've been privileged to know your heart, Odin. I know you're a warrior. And I know you are going to face Forneus as soon as you get the chance. But heart is not enough to win that battle. We must also use strategy. I'm asking you to wait before facing the king."

"I don't have that option," Odin said sternly. "I have to face him now."

"If you wait, I can offer an army," Haren said. "Not now, but soon. I can organize thousands to march in your shadow. If you lead them, we can win. If you lead them, we will have a chance."

"And what of Galian?" Odin asked. "If I wait, what are his chances? My next move depends wholly on his condition."

Haren's tone turned solemn. "Then, for all of us, let us pray that he is holding on."

As Odin took a deep breath, Adara arrived with her tools: a leaf of tobacco, a book of matches, and a tobacco pipe.

"How does this work?" Odin asked her.

"You're about to see," she replied.

Adara then packed her pipe with the tobacco, struck a match, and after lighting the tobacco, she took a long inhalation of the smoke. After she had held the smoke in her lungs for nearly half a minute, she put her mouth over the cylinder's protruding tube, her eyes began to sparkle with a vibrant green, and she exhaled the smoke into the cylinder.

Adara repeated the same rite four times until the cylinder was filled completely with white smoke. With a firm hand, she then sealed the cylinder's tube and stepped back to watch.

Odin was uncertain of the significance of Adara's ritual, but after a short moment he became startled as the smoke-filled cylinder activated. The smoke began to swirl and churn in wild gusts, and as the speed of the smoke increased, it wound into a perfect column. As the cyclone spiralled, there was a green flash, and the twisting column burst vividly into a deep flaming orange.

There appeared to be a great number of white skeletal figures slashing around the column's inside. Odin looked inquisitively into the column, but as he suddenly realized what it was, he stumbled back. The column was the Soul Cauldron. The smoke had transformed into a living vision of Forneus's soul prison.

As the countless skeletons began to crash around the Cauldron with even more fervour, Odin became curious of their awareness.

"Do they see us?" he asked Adara.

"Not yet," she answered, "but they will soon. You ask because of my father, don't you?"

"Actually, yes," Odin replied. "In his visions we were invisible."

"My dad is gifted to see into the past," Adara said. "He doesn't contribute to the visions, so no detection is possible. With a Shamance we see the present. That," she explained, pointing to the smoke, "is happening right now."

As the Shamance started to move deeper into the Cauldron, Adara called out her final warning.

"Brace yourself! We're about to enter!"

Heeding the warning, Odin made an effort to brace himself. There was no adequate preparation. As the Shamance entered completely into the soul prison, his senses cringed as the carnage of the Cauldron overtook the glass cylinder. The sound was like a symphony of torturous screams, doused in the odour of sulphur and amplified by the sight of hellish slashing flames. It was truly Hell.

Because Adara was guiding the Shamance, the impact of the Cauldron hit her tenfold. It was as if she was one of the souls being tortured. As the Cauldron's flames dominated the tube and the glass cylinder erupted into a vision of blazing fire, Adara began to stagger back and forth. And with her body beginning to feel like it was being torn apart, Adara's hands reached for Odin's and Haren's shoulders.

Understanding exactly what she had asked of Adara, Haren braced her and stood attentively at her side.

"Can you hold it?" Haren asked. "Is this too much?"

Adara's reply was stuttered. "It's too late to go back now," she said. "They've already seen us."

"Already?" Haren said with alarm. "That's impossible."

In fear, Haren turned back to the Shamance and was startled to see that a number of white skeletons had identified the Cauldron's intruders and were furiously pounding their fists upon the glass cylinder. As the skeletons eyed them, the gravity of the dilemma seemed to fully hit Haren, and she became unsure of the rite.

"Adara, we can still get out," she said. "It's not too late. There is no need for martyrdom. We'll find another way."

The sinister faces of the skeletons compelled Adara to agree, but even as the torture of the Cauldron coursed through her, she knew she couldn't surrender.

"I can do this," she stammered. "Just look for Galian."

As Adara's posture began to bend under the weight of the Cauldron, Odin was deeply regretful of what she was experiencing. However, as he braced her, he also knew she was right. It was too late to go back.

With her legs' wobbling and staggering, Adara forged her mind even further into the depths of the Cauldron. The Shamance had begun near the top of the Cauldron, and as it began to descend into the prison's depths, Adara, Haren, and Odin became full witness to the horrific scenes of the Cauldron's torture. A number of discernible bodies were being ripped apart by the skeletons, and then like vultures, countless skeletons began to spar with each other and scavenge the torn body parts.

As Adara's weight fell almost entirely onto Odin, she whispered weakly to him.

"Keep your eyes open," she said. "If your brother is still alive, he will no doubt be near the bottom."

Understanding the great urgency, Odin scanned the Cauldron for any sign of his brother. As Adara continued to navigate through the Cauldron, the flames seemed to grow more intense, and more skeletons began to butt and smash into the glass cylinder.

"Odin, we have to... we have to close the Shamance," Adara whimpered. "The glass... the glass is going to break."

With his time and heart fading, Odin desperately searched the bottom of the Cauldron.

There was no sign of Galian.

Odin was torn. But he knew he couldn't ask Adara to suffer anymore.

However, as Adara raised her hands to extinguish the Shamance, Odin caught a small glimpse of the Cauldron's floor and, more importantly, a body sitting in cross-legged meditation.

"There!" Odin shouted as he pointed frantically into the Cauldron. "I saw him. Galian's there!"

"Are you sure?" Haren asked. "You must be sure."

"Yes. I'm sure. There," he said as he pointed again.

As Adara's head nodded clumsily with exhaustion, somehow she managed enough energy to drive the vision down to where Odin had directed her.

As she hit the Cauldron's floor, she saw what Odin had.

Galian sat at the Cauldron's absolute depth, shaking violently as the skeletons ripped and tore through his body. Galian's body was badly damaged from the assault, and his face wretched with the great pain of the pillaging.

Tortured by the sight of his brother's anguish, Odin began to scream at Galian. It was useless. The Cauldron's pitch was too loud. Odin then waved his arms wildly, trying to catch Galian's eye, but he quickly realized Galian wasn't given the Boatman rite. He had no eyes.

"He's in... he's in so much pain," Adara cried as tears welled in her eyes. "But he makes no sound."

"He can't speak," Odin said gravely.

"Oh, Odin...," Adara cried. "He is going to die... he can't hold on. There's no way..."

As more skeletons began to bash into the glass, the cylinder began to crack.

"Close it!" Haren commanded as the glass started to shatter.

Adara barely heard. She, exhausted and so overwhelmingly sorry for the pain Galian had been dealt, could barely think. However, as Haren braced her shoulders and called her to attention, Adara quickly recognized the threat. Just as the Cauldron's skeletons and fire began to break from the cylinder, she extinguished the vision.

As the Shamance ended, a cloud of smoke billowed from the cylinder, but in seconds that smoke dissipated, and the only remaining evidence of the Cauldron's depths were its three shaken witnesses.

Consumed like never before, Odin turned and set his furious strides out of Haren's church. Haren sprinted in chase, and after she caught up, she blocked Odin's path.

"Odin, you can't do this alone. Please," she begged, "just wait."

However, as Haren met Odin's furious stare, she knew Odin was not going to wait for an army.

"You saw him," Odin said. There was a rage in his voice — like a smouldering fire that was being just barely contained. "Waiting is not an option," Odin said firmly. "Adara has explained this world to me. There is fear and there is hope. If I must, I will die on the latter."

As Odin's eyes burned, the small, eyeless boy that Odin had seen at front of the church walked next to Haren.

"Morello?" Odin presumed.

Haren nodded.

"Then you, of all people, know I can't wait," Odin said.

Haren shook her head in regret. "Let me give you this then," she said as she drew a plant leaf from a pouch on her belt.

Odin looked to the door and then back to Haren.

"What is it?" he asked.

"Just eat it," Haren said as she handed the leaf to Odin. "It will hide your blue eyes under a cover of yellow."

Odin nodded and then quickly ingested the leaf. In seconds his blue eyes dimmed to the same yellow as the Scale.

"The closer you get to Forneus, the more the leaf will wear off," Haren said. "His presence counteracts its magic. But with yellows, your travel should be less obstructed."

Odin nodded and then opened the twin red doors of Haren's church.

"Which way?" he asked. "Which way to Forneus?"

Haren pointed to a tunnel that went further east.

"That one will lead you as close as any."

Odin nodded, and just before he turned completely out of the church, he offered his hand to Haren.

"You've done a lot for us," he said as Haren accepted his hand. "But now it's on me. If I don't make it, you burn this god-damned land to the ground."

As Haren nodded, Odin hugged her, and after grabbing a torch from the wall, Odin turned and sped down the eastern tunnel.

Haren's gut churned as she watched Odin's departure, but after he was gone, she turned back to her intently watching parish.

"Get battle ready," she ordered. "We're marching on the throne."

The men and women of the church hesitated in the great implication of Haren's order. It was monumental. Even still, Haren couldn't allow for wasted time.

"Now," she commanded to the stalling parish. "Our future hinges on our haste."

Suddenly, Haren's order registered, and the sixty parishioners began to scramble frantically throughout the church.

As her parish collected physically and mentally for battle, Haren strode contemplatively to the massive bronze altar.

At the altar, she pressed her hands into two specific points on the altar's broad side, and as the bronze began to slide back, a large hidden compartment was revealed.

Carefully, Haren reached into the compartment and retrieved a large padlocked box. After she had examined the box, she took off a necklace she was wearing and drew a particular key from its chain. As Haren unlocked the padlock and looked into the deep red blood that filled the box, she was calmed to see it was just as he had left it.

With pleading eyes, Haren looked skywards.

"I'm choosing hope as well," she said. "The timing is off, but the characters are right. In my mind that's enough. Please, fate, make this so."

After a loud huff, Haren reached deep into the blood-filled box, and after her hand found its bottom, she pulled Serich's golden crown out from its crimson sheath.

"Serich," Haren whispered, "forgive me if this goes wrong."

44

As Odin sprinted through the eastern tunnel, he quickly converged on the doorway that led back onto the streets of Animus Letum.

At the doorway there were four armed guards, and as they saw Odin's yellow eyes emerging from the darkness of the tunnel, they immediately drew their weapons. Odin continued to barrel towards them, showing no sign of slowing down.

Just before he reached the guards, Odin tossed his torch just above their heads, and as the guards focused on the flaming projectile, Odin cut swiftly between them.

Before the guards had even realized what had happened, Odin had kicked the door open and dashed back out into hell.

As Odin tore furiously through the roads and alleys of Animus Letum, he did so against all odds.

Truth had said Galian was fading. Impossibility had laid claim to Odin's task. And all reason defied Odin's heart. But it was his brother near death. It was Odin's best friend in jeopardy. No measure of truth, or impossibility, or reason could ever argue his heart out of action. Odin believed he could save him – he had to.

As he ran, Odin was unsure of his path, but as he made sparing glances skywards, Forneus's orange Soul Cauldron – and especially its hellish glow – made his endpoint clear.

Along his path, there were dozens of Scale and Vayne scattered on the streets. However, because of Odin's yellow eyes, the serpent soldiers paid no special attention to him. He was one of their own.

As his determined strides chased down the orange Soul Cauldron, Odin knew that the magic of the leaf would not last, but against that threat Odin had to employ speed. It was not only his ally, it was his strategy.

As he raced over the golden roads, Odin began to converge back onto the long and wide avenue that led directly to the royal staircase. His heart flared as he realized he was almost at the Throne Room's staircase.

However, as he rounded the corner onto the promenade, his sprinting strides were instantly intimidated down to a cautious walk.

Blocking the entirety of the lane was a horde of Forneus's Vayne. It appeared as though Forneus had positioned them there as a measure of final safeguard, a mocking trial of Odin's will.

Odin's heart beat fast in panic. Sweat began to bead on his forehead. His feet started to tread carefully and slowly. As he edged forward, he began to feign a calm stride and assess his chances. He knew, from engaging the Vayne on the way to V, that he was more skilled in combat than the serpents. But he had only fought a band of them – there were literally one hundred of Forneus's bodyguards blocking the roadway.

Regrettably, Odin knew he could not win such a battle. His only advantage was that the magic of the leaf hadn't worn off. As Odin took careful steps, he tried to navigate the clearest route through the serpent mass.

Unfortunately, there was no such path.

The Vayne had amassed a daunting blockade. The only way passed them was through them.

As Odin neared the first wall of serpents and he heard the slow hisses of their breath, they began to sniff the air suspiciously. Rigidly, Odin breached through their first wave expecting a fight. But as he walked further into the horde, the Vayne seemed otherwise uninterested.

Slowly, Odin cut through the myriad of Vayne, but as he brushed against the shoulders of countless serpents, he could not deny his vulnerability. He was amid a maze of armed killers, and his only measure of security was his yellow eyes – a meagre disguise that was fading the further he pushed into danger.

With the Vayne crowding him on every side, Odin slunk down, and as he tried to avoid detection, he used a subtle hand to claim one of the hatchets that hung off his Lyran armour. Carefully, he angled the hatchet's golden head to catch his eyes in the blade's reflection.

As Odin peered down into the metal, his entire body clenched with panic. His blue eyes were emerging from under the yellow camouflage. As Odin cursed under his breath, he glanced again at his eyes in the golden weapon. However, as the sight of a swinging axe mirrored on the blade, spurred only by instinct, Odin managed to drop his head.

The giant axe grazed just over his head and struck heavily into the Vayne in front of him.

The charade was over. The hundred Vayne had turned hostile.

Facing his gauntlet of foes and staring down his fading hourglass, Odin had no ambition to defeat his foes, only to evade them. He could allow for no trepidation or mistakes. His only choice was to run.

Like a wave, Forneus's hunters began to charge inwards. As the serpents converged, Odin took one deep breath and stocked both of his hands with one of the golden hatchets.

"For Galian," he whispered.

Just hearing his brother's name seemed to ignite his soul, and as Odin's blue eyes flared with the fire of a brother's love, Odin erupted into a counter-intuitive barrage through the wall of serpent soldiers.

As Odin darted from left to right, the Vayne's weapons and limbs swung into his path, and like a living labyrinth, every viable pathway that appeared was abruptly closed.

As they converged on him, the Vayne's weapons began to crash against Odin's golden mail. The strikes were growing closer and closer to a death-strike, and as Odin managed to duck to avoid a thrown spear, the horde of Vayne had nearly overwhelmed him.

Odin couldn't allow it.

Desperately, he started to slice his hatchets into the tendons of any and all Vayne within reach, and as blood and guts splashed and sprayed around him, Odin's fervent steps began to exploit the few passages that opened up. As he barreled through the horde, each of Odin's turns met contest, but with the devastating hacks of his hatchets, the Lyran began to push closer to Forneus's royal staircase.

As Odin's exodus became marked by a trail of dead and disabled Vayne, the battle savvy serpents began to form a phalanx at their very rear.

Odin acknowledged the strategy, and as he dashed and dodged through the serpent mass, he launched his hatchets into the knees of the two Vayne at the center of the phalanx. As the center Vayne collapsed, Odin leapt urgently onto their exposed backs and launched himself high over the Vayne's formation.

While airborne, Odin quickly retrieved two daggers from his belt, and as he fell out of the air, he tackled the final two Vayne blocking his path, plunging his blades into their chests as he crashed headlong into them. As the tackled Vayne crumpled backwards, Odin rolled over them, pulled his daggers from their hearts, and then – conscious of his fading time, as well as the small enraged army at his back – he raced frantically up the royal staircase.

45

Odin's ascent of the five-hundred-step staircase should have cost him his breath, but instead, as he climbed the near-endless steps, he was neither fatigued nor unfocused.

He was absorbed in thoughts of deicide.

As his lengthy and rapid strides brought him closer to the stairs' summit, he gripped the daggers in his hands even more tightly.

The titans of the afterlife were about to collide. The Lyran House and the Dark Pool were primed for war, and to the victor went the afterlife – once and for all.

As Odin reached the summit and his eyes gained a clear view of Forneus's court, he immediately identified the occupied throne. With a ferocious scream, he lunged up the last steps and pitched his twin daggers at the throne's cloaked king.

The daggers cut accurately through the air with their promise of assassination, but as they passed the fifty Vayne in the Throne Room, they suddenly halted in mid-air, and fell futilely to the Throne Room's marble floor.

With another roar, Odin broke defiantly into Forneus's court and quickly drew Sleipnir from his belt.

"Forneus!" he challenged. "Face me now! Come measure my wrath!"

Immediately, each of the Throne Room's fifty Vayne, as well as the Vayne who had chased Odin up the royal staircase, converged on Serich's heir. As Odin's eyes continued to scold the king, he quickly disabled all Vayne within reach. However, the Vayne grew quickly in numbers, and in short seconds they had overwhelmed Odin.

Ten Vayne were restraining him and another five were poised behind him, intent on delivering their swords into his heart.

However, just before they delivered the deathblow, Forneus cancelled the assault with a wave of his hand.

Heeding their master, the Vayne relinquished their grip on Odin, and backed off and formed a circle around him.

The amused Forneus, with his orange eyes glaring from under his purple cloak, stood at his throne, and then grinned as he approached the intruder.

"Your wrath?" he mused. "The snake does not revel in hunting the rodent. I desire challenge, and your wrath offers me none."

"I beg you to test that," Odin said as he readied Sleipnir for battle.

Forneus grinned again. "Your heart betrays you. I can hear it. I can feel it beating with your hatred for me. But it was foolishness that brought you here, not bravery. You have followed your heart to your own death. I am merely a consenting hand."

"Your words are wasted on me," Odin said sternly. "But I promise you, before we are done here, you will know a grave silence."

"Like your brother?" the serpent goaded.

Forneus allowed himself a savouring grunt as he closed his hellish eyes.

"I feel him fading," he said as he looked into his Cauldron. "He is so near his end. Both of you, so poised to die."

"You're mistaken," Odin coldly promised. "Our destinies have brought us here, but our fates are not the same. The weaker will fall."

"My condolences," Forneus said coldly.

As he lashed his face with his serpent tongue, Forneus removed his purple cloak and exposed the grisly state of his face and body. His skin had been shed completely to black and green snake scales, and there were countless scars strewn across his serpentine form. Small horns had also begun to protrude from his forehead.

As the sinister orange glow of the Cauldron blushed against his muscular body, Forneus cast his arm out, and with his power, he summoned Serich's mighty staff into his grip.

"I've waited a long time to extinguish the blues," he said.

With another grin, he pointed the end of his staff mockingly at Odin.

"Bring me your wrath."

As the hellish glow of the Throne Room gleamed off Odin's golden armour, the young Lyran bowed his head and swung his mind into a lethal rhythm. He would not lose. Sleipnir would become his scythe and each of her attacks would drive to kill.

With Forneus still mocking him, Odin wound Sleipnir back, and on behalf of the Lyran House, he rushed at his villain.

As he came within range, Odin swung Sleipnir as fervently and accurately as he could; however, Forneus was equal to the onslaught. As the exchange of attack and parry amplified in speed and ferocity, the serpent deflected and dodged Odin's attacks away with ease.

After turning a sequence of Odin's attacks into deflections and misses, Forneus sneered at Serich's heir, and with a pompous grin, he dropped his arms and allowed Odin's onslaught of fists and staff to crash against him.

Forneus's head and body, submissive to the assault, snapped and recoiled against the pummeling. Odin's devastating attacks began to smash and bash Forneus's flesh into a muddle, but still the serpent was unfazed. In spite of the devastating force, the king snickered at Odin's strength, and as panic began to surface in Odin's eyes, Forneus exploded at Serich's heir.

The serpent blasted his right palm into the center of Odin's chest, and after lifting him easily into the air, he slammed Odin violently down onto the marble floor.

Odin smashed heavily against the court and then skidded helplessly across the base of the Throne Room.

"Now you learn the lesson your father did!" Forneus roared.

The serpent paced wildly as if Odin's assault had unlocked his rage.

"I feed on pain!" he screamed. "You cannot defeat me!"

As he savoured his growing rage, the Serpent stretched his arms out to the hellish skies, and with a primal scream, he used his considerable power to shake loose the giant stone columns that circled the Throne Room. The columns cracked and shattered into boulders and then, by Forneus's will, became suspended high above his royal court.

"Let us test your skill!" he bawled.

In rapid succession, the king used his power to hurtle the giant boulders down at Odin.

Cross-haired at the end of the boulders' path, Odin had no choice but to display his skill. He nimbly evaded the first of the boulders, and as the rocks came faster and in greater number, he set his feet into a sequence of quick and evasive steps. Instead of retreating from the onslaught, Odin used his agility to inch closer to his villain. As Forneus scorched two giant boulders at his target, Odin hurdled just above the first of the barrelling stones. As the boulder passed beneath him, Odin kicked off it and propelled himself even further into the air. He grazed just over the second boulder and descended directly at the Serpent. As he sailed down, Odin wound Sleipnir back and then belted her hard across Forneus's jaw.

The impact knocked Forneus emphatically to his knees, but again, after a small moment of suffering, the serpent resurged even stronger.

As he rose back to full posture, he ran his hand across the considerable gash Odin had opened on his jaw, and then he crowed out to the dark skies.

"Oh, great pain," he screamed. "Give me more!"

With another scream, the serpent slammed the mighty staff against the floor, and a torrent of blazing fire began to descend from the skies.

As Odin guarded his face from the plummeting streams of orange flame, Forneus rushed him and began to drive the bladed end of his staff furiously at Odin's heart. Nimbly, Odin used one hand to parry Forneus's attacks, and his other hand to block the streaks of flame.

But his strategy was no longer defensive. It had become desperation.

The combination of attacks was rapidly overwhelming him, and as Odin's vision became momentarily impaired by the falling fire, Forneus clasped his hand around Odin's throat and lifted him easily into the air. In an attempt to break the serpent's grasp, Odin swung his fists as strongly as he could into Forneus's skull, but Forneus would not relent.

As Forneus stared callously into Odin's eyes, he began to crush Odin's throat. With Odin faltering, the Serpent laughed arrogantly and squeezed even more tightly.

"You are a disgrace to the Lyrans," he mocked. "Even your father was more than this."

With his life being throttled from him, Odin fought desperately to wrestle himself from Forneus's grip, but the serpent would not yield.

Instead, the great depths of the king's power erupted. His face turned to a devilish grin, and as his eyes began to burn a deeper orange, countless bullets of fire exploded from his Soul Cauldron. As Odin remained clutched and suspended perilously in the air before Forneus, the blazing bullets began to pelt him in violent succession. The fire missiles smashed into Odin's body so forcefully that his body recoiled like a gale-blown flag. As the Lyran armour began to fall apart, Odin's body began to go limp.

Even still, as Odin hung vulnerably before him, Forneus conceded no strength from his grip. The sneering king was not satisfied with the pain he had inflicted.

With increased malice brimming in his eyes, Forneus then released his vicelike grip and delivered a devastating palm strike to Odin's chest. The impact sent Odin hurtling backwards to the royal staircase, and as he crashed back down against the marble, he tumbled and twisted into a broken heap.

Certain of his imminent victory, Forneus slowly approached his beaten foe.

Odin was bleeding badly, and with most of his armour disbanded, his skin was torn, burned, and charred from Forneus's fireball assault.

"Your father did you no favours," Forneus spat as he neared. "He only prolonged the inevitable. By letting you live, he only gave you more to lose. And now, you lose it all. I bring death to the House of Lyran. I kill the sons of Animus Letum."

Against his damaged and surrendering body, Odin's mind, heart, and soul fought him back to his feet.

"I've seen your fall," Odin said as his balance wavered. "I saw the torture of the Dark Pool streaked across your face. And then I saw you submit to your knees."

"Your point?"

"You are weak of heart," Odin said, "an ailment that even the Dark Pool could not fix. I promise you, I will see you again on your knees."

Forneus laughed. "Then bring me your best. Surely this has not been it."

Odin was nearly broken. Deep within himself, he could feel Death narrowing in for its second kill. However, in tribute to his parents, his home, and his brother, he would not surrender. If this was the final act, it would be his greatest. For Galian, he would die fighting.

As Forneus again lashed his serpent tongue in ridicule, Odin's hand clenched hard around Sleipnir, and with the great fury of a brother's love, Odin erupted at the king.

In devastating succession, Odin smashed his fists, staff, and kicks onto Forneus. Odin's blaze of attack was beyond a speed Forneus could defend against, and as the ferocity of the assault escalated, the serpent tried to counter Odin's attack with an elbow. Odin caught the flying elbow, and after turning Forneus's right arm back, Odin smashed his fist into Forneus's bicep and shattered the serpent's humerus.

The king hissed and immediately recoiled. As Forneus staggered back, Odin hacked Sleipnir repeatedly down into his right shoulder. The succession of blows cracked Forneus's collar bone, and as the overwhelmed king tried to guard his injured right side, Odin locked Sleipnir around Forneus's right hand and used her like a lever to snap Forneus's wrist.

With his opponent's arms incapacitated, Odin kicked Forneus's legs out from under him and smashed Sleipnir repeatedly into Forneus's ribs.

As Forneus lay helpless on the marble, Odin held back none of his rage. He rained his fists and knees down onto Forneus's skull, and as the serpent's body eventually went limp, Odin quickly located one of the daggers that he had brought into the Throne Room.

With raging breaths, Odin stood defiantly over his villain, poised to cut out his heart.

As Odin knelt and tried to plunge the dagger into Forneus's chest, the Vayne sensed their king's vulnerability, and ten of them quickly latched onto Odin's arms.

As they dragged him off their master, Odin fought wildly to break from the Vayne's grasp, but Forneus's faithful soldiers had made sure to trap him. As Odin thrashed, Forneus's voice coughed out, and after a moment of wheezing, the Serpent rose to his feet.

As the king glared at Odin, the look in his eye was different. There was a small element of fear, as if the Serpent had realized he was facing a worthy foe.

Nevertheless, the king twisted and contorted his injured arms, and after his bones healed and set back into place, he grinned pompously at his foe.

"Do not blow into a hurricane," he said. "You only increase the power of her winds."

"Call your Vayne down!" Odin screamed as he wrestled his captors. "Fight me, yourself!"

"As you wish."

The king ordered his Vayne down with a motion of his hand.

As the Vayne relinquished their grip from Odin and backed off Serich's heir, Forneus used his power to lift two of the fallen pillars behind Odin. Odin, oblivious to the floating fragments, advanced on the Serpent. Forneus's eyes lit up with their unholy orange, and he smashed the pillars onto Odin's sides.

The stones exploded against Odin, and after a moment of stillness, Odin crumpled to the Throne Room marble.

With Odin lying motionless, Forneus slowly approached his destroyed prey.

Blood was gushing from every part of Odin's body, and on both of his sides, his rib bones had broken through his flesh.

As Forneus relished his victory, he cruelly manipulated Odin to his knees.

"It's been a pleasure," he mocked as he summoned the mighty staff to his hand. "But this was always how it would end."

After he spat at his foe, Forneus cocked the staff back to deliver the final death blow.

Odin had failed, and as his broken and ashamed eyes stared up at his impending death, he whispered his final words.

"Galian," he wept as his blue eyes flared, "I'm sorry ..."

Proud of the great victory that awaited him, Forneus lashed his serpent tongue across his face. But suddenly, just before he struck down the mighty staff, the serpent clutched his stomach and turned fearfully back to his Cauldron.

Deep in the Soul Cauldron, Galian sat in unfathomable torment. The Cauldron's skeletons plunged and ripped repeatedly through his body, stealing more of him at each dive. The unrelenting torture had lasted longer than Galian could remember. The pain was his only memory. However, as Galian became certain he could last no longer, suddenly a voice – his most loved – coursed through his head.

"Galian," Odin's voice said, "I'm sorry..."

In an instant Galian understood. He knew what his brother had done, and he knew what Forneus was about to do.

Galian's greatest friend – the one he thought he had lost – had come to save him. In spite of it all, Odin was still there.

In his life, Galian had faced down his enemies. He had thrown himself headlong into their embrace, daring them to best his heart. However, at each fight, at each of his trials, there was one line never to be crossed: evil could strike him, hell could test his heart, but if Odin's name was even breathed, hellfire would erupt from the silent monk.

No one harmed Odin.

And as Galian, broken at the base of the vile Soul Cauldron, became aware of the harm dealt to his brother, an anger and fury immeasurable by human emotion began to burn in his soul. With deadly focus, Galian began to rise from the base of the Cauldron.

The Cauldron's skeletons recognized Galian's efforts, and they urgently summoned more of their brethren to try to tear through him.

Galian was beyond their malice.

As the skeletons tried to pierce through Galian's soul, they began to deflect off him in futility.

Galian was enraged. His wrath was swelling beyond godhood.

As he again felt his brother's soul outside of the Cauldron, and then felt the love he had thought he had lost forever, Galian's heart broke.

It was a pain only a brother can know.

As the agony of the fracture echoed throughout Galian's body, it began to surge out of him.

Galian's voice – spoken only once before – began to seep out the name of his greatest friend. And then, having tasted his second sound, Galian's eyes ignited in electric blue, and as he flexed his body with a godly rage, his voice erupted with the sound of his broken heart.

"Odiiinnnn!"

The scream exploded with such primal and thundering ire that the Cauldron – the very epitome of Hell – instantly cowered and exploded against Galian's sheer rage. Like glass, the Cauldron shattered at its base, and as the explosion blasted out, the echoes of Galian's fury smashed the Throne Room's outer columns into rubble. As the courtyard was violently rocked into destruction, Forneus and his Vayne were thrown helplessly to the courtyard's marble floor.

As countless souls were freed of the Cauldron's torture, a flare of a bright blue energy burst across the Throne Room and crashed into Odin, sending him tumbling back down the royal staircase.

The aftershock of Galian's quake rippled throughout the kingdom of Animus Letum for long and heavy minutes.

Intensely shaken by the blast, Forneus strove his best for composure, but his mind was scattered by the bedlam delivered to his Throne Room. Eventually, he regained his focus and began to scavenge his destroyed court for Serich's heir.

There was no sign of Odin.

Furiously, the king turned to his Vayne.

"Find him!" he barked. "He's in here somewh…"

The serpent fell deadly silent as one blue ember and then a flurry of electric blue rain began to fall from the skies.

"Find him!" Forneus screamed again. "Find him, and kill him!"

The Vayne reacted in immediate obedience to the order. The great folly of their hunt was the confusion of its roles. The Vayne thought themselves to be the hunters, but instead, by the electric blue eyes ascending the royal staircase, they were the hunted.

Sensing a great presence at the staircase, Forneus cast his eyes back towards the entrance to his court.

Standing there was Odin. But to Forneus's astonishment, it was not just Odin.

Cut into Odin's face were both his own and Galian's scars from Vinculum Imletalis. Galian's and Odin's souls had merged again to create Daios – perfectly and permanently.

Together they had become the perfect incarnation of warrior.

Recognizing the threat, Forneus immediately set his soldiers onto Daios.

Daios was aware. As he ascended completely into the Throne Room, he stretched his right arm out, and using the power Galian offered, he summoned Sleipnir out from under the courtyard rubble. As the first wave of Vayne tried to converge on him, Daios stretched out his left hand and froze the fifteen Vayne dead in their strides.

Amid the falling torrent of blue embers, Daios raised his arm slowly into the air and the fifteen Vayne were lifted high above the marble court. After a moment of suspension, Daios slammed them so powerfully down into death that the floor beneath them cracked and cratered.

As Forneus eyed the mighty Lyran, Daios returned a piercing stare and then exploded into the center of the remaining Vayne. He combined the combat skills inherited by Odin and the spiritual powers inherited by Galian into a blaze of deadly assault.

He was unstoppable.

As the Vayne rushed him, Daios disarmed the serpent soldiers with a wave of his hands, and began to slash Sleipnir in lethal arcs. With Daios smashing the Vayne into death, the rapidly dwindling serpent soldiers tried to overwhelm him with their numbers. However, using his great power, Daios hurtled three of the fallen column pillars directly into their cluster.

With only a small number of Vayne remaining, Daios swung Sleipnir into an impossibly fast sweep, and after casting the last ten Vayne airborne, he waved his hand and flung them helplessly down the royal staircase.

In moments, Daios had killed all of the serpent soldiers.

Only the Serpent Messiah remained.

As Daios's raging blue eyes locked onto Forneus, the king stared intently back.

"Finally," he seethed, "a challenge."

"You're beaten already," Daios said coldly.

His eyes turned deadly as he quoted the Serpent: "I am merely a consenting hand."

"You are not better suited than your father," Forneus spat. "Like him, you believe in virtue. Like him, you cower against the great truth of this land."

With hatred in his eyes, Forneus cast out his hand, and one of the daggers Odin had carried into the Throne Room soared into his grip.

As he hissed and snarled, Forneus wrapped both of his hands around the dagger and raised the blade to his throat.

"And that truth is simple: you must bleed for the crown."

With a deep growl, Forneus stabbed the dagger into his own neck, and as his body began to shake violently, he guided the blade slowly down his throat. As green ichor poured profusely from him, Forneus used the dagger to cut a tear down the center of his chest and stomach.

After he had completed the cut, Forneus was crippled by the gash. His body was shaking violently, and he had been reduced to a slumped over agony.

However, after the pain brought him to his knees, Forneus's whimpers soon turned to rapid breathing. The Serpent's mind and soul began to surge with new power, and as Forneus's forearms and fists exploded into blazing flames, the Serpent blasted upwards, and a hellish twenty foot high fire erupted around the outer ring of the Throne Room.

Amid the orange inferno, Daios's electric blue eyes stared daringly at his foe.

"Bring me your best," he snarled.

"I bring you Hell!" Forneus screamed through the flames.

The Serpent wound back his flaming fist, and as he launched a punch, a fireball exploded from his hand and scorched across the Throne Room. As the missile closed in on him, Daios used his considerable power to swat the fire bullet out of the air.

With murder in his gaze, Daios dared the Serpent to bring more.

"You'll have to do better," he said.

"Careful what you wish for," Forneus fired back.

The irate king threw his fists in wild succession, and as dozens of fireballs blasted at Daios, Forneus summoned the mighty staff and stormed directly at his foe.

With intense focus, Daios swatted each of the fire bullets out of the air, and as he knocked the last one down, he drove Sleipnir into the marble floor and vaulted himself at the oncoming serpent. As Daios reached the peak of his vault, he rocked a devastating kick at Forneus's skull. The incredible impact knocked Forneus into a spinning tumble, and as the king crashed back to the floor, Daios stood ominously over him.

"Your reign is over," Daios seared. "I am your death."

After a furious exhalation, Forneus pounded his flaming fists into the marble, and rose angrily to his feet.

"You think you've tasted hell?" the serpent seared. "You have only scratched its surface! Cower, Lyran, for now I bring you to its depths!"

Forneus lunged at Daios, and as the outer court burned with roaring orange flames, the king launched a blazing assault at his rival. Daios dodged and parried the onslaught of flaming fists, until, as he tried to guard against one of the attacks with Sleipnir, the impact of Forneus's punch shattered the bow-staff into fragments.

Without a weapon, Daios used his arms to shield himself, but as the incredible weight of Forneus's attacks thrashed against him, Daios knew he could not withstand the barrage.

Instead, as Forneus threw a heavy right hand, Daios weaved away from the attack, and once Forneus's momentum carried him off balance, Daios delivered a kick into Forneus's chest and sent the king tumbling back down against the marble.

Enraged at the futile state of his attacks, Forneus rose furiously to his feet and bashed his flaming fists repeatedly into his own face. With even more bedlam burning in his eyes, the Serpent used his power to lift five giant pieces of column into the air.

"There can be only one king!" he screamed at Daios. "One of us needs to die!"

As the suspended columns surrounded Daios, the Serpent roared in fury and then threw his arms violently down to the floor. Immediately, the five columns scorched inwards at Daios, and as they barreled towards simultaneous impact, Forneus again exploded across the Throne Room. With the columns a mere second away from collision, Daios drew from the depths of his might, and just before impact, he launched a wave of power outwards that smashed each of the five columns into rubble.

As Daios stood defiantly amid the dust and debris, the king let out a furious scream and leapt headlong at his foe. With a quick deke, Daios altered his step, and after catching the flying serpent, he turned Forneus's momentum into a powerful slam.

Forneus smacked hard against the marble, and as his back broke from the crash, Daios used his power to raise the Serpent back into the air. With Forneus suspended perilously before him, Daios pulled Forneus powerfully back and smashed his knee into the back of Forneus's skull.

The devastating force snapped the king's neck, and as Daios relinquished his hold of the king, the outer ring of fire extinguished, and Forneus's limp and lifeless body fell back to the stone floor.

With his opponent broken, Daios summoned six spears from the heap of dead Vayne and slowly approached the battered Forneus.

Forneus began to cough up more green ichor, and again, after a succession of wheezes and gasps, the Serpent's voice turned to a sadistic cackle.

However, as Forneus tried to rise, Daios halted his movement with a motion of his hand and slammed Forneus so forcefully back down against the marble that the floor fractured beneath him. As Forneus screamed and fought furiously to rise, Daios suspended the six spears methodically over him, and electing to trap the king, he plunged the spears violently down into the serpent. The spears pierced though both of Forneus's feet, knees, and hands and pinned the Serpent helplessly against the marble floor.

Rendered defenceless, Forneus's voice crowed throughout the Throne Room.

"You do yourself no favours!" he screamed. "You are only courting your defeat! You will lose, son of Serich, I promise you!"

"I told you I would break you to your knees," Daios said defiantly. "This, serpent, is how it ends."

As blue embers fell like rain, Daios summoned a dagger into his grip and clutched strongly to Forneus's skull. Desperately, Forneus tried to wrestle, but with great poise, Daios put the blade against Forneus's scales, and after a powerful stab, he used the dagger to slice into the back of the Serpent's neck.

"No!" Forneus screamed as he realized Daios's intent.

Wildly, the serpent tried to break free his pinned legs and hands; however, as he bucked his appendages, it was his flesh and bone that broke.

After using the dagger to complete a deep cut into the back of the king's neck, Daios reached his right hand deep into Forneus's wound. With blue embers lighting the scene, Daios searched the gash, and after hearing a loud hiss, he clutched his hand around its source and ripped a four foot snake out of the considerable tear in the screaming king's neck.

The snake, the great evil that had bonded with Forneus at the Dark Pool, hissed and snapped its jaws at Daios.

With godly conviction, Daios clenched tightly to the snake's neck and stared remorselessly into its orange eyes.

"Your trail of death is avenged," he said.

Using his dagger, Daios began to saw through the snake's neck, and after a succession of powerful slices, the snake's head fell lifelessly to Throne Room floor.

With a disgusted grimace, Daios tossed the snake's dead body to the ground, and looked over the defeated Forneus.

The hellish orange hue of Forneus's eyes had disappeared, and, instead, the great traitor of Animus Letum looked painfully up at Daios with his natural purple eyes.

Forneus trembled as tears streamed from his face. The man had separated from the monster, and as the leftover man looked helplessly up at Daios, his eyes pled for pardon.

"I'm sorry," Forneus wept. "I am so sorry."

"That is not enough," Daios ruled.

"Kill me..." Forneus begged. "Kill what's left..."

As terrified tears streamed down Forneus's face, the sheer horror in his eyes implied that Serich's faithful general had never died. It was as if he had survived inside the monster and watched helplessly as the Serpent tortured an entire world.

"Kill me!" Forneus screamed. "End me! End my torture!"

Daios consented.

In the name of the Throne's Eye and the Lyran House, Daios plunged his dagger deep into Forneus's heart.

Forneus gasped in pain, and as Daios twisted his blade, Forneus expelled an airy scream, and fell to death.

The great villain of the afterlife was no more.

As Daios surveyed the destruction streaked across the Throne Room, he saw Haren ascend to the royal court carrying the crown of Animus Letum. Haren was quickly followed by Adara and nearly one hundred of her armed parishioners.

Haren looked, baffled, over the destruction in the Throne Room. She was awestruck by the great feat she thought Odin had accomplished. As she looked at her old friend, she quickly realized the truth.

"Daios..." she whispered

Daios smiled back.

The Sons of Animus Letum

"A little late," he said.

"Fashionably late," Haren corrected as she held up the crown.

However, Daios could not yet accept the crown. He needed to commit one last deed before he could be anointed.

With an air of royalty, Daios took his rightful seat on the throne of Animus Letum. After pressing the button on each of the throne's arms, two blades appeared, and Daios ran his palms over their edges. As he reclined on the throne, Daios's blood flowed slowly towards the crater that Galian's thunderous scream had left, and as the blood reached the base of Forneus's expired Soul Cauldron, blue electric snaps cracked across the Throne Room. The cracks increased in volume until, with a sudden and thunderous boom, a massive pillar of electric blue energy burst up from the base of the crater.

The new Soul Cauldron and the new reign had been born.

As Daios's blue Cauldron burnt through the dark clouds above and opened the skies to the first view of the night stars in twenty years, Haren approached the king and offered him the crown.

"My king," she said with a smile. "This is yours."

Daios bowed to Haren, and after accepting the crown with careful hands, he placed it on his head.

In an instant, an incredible rush of godly power awoke in Daios's mind. His royal eyes grew wide, and as his soul surged with the level and extent of his inherited strength, Daios gained every power, thought, and memory ever held by a king of Animus Letum.

By his inheritance, Daios had become a deity. He had become the ruler of the afterlife.

As Haren and her hundred followers recognized that truth and humbled themselves to a knee before the new king, Daios accepted his birthright.

The new reign – the promised redemption of Animus Letum's soul – had come.

The Lyran House had taken reign of the afterlife once more. But for the first time ever, heaven needed to be built on a foundation that had suffered nearly a quarter-century of hell.

For this reason, Daios chose edelweiss as his bloom.

During Forneus's rule, the people of Animus Letum had become a mirror of the nature around them. They had been scarred and broken. They had lived in an age of decay. But like his bloom, Daios would forge beauty from bleakness. Like edelweiss, Animus Letum would rise mightily from the barren rock.

The age of Daios had begun.

Andrew F. Whittle

The Sons of Animus Letum

*

After I had delivered Odin across the seas of the afterlife, I, both patient and invested, waited on the banks of Animus Letum's mainland. Bound to my shackle, I acknowledged Odin's pursuit of the impossible. I did not pray, but begged. Fate, I implored, bestow speed and courage upon Odin's task. Endow our great legend's seed with the might of our even greater hope.

And fate was good.

From my boat, I heard first the thunder of a brother's love, and I saw second the blue light of Animus Letum's true blood. Serich's great act of martyrdom, his payment of immense faith, had come to find its heirs atop the throne.

My thankfulness found me in a daze of jubilation. I, in memory of those lost, made time to grieve the black dusk that the serpents had felled on our land. But I then, with greater heart and more time, celebrated the beautiful dawn that was rising.

I must have lost nearly an hour to my revel. As I lay on my back, savouring the night stars I had not seen in an age, one bright star seemed to soar and dive down to me.

I stood up, alerted by the falling light, but as it grew close, I froze in awe. The new king, using his inherited power of flight, was the star.

As he descended from the skies with infinite poise, he landed his feet gracefully onto my bank.

"My king," I welcomed as I dropped to a knee, "thank you for making time. You have come a long way."

Daios nodded.

"Your scar," I noted of Daios's mirrored marks. "It has grown a twin."

"I am no longer the man you transported," Daios informed. "Odin's entirety was merged perfectly with his brother's soul to create me. I am Daios."

"You are both?" I asked.

"Both as one," Daios replied.

"That certainly resolves any of the quarrels posed by two heirs," I said with a smile.

Daios nodded and then pointed to my shackle.

"I come with a gift," he said.

"What gift?" I asked.

Daios smiled at me, and with a flick of his hand he broke open the shackle on my right ankle.

I immediately crouched down and began tend to the wound that the chains had guarded from me for nearly a quarter century.

"It hurts so good," I laughed.

I then looked up at the new king. "I think this wound can heal now."

As Daios smiled and then extended his hand to me, I took it in thanks.

"I often feared I'd be chained here forever," I said.

"I hope now that you will find a place in my court," Daios said.

I smiled, but declined.

"Your court is fine without me. Besides, I have a job here, with this boat."

"But you fear this labour," Daios reminded me.

"I fear not having a choice," I amended. "The people need to be brought to your kingdom, and I can offer them that travel."

After bowing, I stepped back into my boat.

"People deserve your reign Daios, and I wish to deliver them to that privilege."

"As you wish," Daios said. "But if ever you seek leave of your duty and wish to join me, simply set your strides to my throne."

"I'll remember that."

Daios offered a respectful nod, and after ascending effortlessly into the air, he soared back into the starry night of Animus Letum.

I watched his flight until he disappeared, and then I picked up my oar.

"Unbelievable," I marvelled as I set the oar into the water. "Couldn't have written it better myself."

The Sons of Animus Letum

**

After I had reached the Isle of the Lost, it was not long until my workmate Zyled brought me a soul who had been given the Boatman rite.

I offered Zyled the customary gems for his work, and then addressed the very first man I would bring to the kingdom of Daios.

"You have no idea how great your timing is," I said to the tall and slender man carrying a cloth covered box.

The man simply nodded.

"If you'll hold still," I said, "I'll fix those eyes of yours."

After the man nodded again, I knocked my hand into the back of his head and caught the coins that fell from his eye sockets.

"Not bad," I measured of the coins.

As I looked up to the man's eyes, I stumbled back, shocked by the hue that was staring back at me.

The eyes were blood red: a colour of pure evil.

Before I had any chance to act, the man drew a dagger and pointed it to my throat.

"Get in the boat," he said.

"And if I don't?" I challenged.

The man laughed. "Bravery doesn't suit you, Charon. Let me make this simple: if you have any intention of seeing Adara again, you'll get in the boat."

Upon hearing my daughter's name, my voice turned fearsome.

"How do you know that name?"

"I know what I must," the man replied. "This moment has been years in the making."

As the man continued to point his dagger to my throat, I tried to weave and displace it from his hand. However, the man was clearly experienced in combat, and as I tried to reach for the dagger, he jolted my abdomen with a strong kick and flung me helplessly into my boat.

"We should have done it the easy way," the man said.

Arrogantly, the man stepped into my boat and then laid his cloth covered box on the floor. As I clutched my injured stomach, he pushed off the dock and then dropped an oar onto my back.

"Don't test me again," he said. "Your life and Adara's life depend on it. Besides, there is someone on the mainland whom I would like you to meet."

The man reclined confidently on my boat, daring me to make a mistake.

I knew I couldn't. For my daughter, I had to set my oar into the water – for my daughter, I had to knowingly bring evil into heaven.

As I sculled across the sea, the man did not say another word. However, as we neared the mainland and he saw a giant figure draped in a massive black cloak on the shore, he became noticeably excited. I paddled suspiciously to the shore, and the moment I docked, the man leapt from the boat and knelt before the cloaked giant.

"I bring them back to you," the man said as he held out his draped box.

The dark figure responded with an inhumanly deep growl.

"You have done well, Usis," he commended.

As the giant removed his hood, fear struck hard into my heart.

"Malum Ludus!" I gasped.

Ludus shot me a cold grin and then received the box from his apprentice. The Great Terror opened the box and retrieved both of his red, pulsating eyes.

I knew I needed to warn my king.

Ludus began to insert his eyes back into their vacant sockets, and I began a desperate sprint to the Throne Room. As Ludus's eyes became fixed back into his skull, his power instantly returned. Ludus cast his eyes on me, and after reading my fear, the chain shackle that was still attached to my boat hunted me like a serpent does it prey.

The chain caught me in seconds and snapped painfully around my ankle.

I was a prisoner once more.

I tried desperately to wrestle the chain off, but it was no use. Ludus had realized my greatest fear.

Usis shot me a mocking smirk and then turned to his master.

"What is our next move?" he asked.

"Incite madness," Ludus replied. "We must break the king."

"How?" Usis wondered.

"The greatest fear of all kings is the suffering of their people," Ludus said.

With a snicker, his mouth turned to an evil and salivating grin.

"It is time, my apprentice, to finish the Master Labyrinth."

Ω

The Sons of Animus Letum

Contact the Author:

Email: whittlea8@gmail.com

Or

Twitter: @AFWhittle

Or

Facebook: The Sons of Animus Letum

Made in the USA
Charleston, SC
17 December 2015